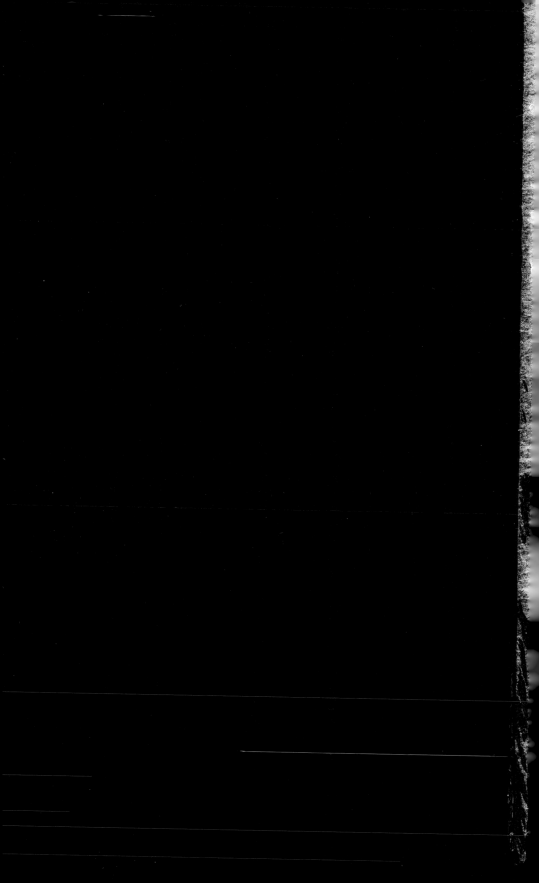

Incendium

Also by A. D. Swanston

The King's Spy
The King's Exile
The King's Return

Incendium

A. D. Swanston

BANTAM PRESS

LONDON • TORONTO • SYDNEY • AUCKLAND • JOHANNESBURG

TRANSWORLD PUBLISHERS
61–63 Uxbridge Road, London W5 5SA
www.penguin.co.uk

Transworld is part of the Penguin Random House group of companies
whose addresses can be found at global.penguinrandomhouse.com

Penguin
Random House
UK

First published in Great Britain in 2017 by Bantam Press
an imprint of Transworld Publishers

A CIP catalogue record for this book
is available from the British Library.

ISBN 9780593076248

Typeset in 12/16.5pt Caslon Classico by Falcon Oast Graphic Art Ltd.
Printed and bound by Clays Ltd, Bungay, Suffolk.

Penguin Random House is committed to a sustainable
future for our business, our readers and our planet. This book
is made from Forest Stewardship Council® certified paper.

MIX
Paper from
responsible sources
FSC® C018179
FSC
www.fsc.org

1 3 5 7 9 10 8 6 4 2

For Susan, with love

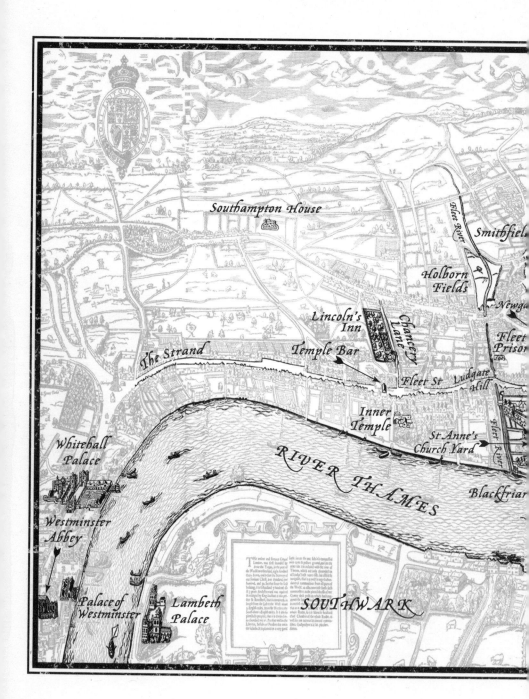

Sixteenth Century

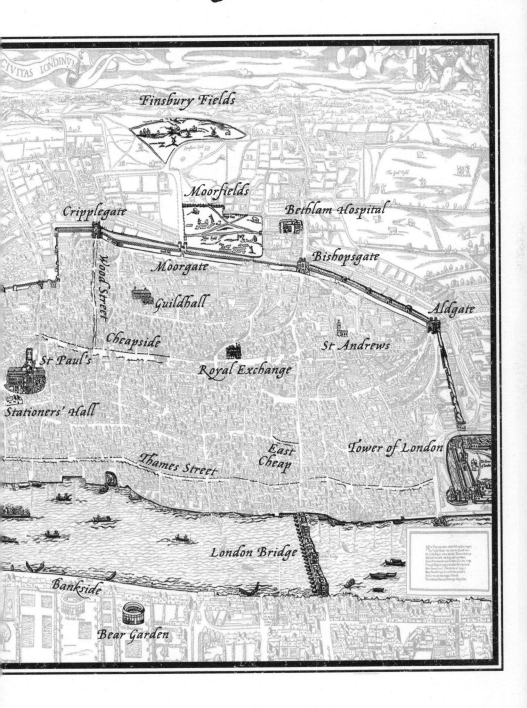

CHAPTER 1

London, June 1572

The two figures outside the narrow house beside the Cripplegate cobbler's shop were unremarkable — both of middling height and wearing white kersey shirts and black breeches with grey hose, soft caps pulled low over their brows, and short capes. They could have been scriveners, clerks, or members of any one of numerous respectable trades.

One had crossed the river from Southwark by row-boat and thence come on foot to Cripplegate. The other had come by Fleet Street and Smithfield. The guards at the city gates had not detained them. They had met at the house and had waited in the shadows until dawn before knocking on the door. They were in no doubt about its being the right house — it exactly matched the description they had been given.

Early as it was, they were not surprised that their knock went unanswered. One of them tried again, this time with a little more force. He did not want to wake inquisitive neighbours by shouting or forcing the door. But he did want to get the job done and be gone before day women carrying milk churns and fruit-sellers and poultry-men arrived through the Cripplegate to tout their wares. The risk of being marked and remembered then would be high.

From an upstairs room they heard the sounds of movement. A window creaked open above them. 'What churl calls at this hour?' demanded a petulant voice, made hoarse by ale and sleep. 'We are not yet risen.'

One of the men glanced down the street to make sure they were not observed. 'Do I address Mr Houseman?' the other asked politely, his voice that of an educated man.

'You do, although I would you did not. I do not welcome visitors when it is scarcely light and I have not yet filled my piss-pot.'

'The hour cannot be helped, sir. We are sent from Stationers' Hall on a matter of great urgency.'

'What can be so urgent that it has taken me from my bed and my wife?'

'If you would be good enough to open the door, sir, we shall be able to tell you. We will not detain you for long and you will soon be back in your bed beside your wife.'

'Come back later, damn you, when I am risen.'

'We are messengers, sir, and must be on our way. We carry important news for all members of the guild. Our instructions are not to delay.'

They heard an oath and the window was closed with a force that rattled its frame. At first, they thought that Houseman was going to leave them to kick their heels. Then there were footsteps on the stair, a key turned in the lock and the door bolts were drawn back.

They waited until the door was opened an inch or two, put their weight against it and crashed into the house, knocking Houseman to the floor. They were on him immediately, one forcing into his mouth the tip of a heavy knife of the sort that a butcher might use, the other tying his hands and feet with short lengths of rope. Houseman could do nothing but struggle feebly and make mewling sounds deep in his throat.

As soon as he had made the knots fast, the other dashed up the stair. Houseman's wife had heard the commotion and was standing in her nightgown at the top. At the moment she opened her mouth to scream, he grabbed her hair and held a slim dagger to her throat. They had not brought firearms for fear of a neighbour hearing a shot. The scream was stifled. He growled into her ear, 'Not a sound, woman, or you will die like a stuck pig and pleading for quarter.' He forced her down the stair and into a small parlour.

Her husband was hauled in behind her and lay helpless on the floor. One stood silently over Houseman, the other held the woman. 'Now, you will tell us what we want to know or your wife will be stripped and swived before your eyes. And not by me, by this.' He held up the dagger. 'She will not enjoy it. And you will not enjoy the taste of your own pizzle.'

The knife was pulled from Houseman's mouth, bloodying his lip, and pressed against his cheek. He managed a strangled croak. 'Do not harm her. Take what little we have and go.'

'It is information we seek from you, bookseller, not your money.'

'What do you wish to know? I will tell you if you do not harm my wife.'

'Very well. If you lie or the woman screams, she will die. Do you understand?' He held his blade under the woman's chin and pressed it into her flesh just hard enough to draw a trickle of blood.

'I do.'

'Good. What do you know of *Incendium*?'

Houseman had recovered a little courage. '*Incendium*? I am a member of the Stationers' Company. I read Latin. Of course I know what it is.' The blade cut down the length of his wife's nightgown, revealing her breasts and belly. She was a comely woman, plump and smooth-skinned.

At a signal the knife was pressed harder into her husband's cheek. 'That is not the answer we seek.' The man holding her smirked. 'On second thoughts, perhaps I shall take her first.'

'For the love of God, husband, do as he asks,' sobbed the woman. Despite the warmth of the house, she was shaking. There was a sharp smell of piss from the puddle at her feet.

'Swear that you will not harm her further.'

'She will not be harmed if you tell us what we wish to know. What do you know of *Incendium*?'

'It means fire. I have heard it spoken in the Hall.'

'And?'

'I believe there may be a body among the stationers who call themselves by this name.'

'How do you come to believe this?'

'A word here and there. Whispers overheard. Nothing more.'

'What purpose has this body and why would it choose such a name?'

'I do not know.' The point of the dagger traced a line of blood from the woman's throat to her belly. She bit her tongue and managed not to cry out. 'If you hurt her, I shall say nothing more.' The words came out in a desperate gasp.

'You do know. You have been asking questions. Why?'

'Curiosity, no more.'

'What have you learned?'

'I know only that there are those of its members who would see a return to the old ways of worship. That is against no law and there are many in London of the same opinion.'

'Why then stick your nose into it?'

'I have told you. Curiosity.'

'Who knows of this body? Who have you told?'

'I have told no one.'

The man cupped the woman's breast in his hand and reached around her to hold the blade to a brown nipple. 'Are you sure?'

'I have told no one. Would I put my wife's life at stake by lying?'

'Your final chance. What do you know about the word?'

'I have told you what I know. There is no more. Now keep your word and release her.'

'I gave no word.' The knife slashed across the woman's throat. Blood spurted from the wound and she fell dying. The bookseller cried out and tried to get to his feet. He was kicked back by a booted foot.

'You should not have meddled in affairs that do not concern you.' The slim blade sliced again. Blood gurgled from the wound and spread out over the floor. Houseman's eyes opened wide in shock. In less than a minute he was dead.

The killer wiped the blade on his victim's nightshirt. 'Search the house. Find a sack and take what silver and coin there is. We will return tonight to clear away the blood and get rid of the bodies. There must be no trace left. Make haste.'

It did not take long. They found little money and few pieces of value. One of them took the key from the door and locked it from the outside. They went quietly back the way they had come and were seen only by a single night-soil man who paid them no heed. By that night all traces of the murders would have been removed.

CHAPTER 2

That same morning, the second day of June, Christopher Radcliff awoke early, rubbed sleep from his eyes and cursed himself for having finished the bottle of sack before retiring. He struggled to his feet, splashed his face with cold water from the ewer in his chamber and ran his fingers through his unruly mop of yellow hair. A glance in a hand mirror that had once been his mother's, and he reckoned himself presentable enough. He slipped on a much-mended white shirt and a pair of black breeches. He eschewed London fashion and was never comfortable in a doublet, which made him feel like an uncommonly tall jester at the court of King Henry.

After nearly two years in London he had become accustomed to a bed too short for him — at an inch above six feet, most beds were too short for him — but last night, despite the sack, he had slept fitfully. He did not relish the task he must carry out that day.

In the kitchen, he swallowed a slice of cold chicken, washed it down with a beaker of small beer, and left the house as the bell of the church of St Martin rang out six. He tucked his poniard, its blade so slim that it was almost a needle, into his belt, locked the door carefully behind him lest thieving eyes were watching, looked up and down the street, saw nothing untoward and set off for the river. As always, he wore his academic gown and cap.

The Earl of Leicester's message had arrived the previous evening. The queen had travelled by royal barge from Whitehall Palace to the Tower and there spoken privately to the warden. The execution of Thomas Howard had been set for eight. The earl had instructed Christopher to attend and to report to him at Whitehall Palace immediately afterwards. That the earl preferred not to be there was no surprise — his own father, John Dudley, Duke of Northumberland, had died under the executioner's axe and the earl himself, together with his brothers, had languished in the Tower under sentence of death. There was nothing the earl would wish for less than to witness another execution in that dreadful, menacing place.

Twice that year the queen had signed the death warrant and twice she had rescinded it at the eleventh hour. On the first occasion a furious mob of disappointed onlookers had taken out its anger on the vagrants and whores who infested the narrow lanes and alleys around the Tower, cracking heads and breaking bones. On the second, the crowd was appeased by the spectacle of two lesser executions hurriedly arranged to provide their entertainment.

This time, surely, there would be no reprieve. This time the Duke of Norfolk, the queen's cousin, would die on the scaffold. And he would die as plain Thomas Howard. He had been tried and found guilty of plotting her death, and sentence would at last be carried out. And, at the Earl of Leicester's command, his chief intelligencer in London, Dr Christopher Radcliff, would be there to witness his death. Whether to be pleased or vexed that he was the one to take the earl's place, Christopher was unsure. Did it put him on the top of the dung heap or underneath it?

In one respect, Norfolk was fortunate. Thanks to his position, he would not face the gruesome end that awaited other traitors. He would not be hung by the neck, cut down while still alive, sliced open, his entrails burned before his eyes until finally his body was hacked into four pieces. As the queen's kinsman, Norfolk had been granted a swift end. He would be killed by a stroke of the axe, albeit on Tower Hill in full public view, not, like the queen's own mother, within the private confines of the castle.

Norfolk's death would mark the end of what had become known as the Ridolfi Plot, named for the Florentine banker who had devised and financed it. Christopher had wondered if the queen might have been more merciful if the plot had not followed so soon after the uprising in the northern counties, a rising led by the earls of Westmoreland and Northumberland. The queen's advisors, the Earl of Leicester foremost among them, had finally persuaded her that Howard, royal cousin or no, had to die. Only the queen's mercy had saved him so far. It would save him no longer.

Christopher did not care to ride if he could avoid it and in London travelled on foot or by wherry. To save time that day, he would use the river. He walked briskly down Blackfriars Lane, head down and purse safely under his shirt. Even at that hour, London was awake and there would be cutpurses and pickpockets and maunderers about. Each week he saw more and more of them, lurking on street corners and huddled in doorways — vagrants and paupers pouring in from the countryside where they could not eke out a living on land being enclosed for animals, and could no longer turn to the charity of the old religious houses. For all their extravagance and corruption, the ancient monasteries had provided food and shelter to the poor and sick of their counties. Now London grew larger, dirtier and more overcrowded with each day while Londoners grumbled and cursed and demanded an end to the river of vagrants and harsher penalties for their crimes. But to no avail. A man had only to walk along Fleet Street to see that the problem was getting worse by the week.

On the corner of Pilgrim Street, butchers and bakers were already setting out their stalls and aiming kicks at the half-naked urchins who scrabbled about in the dirt, squabbling over a stale crust or a scrap of offal. The urchins had to be quick. Hungry dogs sniffed about while kites watched hopefully from the rooftops. Christopher saw a bird swoop from its perch, take a morsel in its beak and flap away before it could be frightened off.

A filthy child saw him and dashed across the street to demand a coin. She grabbed his gown and held on like a terrier with a rat until he gave up trying to free himself and tossed a groat from his purse on to the cobbles. She was on it as quick as any rat. He hurried on. Near Blackfriars stairs, a painted orange-seller appeared from a dark doorway, thrust out a hand and grabbed his sleeve. He shook it off with a wrench of his arm. From her he was more likely to buy the pox than an orange.

There was no one else at the stairs and he did not have to wait long for a wherry. Soon enough, a grizzled old waterman with a single eye steered his narrow boat alongside. Christopher handed him a shilling and stepped in. He pulled his knees up to his chin and settled on to a low seat at the rear of the boat. 'To the steps at the Tower. How is the river today?' he asked.

'Stinking like a whore's quim, sir,' growled the old man. 'But calm as a pond, as you can see for yourself, and no tide to speak of. The bridge will not detain us.' When the river was flowing fast, the waters funnelling under London Bridge were dangerous. There were drownings every year. 'Tower Hill for Howard's head, is it?'

Christopher ignored the question. 'Make haste, man. I must be in good time.' He took off his cap lest it be caught by a fluke of wind and lost to the river, and gathered his gown around his shoulders. The wherryman dug in his oar. It caught in the water and when he jerked it out, sent a spray of water over Christopher's sleeve. 'Take care, oaf,' he growled. 'I do not wish to be soaked.'

Even during the summer stench, the river held a strange attraction for him. As different as could be from the quiet Cam which flowed through Cambridge and along which he had often walked after a morning studying or teaching. An ancient path ran beside it to the hamlet of Grantchester, but more often than not he had only swans on the river and cows in the meadows for company.

And to his surprise, he also liked the movement of the Thames, the bustle, the comings and goings of the cargo ships, the wherries and row-boats, the strange languages, the faces and voices of the men and women who made their living by it. The foul-mouthed wherryman that morning was an exception. Most river people were different to the people of the streets. On another day he would have enjoyed the early morning journey and the greetings and insults shouted across the water by the wherrymen. That day, however, his mind was elsewhere. It was on the foolish, doomed affair that, in less than two hours, would send Norfolk to his death.

To the Privy Council the facts had been clear. Norfolk had conspired with others to assassinate the queen and replace her with the Queen of Scots, whom he would then marry. Supported by an uprising of Catholic sympathizers and an invasion force of ten thousand Spanish soldiers, they would restore England to the ways of Rome. That both Norfolk and Mary had been three times married had not deterred Pope Pius from giving them his blessing or from excommunicating the Queen of England from the Catholic Church. To Christopher's mind, the plot had been driven as much by a raging lust for power as by religious fervour.

It had been an absurd plan, conceived in hypocrisy and devoid of reason. And it had exactly the opposite effect to that intended. After the excommunication and the plot's discovery, royal tolerance had been replaced by fear and suspicion and the country was as far from Rome as it had ever been.

The wherryman steered the boat without mishap under the arches of London Bridge and drew up at the stairs just outside the old city wall. Christopher ordered him to wait there for him. 'Fine morning for it, sir,' the man said as Christopher stepped out of the boat, sending a fat rat scurrying down a hole in the brickwork. 'Good crowd, I daresay. They deserve a show after all this time.'

Christopher looked back and snapped at him, 'Hold your foul tongue and pray for the soul of the condemned man.' He was in no mood for banter.

The sun was already hot and by the time he reached the top of Tower Hill sweat was running uncomfortably down his back and into his groin. The day promised to be sweltering. At the top of the hill, a noisy crowd was gathering around the scaffold, newly erected on a small green near the north-west corner of the Tower wall. A line of yeomen, the queen's own bodyguard, in their red and gold tunics and armed with swords and halberds, kept the crowd from approaching too close.

Christopher used his height and reach to force a way through the throng, paying no heed to the curses hurled at him, until he found a place to one side from where he had a clear view of the platform, on which clean straw had been laid and the executioner's block made ready. He could see an open coffin placed behind the scaffold. Above it all, the Tower loomed huge and threatening. How many executions had the ancient building seen in its five hundred years? How many more before it too crumbled away to dust?

The crowd grew until it overflowed into the streets that converged at the green. Christopher scanned it. There were two faces he knew but none he recognized as a relative of the prisoner. It was a gathering of working men and women in leather jerkins and woollen smocks — smiths and cobblers, milkmaids and tavern-keepers — some of whom would have forfeited a morning's pay to be there. Of gentlemen or even working yeomen there were few. He shooed away a child peddling straw dolls dressed in crimson and gold but lacking heads. A vendor went from group to group selling penny buns and mugs of ale for twopence. Another had a tray of oysters fresh-lifted from the beds downstream. Trade was brisk. The vendors would dine well that day.

Here and there an argument broke out. A fat man was dragged complaining to the back to allow others a better view and a mother with a bawling child was told to take it home lest it be put to sleep on the block. When they had to, the yeomen guards used the shafts of their halberds to keep order. Christopher watched and listened. The earl would wish to know the mood of the crowd.

A cry went up and Christopher instinctively turned his head to follow the general gaze. As he watched, the executioner and his young assistant, both gloved and masked, emerged from the Postern Gate in the Tower wall. They were followed by the prisoner, his hands tied and surrounded by a troop of guards. Christopher had never before set eyes on Norfolk, so could not be sure how imprisonment had affected him, but for a man of only thirty-six years he appeared diminished — round-shouldered, head bowed, an air of fatigue about him — the mien of a much older man.

Not for the first time, Christopher wondered how he would

conduct himself were he on the way to the scaffold. Would he hold his head high and stand by his principles or would he declaim his innocence and cravenly plead for mercy? How could a man know such a thing about himself until it happened?

The prisoner was accompanied by John Foxe, once Norfolk's tutor, Alexander Nowell, Dean of St Paul's, and a third man whom Christopher did not recognize. The crowd erupted as if to send the condemned man on his way from this life to the next with their cries ringing in his ears. Looking neither right nor left, Norfolk ignored them all. When he stumbled, Foxe extended a hand to steady him. Norfolk recovered his footing and raised his eyes to the platform. His face betrayed no emotion. Christopher watched, if not with admiration, at least with respect.

Assailed by raucous shouts of 'traitor' and 'papist coward' and 'hang him and draw him', the little party progressed steadily to the scaffold. A bun was thrown at the prisoner and a screeching hag reached out as if to scratch out his eyes. One old man fell to his knees in front of him and in a pitiful croak asked God to be merciful on a sinner. He was swiftly bundled aside by a guard.

The duke climbed the scaffold and stood facing the crowd. Gradually the hubbub died down. When he could be heard he spoke in a clear voice. 'I do not fear death. I have never been popish and I have been loyal to the queen and to England. I know nothing of Spanish plots and my guilt, if guilt it is, lies in my innocent communication with the Queen of Scots, which has been spoken of by my enemies as evidence of treason.'

The audience muttered among themselves and shuffled their feet impatiently. They cared nothing for fine words. An officer of the guard, sensing their mood, gruffly urged the prisoner to cut short his address. The good people of London, he said in a voice that could be heard around the green, had come to see justice done, not to listen to long speeches.

When Norfolk fell silent, the executioner knelt before him to ask his forgiveness and was given a small purse of coins. The prisoner then read aloud the fifty-first psalm, substituting, at one point, 'England' for 'Jerusalem'. Finally he embraced his tutor and the dean, refused a blindfold, removed his cloak, cap and doublet and knelt to put his neck on the block. Christopher kept his eyes open. The earl would wish to know if there had been any mishap. The executioner raised the axe, paused for a moment and brought it down squarely on the exposed flesh. The head fell, blood gushed and the crowd bellowed its approval. The executioner picked up the severed head and held it up by the hair for it to see its detached body. In a second or two, it had been done. Thomas Howard was dead. Christopher closed his eyes and muttered a brief prayer. The crowd cheered. For some, just one more execution. For others, the death of a traitor. For almost all, a morning's entertainment and a quantity of ale. Slowly, laughing and chattering, the crowd began to disperse, leaving but a handful of women on their knees, weeping and wailing and calling down God's mercy on the dead man.

It was over. Christopher used a sleeve to wipe sweat from his brow and was about to return to the steps when he felt a tug on his sleeve. Expecting a cutpurse or pickpocket he turned sharply. A slight figure, perhaps a foot shorter than he, stood behind him, face half hidden under a hood and dressed modestly in grey. 'Joy of the day, Dr Rad,' said the figure in little more than a whisper. 'Thought I might find you here.'

Christopher glanced about. 'Ell, what are you doing here? This is no place for a lady and we might be seen.'

The woman stifled a laugh. 'Lady, eh? That's new. And there's no eyes on us. They're all chittering and chattering about the duke with no head.'

'What is it, Ell?'

'Thought you should know, doctor. Had a man in the house two nights since. Went with the dark girl, Sal. Beat her about horrible. Face cut and bruised and bleeding from inside. Poor thing. Pretty girl she is. Won't be able to work for a good time, now.'

Again Christopher looked about. 'I am sorry for it, Ell, but such things are not uncommon in your line of work. Why do you tell me?'

'Big bugger, he was. Hair the colour of a rusty nail. Spoke different, Sal says. Not English. Might have been Scotch.'

'And?'

'He was boasting about how he was going to rescue the Scotch queen and set London ablaze. Spoke of fires and flames and slicing the queen's head from her shoulders. Sal said he had the look of Satan in his eyes. Frightened she was. And then he started knocking her about. Got away before any of us could stop him.'

'Did you see him?'

Ell shook her head. 'He'd gone when I heard Sal crying out. We did the best we could for her but she's in a poor way.'

'Drunk?'

'Drunk as a French lord, but still capable and frightening. Thought you should know.'

Christopher took a crown from his purse and slipped it to her. Ell received a coin whenever she brought him intelligence, whether it had worth or not, and she expected more than a shilling or two. 'I can earn a shilling lying on my back,' she had once chided him. 'When I am on my feet, I expect more.' It mattered not. He reclaimed his expenditure from Leicester's comptroller. 'Probably nothing in it, Ell.

Just a fanciful rogue in his cups with a taste for a woman's blood.'

'We get plenty of them, doctor. This one seemed different, Sal said. Thought you should know.'

'You were right to tell me, Ell. Be off now before we're seen.'

Ell pushed her hood back an inch and grinned. Brown eyes and rosebud lips in an oval face framed by auburn curls; it was no wonder that she was in such demand. She could easily have passed for a lady at court. Only her words revealed her for what she was. 'Come by soon, doctor. And don't forget, not so much as a farthing to you. You're a handsome gentleman and it'd be a treat after all the ugly fat pigs I have to spread my legs for.'

Christopher shook his head. 'Thank you, Ell, it's a tempting offer but I'm well served.' He grinned. 'And I wouldn't want the pox.'

Ell's voice rose. 'You won't get no French welcome from me, doctor. I always wash out thorough afterwards.' She wagged her finger at him.

'Ssh, Ell. Thank you for finding me. Go safely.' He watched her leave before walking down the hill to the stairs. A lovely lady, a valuable intelligencer and a whore. He knew of no other like her. He had once asked how she had come to be an intelligencer for his predecessor. She had grinned and held a finger to her lips. 'Couldn't say, doctor. Just one of those strange things that happen in a lady's bed chamber.' In return, she had asked him why he was a doctor. When he told her that he had studied long enough to be a teacher and 'doctor' simply meant 'teacher', she had laughed and said, 'Well then, I must be a doctor too. I've been at it long enough and I've taught my gentlemen a thing or two.' A whore, but a rare one.

The one-eyed wherryman was waiting. 'Did they show him his body, your lordship?' the man asked with a lewd grin. 'They do say the head lives long enough to see the body for itself.' Christopher ignored him. 'Back to Blackfriars, is it?'

'To Whitehall steps and be quick about it,' replied Christopher shortly. The earl would be waiting.

The wherryman spat into the river and fixed him with his eye. 'An extra threepence to Whitehall, it will be.' Christopher did not bother to argue. The fare was of no consequence. The earl had never baulked at the expenses he incurred in the course of carrying out his duties.

As the sun had climbed so had the stench of the river. Bloated animal carcasses floated among the refuse of the villages upstream and the excrement and debris of the city, forcing Christopher to hold a corner of his gown to his nose and to keep his gaze firmly on the trees and meadows on the south bank. The wherryman struggled against the flow, especially where it strengthened under the bridge, so that they took twice as long to reach Blackfriars as they had to reach the Tower. By the time they rounded the sweeping bend in the river and Whitehall Palace came into view, Christopher was grinding his teeth with impatience. He wanted to make his report and be done with it.

The wherryman pulled up against the pier commonly known as Whitehall steps and tossed a rope over a large stone placed there for the purpose. Not even waiting for the boat to settle in the water, Christopher handed the wherryman a few coins, received a vulgar grunt of acknowledgement and stepped out on to the pier. He hurried up to a private gate near the royal chapel. His face was well enough known to be admitted without fuss, but still a guard escorted him to the earl's apartments. In a palace of fifteen hundred rooms, dozens of galleries and corridors, a cockpit, a tiltyard and a tennis court, it was not difficult to lose one's way. In frivolous mood,

Leicester had once insisted that there were lost courtiers still wandering the passages from the days of King Henry. Whitehall Palace was larger than many villages.

When first he had entered the place he had found its size and splendour overpowering: wherever he looked, an unmatched show of wealth, a strange silence, and a hint of menace. A new official royal residence – much of it built and restored by the queen's father – it watched over the law courts and parliament at Westminster, as if to make clear to any man who doubted it that it was the monarch who ruled England. Christopher was now accustomed to it, yet still Whitehall Palace could be unsettling.

The royal apartments stood to the left of the gate by which he entered, their windows looking out over the river. Following his escort, he climbed a flight of steps and passed along a gallery overlooking the queen's garden, where neatly trimmed grass walks separated rows of square beds filled with red and white roses, set around a stone fountain gushing water pumped from the river. At the edge of a dirty, coal-smoked, bustling city the garden's beauty was almost mystical. A game was in progress on the bowling green. He could just make out the gentle clunk of bowl on bowl and the muted voices of the players. On the morning of the execution of a kinsman of the queen, the game, it seemed, might be played but voices must not be raised.

The earl's apartments were guarded, as always, by a yeoman either side of his door. Again, Christopher was admitted without fuss and entered an antechamber from which an imposing carved door led to the earl's office. His escort knocked, and he was ushered in. For once, there was no waiting for the earl to be ready for him. The door was closed behind him.

It was a room he had come to know well – large and airy,

immaculate and sumptuously furnished with intricate Italian and French furniture and rich Flemish drapes. On the walls hung a huge arras, a fine portrait of the queen and smaller ones of the earl, his father and his late wife, Amy Robsart.

The queen's portrait dominated the room. It showed her at her most regal — bejewelled, elaborately costumed in purple and gold, looking down on the observer, unsmiling, unforgiving, a haughty set to her mouth. Her skin showed no sign of the smallpox she had suffered ten years earlier, although whether that was the work of nature or of the artist, Christopher could not tell. He had seen the queen only once, and that at some distance when she was walking with her ladies in the garden. At least that was once more than most of her subjects could boast. He sometimes thought that unswerving loyalty to a prince one has never set eyes on and is thus not able to picture in one's mind, cannot be easy. That is not to say that the queen hid herself away, far from it. Her progresses around the country were designed, in part, to show herself to her people. But did a Cornish miner or a Lancashire shepherd who had never seen a proper likeness of her not wonder about the appearance of the woman to whom he owed his loyalty?

There was another thought — disloyal, even treasonous — that always came into his head when he looked at that painting. How did Her Majesty appear when she woke each morning, dishevelled from sleep and clad only in her night attire? Was there an artist skilled enough to make her regal then? He doubted it. It was said that she took two hours or more to dress and complete her toilette.

Leicester was known for his looks, but in this portrait, smaller than that of the queen, he appeared to Christopher more formidable than handsome — slim and athletic, a narrow face, with a long, straight nose, dark eyes and a neat pointed beard. The artist had sought to portray him as a statesman by dressing him in black and giving him a tiny twist of the lip and a knowing look in the eye. It was the eyes that drew the observer in.

The earl was alone, sitting at his magnificent walnut writing table. On a matching, smaller table stood a chess board set with ivory pieces and a cylindrical brass clock. Despite the heat, he wore a tight-fitting doublet of black cloth embroidered in red and gold over a snowy-white shirt. His hair was coal-black and swept back from his forehead. Even the hair at his temples showed no sign of grey. He put down the document he was reading but did not rise. 'Dr Radcliff,' he asked without preamble, 'what news do you bring?' The voice was low and musical.

Christopher removed his cap and bowed his head. The earl placed a high value on courtesy, seldom lapsed from the highest standards himself and expected the same from every rank of society. Christopher had heard him, on a single day, reprimand a senior palace official for a rude interruption and praise a humble servant for careful attention to his wishes. 'I have come directly from the Tower, my lord. The deed is done.'

Leicester nodded and peered at him from under his heavy lids. 'You will understand why I did not myself attend.'

'Of course, my lord.'

'Was it swift?'

'It was.'

'The queen will be glad of it. She deplores unnecessary suffer-ing. Did he speak?'

'He did. He claimed never to have been popish and proclaimed his innocence and his loyalty to Her Majesty.'

'Popish. Was that the word he used?'

'It was.'

'Why that word, do you think?'

'I too wondered that. Perhaps he was trying to disassociate him-self from the pope's unholy bull, without exactly denying his Catholicism.' The papal bull, the so-called *Regnans in Excelsis*, which had excommunicated England's Protestant queen and had called on all Catholics to rise up against her, had been taken by the Privy Council as tantamount to a declaration of war. It had undermined the last of the queen's natural tolerance and could scarcely have been more damaging. Now the words 'Catholic' and 'traitor' were as good as synonymous.

'He said nothing that might anger or embarrass her or her counsellors?'

'He did not.'

'That is as well for us and for his family. They need suffer no more. And the crowd?'

'Entirely loyal. I knew only two faces. The Earl of Oxford's man and an occasional agent of my own. There was no sign of malcontents and no unrest of any consequence. Although I fancy it might have been otherwise had there been another reprieve.' Christopher did not mention Ell's intelligence for fear of setting alarm bells ringing unnecessarily. He heard rumours of plots to assassinate the queen almost every week.

'Indeed, and I thank God it is done. Her Majesty came to see the necessity of the matter, although she is melancholic and I fear will remain so for some days. She feels the pain of others, as I feel hers.' He sighed. 'And now we must deal with the troublesome Queen of Scots, although this is not the time to broach the subject with Her Majesty. She must be allowed to grieve for one kinsman before burying another. It is inconvenient that both Lord Burghley and Sir Francis Walsingham are in Paris. England needs their wisdom at such a time.'

Christopher remained silent. The earl's mood was unsettling but he had learned to interrupt neither his words nor his thoughts. Leicester and Walsingham were close but his rivalry with the scholarly, cautious Burghley was long-standing. Perhaps there had been a rapprochement. Christopher had delivered his report and waited to be dismissed. Instead, the earl rose from his chair. They were almost equal in height. Indeed, in a light mood the earl had once commanded a servant to judge who was the taller. The wise fellow had declared the contest a draw, before waiting for the earl to turn his back and then indicating to Christopher with his fingers that he had it by an inch.

The earl took the cylindrical clock from its place on the table and turned it over in his hands, holding it as gently as if it were a piece of fine porcelain. 'It has never worked, you know,' he said almost to himself. 'It was a gift to Her Majesty from an admirer in Bavaria. The foolish man also sent a letter declaring undying love and a portrait revealing him to be a grotesque. The queen did not trouble to reply and gave the clock to me.' He looked up and smiled. 'I am sure Her gracious Majesty believed it sound.'

He replaced the clock and walked to a tall window from which he could gaze at the garden below. When he turned to speak again his tone was businesslike. 'Since you came to London, doctor, you have served me well. I trust you do not regret leaving the academic life. How long is it since you left Cambridge? Two years?'

Christopher hesitated. With Leicester it paid to choose one's words with care. 'A little more, my lord. I found London difficult at first but now I am accustomed to it and to my work. Although I would sometimes wish for something more demanding.'

'Most tactful, doctor.' Leicester smiled his sardonic smile. 'I am aware of your wish to advance yourself and indeed I might just have something more demanding for you.'

Christopher watched him carefully, wondering where this was leading. The earl had lately taken to confiding in him rather more than was comfortable. It was a facet of the man's temperament that was becoming more pronounced — one day firm and decisive, the next strangely uncertain. Perhaps it was a consequence of the strain he was under and the one side sought to hide the other. Even strong, rational men could waver under the weight of something beyond their control.

'While Burghley and Walsingham are absent, new voices are heard at court,' Leicester went on. 'The Earl of Oxford entertains us with his poetry and Sir Christopher Hatton has danced his way to the captaincy of the queen's guard. High office for one so young.' Christopher, of course, knew this, but remained silent. Again the dark eyes and the hint of a smile. 'I speak more candidly than perhaps I should, doctor, because I tire of my own company and because I must be sure of your continuing loyalty.'

The comings and goings of the royal court were no secret. In certain Westminster taverns, conversation was of little else. Still, Christopher was taken aback by the earl's directness. 'My lord, you are of course assured of my loyalty at all times.'

Leicester held up a hand. 'I do not suggest otherwise. I do say, however, that there are others who would value your services as highly as do I. The queen likes to call me her "eyes". You are my eyes.' He paused as if a thought had occurred to him. 'Although, like the giant Argus Panoptes, I have one hundred eyes.' Christopher suppressed a smile. Leicester was clever and perceptive but he was no classical scholar and liked to show off what learning he had. 'I would not wish you or any of my eyes to keep watch for another.

You will tell me if you are approached, doctor, will you not?'

'Naturally, my lord, I will.'

'Good. That would be best for both of us. Unsurprisingly after this latest plot, the court, like the country, is nervous. King Philip lurks in the Escorial Palace like a spider in its web, making no secret of his wish to send a Spanish fleet across the narrow sea — too damnably narrow for my liking — yet it is closer to home that vipers lurk unseen. There are rumours, as there always are, but lately I sense in them more venom.' He paused to take a sip from the glass at his hand. 'At least we now have reason to think that we have an ally in France. The treaty recently signed at Blois is a welcome step forward and Queen Catherine is pressing the suit of her son the duc d'Alençon. Walsingham describes him as an ill-favoured dwarf with a poxed face and the charm of a hog, but one hopes he exaggerates; and a brother of the French king married to the queen of England would certainly make the Spaniard think twice before launching his ships.' Again he paused. 'But what have you heard, doctor? Has any new word of insurrection reached your ears?'

'The usual idle talk, my lord. Since Ridolfi's plot was discovered, the stuff of inns and taverns, nothing untoward. I would have informed you had it been otherwise.'

Leicester nodded. 'Of course, of course. But be vigilant. Lurking papists, Scots and Spanish, the enemy is not only at our gates but clambering up our battlements and hacking away at our drawbridge. Her Majesty, as always, is steadfast yet I detect anxiety in her. She speaks of our godly country being surrounded by the forces of evil and of the need for courage in the face of adversity. To defeat the evil we need accurate intelligence and it is our task to obtain it. From Paris Walsingham sends me frequent reports, but he is naturally cautious in what he writes. He fears that his letters will be intercepted and decrypted.' Leicester shook his head. 'There was never a more loyal or more able servant of England than Sir Francis. We too must be as steadfast as the queen and ever on our guard, doctor. ' For a few seconds, the dark eyes held Christopher's before the earl returned to his seat.

'You mentioned something more demanding, my lord?'

'I did. A letter has arrived from Walsingham. He asks that a reliable man be sent to Paris. He has intelligence which he does not care to commit to paper or to entrust to a common messenger. It occurs to me that you might be the very man for the task.'

A messenger. Not precisely what Christopher would have wished for. 'My lord, my French is adequate, but I do not know the country. Perhaps another man would be more suitable.'

Leicester waved a hand dismissively. 'Tush, doctor. Spare me the false modesty. I do so dislike it. I shall think on the matter.' His mood lightened. 'Now, you must excuse me. I have a thousand details regarding the queen's progress to attend to. She will be visiting Kenilworth. That is excellent news, is it not?' Kenilworth Castle, once the home of the earl's late father, had been restored to him by the queen and refurbished with scant regard to cost. The earl had never been a man to count the pennies. Christopher had been there twice and found it almost overwhelmingly magnificent. The queen's summer progresses, for which, as Master of the Horse, Leicester was responsible, were Herculean feats of organization that he appeared to revel in. 'Her household will be the largest ever — almost fifteen hundred in all.'

The previous year, Christopher had seen the progress setting off from Whitehall. Until then, despite the numbers spoken of, he had not fully appreciated the scale of it. Only when he saw it for himself did he begin to realize what was involved. Not just more than a thousand men and women, all of whom had to be fed, but horses, carriages, wagons, provisions, clothing, and all manner of items that the royal household might require on a progress lasting several weeks, from furniture to feather pillows. Whether the expense was justified at a time of such hardship, he doubted.

There was a knock on the door. 'Another visitor,' grumbled Leicester. 'There will be no peace today. Enter.'

A young man of little more than twenty entered and bowed to the earl. He was clean-shaven and sandy-haired, with clear blue eyes and an open countenance. He was gowned, dressed as a clerk, and carried a sheaf of documents.

'Ah, Mr Berwick,' the earl greeted the young man with a smile. 'How fares the queen today? Have you attended her?'

A paper slipped from the young man's grasp and he had to stoop rather clumsily to pick it up. When he rose the embarrassment on his face was almost comical. Christopher felt a twinge of sympathy for the fellow. A year ago, he too might have been discomfited at such a trifling mishap.

'Her Majesty is in low humour, my lord. She has received the news of Howard's death and grieves for his family.' The young man's voice was so quiet that it was scarcely above a whisper. 'Fortunately, Dr Caius has arrived from Cambridge. He is with her now. He has ordered the queen's ladies to keep her windows closed and for a harpist to play outside her chamber.'

Christopher had once met John Caius, who was not only Master of the Cambridge college that bore his name but also president of the Society of Physicians and the most respected man of medicine in England, and had found him somewhat dry. In keeping with his elevated position he had changed his name from Kays to Caius, although the words were spoken alike.

Leicester turned to Christopher, a tiny smile playing around the corners of his mouth. 'Dr Radcliff, Mr John Berwick, not long arrived from the north, where his father, as loyal and brave a man as any in England, died in the uprising. The queen has instructed me to guide you through the mysteries of the court, is that not so, Berwick?'

'Indeed, my lord.' Again Berwick bowed politely. 'And I shall serve Her Majesty as devotedly as did my father. And you, Dr Radcliff, are you also a physician?'

'I am a Doctor of Law, sir. I serve the earl as he commands.'

Berwick inclined his head. 'As do we all, doctor, and I am grateful for his lordship's guidance in my work here. I have much to learn.'

'Then I advise you to apply yourself and wish you success in your studies, sir.'

'What word of the duc de Montmorency, Berwick?' asked Leicester. The duc was coming as an ambassador of the French court, on the pretext of ratifying the treaty and, just as importantly, to promote the suit of d'Alençon.

'None, my lord.'

'Damn the man for keeping Her Majesty waiting. Such discourtesy is not designed to win royal favour. His brother, the mincing duc d'Anjou, had been bad enough. Do you remember the sermons preached against him and the bawdy songs? Let us hope that Her Majesty is not insulted, eh, Berwick?'

'Indeed, my lord.'

'Now let us attend to the progress. Every detail must be perfect for Her Majesty. I shall tolerate nothing less.' Christopher had no doubt of it. Leicester's skills in organization and his attention to detail where the queen's entertainments were concerned were legendary. 'I thank you for your service this day, doctor. And remember, vipers lurk.'

*

The walk back to Ludgate Hill took Christopher along the Strand. In Cambridge most of the old religious houses were now colleges. Here they were rapidly making way for grand mansions and elegant brick-built houses whose flower gardens stretched down to the river. Thence down Fleet Street, ever a jumble of carts and horses and carriages and home to a cluster of printers and small shops. He took care to avoid the heaps of horse dung and the grasping hands of beggars, paid a penny for a broadsheet from a boy outside a printing house and pushed open a narrow door beside it.

The shop was dark enough for candles to have been lit. It was empty but for three pine chairs and a low table on which stood a set of weighing scales and a neat row of graduated brass weights. Motes of dust danced in the candlelight. A small man, black-eyed and red-bearded, soon appeared from the back. He peered at Christopher through a pair of thick spectacles. 'Christopher, here is a surprise. I wish you joy of the day.'

Fifty years had passed since Isaac Cardoza's grandfather had fled the Catholic inquisition in Portugal and arrived with his wife and young daughter in London. Isaac, a goldsmith and occasional banker, had chosen to carry on his business away from the clutter and bustle of the city and had discreetly set up shop in Fleet Street, near the many goldsmiths and silversmiths in the Strand and where, he said, his customers had more time to sit and talk. It amused him to use an Italian word, *chiacchierare*, to describe their chatter. He said that an intelligent man might divine its meaning without knowing a word of Italian.

Soon after his arrival in London, Christopher had sold Isaac a ring once owned by his mother. He was uncomfortable in doing so, but he needed the money and persuaded himself that the sale would mark a fresh start in his life. Isaac had sensed his feelings and they had fallen into conversation. 'We Jews prize money and knowledge above all else,' he had said, 'and we never tire of acquiring both.' Christopher had swiftly recruited him to his network and they had become friends. It had been Isaac who had first got wind of the Ridolfi Plot.

'I am well, Isaac, thank you. How fare your family?'

'Also well. I hope you will break bread with us one day soon. Ruth is eight years old now. A clever child. Already she knows much of the Talmud. You would enjoy talking with her.'

'I would, Isaac. It has been a sad day for England.'

'The execution? Did you attend?'

'From duty only. The earl commanded me to go. It was an experience I would rather forget.'

'Have you come now from Whitehall?'

'I have.'

'Yes. Your face reveals it and your spirit is not calm. You are under strain. For the sake of your health, should you not return to your teaching?' Isaac knew only that Christopher had once taught law. He did not know, nor did any of his intelligencers, why he no longer did so. Christopher intended it should stay that way.

'No, Isaac, I have chosen my path and am reluctant to abandon it.'

'As are we all. To do so is to admit failure. It is God's way of testing us. He wishes us to choose not what is best for ourselves but what is best for others. The choice is not always easy.'

'Wise words, Isaac, as ever. Have you news for me?'

'Except that business is difficult, very little. I can buy as much gold and silver as I wish, and at good prices, but finding a customer for it is not so easy. Even for us Jews, times are hard.'

'Nothing at all?'

'Some nonsense from France, no more. A mischievous story about the French queen sending every unmarried male member of her family to London and asking our queen to choose one. Even for a Medici that seems unlikely.'

Christopher laughed. 'Anything else?'

'In Paris there is much talk of the forthcoming wedding and hope for the peace it should bring.' The marriage of the French king's sister Margaret to Henry of Navarre was planned for the end of August. Raised as a Protestant, Henry would be crowned King of Navarre before the wedding. Leicester had not mentioned it but it was another reason for hope. It was said that Queen Catherine had worked tirelessly to secure the match. The recent treaty, a son married to the Queen of England and a daughter to a Protestant king would surely bring peace to both countries and make King Philip think twice before launching a Spanish fleet.

'Let us pray that it does. Thank you, Isaac. *Shalom.*'

'*Shalom*, my friend. I will send word if I hear anything more.'

The house on Ludgate Hill, backing on to the ancient city wall, had been arranged for Christopher by the earl's staff. It was small, but well built of timber and brick with a tiled roof. The furnishings were simple but adequate — much as they had been in his tutor's room in Pembroke Hall — and he paid only a trifling rent.

When first he had come to London he quickly realized that he must attend to the everyday things he had taken for granted in the college. He had no kitchen staff to provide his meals, no servant to clean his room, no laundress to wash his clothes. For several weeks he floundered, until he found a suitable housekeeper, Rose Crouch, an elderly widow in need of the money. Rose knew her way around the markets and could make a few shillings go farther than ever he could. He slept in a chamber on the upper storey and worked in a room beside the kitchen which would once have been a parlour but served well enough as a study. Compared to his room in Cambridge, the house was almost capacious.

Rose was in the kitchen, preparing his dinner. She was a tiny soul, white-haired and wrinkled, and a little bent in the back, as befitted her name. She bobbed a curtsy when he walked in. 'Good day, doctor. I did not know if you would return for dinner, but I have prepared it anyway. You must eat to keep up your strength.' Her voice was as tiny as she was.

'Thank you, Rose. I was called away early. Dinner would be welcome. I will take it in my study.' It was something he often did when working or when he just wanted to sit and think.

'Very well, doctor, but be sure to leave nothing uneaten.'

'I shall eat every scrap. And kindly open the windows. The house is like a smithy.'

The old lady was aghast. 'Doctor, there is talk of the hot weather bringing plague. You should beware inviting it into the house through an open window. Better to keep them tight shut.'

'And die from a lack of clean air? I think not, Rose. I will see to it myself.' Before going to the study he went around the house opening every window. It made little difference. The house was still hot and airless.

The study was a plain room with oak chairs, a writing table, and, placed carefully to one side of the table, his writing materials. Christopher was particular about these. From the stationers' market outside St Paul's he bought only the best duck-feather pens, good oak-apple ink and well-made rag paper, uncontaminated by foul water or scraps of hemp. His pens, sharpened to a fine point with a small pen knife, stood in a cylindrical wooden holder; his paper was piled neatly and covered with a linen cloth to protect it from dust. As a child he had been taught by his father to form his letters properly and to treat each page of script as a gift to its recipient. Well produced, the gift would be appreciated; hurried and untidy, it would not. The advice had never left him.

A small window overlooked a narrow alley that ran between the house and the city wall. A fire kept the room warm in winter. Rose knew that unless the house was alight or the queen herself came to call, the doctor was not to be disturbed in the study.

She brought him a dish of onion soup and a plate of mutton with manchet bread and left him to eat. The soup was good but he found when he speared his knife into the meat that he had lost his appetite. It was not the meat, which was about as tender as could be had in the markets. It was that there had been a quiet integrity to Norfolk's address that rang true. Both he and his wife had demonstrated their loyalty to the queen — a loyalty that seemed to Christopher to be genuine. The duke had acted foolishly in engaging so intimately with the Queen of Scots, but his greater mistake had been to have made enemies not only of Leicester but also of Lord Burghley. Whether for his alleged treason or merely for past grievances, the treasurer and the earl had between them ensured that Norfolk paid with his life.

Christopher forced down the mutton and pushed away the plate. There was something more troubling him. Was it that Leicester had never before spoken to him so unguardedly? Was his warning of an approach by Oxford or Hatton or some other unnamed courtier well founded, or was it mere conjecture? Did he have specific evidence of insurrection? Had one of his eyes seen something or one of his ears heard something? If so, why had he not passed the information on? Any fact, any detail would make Christopher's job easier. Perhaps the earl's trust in him was not as absolute as he claimed. Or was it the earl's own position that troubled him? In the whispering world of the court, had he suffered some setback or somehow incurred the queen's displeasure? If so, he would be doubly anxious that her progress should be a triumph and would think of little else.

And what intelligence did Walsingham have that was so sensitive that he would not put it in writing? Leicester troubled, Walsingham anxious, a wild-eyed Scotsman promising the death of the queen and the destruction of London. What might be coming next? He did not wish to travel to Paris but if the earl ordered it, he would have no choice but to go.

A pile of reports from his network of agents awaited him. Some agents he had inherited from his predecessor, a victim of the bloody flux; others, like Isaac Cardoza, he had recruited himself. It was Christopher's task to read every report and either act upon it or, if he thought the safety of the realm might be in imminent danger, to pass it on to Leicester. Much of what he read would be trivial – an angry word overheard in a tavern, a set of rosary beads found in a purse, a joke at the earl's expense – but occasionally, just occasionally, two or more reports would come together and point at something more serious. A name, a place, a word incautiously spoken. It was akin to searching for gold in a Welsh stream. Long, tedious work in the hope of uncovering a speck of bright yellow metal. Grateful as he was to Leicester, after two years he longed for something more.

He sat stretching the last two fingers of his right hand, which were bent inwards so that they almost touched his palm. He knew neither the name of the condition nor if there was a remedy for it, only that it was getting worse. A physician had suggested rheumatism, an apothecary a disease of the skin. Both had recommended the letting of blood and ointments that had proved useless. He pulled the fingers straight, only for them to return immediately to a bent position. There was no pain, merely the irritation of having to hold a pen or beaker or spoon with two bent fingers. If it got much worse he would be forced to write with his left hand.

The broadsheet exhorted him to pray daily for the safety of England and of her queen. Once he would have happily done so, but now he rarely prayed other than in church and even then the familiar words sometimes rang hollow. It also advised him to be alert to Spanish spies and Catholic priests and reminded him that the queen had commanded that fish be eaten not only on Fridays but also on Wednesdays. This was not a matter of religious practice, but in the hope of supporting the ailing fishing industry. Christopher grinned. It was a royal command that he chose privately to ignore. As a child he had once choked on a fishbone stuck in his throat. Only a mighty thump on the back from his father and a pot of ale had saved him. Since then he had eaten fish only when he had to and when he was sure that all the bones had been removed, even during Lent.

He put the broadsheet aside and took a report from the top of the pile. He gazed at it for a while, realized that he had taken in not a word and put it too aside. What was it that Leicester knew or suspected? Where were the vipers lurking? What did Walsingham know? And would he receive an approach from a rival of the earl? If so, what would he do about it?

He tried another report. It might as well have been written in Hebrew. He threw it down and stood up. The room was stiflingly hot and his thoughts were jumbled. He called for Rose. 'I must go out again, Rose.'

'Out again, doctor? To Wood Street would it be?'

'It would, Rose. And kindly close the windows before you leave. We must not invite thieves, never mind plague.'

Rose snorted her disapproval. 'I wonder that Mistress Allington does not send you on your way, a respectable lady such as she. If you will not marry her, there's many better who would.'

'I daresay there are, Rose. Have I another clean shirt? This one is for the wash.'

'In your bed chamber, doctor, same as always.'

Christopher found a shirt and put it on. 'Thank you. My dinner was good.'

'Perhaps Mistress Allington will give you another dinner. Wouldn't do you any harm. Put some flesh on those bones. Thin as a pike staff, you are.'

'Good day, Rose. Do not forget the windows.' He knew that every window would be closed within five minutes of his leaving. As he opened the door, Rose muttered something that he could not make out. He laughed quietly, closed the door carefully behind him, touched the handle of his poniard to make sure it was safely under his belt, and set off for Wood Street.

The quickest route — one which for a year he could not steel himself to take — was around the prison at Newgate, where ancient houses huddled together against the threat of fire and disease, and vagrants and maunderers and queer birds just out of the gaol infested the lanes and alleys and eked out a pitiful existence as best they could. It was an area of stews and hovels, drabs and scroyles, which honest men avoided, especially at night. Here one saw neither coach nor carriage, nor even a pony. They would have made targets too tempting for a starving man to resist.

For weeks the weather had become hotter and more humid — as if the city's buildings and streets were soaking up the sun's rays, firing them up and hurling them back with twice the ferocity. There had been no rain, the Fleet river had slowed to a muddy trickle and there was barely a drop of fresh water to be had.

And as the temperature rose, so did the stench not only from the river but also in the streets. The foul miasmas that carried disease thrived in the summer, sometimes disappearing altogether in winter. Unless the weather broke, it would not be long before the plague that had killed his parents arrived and the physicians departed in haste for the countryside, leaving the sick to the quacks and charlatans who were only too eager to put on plague masks and take their places. That fearful, hateful disease could fly through houses and streets and wards like a carrion crow, spreading its poison and sparing neither young nor old, neither rich nor poor. Some said it was merely God's way of punishing sinners. Others that it was the work of witches and papists, somehow enabled by the devil to conjure up the miasmas.

As he made his way through the narrow streets he could not help glancing at doorways. If there was plague in a house, a red cross must be painted on the door. The plague doctors and the women who searched corpses for signs of the disease would arrive and the house might be closed up with the living inside it. In the endless fight against plague, such harsh steps were necessary.

He had as much reason as any to hate the disease. His father had woken one morning to find the tell-tale black buboes under his arms and had immediately ordered a grave to be dug and spread with clean straw. Not wanting to infect others or for his body to be dumped in a plague pit, he had lain down in the grave and died that day.

And, with his father gone, Christopher had nursed his dying mother by dripping sweet wine mixed with water on to her parched lips, and wiping her burning brow with a damp cloth. To no avail. After three days of torment, she too had succumbed. He did not understand why he alone had been spared.

He closed his ears to the pitiful cries from within the prison walls, just avoided colliding with a ragged beggar, shook thoughts of plague from his mind and quickened his step. Rotting food and human waste in the gutters around Newgate fed dogs and rats, and he had to take particular care where he stepped. Twice he slipped on something foul and only just avoided tripping on to the cobbles.

By contrast, Wood Street ran through a ward in which the merchants and officers of the city were busily clearing away mean hovels and crumbling cottages to make way for their new homes — like many to the north and west of the city a forward-looking, confident street, largely unencumbered by poverty or filth.

Katherine herself opened the door. Morning or evening, heat or cold, in silks and satins or in nothing at all, to Christopher's eyes Katherine Allington could only look beautiful. Flame-haired, green-eyed, smooth-skinned, and when she smiled she showed two rows of perfectly white, perfectly straight teeth.

'Come in, Christopher. I expected you. We will sit in the parlour,' she greeted him. 'Will you take refreshment?'

'I will if you have lemon water.' Katherine's lemon water was boiled with honey, left to cool and flavoured with pressed rose petals. She went to the kitchen and returned with a pitcher and two glass goblets. She poured the lemon water and sat down.

The parlour was a small room at the front of the house with latticed windows that looked out on to the street. The walls were bare but for two fine hangings, one depicting the Garden of Eden, the other the story of Noah and his animals on their ark. Christopher knew that they had been embroidered by Katherine's aunt, Isabel Tranter. Two matching oak chairs, each with a high, carved back, rush-padded seat and comfortably broad arms, stood either side of an unlit fire, a small chest between them. The chest, also of oak and with roses and lilies carved on its lid, was low enough to serve as a table.

They sat facing each other. Katherine's hands were clasped on her lap. He saw the tension in them. Her Catholic mother had known Norfolk and had held him in high regard. 'He was brave at the end,' he said gently.

'I am pleased. A good man but misguided. He was not afraid to go to his maker, as none of us should be. Well, it is done and we must pray for peace in England and for Her Majesty's safety.'

'That we must.' Christopher took a long draught of lemon water. 'Excellent. Sweet enough to ward off plague, pestilence and plotters. How fares your aunt in this heat?'

'Isabel is resting. She finds it tiring.' Katherine stood to refill his goblet. 'Did you see the earl?'

'I did. His mood reflects that of the queen and he worries for her health. He did not precisely say so, but I sense that recent intelligence concerns him.'

'Yet the treaty was signed at Blois and Queen Catherine is marrying her daughter to a Protestant prince. Is that not proof of a desire for peace after so many years of bloodshed?'

'Time will tell. Her son, after all, is the one who sits on the French throne, not her, and, having suffered her as regent for so long, he is known to be resentful of her continuing interference. And meanwhile, there is further intelligence that the Spanish are reinforcing their army and preparing their fleet in the Low Countries. From there it is but a hop across the sea to England.'

'I believe you worry too much.'

'Perhaps. But the earl is troubled by something. Still, I have his trust and he knows I do not gossip.' He did not mention Paris. That was a bridge he hoped not to be faced with.

Katherine laughed lightly. 'Yet you have told me.'

'Tush. You are not in the pay of the French king, are you?'

'I might be.' She put down her goblet and stood up. 'Enough of this. Bring your glass to my chamber. We will talk there.'

A flash of green eyes and a toss of auburn hair and Christopher was on his feet, his arms around her. He kissed her forehead and breathed into her ear, 'I must not be too long.'

She put a finger to his lips. 'Be silent. It has been a wearing day. For the rest of it your work must wait at a lady's pleasure.'

Afterwards, and not for the first time, he broached the subject of marriage. Katherine's response was sharp. 'Christopher, we have spoken of this a dozen times. You know why I will not marry you. If I did, you could never be a fellow of Pembroke Hall.'

'But I can never be a fellow, married or unmarried. You know that I am a convicted felon. My life now is in London. Why can we not marry and forget Cambridge? Then we could live together without fear and I would not have to slink through the streets like a night-thief.'

'Because I still believe that one day you may be able to return – as Master of Pembroke, perhaps. I would not want to stand in your way.'

'Master of Pembroke. A fanciful notion. Are you sure that is why you do not wish to marry?'

'That is unworthy of you. I have told you why I will not marry you. Let that be an end to it.'

He had pressed her no more but while she slept, he lay awake, thoughts of marriage and Cambridge and Edward Allington slipping in and out of his mind. He pictured the Doctors' table in Pembroke Hall, a place of conversation and disputation, where he had enjoyed testing his wits against those of his colleagues, and the court behind the college where he played *jeu-de-paume* with Edward Allington. He had loved Cambridge, even during the years of Queen Mary's reign when he was forced to worship in the old way, and had done well. Matriculation as a commoner pupil at sixteen, graduation three years later, a position as a tutor and then appointment as a Doctor of Civil Law. He enjoyed teaching, he had a modest but comfortable living and he hoped one day to join the Fellowship of Pembroke Hall.

But the following year, Edward had fallen from his horse, fractured his skull and died, leaving Katherine a childless widow. Comforting her had been no hardship — Mistress Allington was the object of many a pupil's lust — and they had grieved together. Within twelve months they had become lovers. She had followed him to London, where marriage, until then impossible if he wished to be a fellow of the college, had become possible. But Katherine was steadfast. With no more than her instinct to rely on, she believed he would return to Pembroke Hall; her mind was firm, she would not marry him and that was that.

When he left the house, she was still sleeping. He took the longer route home, avoiding the dark depths of Newgate and approaching Ludgate Hill from the direction of St Paul's churchyard where the stationers set up their stalls every day. It reminded him that he must visit the market again, where Nicholas Houseman might have something for him.

CHAPTER 3

Christopher had not so much recruited Nicholas Houseman to the earl's network as accepted his plea to serve. After his father had been arrested and sent to Newgate for refusing to withdraw his dismissal of the pope as a canting monk, Nicholas had grown up with a burning, consuming hatred of papism. Thanks to him, two writers of treasonous attacks on the queen and her Privy Council were languishing in Bridewell and their printer had lost his licence to trade. Nicholas was a learned man, agreeable company and among Christopher's best agents.

Members of the Stationers' Company were licensed by the City of London Corporation to trade in St Paul's churchyard. Every day but Sunday they set up their wares early in the morning and remained there until late afternoon. From his stall at the north-west corner of the square, Nicholas sold Latin and Greek texts, histories and a few volumes of poetry.

Like the bustling markets at Smithfield and Cheapside, it was a draw for ne'er-do-wells and vagrants. No matter what laws were passed or what penalties imposed, the problem of vagrancy grew worse. What choice had a man who could not feed his family but to leave his village to find work elsewhere? And if he could not do so, and most could not, he was forced to resort to stealing or deception. The city constables were of little use. The stationers employed their own men — men who had served as sailors or soldiers and would otherwise themselves be rufflers, without help and forced to beg and steal — to remove miscreants and to step in when arguments and scuffles broke out.

It was Christopher's habit to browse at other stalls before reaching Nicholas's, sometimes making small purchases as he went. If he were connected to Nicholas, it might one day go badly for the bookseller.

This morning, however, there was an empty space where the stall should have been. 'Haven't seen Houseman for a day or two,' the neighbouring bookseller told him. 'He must be sick. God forbid it's the plague or we're all done for, like as not.' Christopher asked around the market but no one knew why Nicholas was not in his usual place. Perhaps someone at Stationers' Hall would know.

The Hall was close by the yard, in the building that had once been Peter's College. At the door Christopher asked to speak to a warden on a matter of business. He was shown into a rich, high-ceilinged room which evidently served as a place for visitors to wait and for the stationers to sit and talk among themselves. Portraits of distinguished wardens of the company covered the walls, the wooden floor had been scrubbed and polished, the furniture was elegant and expensive. In matters of their appearance and comfort the stationers did not spare expense. The business of printing state papers, new laws and public proclamations, for which they could and did charge almost anything they liked, had filled the company's coffers to the brim.

The man who came out to meet him introduced himself as

James Kaye, Senior Warden of the Company. He was large and florid but, despite the heat, he was flamboyant in a red and gold velvet doublet, black silk stockings and buckled shoes. He wiped his brow with a large white handkerchief, replaced it carefully in a sleeve, bowed politely and asked what he could do for Christopher. Mr Kaye was, like the earl, a man of careful manners.

'I am a customer of Nicholas Houseman and was expecting to collect from him two books I ordered and in part paid for,' explained Christopher, hoping that the deception was not apparent in his voice. 'I fear my money might be lost and am anxious to discover why Houseman is not here.'

At the mention of Nicholas's name, the tiniest hint of a frown passed across the warden's face. 'It is unusual for the price to be paid in advance of delivery,' he said slowly. 'Was there any particular reason for this?'

'Only that the books are uncommon and Mr Houseman asked for my help in providing the funds to acquire them. An illuminated copy of Chaucer's *Tales* and a Latin text of Justinian's *Codex*.' He had had little time to invent the story and to his own ear it sounded hollow. If the warden inquired further about the books, Christopher would be in difficulty. That Nicholas was a member of his network must not become known.

The warden raised an eyebrow. 'Your tastes are agreeably eclectic, sir. May I ask your position?'

'I am a lawyer by profession and a bibliophile by inclination.'

'An admirable combination, sir, and would that I were in a position to assist you. Unfortunately, however, I have not heard that Mr Houseman is unwell or has left London, although we cannot of course be expected to know everything about our members' movements. No doubt he will reappear soon. I do hope as much because there are others waiting for a place in the market. I will keep his stall for as long as I can but if it is unused for more than a few days there will be a clamour for it. I am sure you understand.'

'Of course. I shall hope for his early return.'

'If you would care to tell me where you can be found, I will send word if Houseman appears.'

'Thank you, sir,' replied Christopher, a little more sharply than he intended, 'that will not be necessary. I will call again in a day or two.'

'As you wish,' replied Kaye. 'Now good day, sir. I must be about my labours.'

Nicholas and his wife Sarah lived in a small dwelling by the old wall at Cripplegate. It was typical of the area — one of a number of similar dwellings, built of brick and timber with an overhanging upper storey and a slate roof. A row of almshouses lined one side of the street. Christopher had pulled his cap down over his brow — something he did when wishing not to be recognized. There were times when his height and fair hair were a disadvantage. He waited until the street was deserted before rapping hard on the door. There was no answer and no sound from within the house. He stepped back and looked up. The windows were closed. He knocked again and waited another minute before trying the door. It was locked. He rattled it on its hinges and judged that it was not bolted from the inside.

Even if Nicholas had found it necessary to travel on business — to purchase the contents of a small library, perhaps — would he have left London without informing Christopher? And would Sarah have accompanied him? Christopher did not think so. He pulled out the poniard, glanced about to check that he was not observed and pushed it gently into the lock. Breaking into another man's house did not sit well with him and he had no idea if the dagger would work. He twisted it left and right to no effect and was about to abandon the attempt when he heard a click. He withdrew the dagger and turned the door handle. The door swung open. With another look around, he stepped inside. He closed the door and called out for Nicholas. Still there was no answer.

Three doors led off the entrance hall — one at the back which would open into a kitchen, the others to either side. He tried the door on his left first. Inside were a number of wooden crates and piles of books. Nicholas's store room. He crossed the hall to the door opposite. It opened into a parlour. It appeared entirely as it should be. It was the same on the upper storey. A bedroom, the bed arranged tidily, and a chest of clothes, both Nicholas's and Sarah's. He could not tell if any were missing. The other room was also full of crates and books. He returned to the parlour.

Standing in the middle of the room, he looked around the walls and up at the ceiling. Nothing. He looked down at the bare floor and noticed that he was standing on a large dark stain. He squatted down to examine it. By the roughness of the boards, he thought they had been scrubbed hard. Narrow slivers of timber stood proud and in places the surface of the wood had been scraped away by a sharp tool.

With the poniard he prised off a strip of the stained wood and held it to his nose. There was no smell. He stood by the window and held it up to the light coming through a crack in the shutter. There was a reddish tinge to it. A spilt glass of wine? He thought not. He could not be certain but from the colour and the consistency of the stain he thought it was blood.

Once again he looked in each room and found nothing unusual. Yet he was sure there was something wrong. He realized what it was as he was leaving. He closed the door and looked again. Apart from the books, there was nothing of value. No silver, no coin, no ornament. Had Nicholas and his wife taken what they could carry and disappeared? If so, why? Or had some thief or rogue found a way in and stolen them while the house was deserted? Even if they had, where were Nicholas and Sarah?

He did not attempt to relock the door but closed it carefully. From the corner of his eye he caught movement to his left. He turned sharply and saw a figure disappearing around a corner. He ran to the corner and peered down a narrow lane. It was deserted.

Nothing at all or was the house being watched? Or had he been followed? Cursing himself for an old woman, he took the longer way back to Ludgate Hill, avoiding the evils of Newgate.

Chapter 4

Colombes, France

The three men sitting around the table in the quiet Colombes inn had eaten and drunk well. Their meal had been cooked and served by the son and daughter of the innkeeper. For a handsome price he provided them with a private room, good food and a guarantee that they would not be disturbed. The room was plain — low-ceilinged, panelled walls, and furnished only with a simple beechwood table and three chairs, without adornment of any kind save for a silver crucifix on one wall. It was lit by six wax candles set in brass holders. Having served the food, the innkeeper's son stood guard outside the door.

When they met, it was their habit to use only their Christian names. The oldest of the three and their acknowledged leader, Charles, had passed fifty. His hair and beard were white and his skin the texture of parchment. A priest, he made no secret of his ambition to rise higher in the Church. He used his knife to cut a slice off the shoat, taking care not to touch any other part of the animal with his fingers, and lifted it to his mouth. He followed it with a draught of the excellent claret he had brought with him. No country innkeeper's cellar would satisfy his refined taste. He spoke quietly. 'What news from Paris, Henri?' he asked the young man on his left.

Despite his youth — he was but twenty-two — Henri spoke with the voice of one who believes himself born to rule, a voice that defies argument. He was sharp-eyed and sharp-faced. A neat pointed beard only partly hid a jagged scar down his left cheek. He was a soldier. To some, he was known as 'scarface'. 'Huguenots are already arriving in Paris for this accursed wedding. How the queen can marry her daughter to Navarre is beyond my understanding, although it does present us with our opportunity.' He spat out the words.

'And the heretic Coligny himself? When is he expected?' The uncompromising Admiral Gaspard de Coligny, hated and feared by every Catholic, was the leader of all the Protestants in France.

'A day or two before the wedding, I am told.'

Charles put his palms together in an attitude of prayer. 'When will you receive the weapons, William?'

French was not the first language of the third man although he had been in the country for two years and spoke it well if not in the manner of a Frenchman. William was a large, loud, red-bearded Scot who had joined the rising in the north of England led by the earls of Westmoreland and Northumberland, and had fled to France when it collapsed in ignominy. When he spoke, shreds of meat flew from his mouth. Less than sober when he arrived, he had drunk too much of the priest's wine and was barely sensible. 'In good time. Maurevert will have one. I will dispatch the other as agreed,' he spluttered.

Charles winced. 'And you are sure of the workmanship?' William had approached the priest, claiming to have powerful connections in Scotland and to be an expert on all manner of weaponry. He lived near the seminary at Douai where young Jesuits were being trained for their missions to England, waiting impatiently until he could safely return to Scotland.

'Do not concern your holy head with the workmanship. I will vouch for it,' replied the Scot, using a spoon to shovel spinach into his mouth. In his huge, dirt-encrusted hand the spoon looked like a child's toy. He pulled a green strand from his beard and swallowed it.

Charles ignored the insult. He was not to be fobbed off. 'They are costly and our plan depends on them. Will you test them?'

'Of course I will test them. Do you take me for a fool? I will make sure they work perfectly.'

'And the gunsmith?'

'He is not a danger.'

'Thank you, William. I did not mean to impugn your competence.'

The Scotsman scowled and poured more wine down his throat. 'It is not I with whom you should concern yourselves. While we sit here and talk, the king's mother is not only marrying her daughter to a Protestant, but has sent an emissary to London to ratify a treaty with the perfidious English and to promote the suit of her miserable dwarf of a son.' He tipped the last few drops of wine into his glass. 'Boy, boy,' he bellowed, 'bring more wine!'

'The boy is deaf, William, or had you forgotten? It is as well or you might yet betray us all.' Charles spoke sharply. The Scotsman swore, and growled that the dwarf was cursed with a sickly body and a stunted mind. In the priest's opinion, William had never shown proper respect for the house of Valois. Charles had come to dislike him as deeply as if he were a Puritan preacher.

'What has Montmorency to say?' asked the soldier.

'Much as we expected,' replied Charles. 'He writes that although the witch reportedly found Alençon's likeness less unpleasant than she had been led to believe, she nevertheless laughed at the suggestion of a match and described him as a "little frog". Later she tried to conceal her true feelings by saying that she was too old for such a young man and would disappoint him. She said it would be like a mother leading her son up the aisle. Montmorency is making his way slowly to London. He does not look forward to his audience with her.'

'That is as well.'

'Rats' bollocks,' spat out the Scotsman, thumping the table. 'If the whore is so set on an alliance and an heir, why does she not put a sack over the boy's head and tell him to get on with it?'

Charles glanced at his neighbour and shrugged. He would have to bring the meeting to an end. 'The time approaches to light the fire. Have you anything more from London, Henri?'

'I am told that a possible problem has been dealt with and that there is no reason to delay.'

'What problem?' growled the Scotsman.

'A member of his guild was asking questions. The man and his wife have been silenced. They knew nothing of importance.'

'Is there any reason to suspect the man?'

'None. Merely a tiresome bookseller over-burdened with curiosity.'

'Let us hope so.' A church clock nearby struck midnight. 'Go first, if you please. I will follow.'

'As you wish,' replied the soldier, rising to leave.

'Scotland will not prosper until the Queen of Scots is also the Queen of England. We should be in England, killing Englishmen, not sitting here talking about it.'

The priest regarded the Scotsman as an uncle might regard an errant nephew. 'Be practical, William,' he said quietly. 'We will keep to our plan. So far all has progressed as we expected.'

'The witch, I hear, is in poor health. Her physicians are concerned,' said Henri.

Charles waved a dismissive hand. 'She survived the smallpox, Henri, and she is strong. God will not take her for us. He expects us to do it ourselves.'

'Our rightful queen held prisoner in a damp castle, yet when last we heard in excellent health, the Protestant bastard surrounded by physicians and servants and luxury of every kind, yet sick. Ironical, is it not?'

'We have the weapons and our people are ready,' replied Henri.

'What of the Irishman? What if his attack on the castle fails? What if he proves to be no more than a bag of wind like every other cud-chewing churl from that bog of an island?'

'Enough, William. You have drunk too much. The Irish are our allies and Patrick Wolf is a brave and determined man. He will not fail us.'

'No more will the others,' added Henri, and turned to go.

The Scotsman's head was slumped on the table. Charles made no attempt to speak to him, but waited five minutes before snuffing the candles and leaving quietly. There was little chance of their being seen together by unfriendly eyes, but no point in taking the risk.

To his surprise, Henri was waiting for him outside the inn, the reins of his horse in one hand. 'This cannot go on,' he said. 'The man's a drunkard and a liability. Who knows to whom he might have spoken? When he first approached us, he seemed reliable, but now . . .'

'I fear you are right. His only interest is a Scottish queen on the English throne and a rich reward for his services. In truth, he would not care if she were Catholic, Protestant or pagan. He is uncouth and stupid and only pretends to have faith. Leave it to me. I will deal with the matter when the time is right.'

'It would be as well.' *Incendium* could not be jeopardized.

'Go with God.'

'And you, my friend.'

CHAPTER 5

London

From the fine archway of the Holbein Gate, the main entrance to the palace, Christopher was escorted by a guard to the earl's apartments and asked to wait in the antechamber. The earl, he was informed by a yeoman, was with Her Majesty.

Christopher disliked that chamber. On the occasions when he had been forced to wait there, he had found himself becoming increasingly nervous. Waiting for one of the most powerful men in England in a room furnished with expensive French furniture and decorated with fine paintings of Venice and Rome perversely brought to mind waiting in the foul, foetid, diseased gaol at Wisbech for his turn before the judge at the Norwich assizes. He could not have said why.

It was an hour before the earl arrived, flushed and plainly out of sorts. He swept into the antechamber, saw Christopher and stopped. Christopher jumped to his feet and bowed.

'Dr Radcliff,' said the earl, 'I was not expecting you.'

'No, my lord,' replied Christopher.

'Come in, since you are here.' Christopher followed him into the main apartment and waited for him to speak. But the earl simply poured himself a glass of yellow wine from a decanter, offered Christopher a glass which he declined, and sat gazing at a portrait of his father. The likeness was clear. 'My father, John Dudley, Duke of Northumberland,' he said eventually. 'A good man who served his country as he thought best. He lost his head for it, but I often wish I had his wisdom.' He took a sip of wine and for several minutes sat in silence. Despite the news he brought, Christopher knew better than to rush Leicester in such a mood.

Leicester went on, 'Montmorency has still not arrived but has sent a letter pressing the suit of the duc d'Alençon. The queen has been as tactful as any human being could possibly be but does not take seriously attempts to persuade her of the benefits of the marriage. It seems from his likeness that Walsingham has not exaggerated. I shudder to think of her lying with such a creature but for England's sake I must publicly support the marriage, only because, like the absurd Anjou, Alençon is the French king's brother. Our glorious queen is expected to sacrifice herself to this creature. If only the house of Valois could have offered a more suitable match. I pray she has the courage to refuse.' He took a sip of wine. 'Really, doctor, there are times when I despair of our world. Were it not for my devotion to Her Majesty, I would be tempted to ask her leave to return to Kenilworth to spend my days with my paintings and my books. And my players, of course. Have you seen them? No? Then you must. I shall arrange it.' Leicester shook his head as if to clear it of such thoughts. 'Again I find myself confiding in you, doctor. It must be your scholarly manner. Now, what have you to report?'

'Nicholas Houseman and his wife have disappeared. I fear they have been harmed.'

'Houseman the bookseller?' Christopher nodded. 'What do you know of this?'

'Their house is deserted and Nicholas has not been seen at the market for several days. The stationers know nothing of his whereabouts.'

'Was there any sign of a struggle or of a crime?'

'His silver and valuables have been taken.'

'Could he not have taken them himself?'

'He could, my lord, but I cannot imagine why. He would have told me if he intended to leave London or move elsewhere within the city.'

'Anything else?'

'I found a large stain on the floor of his parlour. I am sure it is blood.'

The earl raised his dark eyebrows. His tone was sharp. 'Whose blood? A cat's? Or could it have been claret? Really, doctor, this is less than convincing and uncharacteristic of you.' Even to Christopher's ears it sounded hollow. 'Have you any reason to suspect that Houseman was in danger?'

'None, my lord. I bring it to your attention only because of your warning. "Vipers lurk" were your words.'

'Hmm. Nothing brewing among the stationers? It was Queen Mary who granted their charter and, although my patronage of the printers is well known, I fear that the stationers have not always been the staunchest of the guilds. It was they who first brought copies of that damnable papal bull into the country and they are not above peddling words of insurrection and incitement dressed up as political tracts. What is more, from the services they provide to the Privy Council and the courts many of their members have become very wealthy men. Has there been no word at all?'

'Not that I am aware of.'

'Then I suggest you do not concern yourself further. Houseman will appear with a perfectly good explanation for his absence. Now, I have more pressing matters with which to occupy myself. Our glorious queen's progress, ratification of the French treaty and Alençon's suit, if Montmorency ever graces us with his presence, our coastal defences which have been sadly neglected from lack of money, and worrying reports from the Low Countries.' He rested his elbows on the table and held his fingertips to his temples. When he spoke his voice was sharp. 'Really, doctor. Do you wish me to investigate this matter myself?'

'My lord, I simply thought to inform you . . .'

'Quite, quite. You did no wrong, doctor. My apologies, I am not myself today. The queen suffers in this heat and I with her. Make inquiries about Houseman but let us not leap to unwarranted conclusions. People disappear for all manner of reasons. I am sure he will appear again unharmed.'

'Doubtless you are right, my lord.'

'Quite so. Now, on the other matter I mentioned, I have written to Walsingham to ask him if it is really necessary to send a man to France. It is not as if I have armies of reliable men from which to choose. I shall inform you when I hear from him. Meanwhile, I travel tomorrow to Kenilworth. There are matters I do not wish to entrust to anyone but myself.'

'When shall you return, my lord?'

'When I am satisfied that all is well for the progress. Now leave me to deal with the troublesome butchers and poulterers who are doing their best to bankrupt the treasury by their prices for meat and fowl to sustain us on the progress. Two pounds for a cow and a shilling for a pair of chickens. Is it not outrageous? I've a

mind to send them to the assizes for thievery. Good day, Dr
Radcliff.'

Later, Christopher sat in his study, stripped to the waist and sipping
from a beaker of small beer. Fretful and ill-humoured after his meeting with the earl, he picked at a plate of bread and cheese.

It had been blood on the floor, he was sure of it, and if it had
become known that Nicholas was his agent, the blood might be his.
And Sarah's. The warden, Kaye, had been courteous but unhelpful
— more interested in collecting rent for the stall than in the welfare of
a member of his company — and a pompous fellow. Christopher
could expect no help there.

The heat was still fierce. The Fleet ditch had long since turned
to mud and Clerke's Well, reliable for as long as any could remember,
was almost dry. Poor Rose had come back in tears from the well with
neither water nor bucket. 'I waited an hour for my turn to fill half the
pail,' she had sobbed. 'Then two foul-mouthed doxies took it from
me. There is fighting there.'

He had tried to comfort her by saying that it would rain soon but
in truth he had no more idea than the next man when it might do so.
There was no clean water to be had south of Moor Fields, where
even the ancient spring that had served Londoners for centuries was
all but dry.

The queen's health continued to be worrying. She was a woman
renowned for her robust strength. Even the smallpox had not
weakened her. They said that she often stood for two hours or more
while her courtiers prayed silently that she would sit down so that
they might do the same; she enjoyed riding and hunting and tired no
more quickly than a young man.

Yet her malady had continued for some weeks. God willing, the diversions of her progress would finally rid her of it. The Spanish ambassador's dispatches would be keeping King Philip and his court informed of her every cough and sneeze. If she died, a Spanish fleet would be on its way from the Low Countries within days, and then who knew what the Scots and the French might do? Treaties, ratified or not, would count for nothing and without its queen around whom to rally, England would be at their mercy. That much Leicester had made clear.

At least the Privy Council had belatedly roused itself. The defences at Southampton and Tilbury were at last being strengthened and in the shires the mustering of men up to the age of forty had begun. The news sheets were urging every man and woman to pray earnestly for westerly winds to keep Spanish ships in their ports.

How much notice the men and women of London took of this advice was open to doubt. The Privy Counsellors did not always seem to remember that the goodman striving to make a living from selling his vegetables or cheeses and the goodwife scrubbing clothes for a few shillings had more pressing matters upon which to think. Rent to be paid, mouths to be fed, children to be clothed — there was little future in wasting energy worrying about the state of Her Majesty's ships or the intentions of the Spanish king, neither of which they could do anything about.

Had they known that the queen was in her sick bed, gout-stricken Burghley was in Paris with Walsingham and Leicester would soon be departing for Kenilworth to prepare fireworks, they might have been less sanguine. Christopher would not have cared to be the one to explain this to them.

The weather broke that night. In the early hours he was woken from an uncomfortable half-sleep by the crack of thunder and the pounding of rain on the roof. It brought blessed relief from the heat and would be washing the streets clean of muck and breathing life into the Fleet river which carried much of it down to the Thames.

He rose and peered out of the window of his chamber. A bolt of lightning lit up the sky, followed at once by a thunderous crash. Sheets of rain fell like a waterfall. He pushed open the window and, for the pleasure of it, held out his arms. Even his bent fingers seemed to benefit from the rain's touch. Refreshed, he lay down and listened to the storm.

At dawn it abated and he rose to go to his study. Rose would come soon to prepare his breakfast. He would work until then.

For an hour he worked steadily, reading each report and making notes in the margins. His training in the law had equipped him well for such a task and a small pile of papers requiring more attention was dwarfed by another which would serve other purposes.

The church bell had chimed seven of the clock when there was a knock on the door. Thinking Rose had arrived early, he went to open it. Outside stood a young man whose face was familiar but which he could not place.

'Dr Radcliff,' the man said, bowing politely, 'my apologies for calling at such an early hour. I assumed that the storm would have woken you and thought to take advantage of the cool air.'

The visitor spoke well and was dressed as a gentleman in a wide-ruffed shirt, a fine doublet and silk hose. He was narrow in the shoulder, several inches shorter than Christopher and smelled of lavender. Clean-shaven and clear of eye, he looked honest enough but what his purpose might be at that hour Christopher could not guess. 'May I know your name, sir,' he inquired testily, 'and the nature of your business?' It was not unknown for armed thieves to gain access by such a pretence.

'My name is Roland Wetherby, doctor. I come from Whitehall Palace.' Not many men knew both of Christopher's connection with Whitehall and where he lived. If this man was a thief, he was an unusually well-informed one. He invited Wetherby in and offered him refreshment.

'Thank you, no, doctor,' replied the young man, 'I do not care to take strong drink. I find it dulls the senses.' Christopher resisted the urge to tell him that his father had once warned him against trusting any man who did not drink wine.

'Well then, Mr Wetherby, what brings you here?' he asked, waving a hand over the table. 'As you see, I am at work.'

'Indeed, sir,' Wetherby replied, adjusting his doublet, 'as am I, and I shall not detain you for long. Before I explain why I am here, however, may I have your word that you will keep that of which we speak to yourself?'

'You may not. I do not know of what we might speak and I will not be bound by any promise.'

Wetherby nodded. 'I thought you would say that, doctor, as would I in your place. No matter. I have been sent with an invitation for you to meet with my employer at an early date.' There was a hint of effeminacy about Wetherby's voice and manner — an occasional lisp, a delicate gesture.

'And who, if I may ask, is your employer, Mr Wetherby?'

'I am engaged by Mr Thomas Heneage.' So Leicester was right. There were others in Whitehall interested in Christopher's work.

Thomas Heneage had a reputation for blunt speaking and driving ambition. He had taken advantage of Leicester's fall from grace after the sudden death of his wife and become a favourite of the queen. Not a man to be treated lightly. 'Heneage. Treasurer of Her Majesty's Privy Chamber and a man of influence. A fine dancer, too, I hear.' He could not resist the jibe. And now he recalled seeing Wetherby's face in the palace.

Wetherby shrugged and put a forefinger to his chin. 'Be that as it may, Dr Radcliff, Mr Heneage has matters of importance that he wishes to discuss with you.'

'What matters?'

'That is not for me to say, doctor. I am merely a humble messenger.'

Christopher rubbed his hand and tried to straighten the fingers. It was a habit he had acquired when needing time to think. The fingers remained stubbornly bent. 'Your employer could have contacted me himself. Why has he sent a messenger?' He was not going to make it easy for Wetherby.

'He did not care to commit his thoughts to paper and preferred an informal approach.'

'Mr Heneage will of course be aware of my work for the Earl of Leicester. Does the earl know of this approach?' It was disingenuous, but he could think of nothing better.

'I think not, doctor. My master is a man of discretion.'

Christopher could easily have declined the approach there and then – pleaded his loyalty to Leicester and sent Wetherby on his way. But he did not. Leicester's warning had piqued his interest. 'This has come as a surprise, Mr Wetherby,' he said. 'You will under-stand that I must give the matter thought. I am presently much occupied with my work, but kindly inform your employer that I will respond to his request by the end of the month.'

'Must he wait so long for a simple meeting? He will be dis-pleased. Mr Heneage is not a man to cross.' Wetherby's tone had become harsher.

The pile of reports was staring at him and he and his visitor had danced long enough. 'Come now, Mr Wetherby, we both know that any meeting between Mr Heneage and myself would be far from simple. If he is unwilling to wait, I must respectfully decline his request.' Christopher peered hard into the young man's eyes and saw him shrink back just a little. 'I am sure you understand my position.'

Wetherby looked so put out that Christopher felt a twinge of sympathy. The young man would have to report back that Heneage must wait for a reply. Heneage would be disappointed and Wetherby would bear the brunt. Such was the life of the messenger in the circles in which they moved. Wetherby stood up. 'Very well, doctor. I will deliver your reply to Mr Heneage. He will be displeased, but if you are adamant, there it is.'

'Indeed. There it is.' Christopher thanked him for calling and promised to contact him. He was in no doubt about Heneage's intentions. He would question Christopher about his work, assure him of the high regard in which he himself was held by the queen, hint at Leicester's star being on the wane, and offer him a position on his staff. He would try to barter Christopher's contacts and information for his own patronage.

The earl had foreseen it. A learned man he might not be, but shrewd he certainly was. Despite the death of his wife, rumours of dalliances and various financial misfortunes, he had survived in the whispering corridors of Whitehall Palace for fourteen years and still enjoyed the queen's trust. What was more, Christopher owed much to Leicester and had no intention of changing horses.

Rose arrived soon after Wetherby had left. Although it was no longer raining, she was cold and wet and again in tears. Christopher found blankets for her and sat her down in the kitchen while he prepared breakfast. She was too bedraggled to argue and sat in silence while he fussed about with bread and eggs.

She told him that part of the thatch on her cottage roof had collapsed in the storm and she had spent the night trying to save her few possessions. He asked her gently what she had lost. 'My chair will survive, and the bed, although the mattress is fit only for the fire. The clothes will dry out. Our Lord is angry with us. No water for weeks and then a flood. How have we angered him that he punishes us so?'

'I know not, Rose. What is to be done about the roof?' he asked.

'My sister's boy can turn a hand to thatching,' she said. 'He will repair it if I give him a shilling or two.' Christopher took some coins from his purse and put them in her hand. Rose must have a new mattress and her roof repaired and he must have a housekeeper. He cared little for the cost.

'If you need more, Rose, tell me,' he told her. 'I will help if I can.' Rose departed gratefully clutching the coins. He had work to do and then he would lock up the house and visit Katherine.

The storm had indeed washed down the streets and made the drains flow again. Glass-sellers and herb-sellers and flower girls were back on the streets and even Newgate seemed a little less foul. Christopher walked briskly.

If Katherine was surprised to see him again so soon, she did not show it. She asked if he had enjoyed the storm. 'I did,' he confessed, 'although poor Rose did not. Her roof has fallen in.'

'I will call on her,' replied Katherine. 'I heard word that the queen is still unwell. They say that her stomach is disordered. Could the condition have been brought on by the strain of Norfolk's execution, do you think?'

'She is unwell, but I know nothing of such matters,' replied

Christopher, although he did recall a physician explaining how the body's humours can be affected by the state of the mind. Fear and guilt, in particular, the physician had said, create black bile and cause the digestive organs to malfunction. But medicine was best left to the physicians. When it came to sickness, he was squeamish. Nursing his dying mother had tested him to the limit.

He did not mention Roland Wetherby or Thomas Heneage or even the Earl of Leicester. He knew that Katherine could tell that his mind was preoccupied and was thankful for it. They did not need words to be comfortable in each other's company. It was mid-afternoon by the time he left Wood Street.

CHAPTER 6

The fields at Holborn lacked the charm of the meadows that bordered the Cam but they were pleasant enough to stroll in on a bright summer morning. While they studied their briefs and pleaded and argued and bickered, the lawyers of Lincoln's Inn left their mounts, tethered or hobbled, to graze there. In the winter, they rented the Holborn stables and paid for fodder. Christopher had wondered sometimes how he would have fared in the profession had he come to London to practise law. Not well, he had concluded. He was more suited to teaching than the rough and tumble of the courts.

'Vipers lurk,' the earl had said, yet had shown scant interest in Nicholas and Sarah Houseman's disappearance. Too much to concern him elsewhere no doubt. But Christopher knew something evil had befallen them. Their sudden disappearance was out of character. The thought had gnawed away at him since Leicester had departed for Kenilworth three days since. What he lacked was proof. A bloodstain on the floor was not enough.

It was not far from Holborn to the Cripplegate and by seven of the clock he was standing outside the house. The street was waking up. Milkmaids and pie-sellers hawked their wares at the gate. Doors were opened and buckets passed to the night-soil men. The cobbler's shop was unshuttered. From Nicholas's house there came neither sound nor movement.

He saw no one watching or paying him any attention at all. He pushed the door to the house. It did not move. Quite sure that he had left it unlocked, he tried again. Still it did not move. Had the Housemans returned and were asleep? He picked up a small stone and lobbed it against the window on the upper storey. Nothing. He threw another stone, this time harder. Still nothing. He called out, quietly at first, then louder. A few heads were turned towards him and the cobbler, a dishevelled old man with a face like his own shoe leather, emerged from his shop. 'Not there,' he grunted. 'Haven't seen them for days.'

'Have you seen anyone else at the house?'

The cobbler scratched his head. 'Not that I recall. Never saw much of them, either. Kept to themselves. I do know he worked in the market at St Paul's. You could try there.'

'Thank you, goodman, I shall. But first I must be sure that all is well in the house. Nicholas and Sarah are my friends. I have a key.' The cobbler shrugged, grunted again and limped back into his shop.

Another quick look around and Christopher pulled out the poniard. Into the lock went the point, he gave it a firm twist and the lock snapped open. Hoping he was unobserved, he slipped into the house and closed the door behind him. Whoever had locked it, it had not been Nicholas or Sarah, and that person knew that someone else had been there. The fleeting figure who had disappeared down a lane? A thief? A killer?

The house appeared just as he had seen it before. Up the narrow flight of stairs, crates of books, a tidy bed and a clothes chest. But when he opened the wooden chest, it was empty. The clothes would have had some value, they would not have been heavy or difficult to move, and a thief might have returned to take them. A thief who had found the door unlocked and had re-locked it. And who might have been the figure he had seen. And who had left a bloodstain on the floor.

The stain was there — if anything, redder and more obvious than before. A trick of the light, perhaps. Christopher lay on his stomach and looked as closely as he could. Not wine, not dye. No dog, no cat, no body. But blood it was.

This time when he left he used the sharp point of the dagger to lock the door behind him. There was nothing to be gained by telling the felon that someone had been to the house again.

The market in St Paul's churchyard was busy. He went slowly from stall to stall, examined a book or two and made his way to Nicholas's place.

He expected Nicholas's stall to be empty. It was not. A young man selling writing materials had taken it. He chose a pot of ink and a handful of duck-feather quills and asked the man where Mr Houseman was. 'I could not say, sir,' the stationer replied, unable to look Christopher in the eye. 'The warden granted me this place and I am grateful to have it.'

'Does that mean that Houseman has lost it?'

'The warden promised that I should not have to give it up and I shall not. Mr Houseman will have to take another place.'

Christopher thanked him and made his way across the yard to Stationers' Hall. He asked for Warden Kaye and, as before, was admitted by a servant and shown into the grand reception room. When the florid warden appeared he showed at first no sign of recognizing Christopher. He introduced himself. 'I am James Kaye, Senior Warden. You asked for me.'

'I did, Mr Kaye, and we have met before. I am Dr Christopher Radcliff. I came to inquire about the bookseller Nicholas Houseman. Has there been any word of him?'

Kaye's greedy eyes looked surprised. 'Forgive me, Dr Radcliff, I am a busy man and had forgotten your face. Now that you mention Mr Houseman, I do recall our previous meeting. But I regret that I can be no help to you. Either he has left London or something untoward has happened. The city is so busy these days and accidents are frequent.'

'Have you visited his house?'

'I myself, of course, have not, but I sent a servant there. He reported that the door was locked and there was no sign of Houseman. The neighbours also knew nothing of him.'

'Or his wife?'

'Or his wife, doctor. Now, I have an election of officers to arrange. You will forgive me if I wish you good day.'

'What if he returns? Will he have back his place in the market?'

'I regret that he will not. I have given it to another. We cannot afford the loss of revenue from empty stalls. I am sorry you have wasted your money but, really, I cannot help you further. Good day.'

Christopher shrugged. 'Then I fear I must forget the matter. My thanks, sir.'

A self-regarding popinjay was Warden Kaye. He had lost no time in passing Nicholas's stall to another and Christopher trusted him not an inch. A quick visit to Cripplegate by a servant, no sign of Nicholas, a fee from the new stallholder and coins in his purse. Greedy and self-regarding.

The markets in the streets and alleys around Cheapside were always busy, as crowded as any London market and as noisy. Poulterers and cheesemakers, honey-sellers and bakers, milkmaids and butchers smeared with blood and offal, all went about their daily business, competing to catch a customer's eye and relieve her of a shilling or two, while cutpurses and pickpockets and all manner of others who scratched a living outside the law went about theirs. The smells were smells of blood and bodies and filth.

Working his way through the throng and around the sacks and barrels of the vendors and the heaps of dung deposited by their horses, Christopher was pushed and jostled and elbowed. He pulled his cap down low over his eyes, kept tight hold on the purse tucked under his shirt, and felt the needle-point of the poniard with his finger.

Turning off Cheapside through a low archway and into one of the dozens of unnamed lanes that criss-crossed the ward, he was not entirely sure that he had picked the right one. He came here infrequently and usually at night when the market was closed. It was dark in the lane, the roofs of the houses either side almost touching and blocking out most of the light. A hag loitering in the shadows saw him and shuffled out. 'Shilling for a fuck, sir,' she croaked, pulling down her filthy rags to expose a withered breast. 'Only two pennies for a feel.' He hurried on, searching for the door he wanted.

He found it just beyond a filthy alley, so narrow that two men could not have walked down it side by side. On the corner of the lane, rats fought over rotting scraps and burrowed into heaps of excrement in search of a morsel. It was not an area often visited by the Corporation's street-cleaners. The stench made him hold his breath. He kicked the fleshless carcass of a rat out of the way, climbed the rickety stairs to the door and hammered on it. It was quickly opened by a big-bellied, grey-haired woman with narrow, suspicious eyes. 'Yes?' she demanded by way of greeting.

'I've come for Ell, Grace,' replied Christopher, anxious to get out of the lane. The woman peered at him.

'Oh, it's you, doctor. Ell's busy. Be a while yet. Why not try another girl for a change? They're all clean.'

'I'll wait. It's Ell I want.'

'Suit yourself. Come in and I'll tell Ell to hurry along.' She led Christopher into a dirty parlour, poured him a glass of yellow wine from a dusty bottle and disappeared. Christopher heard her lumbering up the stair, poured the wine back into the bottle and waited. Grace had never inquired why he only ever asked for Ell and she would never know. Just as he would never know how Ell had become an intelligencer for his predecessor. He had asked but she would not tell him. 'I may be a whore,' she had said, 'but I don't tell tales. You never know when they might come back to tell on you.' A whore she was, and because of it a useful intelligencer. In her bed, with passion spent, many a man had spoken unwisely, little knowing that his words would find their way to the Earl of Leicester's chief intelligencer in London. Ell Cole was a good and trusted agent.

Ell and Grace returned together. 'Here she is, all cleaned up and ready for you, aren't you, Ell?'

'Hello, Dr Rad,' Ell greeted him with a smile. 'Handsome as ever, I see. My most handsome customer, I always say, Grace, don't I?' Christopher grinned. In Ell's company, he invariably found himself grinning. She was what she was and said what she thought — as far from the intrigues and deceptions of Whitehall Palace as he could imagine.

'Maybe you do. Now take him upstairs and earn me my crust,' replied Grace. 'Don't be too long.'

Christopher followed Ell up the stair and along a short passage. From the rooms on either side came the grunts and moans of rutting men and the simperings of their whores. At least every room had a door. Grace's visitors paid for their privacy.

Ell's room was at the end of the passage. She showed Christopher in and offered him her chair. She swept a heap of clothes off the rumpled bed and perched herself on a corner. 'Now, doctor,' she said quietly, 'what brings you here?'

'I have a task for you, if you are willing.'

'Better tell me what it is first, doctor. There are some things I wouldn't do even for you.' She grinned lewdly. 'Although there's no harm in asking.'

'Nicholas Houseman, a stationer who lived with his wife Sarah at Cripplegate, has disappeared. They both have. He is, was, one of mine. If he is in London, I must find him. If he is dead, I want the body.'

'Have you no thoughts?'

'His house has been entered. His silver and coin have gone, and their clothes. There is a stain on the floor which I am sure is blood. The stationers can shed no light. Nicholas Houseman. Around thirty years of age, respectable, educated, a good man. And his wife Sarah. I want you to listen out for whispers. Take care, though. If they were killed because someone knew that Nicholas was an agent of mine, it will be dangerous work.'

'Doesn't sound too wearisome, Dr Rad. I'll listen out. Fancy a rest while you're here? You look tired.'

'Thanks, Ell. Another time.'

Ell threw up her hands in mock astonishment. 'I can hardly believe it. Your lady believes you're swiving me when you've never so much as touched me and here's me offering it to you for nothing and you not wanting it. Bag of eels it is, jumbled up and making no sense.'

'Listen out for word of the Housemans, Ell, please. I need to know what has happened to them.' Christopher stood up. 'How is the girl who was beaten? Sal, wasn't it?'

'Sal's cold in the ground, poor cow. That Scotchman's beating killed her. If he shows his face again I'll cut off his balls and shove them down his murdering throat.'

'Tell me if you see him.'

'I will, doctor. Off you go now. Tell Grace you've had a good time and come back soon.'

Christopher put a half-angel in her hand. 'I shall.'

CHAPTER 7

John Berwick arrived at Ludgate Hill the next morning, while Christopher was at his reports. Rose announced him. 'Mr Berwick is at the door, doctor. Shall I offer him breakfast?'

'Do that, Rose. And show him in, please.'

Christopher rose from his work to greet his visitor. 'Mr Berwick. An unexpected pleasure. How do you fare at Whitehall without the earl?'

'My duties are not onerous, doctor. I deal with such correspondence as I can and send the rest on to him. The earl has made only one request so far and that for a sculptor of subtleties. He has in mind a representation of Kenilworth in marzipan and sugar for the queen's arrival feast and I gather he is dissatisfied with the local man. Happily, I have found the best man in London and put him in a coach to Kenilworth.'

'Then let us hope that the subtlety restores Her Majesty's spirits. Has Rose offered you food and drink?'

'She has, doctor, but I have breakfasted, thank you. I can see that you are busy and will not detain you for long. Before he left, the earl mentioned that an intelligencer of yours is missing. I wondered if I might be of some help in searching for him.'

No fool, young Berwick. Making friends on his way up. 'That is thoughtful of you, Mr Berwick, although I know not what you might do. Nicholas Houseman is a member of the Stationers' Company. No one at their Hall or in the market at St Paul's can shed any light on the matter and there is no sign of him or his wife Sarah at their house.'

'No sign of a break-in or a struggle?'

'His silver and clothes have been taken and there is a stain on the floor which might be blood. That is all.'

'Blood? Do you suspect an attack?' Berwick sounded shocked.

'If I suspect anything it is that a thief or thieves somehow gained entrance to the house — how is a mystery as Nicholas was a cautious man — attacked the Housemans, stole what they could easily carry, and removed the bodies.'

'Indeed, that seems a likely explanation. But did no one report seeing an intruder or hearing a noise?'

'No. The cobbler next door knows nothing and at night that street is unfrequented.'

'Surely he would not have admitted a stranger to his house at night?'

Christopher shrugged. 'I cannot explain it unless the caller was known to him. That also seems unlikely.'

'Was the door locked?'

'It was.' He picked up the poniard. 'I could have been a house-breaker.'

Berwick laughed. 'And ended your days on the end of a rope, doctor. Well, it does seem strange. I will keep my ears open but I doubt I shall learn anything. Do, please, let me know if Mr Houseman appears.'

'Thank you, Mr Berwick. I shall. And call on me if you are in need of help or advice while the earl is away. The corridors of Whitehall are not always easy to navigate.'

'I am learning as much. Good day, doctor. I shall leave you to your work.'

When he had gone, Christopher sat back in his chair. In his place, would he have acted as Berwick had? Would he have called unannounced and offered his help, knowing almost certainly that there would be no help he could give? Probably not, but this was a very clever, ambitious man, to be treated with care. It would be interesting to see how he fared in the future.

Rose stuck her wrinkled head around the door. 'A polite young man, doctor. Did not want breakfast but gave me a shilling for my trouble. Quietly spoken, too. Reminded me of my nephew.'

'Has your nephew mended your roof, Rose?'

'He has, doctor, and I thank you for your help in paying him. Don't know what I would have done otherwise. If there is nothing more, I shall be off. I've left a cold dinner for you in the kitchen. A fresh mackerel with a salad of purslane and cress. Be sure to eat it all.'

'Mackerel, Rose? You know I cannot eat fish. What induced you to buy a mackerel?'

Rose curtsied. 'Oh, I am sorry, doctor. Not mackerel. Mutton, I meant.' He heard her chortling as she left the house.

When Christopher entered the shop, Isaac Cardoza was with a customer. He asked Christopher to wait. 'Sit, Christopher,' he said, 'and you will soon see how hard it is for an old Jew to scratch a living.'

The customer, a large man in a leather jerkin and rough woollen trousers, laughed. 'You are as close to being a thief as a man can be without being hanged for it, Isaac Cardoza. I will take fifteen shillings for the chain and not a groat less.'

Isaac shook his head sadly. 'Fifteen shillings. You would ruin me. I can give you ten.'

'Twelve.'

'Agreed.' Isaac handed over the coins and tucked the chain into his purse. 'Good day, sir. May fortune smile upon you.'

'As it has smiled upon you. You will sell the chain for twenty shillings and still be complaining when next I call.'

'I do not like to ask where he gets the silver he brings me but I know he drinks away whatever I pay him,' said Isaac, when the man had gone. 'Ale for him, a profit for me and we are both content. How do you fare, Christopher? I had not thought to see you again so soon.'

'I have come to ask your help, Isaac.'

'Then if I can give it, you shall have it, my friend.' He locked the door and sat opposite Christopher. 'What is troubling you?'

Ten minutes later, Isaac knew as much about Nicholas and Sarah Houseman's disappearance as did Christopher. He scratched his beard. 'I will make inquiries and ask our people to listen out. Nicholas Houseman, a stationer. Clothes and plate, you say. You never know, something might turn up. Was the plate marked?'

'It might have been.'

Isaac's people, Marrano Jews who had fled the inquisition in Spain and Portugal, lived quietly in the Leadenhall district. They were traders and merchants, tolerated for their business sense and for the intelligence they brought back from Europe. One of them might indeed hear a word. 'Take care, Isaac. If Nicholas and Sarah have been murdered, their killer will be dangerous.'

'I am a Jew, Christopher. I always take care. *Shalom.*'

'*Shalom.* Send word if you learn anything.'

CHAPTER 8

It was the last day of June and still there had been no word from Leicester or from Ell or from Isaac. A tedious time it had been — long days in which Christopher had found it hard to concentrate while waiting hopefully for news that did not come. He had seen no more of Berwick or Wetherby and not much of Katherine. Twice he had walked to Wood Street, only to find her peevish and distracted. 'Now that Isabel is quite well,' she had complained, 'I need work to occupy my mind. I tire of embroidery. Can I not assist you in some way?'

To that he had no answer that would satisfy her. He could hardly ask her to go from tavern to tavern inquiring after Nicholas and Sarah, nor could he ask her to read his agents' reports. He could think of nothing else.

There had been little conversation and no love-making. He could not hide it from himself. He feared that Katherine was moving away from him and he did not know how to bring her back.

The message from Leicester eventually arrived at noon on that Wednesday. Christopher pushed away his plate — on which there had been no semblance of fish — and hurried off to Whitehall.

Leicester was waiting for him. In his hand he held a letter. 'Ah, Dr Radcliff, a reply has at last come from Paris. For some reason its arrival was delayed. Sir Francis insists that I send a most reliable man and suggests that he arrive in the week before the wedding of the king's sister and Henry of Navarre. Be ready to leave at the beginning of August. Sir Francis's agent Tomasso Sessetti will be in Paris at that time and he wishes my envoy to hear what the man has to say.'

'Sessetti, my lord? Italian?'

'A Florentine, but no papist. In Paris there are many Italians spying for one side or another. Sessetti has worked for us since the diabolical *Regnans in Excelsis* was issued by the pope. I know Walsingham holds him in high esteem.'

It was worth one last try. 'My lord, I have been able to find no trace of Nicholas Houseman and am reluctant to leave London until I do. Perhaps you might consider Mr Berwick for the task. He would relish the opportunity.'

'I daresay he would but it is you I wish to send. You are admirably suited and I know I can trust you. Berwick will stay here and report to me.' Leicester smiled encouragingly. 'Come now, doctor, you will be home again within a few days. I will ask Sir Francis to provide you with accommodation. His new house in the Saint-Marceau district, I am told, is very fine. I shall write a letter of introduction for you.'

There was no escape. Walsingham's intelligence must be unusually important. He did not want to leave London and Katherine at such a time, but if he refused Leicester's request, he could not hope for further advancement. 'As you wish, my lord.'

'Good. Now kindly ask the guard to send for John Berwick.' Christopher did as he was ordered. 'I have faith in Berwick,' went on

Leicester. 'Both his parents died during the rebellion in the north. His father was a brave supporter of the Crown. The queen senses the son has potential and wishes to encourage his progress at court. A soft spot, I believe one might call it.'

So John Berwick was indeed making progress in the Whitehall corridors. An ambitious young man and a clever one. The words were out of Christopher's mouth before he could stop them. 'I have been approached by a secretary of Mr Heneage, Roland Wetherby — not a man I warmed to. It seems that Mr Heneage wishes to speak to me.'

Leicester raised an eyebrow. 'Heneage, eh? I have never entirely trusted the man. He is too quick to seek advantage from the misfortunes of others. I had thought Hatton more likely. What did you say?'

'I said that I would consider the request.'

'Good. You will be out of his reach while you are in France. Keep him guessing and do nothing without discussing it with me first.'

When Berwick arrived, carrying a sheaf of papers and dressed, as before, in the drab black and grey of a clerk, Leicester wasted no words. 'Mr Berwick, as you know, an agent of Dr Radcliff has disappeared. The queen will soon leave London on her progress and I shall accompany her. I shall leave matters here in your hands.'

Berwick glanced at Christopher. 'Will Dr Radcliff be travelling with you, my lord?'

'Dr Radcliff will be travelling to Paris. Kindly make arrangements for his journey and furnish him with adequate money. He will need French coin.'

'My lord, Mr Berwick, with respect, lacks experience of intelligence work and is surely occupied elsewhere,' protested Christopher.

He might be going to Paris but he did not want John Berwick using his absence to further his own ends.

'Mr Berwick will serve us well, will you not, Berwick?'

Berwick fiddled with his cap. 'I shall of course do my humble best, my lord.'

'I am sure of it. And you, doctor, will bring back Sir Francis's intelligence. Berwick will make the arrangements and provide you with funds. Please use them carefully. Report to me the moment you are back in England. Now I must attend the queen. Good day, gentlemen. Oh, Dr Radcliff, I think it best if I inform Sir Francis fully of your background. Knowing him, he will only find out for himself if I do not. I am sure you understand.'

'Of course, my lord.' Fully? Every detail? Every scrap and crumb? Walsingham's reaction would be interesting.

As they walked down the gallery, Berwick tried to placate him. 'Dr Radcliff, I do not seek this task. I shall do my poor best while you are in Paris but I fear the earl's mind is troubled by other events. The queen remains unwell and is confined to her apartments. Her condition disorders his judgement.'

'Indeed it does, Mr Berwick. I have no desire to travel to Paris, yet who are we but to obey? Houseman's house is beside a cobbler's shop at Cripplegate. You will need to unpick the lock or find another way in. Search it thoroughly. Look for signs of a crime. There is a stain on the parlour floor. I think it is blood. Examine it. Go, also, to the Stationers' Company. The Senior Warden's name is James Kaye. Try to prick his bubble.'

'I shall do so, doctor, and be assured that I shall do my utmost in your stead. I shall pray for your safe return. Your papers and money will be delivered to your house.' He offered his hand. 'May God protect you.'

Christopher made his way to the gate, where a single figure was waiting. As he approached, he saw that it was Roland Wetherby. 'I heard that you were at the palace, Dr Radcliff, and hoped to speak privately with you,' said Wetherby.

In Whitehall Palace few things went unnoticed. No doubt a watchful guard had sent word to Wetherby. 'I have been with the Earl of Leicester,' replied Christopher, barely breaking his stride, 'and must be on my way.'

'Mr Heneage still awaits your reply. You said by the end of the month.'

Christopher was in no mood to converse with Wetherby or anyone else. 'Mr Heneage must go on waiting. I have urgent business elsewhere.'

He swept through the gate and down Whitehall. Damn Leicester's moods. Nicholas and his wife had disappeared. The earl himself had twice warned of lurking vipers. Christopher was needed in London but had been summarily ordered to Paris, leaving John Berwick, young and inexperienced, to take his place. Why?

'But why, Christopher?'

He had walked directly from the palace to Wood Street to unburden himself to Katherine. 'Sir Francis Walsingham is in Paris with Lord Burghley. He is close to the earl and has requested that a reliable man be sent over.'

'The earl must have other reliable men. Why you?'

Christopher ran a hand through his hair. 'Katherine, I really could not say. He spoke some time ago of vipers lurking, Catholic spies and a Spanish fleet against which we have little defence, and no money to spend on building ships, yet he dispatches me on a long and tiresome journey to Paris. I wonder if he is anxious to be rid of me.'

'Nonsense. It is because he trusts you.'

'Perhaps. He has appointed John Berwick, a new arrival at court, to deputize for me. Berwick is scarcely more than a boy. It is insulting.'

'Berwick? The name is not familiar.'

'I hardly know him. He gives the appearance of an earnest fellow, quietly spoken and respectful. Leicester has taken him under his wing and the young man seems to be favoured by the queen.'

'A future bedfellow? Is he worthy to follow Leicester? Or Oxford or Heneage?'

'Ssh, Katherine. That is mere gossip. And by appearance Berwick is more scholar than lover. Yet favoured, as I, it seems, am not.'

Katherine sighed. 'You make too much of the matter. It is an opportunity for you. Impress Walsingham in Paris and you will impress Leicester.' Her sigh was as theatrical as any of Leicester's players could have managed. 'So I am to kick my heels in London while you travel to Paris. Am I to occupy myself with books and needlework?'

'You have your aunt to consider.'

'Isabel is fully recovered now the weather is cooler. She has no need of me to nurse her.'

Christopher held up his hand. 'Would she examine this? Perhaps one of her potions would help.'

Katherine peered at the hand. 'It is worsening. I will ask her down to look at it. But do not suppose you have ended this discussion. I am no Penelope to be left at home at my tapestry while my husband Odysseus goes off to war.' She shook a finger at him. 'Think on that while I fetch Isabel.'

Isabel Tranter, her father's sister, had never married and, until Katherine had arrived, had lived alone in the house in Wood Street.

Her hair was white, her skin wrinkled and her cheeks sunken into her face, but she was saved from the ugliness of old age by the green eyes that she shared with her niece.

Christopher rose when she entered the room on Katherine's arm. 'Christopher, I am pleased to see you,' she greeted him, with a kiss on the cheek. 'I do not see you often enough. How do you fare with the Earl of Leicester?'

'As ever, madam, up one day and down another. The earl is a demanding task-master.'

'I hear the queen is unwell.'

'Alas, she is. The earl hopes that her forthcoming progress will restore her to good health. And you, are you well?'

'Now that the heat has gone from the air, I am much improved. I thought it would carry me off to my grave it was so fierce.'

Katherine helped her aunt to sit. 'Tush, aunt, you will live to be a hundred. Now, Christopher asks that you inspect his hand. Perhaps one of your spells might improve it.' Katherine enjoyed teasing the old lady and often accused her of witchcraft for her knowledge of plants and what they could do for ailments and wounds if correctly used. Isabel, too, enjoyed it. In the privacy of her house, she even occasionally pretended to cast spells.

She took Christopher's hand in hers and tried to stretch the fingers. Then she rubbed the knuckles and pressed her own fingers into the palm. 'It has worsened since last I saw it. Did the vervain not help?'

'I fear not. The last two fingers seem to bend a little more each day.'

Isabel sat stroking the hand and thinking. Eventually she looked up. 'We will try a mixture of dandelion and lavender with a drop of apple vinegar. I have them all in the kitchen.'

'What do you think causes this?' asked Katherine.

'I do not think it is caused by a disorder of the humours or another internal problem because it has brought on no fever or sickening. The problem lies in the hand itself. Do you write every day, Christopher?'

'Most days.'

'And it is only your right hand that is affected. The holding of a pen for long periods might be to blame. I will make up the ointment.'

When Isabel had left them, Katherine asked, 'When shall you go?'

'In a few weeks, before the wedding of the French king's sister to Henry of Navarre. Berwick is making the arrangements. I also had an approach from Thomas Heneage's man, Wetherby, some three weeks back. He wants to meet me.'

'Why would Thomas Heneage wish to meet you?'

'He wishes to employ my services.'

'Have you told the earl?'

'I have.'

'Then doubtless that is why he is sending you to France.' Christopher let it go. Better that Katherine should not know about Nicholas Houseman. 'And I shall accompany you.'

'You are in jest, I hope.'

'I am not. I shall accompany you.'

'What? You cannot possibly accompany me. It is an absurd suggestion. The journey might be hazardous. The earl would never countenance such a thing.'

'Would he not?'

'No, Katherine. You know well that he would not. And without his authority to travel, to do so would be illegal.'

'Will you ask him?'

'No, Katherine, I will not allow it. You must have an ague coming on. Put the foolish notion from your mind. I shall go alone. Let that be an end to it.'

If they argued further, she would speak of Bess of Hardwick, the Countess of Shrewsbury, perhaps the richest woman in England. Then she would mention Boudicca and Jeanne d'Arc. And, if he had not yet surrendered, she would ask him if, to his knowledge, their monarch wore a codpiece. Katherine Allington had no more time for the so-called frailties of her sex than any of them.

He was spared more by Isabel returning with a small jar. 'Here it is,' she said. 'Rub it into the hand every morning before prayers and every evening when you retire. Write as little as you can.'

Christopher took the jar. 'Thank you. I shall take it with me to France.'

'To France? Are you sent there by the earl?'

'I am.'

'I have offered to accompany him but have been rejected. It seems that my help is not wanted,' said Katherine. Like any woman, petulance did not improve her looks.

'I have explained to Katherine — not that it needs explanation — that it is not possible for her to travel with me, Isabel. Please persuade her to put the matter from her mind.'

'It is indeed a foolish thought, Katherine, as you must know. Your place is here until Christopher returns. How long shall you be away, Christopher?'

'No more than two or three weeks, God willing. I must leave in early August. I do not relish not being in London and will return as soon as I can. Now, forgive me, I have much to do before I leave. Thank you for the ointment, Isabel.'

Katherine's voice rose. 'Much to do including visiting your whore, I daresay. Go, Christopher, and take the doxy with you if you must. It is no longer of any account to me.' She pushed past him and out of the room.

'I am sorry, Isabel,' said Christopher. 'But rest assured that I shall be taking no whores. Do you think Katherine is serious?'

'It can be hard to tell with her, but I think not. The idea is too absurd. She is merely striving to make the point that she does not relish being left alone with little to occupy her. I shall endeavour to restore her spirits.'

Christopher stooped to kiss the old lady's cheek. 'You are kind to us, Isabel. Few would tolerate us with such discretion. A convicted felon and your niece, a young widow. You keep our secrets as if they were your own. We owe you much. I hope it does not embarrass you.'

Isabel smiled. 'Never. Katherine's happiness is all I care for and I know she is happiest with you. I am too old to care much for the opinions of others. Apply the ointment each day and return safely.'

'I shall be sure to do both.'

CHAPTER 9

August, France

He had told Rose that he was travelling to France and asked her to look after the house while he was away. 'Be sure to take care, doctor,' the old woman had said. 'They say they eat strange beasts, the French, beasts we have never seen in England.'

'I shall take care, Rose,' he had assured her, 'and eat only that which I recognize.'

He travelled by barge to Tilbury and there boarded a packet-boat for Calais. The westerly winds that had kept England safe from the Spanish fleet were still favourable and they crossed the narrow sea in only a few hours. Just as he enjoyed the Cam and the Thames, he found that he enjoyed the sea. For much of the journey he stood by a mast, feeling the wind on his back and the sun on his face, and watched the French coast turn from a hazy grey outline to green fields and small villages. His next steps on land would be his first outside England.

In his bag, wrapped in a spare gown and hidden among changes of clothes, he carried a heavy purse, a letter from the earl authorizing him to travel to France on government business and another addressed to Sir Francis Walsingham. He had not called again at Wood Street and half-wished that he had.

The hope that French highways and French inns would be more agreeable than those at home proved forlorn. After four days and three uncomfortable coaching inns, he arrived at last at the outskirts of Paris. He had been forced to employ a new coachman at each inn. None had wished to travel further than a day's journey, unwilling to venture too far from their homes. The inns had been rough — hard beds, poor food, surly serving girls — and he could not find a woman at any of them to wash his linen. The highways — until the last twenty miles to the city walls, where they had been levelled and paved — had been rutted and uneven.

Alone in the coach, he had only his thoughts for company. No London intelligencer could be wholly ignorant of affairs in France. The earl had spoken about them and had even shared with him some of Walsingham's dispatches. One thing only was clear. In a country divided by intractable faith and bitter hatred, factions, both Catholic and Protestant, rose and fell on the shifting sands of royal influence and popular support.

For thirty years the established Catholic Church had faced the growing challenge of the strict Protestantism preached by the German monk Martin Luther and, after his death, by his followers. And for a decade the Protestant Huguenots, now led by the austere Admiral Gaspard de Coligny, and the Catholics — led by the duc d'Anjou, the king's brother, and Henri, duc de Guise — had been at each other's throats. Yet now, evidently as a sign of her wish for reconciliation, Queen Catherine was to marry her daughter Margaret to a leading Protestant, Henry of Navarre. Could it be this about which Walsingham had intelligence, and, if so, how might it affect England?

When he was not thinking about France he was thinking about the Housemans. He could not explain their disappearance without leaving a trace of why or where. Nicholas was a valued agent, one of his best. He would surely not leave London without a word and if he had somehow been discovered and disposed of, others would be in danger. Would he return to find that Ell Cole or Isaac Cardoza had also disappeared? He had sat drumming his fingers impatiently on the seat of the coach. He should be in London, not acting as a messenger.

As for his task, was it really something the earl could only entrust to a 'reliable' man or was it just a sign of his displeasure at the disappearance of an agent — if the queen's humour had been low and her temper short, he was capable of such an irrational action — or did he have another reason to send Christopher out of the country? Did he want to give John Berwick a chance to prove himself? If the young man had the queen's favour, Leicester might see him as a means to promote his own cause.

It had been at night that he had thought most of Katherine. Narrow, dirty beds did not make for restful sleep and each night he had lain awake thinking about their parting. Her demand had of course been absurd, even dangerous, but for all her intelligence, Katherine was a woman who could be unreasonable if she did not get her own way. And whether her oft-voiced feelings about Ell were genuine or simply put on as a warning, he still did not know. Nor did he know how he would find her when he returned. Still angry? Petulant? Remorseful? Much as he had come to love her, she was not an easy woman to understand.

They had passed through flat, green countryside, dotted with small farms and villages, and broken up only by copses of oak and elm. As they approached Paris, the number of travellers on the highway increased. Not only farmers and tradesmen taking their wares to market but parties of a dozen or more, men and women, some riding, most on foot, all making their way to the city. At a halt to water the horses, he asked a traveller his business. 'To Paris, for Navarre's wedding,' replied the old man. 'I would see peace before I die.' They were Huguenots, determined to see for themselves one of their own married into the royal family of Valois. Perhaps the wedding would indeed bring peace.

But a mile or so outside the walls, they passed clusters of tents and groups of armed men on either side of the road. Most were dressed as working men and carried muskets and knives. Their officers held pistols and swords. They too were Huguenots.

Inside the city wall, they drove along a broad street that stretched down to the Seine. At first sight Paris was not only far, far larger than London, it was also subtly different in other ways. The houses were taller — up to five storeys — the churches were grander and more numerous and the public buildings more elegant. Yet the difference lay in more than that. Above all, London was a city of commerce. Thomas Gresham's Royal Exchange, less than two years old, stood proof to this. Ambition, commerce, wealth. If it were human, London would be a clever young merchant looking to make his way in a life of business. Industrious, quick to learn, determined, sometimes brash. Paris would be a learned theologian.

As the coach trundled down the street towards the Seine, Christopher sensed a city more confident in its history, wiser and certainly more pious. The people walked with less urgency, the carriages — many finely finished in brass and gilt — were driven with care. There appeared no urgency. It was a city founded on faith, on beauty, on learning. At the beautiful Fontaine des Innocents, the groups of gowned students brought Cambridge, not London, to mind. In London there were no universities. Paris was the seat of two – one that bore its name and the Sorbonne, both fiercely, unwaveringly opposed to Luther's Protestantism and fearful of its spread. Paris, too, was a centre of printing and thus of the dissemination of information and opinion. The city he had come to was a city not only of theologians but also of artists and writers and scholars.

Christopher smiled to himself. These were fanciful notions. Scratch the surface of any city, even this one, and a man would find disease, poverty and crime. The lanes and alleys of Paris would be as dark and threatening and dangerous as any in London. And in France, violence could erupt without warning. For ten years or more it had done so.

They crossed the river, passed the king's palace, crossed the river again and continued south towards the district of Saint-Marceau. The Seine was wider here than the Thames, slower moving and much less busy. Near London Bridge one might see three times as many barges and cargo vessels.

The coachman found Sir Francis Walsingham's house without difficulty. The footman who opened the door took the earl's letter and left Christopher to wait in a large, elegant reception room, finely decorated with paintings of Paris and a huge Flemish arras. An oriental carpet covered the floor; thick velvet drapes hung at the windows. A row of high-backed chairs lined one wall, ready to be put to use when needed. Christopher, a little nervous and tired of sitting in coaches, ignored them and remained standing.

In due course, the footman returned and escorted him to Walsingham's study. When Christopher entered, unrefreshed and concerned at how he must look, the ambassador was holding the letter in his hand. He was several inches shorter than Christopher, his neatly trimmed hair and beard a mix of black and grey, his expression not unkind. He wore a simple black coat, white ruffs at the neck and sleeves and black hose. The sharp eyes ran over Christopher. 'Welcome, Dr Radcliff. The earl must think highly of you to entrust you with this task.'

Christopher bowed his head. 'I hope so, sir, although I know only that I am to carry a message back to London.'

'You will discover more tomorrow, doctor. Signor Tomasso Sessetti, one of the many Italians now in Paris and a good friend to our country, is coming. Until then, make yourself comfortable. The servants will bring supper to your room and will provide you with whatever you need. If you are like me, a hot bath after your journey would be welcome.'

'It would, Sir Francis. Thank you.'

The door opened and a small woman, modestly dressed in grey and wearing a white cap, entered. Her face was oval, her eyes brown and her skin clear. Not a beautiful woman nor a plain one. Her eyes held a hint of sadness. Walsingham introduced his wife. To Christopher's inexperienced eye, Ursula Walsingham had been carrying her unborn child for about four months. 'I heard you had arrived, Dr Radcliff,' she said in a quiet voice. 'Welcome to our home while we are in Paris.'

Christopher made what sounded to his own ears a clumsy attempt at a compliment about the house. 'We moved last year from Faubourg Saint-Germain,' she replied. 'Here, we are among the Huguenot community and much more comfortable. We worship with them at their church. They call it *Le Temple*. I go there to remember my sons.'

'Ursula lost both her sons by Sir Richard Worsley in an accident,' explained Walsingham, with a smile at his wife. 'Happily we now have Frances, who is five years old, and a second child due in January.'

'I shall bear my confinement in London,' said Lady Walsingham. 'I would rather our son be born in England. But you must be tired, doctor. The servants will bring you hot water. We will see you tomorrow.'

'Sleep soundly, for we have much to discuss,' added her husband.

Christopher was indeed tired. With a sense of relief, he took his leave. His bed chamber was as lavish as the reception room. The bed was wide and framed in a light-coloured fruit wood and its cover was embroidered in red and gold. Two carved, padded chairs in the same wood stood either side of a round table, the edge of which had been inlaid with gold leaf. The clothes chest and wash stand, both finely carved, were oaken. One wall was almost entirely taken up by a gilt mirror. He took a look at his face and grimaced. It had been a long journey.

CHAPTER 10

Colombes

The three men had gathered in the same room in the inn at Colombes, not far north of Paris. It had been more than two months since their last meeting. Clean rushes had been spread on the floor. The candles flickered in their holders and cast shadows on the walls. The innkeeper's son had served their meal and now stood outside the door with instructions to admit no one.

Charles, the priest, spoke first. 'This monstrous union will soon take place and our work will begin. Coligny will soon arrive.'

'I have identified twenty heretic leaders already in the city,' spat out the scar-faced soldier. 'God has given us our chance.'

'When?' growled William the Scotsman. He was already half cut and slurring his words. He tore a leg off a roast chicken and began to gnaw at it.

'After the wedding,' replied the priest. 'I have alerted Maurevert. Soon, William, soon you will be on your way.' It was, thought the priest, as devious a remark as he had ever uttered. 'Has there been news from England?'

'I have heard nothing since we last met,' replied the soldier. 'With my cousin locked up in that damned castle, it is near impossible for her to send word. I do manage to speak to her through her priest but she does not reply for fear of discovery. That would certainly mean her death. I pray daily for her.'

'As should we all. Has the other weapon been dispatched, William?'

'As I said it would. It went hidden in a shipment to London. Our friend will receive it and hide the weapon in a secure place. He assures me it will be well concealed.'

'Good. And in London, Henri?'

'It goes well. They are ready when we give the order and there have been no difficulties since the minor one I mentioned when we last met. They await our word.'

William thumped the table with the haft of his knife. 'Then why do we not get on with it? Why the delay? The witch must die and the sooner the better.'

Henri poured more wine into his glass and spoke gently. 'Be calm, William. All will be well and the Scots queen will soon be in her rightful place. For her sake, we must be cautious. Now let us drink to success.' He held up his glass. '*Incendium.*' William emptied his glass and Henri refilled it again.

The priest stood up. 'When next we meet, it will be done and we shall have taken the first step towards achieving our godly purpose. Then you will both come to my house to celebrate. There will be no more skulking in dark inns. Good night, gentlemen. Go with God.'

It was a moonless night, the sky covered by dark cloud. In the woods nearby, a fox barked. Outside the inn, Charles waited in the shadows. After five minutes, Henri appeared. 'Barely sensible, Charles,' he said. 'I refilled his glass twice more. There is no need for you to wait. I will make sure it is done as we wish.'

'No,' replied the priest, 'I must see it for myself. Then, if any-thing goes wrong, you will not have to explain it to me.'

'Thoughtful, as ever, Charles. Where are they?'

'Watching from the trees. Have no fear. They are the best money can buy.'

Ten minutes later, the door of the inn opened and William stumbled out. The two men stepped back into the shadows. He walked a few paces towards the post to which his horse had been tethered, stopped and turned to face the wall. He unfastened his breeches and, with a grunt of satisfaction, began to piss against it. When the fox barked again, he gave no sign of having heard it.

Two dark figures emerged from the woods and moved silently up behind him. William Mackay heard nothing. One of the figures produced a length of twisted rope, the other a long knife. In a trice, the rope was round the Scotsman's neck and the dagger lodged in his back. His bellow of pain was cut off by the rope with which the assassin squeezed his windpipe. The dagger was withdrawn and plunged again into their victim's back. He slumped to the ground. The rope was removed and his throat cut.

The priest and the scarred soldier had seen it all. They exchanged a look and smiled. 'They will dispose of the body,' whispered the soldier. 'It will not be seen again. Farewell, Charles.'

The priest watched him mount his horse and disappear into the darkness. An extraordinary man. So young, yet God's fire ablaze in his heart. Nothing would deter him from achieving his godly purpose — not the weakness of an ally, not the heretic Coligny, not the blood of Frenchmen. He crossed himself. They had planned for this and the wedding had given them their opportunity. May God guide their hands in what lay ahead.

CHAPTER 11

Paris

'You are wondering why I asked the earl to send a special courier,' said Walsingham, 'when there are couriers aplenty travelling back and forth between London and Paris. Am I right, Dr Radcliff?'

They sat either side of Walsingham's writing table in his handsome library. No sound penetrated from outside nor was there a clock. It was a silent room, a room for study and privacy and contemplation. The walls were lined with beautifully bound, expensive books, but on his table documents were strewn about like autumn leaves. Only a man of self-confidence and capacious memory could operate in such disorder. Christopher knew that he could not.

'You are, sir,' replied Christopher. 'Might it be wise to deal with that question before we discuss anything else?'

'In good time. First, you must know that the earl has provided a full account of you.' He held up Leicester's letter. 'Very thoughtful of him. I would otherwise have had to make my own inquiries. You have led an unusual life, Dr Radcliff.' Christopher inclined his head in agreement but said nothing. He could not be sure what Leicester had written. Walsingham went on, 'How did a Doctor of Law at Pembroke Hall and recruiter for the Earl of Leicester come to be caught up in a tavern brawl?'

Christopher stretched the fingers of his right hand and tried to relax his shoulders, still tense from the journey. He had expected this from Walsingham and had prepared his response. 'It was on the day my mother died. The plague took her as it did my father and many others in Wisbech. For three days I had watched her die. We buried her with my father.' He did not look directly at Walsingham but was aware of his keen eyes watching. 'That evening I drank too much ale. A fight broke out — I cannot remember why — I lashed out, a man fell and his head struck the flagstones of the floor, causing him to lose much blood. He died. It altered the course of my life and has been on my conscience ever since.'

'You lashed out. Have you a temper, doctor?'

Christopher shook his head. 'Rarely. I was driven by ale and grief.'

'If what you say is true, it was an accident.'

'It was, but six witnesses, friends of the dead man, testified against me at the assizes. They claimed I had intended to kill him. I was fortunate to escape the rope.'

'And then what?'

'I was sentenced to eight years' imprisonment in Norwich gaol.' Christopher laughed lightly. 'Not much different from hanging except that death comes a little more slowly. But again I was fortunate. I survived eight weeks before the earl arranged my release.'

'Not a happy eight weeks, I daresay. It must pain you to speak of it.'

'It does, sir. A man who has not known for himself the misery and degradation of such a place cannot begin to understand it. I would rather face a bloodthirsty Tartar horde than experience it again. Even now, I have a dread of prisons.'

'And after your release?'

'By the grace of the Master, I returned to Pembroke for a short time, but of course as a felon I could not go back to teaching there. The earl offered me a position on his staff in London, a position I have held for a little more than two years. I owe him much.'

'Good. That is entirely consistent with the earl's account. I thank you for your honesty. We live in confusing times, doctor, and I have found it best to trust as few men as possible. But the Earl of Leicester I have known for many years and would trust with my life. In you, despite your story, I have no doubt he has chosen wisely.' Christopher inclined his head in acknowledgement. 'Now, as to why you are here.'

Walsingham stood and walked slowly around the library, as if gathering his thoughts. 'The truth is that I have been concerned for some time about the loyalty of our couriers. Messages have gone astray and there is reason to believe that our ciphers are being broken. Two of the pope's own cryptographers are known to have arrived recently from Rome. The new pontiff has lost no time in allying himself to the house of Valois although he is ill-disposed to the wedding.'

'Can these leaks in the dam not be plugged, Sir Francis?'

'We try, of course, but seem always to be one step behind. One bad apple is thrown out and two more appear. That is why I asked for you, or someone like you, to be sent here. You will commit everything you learn to memory and nothing to writing. That must be clearly understood.'

'It is understood, sir.'

'Very well. Tell me how the earl fares at court. He is cautious in his letters.'

'The earl is well but has been concerned at the queen's health and humour. They have suffered since the latest plot and the execution of her cousin Norfolk. He hopes her planned progress to Kenilworth and Warwick will lift her spirits. The duc de Montmorency's visit will not, he thinks, be a success. The earl confided in me that he dreads the thought of the duc d'Alençon marrying our queen but is obliged publicly to support a possible alliance with France. Such a conflict is not easy for him to bear.'

'No, that I can understand and it is concerning. In matters of conscience the earl is a straightforward man, not given to dissembling or hypocrisy. Indeed, that is what I most admire about him. The very idea of his having ordered the death of his own wife is absurd and abhorrent to me, although the rumours persist, even here in Paris. Poor Robert was devoted to Amy and was distraught at her loss. She was a sick woman, you know. A fall might easily have killed her.' Walsingham paused. 'And your work, doctor — how did the earl feel able to release you from your duties?'

'Sir Francis, you requested a reliable man. To oblige you, the earl had to release someone from his staff. I would not have been the only suitable choice.'

'Yet he chose you. Can you tell me why?'

'One of my agents, Nicholas Houseman, has disappeared, his wife with him. The earl thought it opportune to send me here and to appoint another to investigate the matter.'

'And who was that?'

'Mr John Berwick, a young man newly arrived at court and favoured by the queen. I found him decent and studious. He will serve the earl well.'

'Good. That too is consistent with everything the earl wrote in his letter. *Semper veritas.* Like the earl, I have not opposed Alençon's suit, chiefly because he is much less mulish than his brother Anjou in the matter of worship. Not opposing, of course, is not the same as supporting. That I have not done, largely because I do not believe that it will go ahead.'

'And how can I be of assistance while I am in Paris, Sir Francis?'

'Today you will meet Signor Tomasso Sessetti, one of my most valuable intelligencers. Signor Sessetti is an unusual man. He is a Florentine with no love of Pope Gregory or, indeed, of papism. He moves in the highest and the lowest circles with equal facility. After that, we will see how matters develop.'

They met in the library. Tomasso Sessetti was a slight, swarthy man with coal-black hair, a nervous manner and watchful eyes. His beard was short and pointed, his mouth uncommonly small. It would have been easy to distrust him. Christopher tried not to. They sat at a small round table, a bottle of white Burgundy wine and three glasses in front of them. Walsingham filled the glasses, explained Christopher's presence and asked Sessetti to tell them what he knew.

'England and France have agreed not to take up arms against each other and to come to each other's aid if asked to do so,' began the Florentine, his voice betraying some nervousness. 'This agreement was a prelude to a possible match between Queen Elizabeth and a French prince and is of course aimed at keeping the Spanish at bay.'

Walsingham interrupted. 'Although King Philip will not easily be deterred. He is bent on ridding the world of every Protestant — man, woman and child.'

'As Sir Francis says. The French ambassador, the duc de Montmorency, will by now be in London to ratify the Blois treaty and to promote a marriage between your queen and the king's brother, the duc d'Alençon. I understand that even if she does not agree to the match it should not alter the terms of the treaty. Our problems lie elsewhere.'

'In France?' ventured Christopher.

'Exactly. First of all, the wedding of Henry of Navarre to Margaret of Valois will take place the day after tomorrow. Navarre has invited many prominent Protestants to attend the ceremony, including their leader, Admiral Gaspard de Coligny. The admiral will be vulnerable and there are rumours of an attempt on his life. If that were to happen, there would be more than just his blood on the streets of Paris.' Christopher did not ask how Sessetti knew this. Walsingham would have intelligencers all over the city.

The Florentine went on, 'Second, agents from Scotland are here to rally support for their queen's cause. They mix with the émigré community and talk openly with members of the Guise family.'

'Would the Blois treaty not preclude such support?'

'It would,' replied Walsingham, 'and that is what most alarms us. We fear that there is a plot to flout the treaty by an alliance with the Scots and another attempt on the English throne. Queen Catherine, however, is marrying her daughter to a Protestant and has sent Montmorency to London to promote the suit of d'Alençon. That suggests that if there is a plot, she does not know of it. A Medici she may be, but could she act as deviously as that? I think not.'

Sessetti went on, 'During the last twelve months I have culti-vated the society of a Scotsman by the name of William Mackay, who is known to us for his part in the uprising led by the earls of Northumberland and Westmoreland. He fled to France after its failure. He is an ill-tempered drunkard with a loose tongue. With a barrel of wine inside him, he recently hinted at a plot to free the Queen of Scots from her confinement in Sheffield Castle.'

'Most worrying is the possible involvement of Henri, duc de Guise,' added Walsingham. 'He has always believed Coligny to have been responsible for his father's death at Orleans and has sworn revenge. As a young man of less than twenty he fought with distinction at Saint-Denis and Jarmac and now, despite his youth, commands support throughout France.'

'And the king,' asked Christopher, 'is he involved?'

'He keeps his mother at a distance and is closer to Guise despite the history of bad blood between the houses of Valois and Guise. He may well know things that she does not, but we have no knowledge of what they might be,' replied Walsingham.

Sessetti rose and looked out of the window. When he spoke the nervousness in his voice had gone. 'Mackay has even let slip, admittedly when barely conscious, a name. *Incendium.*'

Walsingham refilled their glasses. '*Incendium.* The word itself is frightening enough. It brings to mind brave men dying at Mary Tudor's command in unspeakable agony for their faith. And if Guise is part of it, even worse is possible.'

Mary Tudor. More than three hundred burned at the stake for their faith. Nicholas Ridley, once Master of Pembroke Hall, one of her last victims. Christopher remembered the mourning in college all too well. A service had been held for Ridley's soul, although perforce in a chapel compelled to embrace the trappings of Catholicism. 'Has Mackay mentioned other names?' he asked.

'No. However, he has suddenly disappeared. He has not visited any of his regular drinking haunts and he was not at his house in Douai when I called.'

'Could he have suspected you?'

Sessetti shook his head. 'I am sure not.'

'Might he not have returned to Scotland?'

'Possibly, but the ports are watched and the risk would be high.'

'What do you suspect?'

'If he is working with Guise, that he opened his mouth once too often and has been disposed of. Guise would not be deterred by scruple.'

'Have you grounds for believing this, Signor Sessetti?'

'Only that it is what I would do if an agent of mine habitually drank too much wine and became a liability.'

'You too have recently lost an agent, doctor, although I imagine the circumstances were different,' said Walsingham.

'They were. I trusted Nicholas Houseman as you trust Signor Sessetti.' It was said sharply.

'Forgive me, doctor. I did not mean to imply otherwise. I merely remark the coincidence. That, I think, is enough for now. Admiral Coligny is due in Paris today. I will send word asking him to call.' Walsingham rose to signal the end of the meeting. 'Thank you, Tomasso. We will meet again soon.'

'Sir Francis. Dr Radcliff. Let us pray for rain to douse the fire.'

Admiral Coligny arrived that afternoon. He came alone and was shown into the reception room where Walsingham and Christopher were waiting for him. He wore a simple black doublet, an unruffed shirt and black breeches to his knees. His frame was tall and spare, his eyes dark and unsmiling.

He bowed politely when Christopher was introduced but did

not speak. 'Welcome, Gaspard,' Walsingham greeted him, 'how was your journey?'

'Quite uneventful, thank you. I received your message as soon as I arrived and came straight here.'

They sat and waited for a footman to bring wine. When they were alone, Walsingham spoke first. He came straight to the point. 'We have intelligence that an attempt is to be made on your life, Gaspard. While in Paris, as leader of the Huguenots you are like a stag in the sights of bowmen.'

Coligny raised an eyebrow. 'We?'

'Tomasso Sessetti.'

'The Florentine.'

'Just so. He believes that your assassination might even have the approval of the king.'

'For some time I have been on good terms with his mother the queen, who speaks only of peace and reconciliation, but her influence with her son is waning. He listens more to his mistresses. What poison they drip into his ear, I know not.'

Walsingham pressed on. 'We also believe that your death could be part of a much larger plot, involving the Queen of Scots and therefore also the Queen of England.'

'How so?'

'An attack on Protestants in France, a Catholic uprising in England and an attack by the Scots. Sessetti has heard a name. *Incendium*. It speaks for itself.' Christopher held his tongue, although Walsingham had exaggerated what they knew, perhaps suspecting that Coligny would dismiss an attempt on his own life as of little consequence.

'*Incendium*,' repeated the admiral. 'If such a plot exists, you may be sure that the Guise family will be involved. The duc has wished me dead since the death of his father at Orleans, for which he holds me responsible, and he is a cousin of the Queen of Scots. For nine years I have lived with the knowledge that an assassin might lurk around the next corner and I will not hide myself away now. I must be seen at the wedding. Hundreds of our people will be there. It should be a time of reconciliation and joy and I must attend. If he wishes it, God will protect me.'

'I knew you would say that, my friend,' replied Walsingham, 'and you are right. Not only must you attend the wedding as leader of your community but if you do not, the plotters will smell a rat and our agents will be in danger. However, I urge you to take precautions. Your death would be a disaster for France and perhaps too for England.'

Coligny's mouth twitched in a brief smile. 'You overstate my importance, Francis. If I were to fall, there are twenty more to take my place. The Huguenot community seeks peace, not bloodshed, despite the wrongs we have suffered at the hands of the Valois and the Guises. The men encamped outside the city walls are merely a precaution. But what of this plot? What more do you know?'

'Little, as yet. Sessetti is trying to discover more and Dr Radcliff will report to the Earl of Leicester.'

'And I will instruct our people to find out what they can. Is the Queen of Scots adequately guarded?'

'She is. Leicester tells me that since the Ridolfi affair her every word and action are monitored and noted down. Only her priests may visit her and they are closely watched.'

'*Incendium*. The name brings to mind images of the bloodthirsty Mary Tudor dancing round pyres of burning Protestants.'

'It does. And you, Gaspard, can you not imagine Huguenot

corpses being thrown gleefully on to fires lit by the king?' replied Walsingham.

'I wish I could not,' replied Coligny. 'And what are your thoughts, Dr Radcliff?'

Christopher hesitated. 'The Earl of Leicester believes that in England vipers lurk. Those were his words. If they also lurk in France and if the two nests should conspire to act together, no treaty will stop them. We must find out what, if anything, this plot is and extinguish it.' He found that he was rubbing his hand. Isabel's ointment had had little effect as yet.

'Meanwhile, let us speak the word only among ourselves,' said Walsingham. 'You will note what I have said, Gaspard, will you not? Take great care.'

'Be sure that I shall, my friend, although I have no fear. I must stay here for a few days after the wedding but will be returning to Burgundy by the end of the month.'

'A good man,' said Walsingham after Coligny had left, 'and a brave one. Let us hope that the rumours are no more than idle tittle-tattle, although the duc de Guise is a formidable enemy and the admiral might well be right. If there is a plot to murder the Protestant leader, Guise will be involved one way or another. Queen Catherine has kept the duc at a distance since his short-lived affair with her daughter Margaret, and Margaret is about to marry a Protestant. He will be like a cornered boar — furious and slavering and dangerous.'

'Would Guise have sought the support of the king or would he be acting apart from the house of Valois?'

'The king has given his blessing to the marriage and has recently made approaches to the Huguenot leaders but he is young and easily swayed. He does not have my trust. Spend tomorrow with Sessetti, doctor. No one knows his way around Paris better than him. Pick his brains. The next day we will attend the wedding. I will arrange places for you.'

So no longer merely a messenger. 'I shall, Sir Francis.'

Walsingham nodded. 'I noticed that your hand troubles you, doctor. There is an excellent apothecary not far away. I will give you directions.'

'Thank you, sir,' replied Christopher politely, although he doubted a French apothecary's remedy would serve any better than Isabel's.

CHAPTER 12

The mood in the city was taut as a bowstring. As he walked the city streets with Sessetti, Christopher could see it in faces and in the set of shoulders. Parties of Huguenots, easily recognizable by their sombre dress, strolled in the sunshine. Catholic Parisians about their daily business took care to avoid them. Christopher ignored the curious looks of passers-by, hoping that they were only for his height and hair. A Protestant Englishman might not be welcomed at such a time.

Here and there a scuffle broke out. Near the great cathedral of Notre-Dame, they saw a baker refusing to sell a loaf of bread to an elderly man in a black coat. 'Clear off,' shouted the baker, 'I do not serve heretic visitors.' The old man shouted back that he lived in Paris, spat out a vile curse and went on his way. Some shops were closed. Outside others stood guards armed with dung-forks and timber-axes. Were tension tangible, they could have returned to the Walsinghams' house with a cartload.

They were accosted but once. Near the church of Saint-Sévérin, three sergeants were slaking their thirst outside a busy inn. They saw Christopher and Sessetti and approached them. Despite the early hour, the sergeant who spoke had taken more than a beaker or two of ale. 'One tall and fair, the other small and dark. Both have the appearance of Puritans yet an ill-matched pair. What is your business in Paris?'

Sessetti replied, 'We are in the employ of Sir Francis Walsingham, Her Majesty Queen Elizabeth's ambassador to the French court. We have as much right to be here as any man.'

The sergeant was not to be placated so easily. 'Have you now? And have we not the right to arrest you on suspicion of planning to cause affray?'

'There will be no affray, sergeant,' replied Christopher, keeping his tone even. 'We are here to attend tomorrow's wedding. It will be a grand occasion and a step on the road to peace in your country.'

The sergeant grunted. 'Perhaps. As long as the heretic Huguenots do not cause trouble. On your way, Puritans. We have more important work to do.' His companions laughed and returned to their ale.

'Much like London,' said Christopher, as they walked. 'A man may be judged and found guilty simply for his appearance.'

'It is not so different in Florence either,' replied Sessetti. 'There too a man must dress as his position dictates and poverty is taken as evidence of guilt. The wealthy are seldom brought to account. While the bishops live in their gilded palaces, stuffing themselves with the fruits of the earth and breaking their vows as they wish, the poor die in doorways and under hedgerows for want of food and shelter. It is why I reject the Catholic faith. It is corrupt and hypocritical.'

'In that respect it is not the only faith at fault. I once prayed daily and worshipped as our queen instructs. Now, I find myself doubting the purpose.'

Sessetti looked up sharply. 'Why is that? To be thought *nulla fidians* is as dangerous in your country as in mine.'

'I am not atheistical, merely questioning. Now, enough of this. I shall meet you outside the cathedral tomorrow.' They shook hands and parted company — Sessetti to his family, Christopher back to the house in Saint-Marceau.

Rather to his relief, he found that Walsingham was dining else-where. He did not want to be asked to describe what he had seen and felt in the city. To Lady Walsingham's inquiry, he said only that if the ingredients of tension were fear, anger and hatred, Paris was a place of tension.

The wedding of Henry of Navarre to Margaret of Valois, youngest daughter of Catherine de' Medici and sister of King Charles, was to take place in the parvise of the great cathedral of Notre-Dame. Although Henry's Protestantism precluded him from marrying in the cathedral itself, it would be as lavish an affair as befitted the occasion.

By midday, rows of invited guests, led by the king and his mother, filled not only the grand entrance to the cathedral but also the covered parvise, whose roof was supported by rows of colonnades. Gold and silver sparkled in the sun, red and blue and white shimmered in the breeze. Musicians played and the cathedral choir sang. Flanked by his priests and officials, the Bishop of Beauvais, who would conduct the service, stood unsmiling, his eyes fixed on some point in the distance.

Christopher and Sessetti had arrived early and found a spot from where they could observe most of the congregation. They watched the royal party, France's highest officials, its bishops and judges as they entered the parvise and took their seats. Sir Francis and Lady Walsingham had been placed in the second row of guests. Sessetti pointed out Admiral Coligny, unguarded and seated conspicuously in the front row. 'There he is, doctor. Let us hope that his confidence is justified. On the other side, as far from Coligny as possible, can you see a man with a scar running down his cheek?' Christopher nodded. 'That is Henri, duc de Guise, hater of all Protestants, once close to the queen, now, we think, closer to the king.'

At the front of the congregation sat the bride's family — in the centre of the row the king, the ducs d'Anjou and d'Alençon, and their mother the queen. Even from a distance, Alençon cut a pitiful figure. The man who wished to marry the Queen of England was so short that his feet barely touched the ground and the poor fellow's face resembled nothing so much as a turnip speared by a farmer's fork — a pitted, shapeless lump. Despite his appearance, the duc managed to grin happily throughout, as if thinking that it would be his turn next. Christopher wondered how he compared to the Bavarian grotesque whose clock now stood in Leicester's apartment.

Beyond, the streets were packed with onlookers. For some it was a day of hope. After years of bloodshed, a union between the houses of Navarre and Valois might, just might, bring peace to France at last, a peace for which the king and his family claimed to long. So important was it that even the untimely death of Navarre's mother had not prevented the ceremony from going ahead. For many Parisians, however, the marriage of the king's sister to a Protestant was nothing less than sacrilege. Their pope had condemned it and they condemned it.

If there was to be bloodshed, this was surely where it would erupt. The parvise was ringed by guards armed with halberds and swords but a single pistol shot or a determined attack with a dagger and Henry or Margaret would die. So, doubtless, would the assassin but he would have volunteered for the task in return for the security and comfort of his family.

For nearly two hours they stood and watched, while Charles, Bishop of Beauvais, conducted the wedding. Sessetti quietly pointed out figures he recognized while Christopher thought of Katherine and whether one day she would relent and agree to marry him, albeit in a ceremony a trifle less grand than this one.

Eventually it was over. There had been no outcries and no disturbances. The congregation had prayed for the happiness of the union and cheered as the newly wedded couple were taken by carriage to the Tuileries Palace where the wedding feast would be held. Their guests followed them and the onlookers, Sessetti among them, dispersed. Christopher made his way through the crowds back to Saint-Marceau. For all the tension he had felt in the city, a lavish wedding appeared to have brought peace. At least a temporary peace.

Chapter 13

Christopher heard the shot on his way to the apothecary recommended by Walsingham, a few days later. Before he could react to the shot, there was another. It had come from not far off. He quickened his pace.

Two streets away, a crowd was gathering outside a narrow house — one of a row on either side of the street. Men were shouting and women screaming. He pushed his way through to the front where a figure sat nursing a shattered arm. It was Admiral Coligny.

Ignoring protests from the onlookers, he squatted down beside the wounded man. There was little blood and he was conscious. The admiral recognized Christopher and held up his right hand. The small finger was hanging by a thread of skin. 'A minor injury,' he said in a calm voice. 'I fear that the other is more serious.' Christopher looked at it. The elbow was shattered and the lower arm hung limply at his side. Even if the admiral survived, he thought that the arm would not. Coligny's face was set with pain, but in his eyes Christopher saw only a fierce determination.

'Did you see the man?' asked Christopher.

'He fired from a window of the house. Fortunately for me his aim was poor. I caught only a glimpse before the second shot.' Coligny was fading. His voice was a whisper.

Christopher looked up. An upper window of the house was open but there was no sign of an assassin. The crowd around them had grown. Coligny's two guards were hammering on the door and trying to break it down. Others shouted for help. A young woman knelt beside him and crossed herself. 'It is Admiral Coligny,' she said softly. 'May God take vengeance on whoever did this.'

'He must be taken home and a surgeon sent for,' said Christopher. 'Can you find a reliable man to help you, mistress?'

The woman nodded. 'I can, sir. My husband will assist me.' She spoke rapidly to the man behind her, who stepped forward and helped the admiral to his feet. 'Come, sir,' she said to him, 'we will escort you home and I will fetch the surgeon.' Coligny made no effort to resist and allowed the man to put an arm around his waist to prevent him from falling. He stumbled and the blood drained from his face, as if he had suddenly realized how close he had come to death. He made no sound.

The two guards had managed to break in. Christopher followed them inside and up the stair to the bed chamber overlooking the street, from where the shots must have come. The chamber was empty but the acrid smell of powder hung in the air. They split up and searched the house. In the kitchen, Christopher found a window open. He clambered out into a small yard enclosed by a low brick wall, easy enough for a man to climb over. At the foot of the wall, half hidden by a patch of long grass, there was a glint of metal. He bent down and saw that it was a pistol, no doubt abandoned by the fleeing man while making his escape over the wall. He had panicked and tossed it away rather than be caught in possession of it. Christopher picked it up by the stock and hefted it in his hands. He had never seen another like it. There were two wheel-locks, two pans, two dogs, two springs and two barrels, both unusually long. Although heavy, it was well balanced and finely made. The length of the barrels would give it greater accuracy. They were still warm to the touch. Holding it carefully, he climbed back into the kitchen. He took off his cloak, wrapped it around the gun and held the garment loosely as if he had removed it for ease of movement. There was no point in following the fugitive. He would have disappeared into the cobweb of narrow lanes that wound through the area.

Christopher returned to the street. There was still a crowd outside. 'Whose house is this?' he called out. There was no response. He tried again. 'Does any man know to whom this house belongs?'

'It has been empty for months,' croaked an old woman in a timid voice.

'An empty house, while others starve,' growled a rough-looking man behind her.

'It is the ungodly who starve,' shouted another voice. 'God feeds the righteous. And you, sir, you are not a Frenchman. What business is this of yours?'

'I am a friend of France, sir, and a lover of justice. An attempt has been made on a man's life. A cowardly attempt, from which he could not defend himself. Now let me pass. I must report what has happened.'

Very quickly the street was in uproar. Fists were waved and sticks brandished. Lines were drawn and a man fell, struck by a stone. Uproar became violence. Men and women bellowed in anger and screamed in pain. And blood flowed.

Christopher detached himself from the edge of the melee and made his way quickly back to Saint-Marceau, the pistol still wrapped in his cloak and safely in his hand. He brushed past the footman and did not bother to knock on the study door. Walsingham was at work behind his writing table. 'Sir Francis, there has been an attempt on the admiral's life and there is trouble in the streets.'

Walsingham was on his feet. 'Does Coligny live?'

'He does. Two wounds only, one more serious than the other.' He placed the pistol on the table. 'This is the assassin's weapon. A pistol with two firing mechanisms and two long barrels.'

Walsingham picked up the pistol and turned it over in his hands. He squinted down the barrels and tested the trigger. 'Thank God they did no more harm. Come, we must see what is happening on the streets.' They left the house and set off on foot. Horse or carriage would be an encumbrance if there were crowds abroad.

'It happened outside an empty house,' Christopher told him as they hurried on. 'Someone knew that the admiral would be passing.'

'If he had been to the palace it would have been known. He was unwise to travel on foot.' Walsingham was panting. 'We will go there.' Nearer the palace the crowds became thicker and they had to force their way through knots of angry townsfolk. Word of the shooting had spread fast.

Outside the palace a group of angry Huguenots, distinguished by their sombre dress, were held in check by the guards. On the other side of the entrance, a larger group faced them in sullen silence. They too were held back by halberds and short pikes. Inside the gates, a row of guardsmen stood ready.

Walsingham approached a nervous captain of the guard. 'I am Sir Francis Walsingham, captain. Admiral Coligny has been shot. Is the palace secure?'

'It is, sir,' replied the captain, 'for the present.'

They avoided the crowds and retraced their steps towards

Saint-Marceau. If the royal family were safe, the militia should bring the trouble under control without difficulty. If the palace walls were breached, however, it would be a different story.

Approaching the Petit Pont they found their way blocked by a mob armed with clubs and knives and axes. Walsingham, seemingly unafraid, held up his hands in a gesture of peace. A tall, elegant man with white hair swept back from his brow stepped forward. Behind him, voices shouted that they were Protestants and should be thrown into the river. 'Who are you?' demanded the tall man.

'We are Sir Francis Walsingham and Dr Christopher Radcliff,' replied Walsingham calmly. 'We serve Her Majesty Queen Elizabeth and are on our way to my house in Saint-Marceau. Kindly let us pass.' Christopher stood at his shoulder, his arms crossed in defiance and so that he could feel the hidden shaft of the dagger in his belt.

'That Protestant witch,' bellowed a rough voice. 'If the whore were here, I would throw her to the fish myself.' His cry was taken up by those around him, who moved ominously forward brandishing their weapons. The two Englishmen stood firm. To run would be fatal. They would be caught in seconds and dispatched with a blow to the head or a knife in the ribs. Unless this mob stood aside, they could not go forward. Christopher stole a glance over his shoulder. Nor could they retire. The north end of the bridge was also blocked.

Walsingham spoke again, his voice still strong and even. 'Your quarrel is not our quarrel. We wish only to go home. Do you intend to attack two unarmed Englishmen? Hardly the behaviour of a civilized Frenchman.'

'It would be an act of cowardice,' added Christopher. He stole another glance. The men behind were advancing slowly, weapons raised. 'Fifty Frenchmen faced by but two Englishmen, who mean you no harm? What justice is there in that, sir?' He sensed the men behind coming closer. For a long minute, the Frenchman stared at them. Then Christopher felt a sharp point at his back. Had Walsingham not laid a hand on his arm, he would have turned to face it. He braced himself.

The white-haired leader spoke. 'These men are not who we seek. Let them pass.' The point was withdrawn and reluctantly, muttering and cursing, the mob parted. As they passed, Walsingham quietly thanked him. 'Go straight to your home,' said the Frenchman. 'It is not safe on the streets.'

Christopher ignored a shove in the small of his back and a volley of spittle on to his cheek and followed Walsingham through the crowd and over the bridge. On the other side, he wiped his face with a sleeve. 'I fear this is only the beginning,' he said.

'The fellow was right,' replied Walsingham. 'It has spread through the streets like fire. We must go home at once and stay there. Thank God Coligny lives. If he had died, Paris would already be in flames.'

'Fire and death in the name of piety.'

Walsingham's footman opened the door. He held a loaded pistol. 'Lady Walsingham is in the sitting room. I will bring wine,' he said, locking and bolting the door behind them.

Ursula Walsingham sat with her hands clasped protectively over her unborn child. She rose from her chair to embrace her husband. 'Are you hurt?' she asked.

'We are not. Only shaken. It was like a thunderstorm erupting from a blue sky. One moment all serene, the next an angry mob roaming every street.'

'Is it true that the admiral has been shot?'

'He has, but by the grace of God he lives. Dr Radcliff saw him after the attack.'

'He was fortunate, madam. A finger lost and an elbow shattered. The attempt on his life that we feared has failed,' said Christopher.

The footman entered, carrying a silver wine jug and three glasses on a silver tray. He filled the glasses with a pale wine and retired. Walsingham passed them round. He did not mention their experience on the bridge.

Lady Walsingham dabbed her eyes. 'I pray the admiral lives and that there will not be another attempt. If there is, the city itself will explode.'

'Tension has turned to menace and thence to bloodshed,' agreed Walsingham. 'If the city is not to burn to the ground, the king himself must act. He must speak to his people and call for peace. He must command the militia to maintain order. He must forbid the carrying of weapons in the streets.' He sighed. 'Of course he will do none of these things.'

Tomasso Sessetti arrived just after dark. 'Forgive my calling at this hour, Lady Walsingham,' he said, a little out of breath. 'I did not care to be caught on the streets. It has been mayhem.'

'What news do you bring?' asked Walsingham.

'Coligny lives. He is at home. Queen Catherine has already visited him.'

Walsingham raised his eyebrows. 'I suppose it might help calm the mood.'

'Francis,' said Lady Walsingham, 'you are harsh on the woman. She has befriended the admiral. It is her son who cannot be trusted.'

'After today, I trust neither of them.'

'The city gates have been closed and blockaded against Coligny's army,' went on Sessetti. 'Coligny was shot from the window of a house owned by the duc de Guise. Among the Huguenots there is talk of an invasion of the Louvre Palace. I fear that tomorrow will bring more bloodshed.'

So Coligny was right. The Guises were involved. More than involved, probably. 'Signor Sessetti, have you heard more talk of London?' asked Christopher.

'None, doctor. My agents have learned nothing.'

That was a blow. Now that violence had erupted in Paris, London was in danger. They needed intelligence and quickly. Walsingham asked Christopher to fetch the pistol from his study. 'This is the weapon used by the assassin,' he said, taking it by the stock and passing it to Sessetti. 'In his haste to get away he abandoned it behind the house.'

Sessetti turned the weapon over in his hands, before pointing it at a painting of a young woman at her sewing, and, as Walsingham had done, sighting along the barrels. 'This is the weapon of a wealthy man. It would have been very costly,' he said, 'and it is unusual. Few gunsmiths could have made it. A single trigger for two barrels, one above the other, each with its own pan and wheel-lock. The forward dog can be swivelled to one side.' He held it up for both of them to see and demonstrated. 'The barrels are long and narrow, requiring small bullets.' He weighed the pistol in his hand. 'The stock is short, much like that of a dag, and unembellished — surprising in a weapon as fine as this. It is made of a wood heavy enough to balance the weight of the barrels. It is not a wood I am familiar with.'

'Why such a plain stock, do you suppose, Signor Sessetti?' asked Walsingham.

'If it had been commissioned by a rich man for his own safety, one would expect the stock to be engraved or inlaid with silver,' replied the Florentine, placing the pistol on the table. 'This was never intended as a demonstration of wealth. I would guess that the shortness of the stock is for ease of concealment. It is a weapon designed purely for accuracy, but it is heavy and would need practice. Thus the lack of embellishment.'

'By an assassin,' said Christopher, 'or a would-be assassin. Fired and discarded. How fortunate that it proved less accurate than he expected.'

'It would seem so. Its weight might account for the admiral's escape. That and the fact that he was moving.'

'You are well informed, Signor Sessetti,' said Walsingham.

Sessetti grinned. 'My family are gunsmiths, Sir Francis. Had I not taken a different path, I might have become one myself. This is a beautifully made pistol. In the right hands it would be most formidable.'

'Do you know who might have made it?'

Sessetti turned the gun over and examined the underside of the stock. 'I thought as much. It is marked *PC*. There is a very fine gunsmith near the Porte Saint-Jacques named Pierre Caron. This is his work.'

'We must pay Monsieur Caron a visit,' said Christopher.

'I doubt he will tell us anything. Gunsmiths are secretive creatures.'

'We can but ask.'

'And we have no other scent to follow,' said Walsingham. 'Go early tomorrow and hope to learn something from the gunsmith.'

All through that night a steady flow of refuge-seekers arrived at the house. Among them were diplomats, merchants and a number of Walsingham's intelligencers. A little after midnight, Sir Philip Sidney,

Leicester's nephew, arrived. An elegant young man, not unlike his uncle in looks, he wore a fine sky-blue doublet embroidered with gold thread and white hose — to Christopher's eye a little too elegant for the occasion. Walsingham introduced them.

Sidney tried to make light of their predicament. 'When Her Majesty asked me to travel with her embassy to Paris to negotiate a marriage with the duc d'Alençon, I did not expect to confront violence on the streets and witness an attempt to murder Admiral Coligny. Had I been warned, I should have made an excuse and remained in England. Still, I should be grateful. It gives me the opportunity to sample some of Francis's excellent cellar. I do hope there will be enough for all.'

It was braggadocio of course. In truth, none of the refuge-seekers had relished the thought of being cornered by the mob or trapped in their own home and forced to defend themselves. They felt safer in the house of the English ambassador. Christopher and Walsingham had been fortunate. Few of the rampaging Catholics intent upon violence would be deterred by a victim's country of birth. A Protestant Englishman was as much a Protestant as a hated Huguenot.

To Christopher's surprise, when on the bridge and faced by an angry mob he had felt calm and alert. Now, trapped in the Walsinghams' house, he simply wanted to escape, to get out of Paris and back to London. Suddenly, his message for the earl had become even more urgent. And he wanted to make his peace with Katherine. Over the coming days, news from France would filter through to London. The broadsheets would carry a report of the attempt on Coligny's life. Katherine would be worried. At least he hoped she would be worried.

By two in the morning, the house was crammed and every chair and bed taken. Christopher had given up his room to a merchant's wife and daughter. It was not a night for sleep or for words. Conversation was brief and voices hushed. Everyone awaited news. Despite her condition, Lady Walsingham bustled about, making sure all were as comfortable as possible and, like Sidney, doing her best to keep spirits high. 'I fear that we shall run out of food and drink if we are confined here for more than a day or two,' she warned them. 'I shall be forced to ask for volunteers to go about foraging.'

At dawn, Christopher and Sessetti left the house by a servants' door at the back. Sessetti led the way, the pistol in a bag over his shoulder. They went carefully, avoiding the busier parts of the city and alert to sounds that might mean trouble. Sessetti checked around every corner before signalling Christopher to follow. The night, however, had brought an eerie calm to the city as if it were a volcano preparing to erupt. They saw only the habitual early risers − pure collectors, night-soil men, a milkmaid − who paid them no heed, a beggar or two and a few who had spent the night drinking and been unable to make their way home. These lay prostrate on the street, oblivious to all around.

Margaret of Valois had married Henry of Navarre; Coligny had been shot but was alive. Neither Catholic nor Protestant rejoiced.

They found the premises of Pierre Caron near the Porte Saint-Jacques on the eastern edge of the city. From the outside it was an unremarkable place, a little run-down and in need of restoration. Sessetti knocked on the door. After a minute, he knocked again. They heard bolts drawn back and a key turned in the lock. The door was opened by a squat woman of about forty years with a broad peasant face and thick, rough hands. She was wearing a leather apron over her smock. 'We have come for Monsieur Caron,' said Sessetti. 'Is he here?'

The woman ignored the question. 'Who are you and what do you want with my husband?' she asked. Her speech was coarse, in the manner of a country woman, and her eyes narrowed in suspicion.

'We are interested in his work, madam,' replied Christopher gently. 'There is no cause to be alarmed.' He used the polite term of address in an effort to reassure her.

She was unconvinced. 'What is the nature of your interest? We are good Catholics and keep to ourselves.'

'I do not doubt it. Our interest is in Monsieur Caron's workmanship, not his beliefs. Is he at home?'

Again the woman eyed them suspiciously. 'I have not seen him for several days. I do not know where he is.'

Christopher and Sessetti exchanged a look. 'Is it usual for him to be gone for so long?' asked Sessetti.

'That is no concern of yours.' She spoke sharply but her manner was masking uncertainty, even fear.

'Perhaps we can help find him, madam. It is uncomfortable standing in the street. Would you allow us to enter?' She hesitated before stepping back to let them in.

The room they entered was a workshop. A long oak table littered with bits and pieces of firearms — barrels, handles, firing mechanisms and oddly shaped lengths of metal, waiting to be fashioned into triggers and hammers — ran the length of it. The gunsmith's tools lay on another, smaller table at the back. A rack of unfinished muskets covered one wall. A glance at their elegantly carved, gleaming stocks was enough to know that the clutter was that of a highly skilled man whose work was his pride.

The woman watched them intently. 'How do you know of my husband?' she asked.

Sessetti took the pistol from his bag and handed it to her. 'Did your husband make this?'

She barely looked at it. 'He did. Pierre is the finest gunsmith in Paris. See how the weight of the barrels is exactly balanced by that of the stock. Few are capable of such fine work.' There was respect in the rough voice.

'The design is unusual. Do you recognize the pistol?'

The woman handed it back. 'Who are you and why do you wish to know? Where is my husband?' The fear had gone from her voice. 'I will answer no more of your prying questions until you tell me. Where is he and where did you get this gun?'

Christopher knew that his height could be intimidating. To reduce it, he perched on a corner of the long table. 'Madame Caron, we do not know where your husband is but I assure you that we mean you no harm. If we did, you would already be dead. This pistol was used in an attempt to murder a man in the street. We must discover the identity of the man who fired it.'

'You will be helping the cause of peace if you can tell us for whom your husband made this pistol,' added Sessetti.

'And if I do not?' She clenched her hands almost in an attitude of prayer. Her tone was defiant but she was hiding something.

'Then we will search these premises for anything that might lead us to him and we will pass your name to the authorities.'

'You claimed only to be admirers of Pierre's work. Who are you to threaten me with this?'

'We do not mean to threaten you, madam,' replied Christopher. 'We are employed by Sir Francis Walsingham, ambassador to Paris for Her Majesty Queen Elizabeth of England. Both our countries are in danger. We must find the man who ordered this pistol.'

The woman's resolve wavered. She shook her head and dabbed

at her eyes with a scrap of linen. 'I told Pierre not to trust that man. He spoke like a Dutchman and he reeked of strong drink.'

'What man?' asked Christopher. 'Do you know his name?'

'I do not. He came only a few times while Pierre was making the guns and never gave his name. I was frightened of him.'

'Guns? Are there more like this?'

'The man ordered a pair. He said they were for his own protection. We did not believe him but he was willing to pay three times the normal price for such pieces on condition of our silence. Now my Pierre has disappeared and I fear he is dead. He should never have accepted the order.'

Two double-barrelled pistols – one used in an attempt to kill Admiral Coligny, the other to kill whom?

'Can you describe the man who ordered them?' asked Sessetti.

'I can, sir. He was loud and, as I have said, he smelled of drink. A big, rough man, with an odd way of speaking. Dutch, perhaps, or German. Not French. A big, straggly red beard.'

'Did he pay for the pistols?'

'He did. One half when he placed the order, the other half when he collected them.'

'When was that?'

'Two weeks since. Pierre disappeared the next day. I have asked around but no one has seen him. He went to buy food at the market and had some of the money with him. He is a decent man and a good husband. He would not have run off and left me alone. I do not know what to do, especially with the city as it is. They say someone tried to murder Admiral Coligny.' She paused as if a thought had occurred to her. 'Was this the gun that was used?'

'It was, madam, although your husband is not implicated in the crime. He could not have known the purpose for which the pistols were intended. And, by the grace of God, the assassin missed his target. The admiral is alive.'

'I thank God for it, although the Huguenots have themselves committed many crimes. Do you believe my husband dead?'

Christopher stood. 'I cannot say, madam. My advice is to stay here, go out only when you must and pray for his safe return.'

'Will the foreigner come again?'

'I think not. Keep the door locked. You will be safe here. We may return.' Sessetti replaced the pistol in his bag and opened the door. He looked up and down the street before motioning Christopher to follow. The door was immediately locked and bolted behind them.

'Large and loud and rough, drink-sotted and not French, with a red beard,' said Sessetti, as they made their way back to Saint-Marceau. 'Could it be anyone but Mackay?'

'Let us assume that it was Mackay. But why did he spare the woman?'

'I imagine he himself was disposed of before he could return to kill her. As for her husband, if she sets eyes on him again it will be as a corpse dragged from the river.'

They made their way back to Saint-Marceau, where they found servants handing round food and drink and Walsingham taking breakfast with Sidney in his study. Walsingham's eyes were red and his face drawn. 'What did you learn from the gunsmith?' he asked without preamble, courtesy for the moment forgotten.

Christopher told them what they had discovered.

'So the pistol intended to kill the admiral has a twin sister whose whereabouts is unknown and Caron is undoubtedly dead, probably at the hands of the Scotsman Mackay. Not a great deal but more than we knew before. The earl must be informed without delay. Prepare to leave, doctor,' concluded Walsingham.

CHAPTER 14

Henri, duc de Guise, and Charles, Bishop of Beauvais, sat side by side on a bench in a corner of the garden of the duc's Paris house. The evening sun was warm and the garden filled with the fragrance of roses and lavender. It was the eve of the feast of Saint Bartholomew, Christ's apostle. A man of healing and peace.

The scar on the face of the duc stood out fit to burst. 'What was his name? Maurevert? Curse the idiot. Mackay assured me he was reliable. How could the incompetent imbecile miss at that range?' If the duc was aware of the date, he gave no sign of it.

The bishop did not respond. He too was furious that the plan had started so badly but he had not risen through the Church hierarchy without learning to control his temper. Coligny should by now be dead and the news on its way to London. With their leader still alive, four thousand of Coligny's men outside the city gates were an immediate danger. If they chose to attack, *Incendium* would be still-born. Everything rested on surprise. Surprise and over-whelming force. The Protestant threat in Paris must be crushed once and for all. He had not suffered the humiliation of conducting the wedding of the queen's daughter to a Protestant only to see the plan fail.

'Calm yourself, Henri,' he said. 'The city gates are barricaded and the palace is safe against attack. We will kill Coligny and proceed as planned. I will instruct Maurevert to finish the job.'

'Bugger Maurevert. The bungling idiot even managed to lose one of Mackay's precious pistols. I will do it myself. Tonight. Coligny is wounded and at home. It will not be difficult. The moment it is done, set your men to deal with the others on the list. Kill them all. When the tocsin bells sound the alarm, God's enemies must be leaderless.'

'As you wish, Henri. Kill Coligny and the bells will ring if I have to pull the ropes myself.'

In the early hours, Guise led six men to the house of Admiral Coligny. To their surprise the door of the house was unguarded. He ordered one of them to break the lock with a pistol and the others to put their weight on it. The hinges broke and the door fell in. Guise was first over it and up a flight of stairs. He shot a man who appeared above him and charged into the first bed chamber. There he found Coligny in his bed, a guard, sword drawn, on either side of it. 'Kill them,' he bellowed. Two shots rang out and both guards fell, blood spurting from their heads. Coligny lay perfectly still, eyes wide and face ashen. Guise stared at the defenceless man.

'I have come to kill you,' hissed Guise, 'as you killed my father at Orleans.'

Coligny could manage only a hoarse croak. 'I did not kill your father.'

'You lie. This day, you will be the first of your ungodly Protestants to die. Many others will soon follow you to hell.' Guise signalled to his men to drag the admiral off the bed. They threw him to the floor, where he landed on his broken arm and screamed in agony. Guise laughed.

Holding the arm, Coligny struggled to his feet and stood facing his attackers. He showed no fear. Guise stepped forward and thrust his sword into his victim's chest. Blood spurted but Coligny did not fall. The duc thrust again and bellowed in triumph as his victim slid soundlessly to the floor. Without checking that he was dead, Guise ripped off the admiral's nightshirt to reveal his naked body, cupped his testicles in his left hand and sliced them off with a knife. He hurled them across the room to splatter against the wall. Again he bellowed with the joy of it.

'Throw the heretic from the window,' he ordered. 'Let it be known that we have rid Paris of a murderer. Find a man to sever his head and burn what is left of him. Send word to the Bishop of Beauvais. The bells must ring. The time has come.'

Christopher was woken from a fitful sleep by the bells. So great was the cacophony that he imagined every bell in Paris to be ringing. He rose and dressed hurriedly.

Downstairs, candles had been lit, men were buckling on sword belts and their wives smoothing out their clothes as best they could. Sir Francis soon appeared, a trifle dishevelled but wide awake. 'It is a signal,' he said, 'an alarm to rouse the city against attack or to signal the start of an attack from within. We will be as safe here as any-where. Do not leave the house.'

Tomasso Sessetti arrived just before dawn. 'Coligny is dead,' he told them. 'I myself saw his headless body being burned in the street. Parties of Catholics are hunting down Protestants. Already there are dozens of corpses in the city squares and fires are being lit on which to burn them. It is too dangerous to venture out.'

'The bells must have been the signal that the admiral was dead,' said Walsingham, 'and for the Catholics to begin their slaughter. The very catastrophe that I feared most and prayed would not happen.'

Christopher closed his eyes. A brave man foully murdered. A rampaging mob intent upon killing and burning. The nightmare was coming true. He took a deep breath. 'I cannot stay here, Sir Francis. If Paris is burning, London will be next. This is surely what was meant by *Incendium*. I must warn the earl.'

Walsingham raised his eyebrows. 'And how will you get out of Paris and back to England alive, doctor? Yesterday it was possible; now, however . . .' He left the thought hanging in the air.

'If Signor Sessetti will escort me to the gate, I will find a coach and take my chances. Will you take me, signor?'

Sessetti looked doubtful. 'No, doctor, the danger would be too great. Let the violence run its course before you venture out.'

'Dr Radcliff,' said Walsingham, 'Signor Sessetti is right. If you are caught by a mob baying for blood your message will not reach the earl. I insist that you wait until it is safer.'

'But yesterday you urged me to go and if Signor Sessetti were to guide me through the city—'

'No, doctor. It is no longer safe to venture out. You will wait until the streets are quieter.' Walsingham turned to Sessetti. 'Dr Radcliff will stay here. In the meantime, keep us informed of what is happening. And I should like you to take a letter to Lord Burghley. He will be anxious for us as I am for him. Can you do that?'

'I can, Sir Francis. And I will bring back his reply.'

'Good. The letter will be ready within the hour. Lord Burghley is bed-ridden with gout. I doubt he is in danger, but I would like to be sure.' From nearby came the crack of musket fire. Walsingham raised his voice. 'No one will leave this house without my permission.'

Through the day more frightened families arrived, seeking the safety of the Walsinghams' house and bringing with them stories of limbs hacked from bodies, heads crushed by cudgels and clubs, and living and dead alike being thrown into the flames of fires fuelled by the timbers of their own houses. Space was somehow found for all. Although supplies of food were running short, no one was turned away.

News of Admiral Coligny's murder had spread through the streets like plague and had been the spark that ignited the powder. Bands of Catholics were rampaging through the city intent upon killing every Protestant they could find, as if they had drunk some devilish potion that replaced reason with an insane lust for blood. Some Huguenots were fighting back but they were leaderless and too few. Unless the Protestant army outside the walls forced its way in, few would survive.

Sessetti returned that evening. 'It was as well I carried this,' he said, holding up a small set of rosary beads. 'Twice it saved me from an axe blade.' Lord Burghley and his household, he told them, were safe. Paris was a slaughterhouse, the streets running with blood and the squares heaped with corpses. Twenty leading Huguenots, among them wealthy merchants, lawyers and soldiers, had been murdered. Gangs of criminals had taken advantage of the chaos and were robbing and killing. The bloodshed had become indiscriminate.

Every room in the house but one was in use. Walsingham had put Sidney in charge of the refuge-seekers. He had ensured that his library remained private and it was there that he sat with Christopher and Sessetti. 'I fear that the delay will try your patience, doctor,' he began. 'The city will not become calm overnight.'

'I urge you to reconsider, Sir Francis,' replied Christopher. 'I must return to England at once. Is the risk not worth taking?' His voice had risen in frustration.

'Events have made me unsure,' replied Walsingham. 'What exactly do we know? That there is a plot which we can only guess involves Mary Stuart and her cousin the duc de Guise, and that there exist two unusual pistols of which we have the one that was used to try to kill Coligny. Without more flesh on these bones, I am reluctant to allow you to risk your life at the hands of a barbarous mob. The earl does not yet know the word *Incendium* but he will soon learn what is happening here in Paris.'

'And he will learn of it before you reach London,' added Sessetti. 'It would be wiser to wait.'

'But is it not certain that the plot also threatens the safety of our own queen?' demanded Christopher. 'The presence in France of the man who has vanished, Mackay, suggests as much. It is another plot to replace Queen Elizabeth with Mary Queen of Scots. What is happening here will happen in London if we do not alert the earl. I must leave Paris and find my way to England.'

'Do you suggest London streets will be full of murdering Catholics, doctor?'

'No, sir. I merely suggest that our queen is once again in danger – this time from a foul alliance between Coligny's murderers and England's enemies. That is enough to endanger her. Two well-placed shots from a single pistol would kill her as certainly as an executioner's axe or a mob of bloodthirsty Catholics.'

'When news of the admiral's murder and its bloody aftermath reaches London,' replied Walsingham, 'the Privy Council will act. The Queen of Scots will be moved to the Tower and refused contact even with her priest, and Queen Elizabeth will cut short her progress and return to Whitehall Palace where she will be protected by her household and her guards. I had hoped, when I asked the earl to send you, that we would know more. We suspected a plot and foresaw the admiral's death but not the extent of what is now happening outside this house. The danger is no longer insidious. It is out in the open for all to see.'

There was a knock on the door and Sir Philip Sidney entered. From his dress and manner one might suppose he had spent a peaceful night in a comfortable bed, bathed and shaved, put on new clothes and eaten a good breakfast. 'Philip,' Walsingham greeted him, 'come in. How fare our guests?'

Sidney took a chair. 'They are complaining of hunger and thirst and demanding to know what plans you have for them. What shall I tell them?'

'Is my cellar empty?'

'Not quite, but I have had the door locked. The kitchen staff say that their cupboards are bare. I could take two men to buy what we can find.'

Walsingham almost shouted. 'No. No one will leave this house until I say so, least of all you. Hunger and thirst we can survive, but not the point of a sword or the blade of an axe.'

Christopher tried once more. 'Sir Francis, I beseech you to allow me to leave. Me alone. No one else need know.'

Sidney laughed. 'I would know, Dr Radcliff, and I would not be pleased. It is too dangerous.'

'Dr Radcliff,' said Sessetti, 'permit me to continue my investigations while you are here. If I discover anything, you will have something more substantial for the earl. Later, when it is safer, I will escort you out of the city.'

'Thank you, Tomasso,' said Walsingham. 'That is how it will be.'

Christopher was trapped. If he disobeyed Walsingham and tried to leave Paris either he would be killed or he would suffer the displeasure of both Walsingham and Leicester. Perhaps Sessetti would uncover something. He sighed. 'As you wish, sir.'

CHAPTER 15

The attack on the house came that night. A gang armed with knives and axes and dung-forks gathered outside, shrieking for blood and hurling stones at the windows. The household was immediately awake and making ready to repel any attempt to break in. Walsingham ordered the women to go to the cellar and the men to arm themselves with whatever they could find or had brought with them.

Twelve men gathered in the hall — Walsingham, Sidney, Sessetti, who had intended to slip away before dawn, Christopher and eight others. Two held pistols, a third a heavy wooden ballow, the rest had swords. Christopher had found a heavy kitchen knife. He looked around. They were an ill-assorted party, poorly armed, confused, frightened. They would be no match for a concerted attack on the house.

A heavy object crashed against the door. It was followed by another and a volley of missiles against the windows. Their attackers must know the house to be full of English Protestants and were bent on breaking in.

Walsingham peeked through a narrow gap between the

shutters. 'About a dozen of them, armed and some with torches. If they put fire to us, we will open the door and attack them. Otherwise we will stay inside.'

'Could we not frighten them off with a few well-placed shots, Sir Francis?' asked an eager man waving a pistol above his head.

'No, sir,' replied Walsingham firmly. 'The risk of retaliation is too great. We will wait and see what transpires. I daresay they will lose interest and seek entertainment elsewhere.'

The shouting and stone-throwing continued off and on for perhaps an hour but there was no attempt to set fire to the house or to break down the door. The defenders stood ready. 'They are more criminals than Catholics,' said someone. 'Otherwise they would have attacked us more forcefully by now.'

Sidney, as was his way, made a joke of the matter. 'I think not, sir. They have received intelligence that this house is defended by a party of heavily armed, fearless soldiers and will not easily be taken. They will soon disperse.' Christopher could not help but admire the young man's cheerful defiance.

And Sidney was right. Deprived of provocation, the mob did eventually lose interest and disperse without setting fires or causing damage. The ladies were brought up from the cellar. While they were being given the last of Walsingham's wine, Christopher saw his chance and approached him. 'Would this not be a good time for me to slip out of the house and be away?' he asked. 'Sessetti can guide me to the gate and I shall be out of Paris by morning.'

'You try my patience, Dr Radcliff,' replied Walsingham curtly.

'And mine is exhausted, sir.' The sharpness of Christopher's response surprised even him.

Walsingham was plainly taken aback. He rubbed his temple with a finger. When he spoke his tone was that of a man resigned to defeat. 'Very well, doctor, if you are determined, go. But you will have to find your own way to Calais.'

They left the house through a kitchen door at the back, as before with Sessetti leading the way, Christopher following with his bag over his shoulder. Keeping away from the main streets, they worked their way through a maze of alleys and lanes. Few lanterns were now lit outside houses and the moon was new. For the most part, they travelled in darkness.

From the left bank of the river came the terrible sounds of fire and burning, despair and death. Neither women nor children would be spared. Nor would the gangs be composed only of men. Women, too, armed with kitchen knives and meat cleavers, would be cutting and slashing and slicing. As they moved quietly through the lanes, Christopher and Tomasso caught glimpses of the horrors and shrank back into the shadows.

Near the church of Sainte-Agnès they heard voices raised in terror. They turned a corner and quickly ducked into a doorway. A troop of Swiss Guards, the king's own guards, had surrounded a terrified, wailing group of women and children in a small square, while a fire was being lit. Their cries of anguish and despair filled the square. Their fathers and husbands and sons lay nearby in heaps of flesh and heads and limbs, their blood running in rivers between mounds of gore, on which squabbling rats were already gorging themselves. Christopher stepped out of the doorway and was immediately dragged back by Sessetti. 'We dare not,' he whispered. 'You must take the message.'

Sessetti was right. If the guards saw them, they too would die. The children were hanging on to their mothers' skirts, some bawling, others struck dumb with fear, and the women were shrieking for mercy. One woman tried to break through the circle of guards. She was cut down by the blade of an axe and stabbed with a sword as she lay helpless on the ground. A small child crawled to her side. His head was instantly hacked from his body. Christopher closed his eyes. He could not bear witness to this barbarity, nor could he intervene. He offered a hasty prayer for the victims. If this was *Incendium*, it had brought hell to France.

The fire was burning. The guards threw the dead woman and her child into the flames and turned their attention to the others. One plucked a baby from its mother's arms, tossed it into the air and laughed mightily when another skewered it with a dung-fork as it fell. The sickly-sweet stench of burning flesh wafted towards them. Christopher's stomach heaved. Sessetti grabbed his arm and pointed to their left, where a narrow alley ran off the square. While the guards' backs were turned, they dashed across and disappeared into it.

'God in heaven,' breathed Christopher, as they emerged at the other end of the alley into a wider lane, the stench still in his nostrils. 'Is this happening all over Paris? It is beyond belief. Women, babes in arms, old men. Has bloodlust taken over the world?'

'It seems that way,' replied Sessetti. 'And the Lord alone knows when the lust will be sated. It is as if the devil himself has descended upon us and is filling minds and hearts with a craving for blood and terror and murder.'

'I doubt it will be contained within the city. Terror is like disease. It spreads on the air from village to village and house to house. The Protestants will retaliate, then all of France will be in flames and England will soon follow.'

'Come, we must get you to the gate.'

To their right three men armed with axes appeared from around a corner. A cry went up when the axemen saw them and they immediately ran at them, brandishing their weapons and shrieking for blood. Christopher and Sessetti turned and ran. But while Christopher's long legs soon carried him away from danger, Sessetti's did not. The Florentine was not designed for speed of foot.

Christopher glanced back, saw that Sessetti would soon be caught and sprinted back to him. He reached him just as the first of the axemen arrived. Christopher had no training in fighting and no experience of it. His action was instinctive. He shot out a long arm and thrust his poniard into the attacker's eye. The eye exploded into a bloody mess, the man screamed and dropped his weapon. Sessetti stooped to pick it up and held it aloft. 'We are not your enemies,' he shouted. 'Take your friend and go. Otherwise, some of the blood spilt will be yours.' For a few seconds their attackers did not move. Then they turned and hurried back the way they had come. Their stricken friend was left where he lay.

There was no time to dither. Sessetti dropped the axe and they were off again. It was not far to the gate, which they found closed and guarded. Stone and timber had been piled up against it, leaving only the Judas gate accessible. They approached a guard with their hands in full view. Sessetti spoke to him. 'My friend has received news from London that his wife and children are sick. He must leave Paris and return at once.' He held out a small purse. 'This for your trouble if you will permit him to leave peacefully.'

The guard's eyes narrowed in suspicion. 'Who are you and who is he?' he demanded, taking the purse and hefting it in his hand.

'We are men of no account. Humble merchants only. Keep the purse, sir, and we will be gone.'

The guard hesitated. 'Just him?'

'Just him. I will return to my house.'

For a moment Christopher thought the guard was going to refuse. He shook his head and turned down his mouth. Then he took a quick look about and beckoned them to follow him. He unlocked the Judas gate and pushed Christopher through. The gate was closed and locked before Christopher could even say farewell to Sessetti.

Outside, it was quieter and almost possible to believe that what he had just witnessed had been no more than a fearful nightmare. Sweat dripped from his brow and ran down his face. His chest heaved and he vomited. Wiping spittle from his mouth, he cast a glance back. From somewhere deep in the city a tower of flame rose into the dawn sky. Then another and another. It was no nightmare.

A straight road ran directly from the gate towards the northwest. Another looped to the right, circling the city wall to join the road north to Calais. A handful of traders stood silently by their carts gazing at the flames. They would not be in the market today.

Of coach or carriage there was not a sign. Nor, oddly, of a Protestant army. He saw only the ashes of camp fires and the detritus left by men living in tents. If news of their leader's death had reached them, perhaps they had melted away.

He had a choice — hide nearby and wait for a carriage or even a farmer's cart, or set off on foot. Hoisting his bag higher over his shoulder, he set off. He was hungry and thirsty but did not stop. The urge to be away from Paris was greater than the need to eat.

He found the road north without difficulty and after about a mile came to a cluster of cottages on the edge of fields. A noisy group of peasant women had gathered in the road. It was not difficult to guess what they were shouting and gesticulating about. They saw him approaching and one called out. 'Do you come from Paris, sir? Is it true what we have heard? Is the city burning? We have seen flames.'

He could not ignore the women. 'It is true, goodwife, and there is violence on the streets. My advice is to stay at home.'

Another woman was sobbing. 'My husband is in the city. God will make a widow of me.'

'Are the Protestant scum killing and burning again, sir?' asked the first.

Christopher swallowed an oath. 'It is difficult to tell what is really happening, but there is fighting and bloodshed. I managed to leave but the gates are closed and barred.'

The woman eyed him suspiciously. 'You are not French.'

'I am English and on my way home. I must get back to my family. They are sick.' This elicited a murmur of sympathy.

'It is a long walk to the coast, sir. Two miles on you will find a farmer with horses. Perhaps he will sell you one.'

'Thank you. I will inquire. Good day, and may God protect you.' Much as he disliked horses, he needed one, and soon.

The farm was a collection of ramshackle timber buildings — a barn, stables and a tiny farmhouse. Chickens and ducks pecked about in the farmyard and a pig, tethered to a post, lay asleep. Christopher called out. There was no reply. In a stable he found an elderly cart horse, such as might be used for ploughing. A saddle and bridle hung on hooks outside the door. He called out again. Still there was no reply.

He took the saddlery from its hooks, opened the stable door and slipped inside. The plough horse took a step back and shook its head. Christopher approached it slowly and managed to throw the saddle over its back. He was intent on securing it under the horse's belly when a voice spoke behind him. 'You are tall for a horse thief and I doubt you will get far on this one. He is old and lazy.' Christopher straightened up and turned sharply. The farmer stood at the stable door, pointing a long-handled hay-fork at Christopher's face.

He raised his hands and bowed his head. 'Excuse me, sir. I had intended to leave money for the animal and will gladly pay for him. I must make my way to Calais without delay.'

The farmer scoffed. 'And how much money had you intended to leave, horse thief?'

'Would five livres be sufficient?'

The farmer's greedy eyes narrowed. It was more than the beast was worth. 'Hand over the money and the horse is yours.'

'I shall need the saddlery.'

'Another two livres.' Christopher nodded his agreement, took out his purse and counted out the coins. The farmer took them. 'You have a full purse, horse thief. Take care on the road. There are plenty who would slit your throat for it. Be gone or I might do so myself.' Christopher stooped to pick up his bag. 'Leave the bag,' growled the farmer.

Not only was Caron's pistol in the bag but also another fifty livres. To get home he would need the money. 'I cannot do that, sir. My clothes and a few small possessions are in it. They will be of little use to you.' As he stood up, he felt for the handle of the dagger.

'Leave the bag and go. You are fortunate that I do not kill you and feed your corpse to the pig. You would not be his first taste of human flesh.' Christopher took the reins and led the horse to the door. The farmer lowered his hay-fork and stepped back to make way for them. Just outside, Christopher stumbled and let go the reins. The farmer laughed. 'Not much of a horse thief—'

The words ended in a strangled grunt. Christopher had grabbed the farmer's wrist with one hand and jabbed the tip of the dagger into his throat with the other. A drop of blood dripped from the wound. He twisted the wrist and the fork fell to the ground. 'You are a fool. You could have had seven livres for an old horse. Now you will have nothing.' He reached around the farmer's head, grabbed a handful of hair and marched him into the stable, the point of the dagger still at his throat. He shoved the man in the small of his back and sent him headlong into a pile of filthy straw. Christopher felt his temper rising. With an effort he controlled his breathing and let it settle. 'You are the fortunate one, farmer. I have seen enough killing today. Otherwise you would die now.' He retrieved the fork and jabbed it hard into the soft flesh of the farmer's thigh. The farmer screamed and clutched the wound. He would not be chasing Christopher down the road. Christopher felt no pang of guilt. The farmer should survive and it had been done out of necessity.

He collected the coins from where they had fallen, swung his bag over the horse's back and mounted. The farmer lay holding his wounded leg and whimpering like a baby. Christopher did not even glance back. He dug his heels into the horse's flanks, snapped the reins and plodded away up the road.

It was a long time since he had sat on a horse and his backside and thighs were soon sore. At the next hamlet he dismounted and stretched his back. He found an inn and ordered food and drink and asked for the horse to be fed and watered. While he was eating, the innkeeper returned from seeing to it. 'That horse will not get you very far, sir,' he said. 'It is old and it favours one leg. I will give you three livres for it and sell you an excellent replacement for five.'

Christopher was suspicious. The last bargain had not gone well. 'Why would you wish to take it off my hands if it is so old and infirm?' he asked.

'You are a traveller, sir, and perhaps unaware of the harsh times we live in,' replied the innkeeper. 'The harvest is poor, the king taxes us beyond our means and many are starving. Horse meat is as good as any when a man's family are hungry. May I ask where you are going?' News of what was happening in Paris seemed not yet to have reached the village.

'I am on my way to Calais, from where I shall find a ship to England.'

'Then you will need a good mount.'

'Very well. Show me the horse and I will decide.'

To Christopher's inexpert eye the animal appeared sound enough. The bargain was soon struck and he set off again. Several days' journey lay ahead before he even reached the coast. Paris was burning, hundreds were dying and in Kenilworth the queen and the earl were dancing and feasting and watching jousts. He spurred the horse into a canter.

Eventually both he and the horse had to eat and rest. The inn he found was filthy and smelled of vermin. He had a thin straw palliasse to sleep on and a bowl of greasy soup with stale bread to eat. He was too tired to look for another inn and there might not have been one for miles. He made sure the horse was well enough stabled and lay down on the bed, intending to be gone again before dawn.

As it often did when he was exhausted, his mind would not allow sleep but wandered from image to image and thought to thought. He worried about Katherine and wondered if she were still in London. He thought of *Incendium* and whether he had really witnessed its first flames. He tried not to imagine what might happen if they spread across the water. And he thought of the day, fourteen years since, that news of Queen Mary's death had reached Cambridge.

He had been a commoner pupil at Pembroke Hall when the news had arrived. He remembered it as a joyous time, a time of celebration and thanksgiving. While others waited for directions from the new queen, the Master of Pembroke had immediately ordered a quantity of English prayer books and called for college services to be conducted in English. In no time every vestige of the old ways had been stripped from the chapel. Gone were the Latin prayer books, vestments and images, gone were the elaborate furnishings, altar cloths and censers. In their place John Foxe's *Book of Martyrs* soon lay, open and much read, on a lectern to the left of the altar. *Cuius regio, eius religio.*

He was woken from a shallow sleep by the innkeeper shaking his shoulder. 'Sir, sir, you must be gone. My cousin has arrived from Paris. The city is in flames. Men and women are dying in the streets. The duc de Guise has sent soldiers out of the city. There is a troop coming this way. I cannot risk their finding an English Protestant under my roof.'

Christopher was instantly awake. 'As well you roused me, land-lord. Prepare my horse if you please. I will leave at once,' he said, climbing off the bed. 'And bring bread and milk. Make haste.'

Downstairs, he swallowed a cupful of milk and put the bread in his bag. Within three minutes he was on the road to Amiens.

He reckoned that he had covered thirty miles when the horse threw a shoe and started hobbling. There were another twenty to go before he reached Amiens. It was too far. He would have to lead the animal and walk until he found a blacksmith. The sun was past its zenith but still there would be a good six hours of daylight remaining. He loosened his shirt and trudged on.

He heard the horses' hooves galloping up behind him long before they rounded a bend in the road and came into view. He led his lame mount to the side of the highway and waited for the riders to pass. They would be Guise's men galloping north to spread the news. He held his breath as they approached, sure that they would stop to question him. They would want to know who he was and where he was going.

Their captain slowed to a walk as he came up and peered hard at Christopher's horse. 'A bad day for you, sir,' he shouted loudly enough for the troop behind to hear, 'but a great one for France.' The soldiers laughed, the captain spurred his mount, and they galloped off. Christopher breathed deeply and watched them go. A great day for France? God in heaven, how could a day of terror and death and destruction be great for anyone or any country?

There was no point in keeping the horse. It was holding him back. He took off the saddle and left the animal to graze on a patch of grass by the road. Someone would be glad of it, if only for food.

At sunset he reached the edge of Amiens, decided not to risk the centre of the city until morning and found lodgings in a coaching inn. The food was a little better and the room a little cleaner. He fell asleep clutching his bag lest a thief slip in and steal it without waking him.

He left at first light and walked into the city, expecting to learn that Guise's men had been there. He would find a coach to take him to Calais. It would be as quick as riding and perhaps a little safer.

The great cathedral towered over the city and he felt himself drawn towards it. He heard the crowd long before he saw it. The open square in front of the cathedral was full of praying, chanting, weeping people. From their sombre dress, many were Protestants. While they prayed aloud for God's mercy, clusters of Catholics clutching rosaries and gathered around the perimeter of the square were silently watching. The air of menace he had sensed in Paris he sensed again. He saw no weapons blatantly displayed but a cloak or a shirt might easily hide a sharp blade or even a pistol. Guise's men had indeed been there and there would be bloodshed. He must find a coach and move on without delay.

He worked his way cautiously around the square, intending to look for a coaching inn on the road north. He did not see the spark that lit the fire but suddenly the silent watchers were among the prayers. They hacked at faces with knives and axes and swung clubs at heads. Others had joined them from the streets, bringing weapons and bellowing for Protestant blood. The Huguenots resisted as best they could. They wrested weapons from their attackers to use against them and fought with stones and sticks and their fists. But they were outnumbered. Their prayers turned quickly to screams and the square to a bloody battlefield. Where Paris had led, Amiens had followed. And it would not be the only city to do so.

Christopher huddled into a doorway and looked around for an escape. He could not risk being caught up in the violence. He inched his way round towards the side of the cathedral, where he had spotted the entrance to a narrow alley. He had almost reached it when he felt his arms pinioned from behind and he was shoved to the ground. He struggled to sit up. Two men armed with cudgels faced him. One demanded his bag. He swung it at the man's face and backed away. A blow from behind knocked him down and he was on the ground again. He tried to get to his feet. Another blow knocked him sideways. The last thing he heard before he passed out was the ringing of the cathedral bells.

CHAPTER 16

Beauvais

The bishop rose from prayer and left the great, silent cathedral of Saint-Pierre through his private door on the east side of the transept. When he had first come to Beauvais he had planted an elm tree in the small, cobbled square there and ordered a seat of carved beechwood set beside it. The tree had thrived and now offered shade from the morning sun. In spring and summer it was where he most liked to sit and think. It was there that he had arranged to meet the duc de Guise.

Guise's ferocity had taken even him by surprise. A courageous soldier, yes, but to have murdered Coligny with his own hands and in such a manner, that was an act of monstrous anger. Anger, and revenge for the death of his father, not the act of a straightforward military man. Three days later and Paris was still burning and blood still flowing. And it would be flowing in cities all over France. Already he had received reports from Rheims and Rouen. The deaths of Coligny and the other Huguenot leaders were necessary and he had consented to them as readily as he had consented to the death of the

English queen. But the slaughter of thousands, women and children among them — that he had not agreed to and could not condone. He had prayed for God's understanding and for his guidance, and for Henri's soul.

It had been Henri's zeal, above all else, that had persuaded him to the belief that *Incendium* could and would succeed. But Henri was only twenty-two years old, proud and headstrong. He liked to boast of being a descendant of Lucrezia Borgia and to have succeeded his father as Grand Maître de France. He had even risked an affair with Margaret of Valois before her marriage, incurring royal wrath. Only his marriage to Catherine of Cleves had restored him to the queen's favour. As a bishop Charles should have been more cautious and done more to restrain the young man.

Henri arrived as the cathedral clock struck noon. He kissed the bishop's hand and took a seat beside him. 'It is more than I could have hoped for,' he said. 'Coligny dead and twenty of his foul lieutenants with him. In a week there will be not a Huguenot alive in Paris. I rejoice at the thought. Our people are taking revenge for the years of poverty and suffering. At last the Protestant usurers are reaping what they have sown and I thank God for it.'

'It is the same in Rouen and Rheims and Amiens,' replied the bishop, hoping that Guise could hear the sorrow in his voice. 'And in other of our cities, I daresay. If the dead are not burned or buried without delay, there will be disease and disease does not discriminate between the godly and the ungodly. Our own people will die.'

'In Paris, the city authorities are dealing with the matter. Burial pits are being dug. Other cities will do likewise. No one wishes to invite disease.' The words were brusquely spoken.

'Yet I hear that bodies lie in the streets and blood runs in the river. There will be retaliation.'

'How can our enemies retaliate if they are all dead?' asked Guise with a smirk.

'I am speaking of our friends in Italy and England. Reports will be exaggerated and stories invented. Already I hear reports that our people are skewering babies and roasting them on spits. The stories may turn our friends against us.'

'My dear Charles,' said Guise, as if he were fifty and the bishop twenty, 'for years, Huguenots everywhere have slaughtered Catholics, desecrated our churches and destroyed the very things we hold most dear. Coligny's army is still at large. Had we not disposed of him, they would have attacked the city and taken control of it. It would have been a catastrophe.'

'Queen Catherine wants an end to the violence. She is most concerned at the prospect of a backlash against Catholics in England.'

'If by backlash the queen means that Alençon now has as much chance of marrying the English witch as does a barbary pirate, she is right. Not that it was ever likely. But what matter is that to us? When the fires are lit in England, the witch Elizabeth will also die. Then Alençon can marry the Queen of Scots. A piglet and a swan. God alone knows what manner of children they might produce.' The bishop ignored the vulgarity. 'And, Charles, I could not stop what is happening here even if I wished to. The people of Paris are with us. They will lay down their weapons only when there is not a single Protestant left in their city.'

The bishop sighed. 'Then I pray that will be soon.'

'God willing, my envoy should reach England by the end of the week. He will contact our friends in London and agree plans for the second part of *Incendium*. The Irishman Wolf is a concern to them, as Mackay was to us. They worry that if we delay too long he and his followers will act out of impatience and rage. That would be fatal.'

'Can they control him?'

'They say so, but not for ever. Mackay, Wolf — allies of necessity, not choice. Uncouth Celts both.'

'But our partners in the eyes of God.'

'There is another slight irritation,' went on Guise. 'We were unable to locate the Earl of Leicester's agent in time to dispose of him and we think he has now left the city. No matter, he knows only what is known to all and can do us no harm. It would just have been gratifying to report that his headless corpse was floating in the river. Favours beget favours. What of the king?'

'His Majesty is as excited as a child with a new toy. He embraced me when I told him of Coligny's death and insisted on hearing every detail. His mother would do well to curb her pup. He may yet prove our undoing.'

Guise stood and pointed a finger at the bishop. 'There will be no undoing. France will be rid of every Protestant usurer and England will follow. And then . . . well, my dear Charles, then we shall see whither the wind blows us.' His tone hardened. 'The Duke of Alba in the Low Countries proceeds too slowly for my liking. He is provisioning his ships and arming his men, but he will not launch the Spanish fleet against England until the witch is dead. I sense reluctance.'

'The pistol. Has it been found?'

'We are searching for it. Meanwhile Walsingham is sheltering English Protestants. Our people wish to see him dead too.'

The bishop put a hand on Guise's arm. 'Henri, I cannot help but feel that would be a mistake. Walsingham is close to the Earl of Leicester. If he were killed, Leicester would insist on retribution. Montmorency, even Alençon if he were in London, would be at risk. The witch-queen would be forced to retaliate.'

'Perhaps so. I will stay their hand for the present, although a house full of English Protestants is a tempting target. I cannot promise that they will be able to resist it.'

'You must make it clear that disobeying your explicit orders would be an act of treason. If they still cannot resist temptation, we shall be forced to disown their actions. That would be taken by our enemies as a sign of weakness.'

'Very well. But I will put no other restrictions on them. The fire must burn itself out.'

'And your men?'

'My force is being assembled in towns throughout the north. The extent of the uprising has occasioned some confusion and delay but all will soon be in order. When the time comes I will command them to move to Calais. Until then they will remain dispersed so as not to attract unwanted attention.'

'Have the English woken up to the danger they are in?'

Guise snorted. 'Their defences are feeble. A few hundred militia at the ports, old cannon, a handful of leaking ships. The witch-queen is notoriously parsimonious. Even in defence of her own realm, she is loath to spend a shilling from the royal purse. And the longer we wait, the more secure she will feel. They will not expect us to sail late in the year. Landing our force will not be difficult and, once landed, the English Catholics will rise up in support. The Scots will join them, the witch-queen will die, her palace will be destroyed, and the Queen of Scots, my dear and righteous cousin, will be crowned queen of England.'

'I pray that you are right, Henri. Bear in mind, however, that the Englishman is a stubborn breed. He might not be as easily subdued as you imagine.'

'Be assured, my dear Charles, that all resistance will be instantly crushed. We have God on our side.'

The priest nodded. 'God wills it.'

When Guise had left, the bishop sat alone with his thoughts. It had started, and it must be finished. For all the unnecessary bloodshed, *Incendium* must succeed.

CHAPTER 17

Amiens

'You are fortunate, sir,' said a quiet voice. 'Bishop de Créqui ordered the bells rung just in time.'

Christopher struggled to open his eyes. A cold stone floor was beneath him, a huge vaulted ceiling way above. He felt for his bag and pushed himself up and on to his feet. His legs shook and his head throbbed. He put a hand to it and felt blood. The floor moved under him and he stumbled. A hand on his elbow steadied him. 'What happened?' he asked, his voice to his own ears no more than a rasp.

'The bells halted the madness for long enough. The bishop opened the cathedral doors and demanded an end to the violence. We brought in as many of the wounded as we could.' Christopher looked about. Injured men and women lay in the pews and on the floor, tended by priests with bandages and bowls of water. The priest who had helped him was fresh-faced and sturdy. 'I am Jérôme,' he said, offering Christopher a cup of water.

Christopher took a sip. 'Has the violence ended?'

'For now it has but it will return. Do not be afraid. You are safe here. Are you hurt?'

'Battered and bruised only. I will mend. There are many in Paris who will not.'

'So we have heard. By killing and wounding we bring shame on ourselves. The bishop has refused to obey the duc de Guise's order to kill the Protestants in the city. He does not believe it is God's wish.'

'Nor is it,' replied Christopher, stretching his fingers. 'My name is Dr Christopher Radcliff. I am an envoy of the Earl of Leicester and I must reach England without delay. Please take me to the bishop.'

'The bishop is at prayer, sir,' replied the priest, 'and may not be disturbed. In an hour I will take you to him. Meanwhile there is food and wine if you wish them. Stay in the cathedral. It is not safe outside.'

Christopher found a seat and waited. His back and arms ached from the blows and there was a trickle of blood from his nose. No serious wounds and no broken bones. Others had been less fortunate. A man screamed when a priest straightened his broken arm to apply a splint and a pregnant woman sat sobbing as her stillborn child slipped from her. The violence had known no boundaries.

The priest returned in an hour and escorted Christopher to the bishop's chamber. Antoine de Créqui was a small man, with white hair swept back from his forehead, a neat pointed beard and dark eyes. He greeted Christopher with sadness in them. 'Dr Radcliff, I understand that you are on your way to England. It grieves me that you have witnessed our people killing each other. They have dishonoured themselves and our beliefs.'

'Had it not been for your intervention, sir, I would have been among the dead. I am grateful.'

Bishop de Créqui smiled. 'Be grateful to God, doctor, not to me.

Our country has been at war with itself for ten years. In God's eyes, we are all guilty. I pray daily for an end to the bloodshed. Now, how can I help you?'

'I was sent to Paris by the Earl of Leicester, principal advisor to Queen Elizabeth. I must return at once to London.'

'So Father Jérôme told me. Yet you would be safer here, doctor,' replied the bishop. 'Will you not wait until God's peace has been returned to us?'

'I cannot. Time is against me.'

'In what manner?'

'There is evidence that the violence in your country will soon spread to mine. I must warn the earl.'

'Do you suggest a plot?'

'I do.'

The bishop's eyes narrowed. 'You are an agent of the Earl of Leicester, doctor, so I shall not ask how you know this because you will not tell me. But for all the blood spilt in our city, you ask much of me.'

'Is transport to Calais so much to ask?'

'In itself, of course it is not. But you are asking me to accept your story. How can I be certain that your intentions are not hostile to France?'

The bishop was no fool. He wanted to be sure. Christopher sighed and shook his head. 'You have only my word, sir.'

'Quite so, doctor. I will ask God's guidance. You will have an answer within the hour.'

The queen herself had once said that all her subjects worshipped the same God. The rest, she said, was mere detail. Gazing at one of the largest and most magnificent cathedrals in Europe, Christopher could not help but think there was more to it than 'mere detail'. Rows of stone pillars, chapels on either side of the nave, a huge, high-vaulted ceiling, statues and paintings on the walls, the windows themselves richly decorated. Not to his taste, not a place in which he would wish to worship, yet mighty and impressive and signalling unshakeable faith. While he sat, the priests continued to tend to the wounded. He heard prayers being said for the dead and saw bodies being removed. A child wailed. An old man called for God's vengeance on the murderers of his daughter. Christopher knelt by a pillar, put his head in his hands and prayed silently.

The bishop returned within the hour. 'It is not yet clear to me what God wishes of me but if, as you say, the peace of England is also at risk, I will do what I can to help.'

'Can you provide a coach to take me to Calais?'

'A coach I can find, doctor. Its safe passage to Calais is in God's hands.'

'The risk is small compared to the danger England is in. I must go. If you can help, sir, I beg you to do so.'

'Very well, doctor. A carriage will be provided for you. Father Jérôme, the priest who brought you in, will inform you when the arrangements have been confirmed. Have you sufficient money?'

'Thank you, I have. I shall be ready.'

A little before midnight, Father Jérôme led Christopher out of a small door half hidden by a buttress on the side of the cathedral. By the light of Jérôme's rush lantern, they walked as quickly as Christopher's bruises would allow, listening out for the sounds of other men abroad at that hour and straining their eyes to see what might be lurking in the shadows. Save for dogs fighting over what was left in the cathedral square, the city was quiet. Yet the air of menace persisted. Likely as not, dawn would bring yet more bloodshed.

Now and again Christopher glanced nervously back over his shoulder to make sure they were not followed. There would be thieves and cut-throats about, hoping to take advantage of the bloody chaos in the city. One corpse more or less would go unremarked.

The coach was waiting for them at the city gate. 'I will leave you here,' whispered Jérôme. 'God be with you.' Christopher thanked the priest and climbed in. The coachman snapped his reins and they rumbled away into the darkness.

Christopher sat back and closed his eyes. He had been rescued from a mob of bloodthirsty Catholics by a Catholic bishop. In London would he find mobs of Protestants seeking revenge?

They stopped at the small town of Abbeville. There the inn-keeper seemed oblivious to what was happening in Paris and Amiens. Guise's men must have ridden north to Arras, passing the western towns by. The innkeeper told Christopher that he was the first traveller for a week. While France burned and the streets of its cities filled with corpses, wise men stayed at home.

They changed horses and were back on the road within the hour. The coachman drove the new horses hard, harder than was safe. Christopher wriggled down into his seat and braced his legs against the one opposite. Twice they bounced off stones large enough to tip the coach sideways but on both occasions it righted itself in time. The coach rattled on, juddering and shaking and giving way to no one. Few English coaches would have withstood the battering it took but French coachmakers were known to be the best in Europe.

One more change of horses and they had reached the town of Boulogne by dusk. In the morning they would reach Calais and from there Christopher would take the first boat across the water.

They found another inn, where Christopher paid for a room.

The coachman arranged stabling before disappearing into the town in search of drink and company with orders to be ready to leave at dawn.

Christopher slept little and was up and waiting for him before the sun rose. From the journey and his night in the town, the fellow looked sick and exhausted. It crossed Christopher's mind to let him be and drive the coach himself. He found milk and bread and forced the man to eat and drink. It was enough. The horses were fetched and they were on their way again.

The quay at Calais was busy. Fly boats and fishing boats lined the harbour wall, their crews busy with rope and canvas and preparing to sail on the next tide. Christopher paid the coachman and suggested he find a bed before venturing back on the highway. He scoured the harbour for a packet boat. There was none.

At the far end of the quay, a family with several items of baggage stood together. A mother and two daughters were crying. Christopher approached the father and asked if they were travelling to England. 'We are, sir,' the man replied. 'My wife and daughters and I. France is no longer safe for us.' He was a slight man, clean-shaven and soft-spoken.

'Where are you from, sir?' asked Christopher.

'We have come from the town of Arras, a city that has been our home for ten years. I doubt now that we shall see it again.'

'Is there violence there?'

'There is, sir. Such violence as I would not wish my wife or daughters to witness. A mob of murdering Catholics — men employed by the duc de Guise, I should not wonder — burst into our church and set fire to it. There were men and women at prayer. They were bound and beaten. Their screams as the flames engulfed the church were beyond imagining.'

'I have come from Paris,' replied Christopher, 'where the streets run with blood. Admiral Coligny is dead and hundreds, perhaps thousands of his followers with him. I am travelling to England with the fearful news.'

'Have you a means of crossing the water, sir?' asked the man.

'I was expecting to find a packet boat.'

'There has been none today and the tide is about to turn. We must find a fisherman or a trader willing to take us. For you that should not present a problem but my family will not be welcome on a small boat. Sailors are superstitious folk. If I had the capital, I would buy a fleet of boats to carry our people to England, where they would be safe.'

Among the smaller vessels, one stood out as larger and better equipped for a voyage beyond coastal waters. It was two-masted, square-rigged and would be a merchant ship, used to plying its trade up and down the coasts and across the narrow sea. Christopher made his way along the pier towards it. The deck was deserted. He called for the captain in French and then in English. A grizzled head appeared from below. 'I am the captain. What do you want?' he demanded in a rough, throaty voice. Christopher guessed that he was from the Low Countries.

'Passage to England, if that is your destination.'

'How much will you pay?' The captain's keen eyes narrowed.

'Ten livres.'

'Fifteen.' The captain held out his hand and watched Christopher take the coins from his bag and count them out. It was as well that he had travelled with a full purse. 'We leave in one hour. Be ready.'

'Where are you headed?'

'Dover. With a cargo of good French wine. One hour.'

*

It was a Dutch trading ship and the hold was full. There was no provision for passengers. As they left the harbour, Christopher looked back to see the family from Arras still huddled miserably together on the quay. God send them a boat and a captain willing to take three women on board.

They were soon on the open sea. Christopher stood by the main mast, willing the ship on and calculating when he would arrive in London. A few hours to make the crossing, a hired carriage to Canterbury and another from there to London. In under two days he would be in Whitehall Palace.

The Dover cliffs were well within view and Christopher had begun to think that he might reach London a little sooner when the storm broke. Suddenly the wind swung to the north-east, bringing with it icy rain and waves that threatened to devour the ship and its crew. While the captain wrestled with the tiller and the crew struggled with the sails, Christopher scrambled below and, ignoring the complaints of his bruised back, squeezed himself painfully between a cask of wine and a heap of sacks. Although the cargo was lashed down, it creaked and groaned and strained against the ropes.

While the storm raged he sat with his back to the sacks and his legs braced against the cask. When he closed his eyes he found that a part of him revelled in the excitement – the screeching wind, the waves crashing over the gunwales, the creaking of the ship's timbers – while another part, a part which he struggled to suppress, saw only a wrecked ship, its sails and masts floating in a tangled heap, and gulls pecking at the eyes of bodies washed up on a distant shore. He had escaped the horrors in Paris and Amiens, but at sea death was never far away. And if he perished, the message he carried would perish with him. Katherine had spoken of Penelope at her spinning wheel. In the midst of this storm, after Paris and Amiens, a lame horse and a greedy farmer, the thought occurred that he was not unlike Odysseus returning home from Troy. Would his journey also take ten years?

When at last the storm abated, they had been blown far to the south. Christopher climbed unsteadily to his feet and pulled himself up the ladder to the deck. From the height of the sun, now just visible behind a bank of cloud, he judged it to be late afternoon.

The captain was bellowing orders to his crew and did not see Christopher approach. 'How long to land?' he shouted into the captain's ear.

The captain shrugged. 'Who knows? We are turning towards England but it will be hard going against this wind. Stay below and I will fetch you when we near land.' Reluctantly, Christopher did as he was bid.

When the shout came, Christopher was dozing with his back propped against a cask of French wine. He went on deck and stood by the mast. He could see land well enough but there were no high chalk cliffs. It was not Dover.

'From the shape of the land, the Isle of Wight,' yelled the captain, as if reading his thoughts. 'We will sail around the eastern coast and make for Portsmouth. But I doubt we'll make land before dark. It'll be a night at sea for us.'

For an hour, and then another, the ship worked its way around the island until it was behind them and Christopher could just see the narrow entrance into Portsmouth's large natural harbour. 'Can we not still reach the port tonight?' he asked.

The captain looked up at the darkening sky. 'It would be foolish to try. There are sandbanks and rocks and these waters are a sailor's graveyard. It was here that your King Henry's *Mary Rose* went down.

We will go in at first light. We have victuals and plenty of good wine to drink. Tomorrow it will be.'

'Captain, I must get to London without further delay. I have urgent business and you are a fine sailor. Can you not try for Portsmouth now?'

'I cannot. Our cargo is valuable. The owners will not thank me for pouring it into the sea. If we were unladen I would be more inclined to try. As it is, we will anchor off shore and wait for the morning.' Another day lost. Christopher cursed, then gritted his teeth and clenched his fists in frustration.

CHAPTER 18

England

The storm had added a day to the journey, and almost a hundred miles in the saddle had done nothing to lessen his dislike of riding. He had bought a palfrey in Portsmouth, sold it to a dealer in Southwark for half the price he had paid and taken a wherry to Blackfriars stairs. Since escaping from Paris, images of women and children mutilated, burned and crying pitifully for God's help had urged him on. Now at last the journey was over. He went briefly to Ludgate Hill, changed his clothes and hurried to Whitehall, clutching the bag in which Caron's pistol had travelled with him from France. He insisted on being taken straight to the earl.

'Dr Radcliff, I am much relieved to see you returned. The stories from Paris are beyond belief.' The earl extended his hand. He was dressed in black as if in mourning, his face drawn and his eyes red with fatigue. 'When the news arrived, the queen insisted on returning at once from Kenilworth. But you must be exhausted. A glass of wine, perhaps? Or would you care for food?' For all his problems, Leicester's natural courtesy had not deserted him.

'A glass of wine would restore my spirits. Thank you, my lord.' The earl called for a servant to bring it and invited Christopher to sit. He raised his own glass. 'By the grace of God, to your safe return, doctor.' They drank and the earl went on, 'When I sent you to France, I little thought that I was putting your life in such danger. I regret doing so.'

'You could not have foreseen it and here I am alive.'

'Indeed you are. Are Sir Francis and his family safe? And my nephew, Philip Sidney? Was there news of him?'

'All were safe when I left. Sir Francis's house had become a refuge from the carnage. Sir Philip was among those who took shelter there and did much to cheer the women and children with his good humour. He sends you his wishes for your good health and his assurance that he will return unharmed. I was fortunate to escape and make my way to England, although it has taken longer than I hoped.'

'His wishes are kindly received. Was it as appalling as we have heard?'

'I doubt any report could have exaggerated it. On the eve of St Bartholomew's Day, Admiral Coligny was murdered most brutally and the Catholics in the city at once set about hacking the Huguenot Protestants to pieces and burning their homes. Men, women, children and babes – they made no distinction.' Leicester put his hands to his head and muttered a few inaudible words. 'There is insanity in their rage and it has spread from Paris. I found much the same in Amiens, where only the goodwill of the bishop saved me from a bloodthirsty mob. France is burning.'

Leicester sighed. 'So there remains at least one godly priest. It is a lamentable tragedy and the queen has been cast again into a mood of utter despondency. She has ordered the court into mourning. That this could happen so soon after our recent treaty and while the French

were promoting the suit of Alençon is beyond Her Majesty's understanding, and my own. What does Walsingham say?'

'Sir Francis believes that the duc de Guise murdered Admiral
Coligny by his own hand and is behind the slaughter. Whether the
king or his mother were aware of his plans, we do not know.'

'Although we hear that the king has sent Coligny's head to
Rome. If that does not suggest his connivance, I know not what
does. Was fear of this slaughter the matter Sir Francis felt he could
not entrust to a messenger?'

'In part, it was. But there is more. His agent Tomasso Sessetti
has heard word of a wider plot, perhaps involving the Scots, and
therefore ourselves. It has a name — *Incendium*. I fear that the
violence and burning in France is part of such a plot.'

Leicester shook his head. 'Another unholy plot. Will we never be
free of them? Our gracious sovereign, fearless though she is, forced to
spend her life in mortal danger and her realm ever under threat.
Spanish, French, Scots, Irish — enemies on every side. Where should
we look for friends? Or are we fated for ever to travel alone?' He
paused. '*Incendium*. The word itself is a warning. The sorceress Mary
Stuart will be behind it, mark my words. And to think that there was
once talk of my marrying the woman. The very thought makes my
blood run cold.'

'There will be plotters in England, my lord, as there are in
France. They will be working together. We must uncover them and
without delay.' Christopher took the pistol from his bag and laid it on
the earl's table. 'And there is this.'

Leicester picked it up. 'Two barrels, longer than is usual in a
firearm of this kind, and two firing mechanisms. Most uncommon
and beautifully made. I do not recall seeing anything like it. What
has it to do with a plot?'

'It is the weapon with which an unknown assassin tried to kill Admiral Coligny.'

'I understood that the Admiral was cruelly hacked to death.'

'He was, my lord, but not before being wounded by two shots from this.'

Leicester weighed the pistol in his hand. 'And?'

'There is another like it.'

'What exactly do you suggest, doctor?'

'There must be a reason for two such weapons. In the hands of a skilled assassin they would be formidable.'

The earl sighted along the barrel. 'A dangerous weapon to be sure, but why do you suppose its twin is not also intended for use in France?'

'Of course, my lord, it might be. But it could equally have crossed the sea and be concealed in London.'

Leicester replaced the pistol on the table. 'Conjecture, doctor, no more. And in any event what is to be done? Are we to question every man in the city or publish the word *Incendium* in a pamphlet, asking for any who have heard the word spoken to come forward? I hardly think so. What we can do is guard our queen night and day and keep her cousin securely locked up in Sheffield Castle. We can trust no one and suspect everyone.'

'With respect, that will not help us discover the conspirators or the nature of their conspiracy. If Her Majesty is to be truly safe, we must do so.'

'I realize that, doctor, and it is you who will ensure that we do discover them. I shall depend upon you. I will instruct John Berwick to assist.'

Berwick. Christopher had given the man barely a thought since leaving Paris. 'And the stationers? Did Berwick discover anything from them?'

'He did not. He does not believe they are in any way to be feared.'

That was disappointing. 'Very well, my lord. I shall expect to hear from Mr Berwick.'

'Find those who would see our queen dead and godly English Protestants slaughtered like their French cousins. Discover their scheming. Bring them to the executioner's block.'

'I shall, my lord.'

'If you do not, as you say, London may go the way of Paris.' Leicester paused. 'One thing more, doctor. I wish you to accept Heneage's request for a meeting. Find out what he wants. The queen trusts the man, everyone seems to trust the man. I do not. Now go, and return with intelligence I can use.' He pointed to the pistol. 'Meanwhile I shall take care of this. Let us keep its existence to ourselves.' He smiled. 'I am pleased to know that you are safe, as the queen will be.'

Christopher put the almost empty purse on the earl's table. 'Thank you, my lord. Here is what remains of the money I took with me.'

Leicester weighed the purse in his hand and raised his eyebrows. 'Your expenses were great, doctor. The purse must be worth more than the coins left in it.' He put it down. 'No matter, doubtless you spent wisely. Go home now and rest. If this *Incendium* is as you think, we shall have much work before us.'

Christopher had been in such a hurry to reach Whitehall that he had barely noticed the clamour or sensed the mood of fear in the streets. Now he did. The Strand was chock-full of horses and coaches, many heading westwards away from the city. A highway that was always busy had become a narrow funnel through which all must pass if they were to reach the safety of the countryside. Arguments erupted, insults were thrown, horses reared and bared their teeth in alarm. Some of the Fleet Street shops had closed their doors and shuttered their windows, as if expecting the enemy to arrive at any moment. Even the goldsmith Isaac Cardoza's door was locked. Rumour had spread and grown and taken strength from each retelling.

Huddles of men and women stood outside doorways and shops while pamphlet-sellers shouted the news from France. Christopher paid twopence for a pamphlet — twice the common price. The printer, a man with an eye for profit, had not waited for the rumours to be confirmed. He warned of a French army on its way to Tilbury and their Spanish allies sailing to Portsmouth and Plymouth. He spared his readers no detail of the killing in Paris and estimated the number of French Protestant dead at 'many thousands'. And he called for the Queen of Scots to be executed immediately. Outside St Bride's church a line of worshippers waited to be admitted. And on Ludgate Hill he passed a company of armed militiamen. The trained bands had been called out. The news had arrived with alarming speed and it would not take much of this to turn a panic-stricken London into a city of blood and retribution. He hurried as best he could through the confusion of bodies and vehicles and arrived back at Ludgate Hill.

Rose was in the kitchen, kneading dough. The wrinkled face split into a toothless grin at the sight of him. 'I saw your clothes, doctor,' she whispered, 'and knew you had returned from France. I feared greatly for you and thank God you are safe.'

'Thank you, Rose. The news has travelled fast. There is killing and burning in the cities there but I am unharmed. I was fortunate.

More fortunate than many. The scenes I witnessed surpass understanding.'

'I wept at the news of such bloodshed. What drives men to kill in such a manner?'

'I can explain it no better than you, Rose.'

'You are fatigued, doctor. You should eat and rest. I am making a stew. I managed to buy a pair of rabbits from an old man who traps them in the fields at Holborn. What I could buy in the market for sixpence now costs a shilling. Is it true that a Spanish fleet has been seen off the Cornish coast, doctor?'

'I could not say, Rose. It is possible but until we see Spanish masts in the Thames, let us be calm and pray for peace.' A thought occurred to him. 'How did you know I was in France?'

'A young gentleman called, doctor, while I was here cleaning. Said he had been sent to make sure the house was safe while you were in France.'

'Did he give a name, Rose, or say who had sent him?'

'No, doctor. I did not think to ask.'

'And his appearance? Did you note it?'

'No, sir. One young gentleman is much like another to me. Have I done wrong?' Rose looked close to tears.

'You have not, Rose. And I am grateful to you for coming here while I was away. I must call on Mistress Allington. Then I shall be ready for your rabbit stew and my bed.'

The study was just as he remembered leaving it and the window was secure. No sign of disturbance, nothing out of place. Had Leicester seen fit to send a man to check on the house or simply to make sure that he had left? Or had Heneage's man Wetherby come to call again? He was too tired to think about it. As soon as he could he would take Rose's advice — eat and rest. But first he must go to Wood Street.

The door was opened by Isabel. Without a word, she took his hands in hers and led him inside. Katherine was sitting in the little parlour, intent upon her needlework. 'You have a visitor, Katherine,' said Isabel quietly.

Katherine looked up from her work. For a moment she neither spoke nor moved. Then she put aside her sewing, stood up and held out her arms. Christopher stepped forward. In his ear she whispered, 'I have prayed harder than I have ever prayed in my life. I hardly dared hope you would return safely.'

He stepped back and placed his hands on her cheeks. 'I thank you for your prayers. They were needed.'

'Sit, Christopher,' said Isabel, 'and tell us what you can bear to.'

He omitted the worst of it, concentrating on the difficulties of the journey, the spectacle of the wedding and the differences between the two cities. 'I heard Italian spoken on the streets,' he told them, 'and German and Flemish. Paris is full of students and artisans.'

'Did you complete your task?' asked Katherine.

Christopher hesitated. 'I brought home a message from Sir Francis Walsingham to the earl, which was my primary purpose. I did not bring answers to all the questions that have arisen.'

'No doubt you will be seeking answers now that you are here.'

'I shall. The earl has entrusted me with the task of doing so.'

'And I shall help you.'

It was no time for another argument. He grinned. 'Perhaps it is I who will help you. But let us talk of this another day.'

She nodded. 'You are much fatigued. Your face is drawn and you are thinner. Another day, but talk of it we shall. Go home and rest and I will call at Ludgate Hill in a day or two. I thank God that he has returned you to us.'

Isabel showed him to the door. 'She has cried every day,

Christopher,' she said, 'for you and for the horrors in France. It is hard for her to accept that those who share her mother's faith have done such things in the name of God and there is guilt in her. Be gentle and let her speak of it.'

'I shall, Isabel. Be sure of it.'

He longed for nothing more than Rose's stew and his bed chamber, but one more task remained. He hurried down Wood Street towards Cheapside. But at Woolchurch he found himself caught up in a troupe of players doing their best to lighten the mood of a small audience with a comical performance involving a green-clad Robin Hood, the fat friar, covered only by a sack, and two boys dressed as doxies and speaking bad French. Within the city bounds, they were acting illegally but the two constables watching did not seem to care. The audience were enjoying the entertainment, the more so when Robin Hood spotted Christopher among them and had them believe that he was one of the players. 'Ah, here is our giant,' he called out, pointing at Christopher. 'Come, sir, you are needed to rescue these poor girls.' The crowd parted to allow Christopher through. Another time he would have played his part, as one was expected to do. Today, however, he could not.

'Alas, sir,' he replied in a loud voice, 'the girls must fend for themselves, but here is reward for your work.' He threw some coins towards the players and slipped away while they scrambled to collect them. Even at such a time, a man must eat. There would be many in France struggling to do so.

He made his way over and around the heaps of horse dung that the Cheapside markets were never without and down the lane to the house. The door was opened by Grace. 'Come in, doctor. You have been a stranger too long. Has another house taken your fancy or have you turned to boys? I don't offer boys, if you have.' Her belly heaved with laughter and her cheeks wobbled. She smelled of burned meat and rotten cabbage.

'Nothing like that, Grace,' replied Christopher. 'Is Ell here?'

'She is, doctor, and free for you. Go up and tell her to earn me my crust.'

Ell was lying on the bed, naked from the waist up and sipping from a beaker. When Christopher poked his head around the door, she put down the beaker and jumped up to embrace him. 'Doctor Rad, you've returned. I feared you might not with all the goings-on in France. Thought you might have had to stay put.' She glanced down. 'Oh, sorry, doctor, I quite forgot.' She stepped back and pulled on a man's undershirt far too large for her. 'Fat fool left it behind. Gor-bellied he was and stank like a donkey.'

Dress her in a silk gown and put pearls around her neck, thought Christopher, and Ell Cole, a Cheapside whore, would grace any noble table. Not just for her looks, although in those she would outshine every rival, but also for her lack of artifice and plain good humour. He realized that he had missed her as he had missed Katherine. 'How are you, Ell? Lovely as ever, I see. If I wasn't so tired I might be tempted.'

She sat back on the bed. 'Well as ever, doctor, and still busy, although I have been worried for you.' She put out a hand to touch his sleeve. 'The stories from France have been enough to chill the blood. My customers have spoken of little else. Is it true what they are saying?'

He put his hand on hers. 'I fear that it is, Ell. I saw things that will never leave me, dreadful, terrifying things. But I am unharmed and safe home.'

Ell wiped a tear from her eye. 'I thank God for it. We heard they were roasting new-born babes on spits in the street and eating them. Are there black cannibals over there?'

'No, that is not true. Best to put it out of your mind. Have you heard any word of Houseman, the stationer who disappeared?'

'I did try, doctor, but you told me to take care, so I went about it quietly. Heard not a whisper. Sorry I can't help.'

'And the man who cut Sal? Any sign of him?'

Ell spat into a pot. 'None, thank the Lord. Evil beggar should be burning in hell. Fancy a wet?' Ell held her beaker out to Christopher. 'Only the one beaker, I'm afraid.'

'Save it for yourself, Ell. Anything else to tell me?'

'Not that I can recollect, doctor. So the killing won't happen here?'

It would if French soldiers arrived on Spanish ships. 'No, Ell, it won't happen here. But keep listening and find me if you hear anything. Any talk of fires or flames, especially. There is a word — *Incendium* — I need to know if you hear it spoken.'

'Funny word. Never heard of it. Where is it?'

'Not where, Ell, what. It means fire. Listen out for it.'

'French, is it? I'll try, doctor. If you're tired, why not lie down for a while?'

'No, thank you, Ell. Kind thought, though. Next time, perhaps.'

Ell let out one of her throaty cackles. 'Next time, my arse. I'm too good for you, Dr Rad, that's how it is. Too fucking good for you. Pleased to see you safe, though.'

She was still laughing when Christopher closed the door. Downstairs Grace was on her settle, snoring peacefully. He left a few coins on a table and slipped out of the stew. Seeing Ell had lifted his spirits but there had been nothing about Nicholas, nothing about *Incendium*.

CHAPTER 19

September

He had dreamed of a dark place far beneath the streets of London, a stinking place in which naked prisoners had only rotting fish to eat. The fish had turned into headless babes and the prisoners into slavering beasts armed with dung-forks. When he woke he was shivering. September had come and the night air was cool. He pulled the bed cover back on to the bed and lay awake until dawn. Would all his nights be filled with such images? Only when he left the house and walked briskly to Fleet Street did the dream fade.

Isaac Cardoza emerged from his back room when he heard the door to his shop open and greeted Christopher with open arms and a wide smile. 'Christopher, you have been a stranger. I feared for you.' He peered at Christopher's face. 'And you are distressed.'

'I have been in France for the earl.'

Isaac threw up his hands. 'We cannot believe the stories arriving from Paris. Are they true?'

'Alas, Isaac, they are. It would be difficult to exaggerate what has happened.'

'There are many who think the terror will cross the narrow sea. If it does, none will be safe. Catholic will kill Puritan, Christian will kill Jew. Are we wrong to be frightened?'

'You are not wrong. England is in danger. I can tell you no more, Isaac, but be watchful. While our defences are strengthened against attack from the Spanish, in Paris and London there are those who wish us harm.'

'I am sure of it. Christopher, I have heard nothing about the man who has disappeared – Houseman – or his wife. Nothing at all.'

'Please keep listening, Isaac. And there is a word. *Incendium*. If you hear it spoken, send word at once.'

'*Incendium*. Fire. I shall. Go safely, Christopher. The distress will pass. *Shalom*.'

'*Shalom*, Isaac.'

In the stationers' market there was no sign of Nicholas, not that he had expected there to be, and the man who had taken over Nicholas's pitch was still there. Christopher browsed the stalls, listening out for gossip. In one corner of the yard, two booksellers were arguing. He edged closer until he could hear what they were saying. 'The cost of the best-quality rag paper will rise, mark my words,' said one, a large, moon-faced fellow.

'Why should the cost of Italian paper rise?' asked the other. 'Mine comes by sea from Genoa. It never touches French soil.'

'Because the merchants will invent reasons to make us pay more. You wait and see. I shall buy every quire I can before they do, and you should do the same.'

Christopher shook his head. In the world of trade, a man must look to his own interests, whether manna was falling from heaven or the earth opening up to swallow entire villages. While those who could departed the city for the safety of the countryside, and those who could not waited in dread for the report of Spanish ships at Tilbury, in the Royal Exchange there would be clever men looking for opportunity from the catastrophe in France and planning ways of profiting from it. It was ever thus.

Outside the church, a face he recognized looked up from the book he was reading and swiftly looked down again. Beside him stood a very young man, dressed, as he was, in a red and gold doublet and a soft cap decorated with a white feather. Taking them for brothers, Christopher approached them. 'Mr Wetherby, I wish you good day. Have you found an interesting book?'

'Dr Radcliff, a joyful day to you. I come from time to time to the market just to see what is new. I find the stationers agreeable company and by their printing of official documents, they provide a valuable service. I should happily be a member of their company, if they were to invite me.' His boyish face had turned red and his words came out in a rush. 'May I present Monsieur Grégory Deschamps, who serves the duc de Montmorency and has accompanied him to England. Grégory, Dr Christopher Radcliff, a member of the staff of the Earl of Leicester.'

Deschamps held out a hand. '*Enchanté*, doctor.' The Frenchman was no more than twenty, clean-shaven, slightly built and courteous in manner. The fingers of both his hands were heavily beringed. Wetherby's brother he was not.

'I have just returned from your country, Monsieur Deschamps,' replied Christopher, taking the hand. 'Words cannot describe the tragedy that has befallen it.'

'A tragedy indeed, doctor. I am happy to be in England at such a time.'

'And you, doctor, how do you fare?' asked Wetherby.

'Also happy to be in England.' Christopher lowered his voice. 'Would Mr Heneage care to meet me now that I am back?'

Wetherby's eyes widened in surprise. 'I daresay he would, doctor. I shall ask him.'

'Thank you, Mr Wetherby. I shall await a reply. Good day, Monsieur Deschamps.' Christopher left Wetherby to his reading.

Outside Newgate prison a noisy crowd had gathered for a hanging. Christopher clutched his purse under his shirt. Money would be changing hands on how long the condemned man would take to die and there would be pickpockets about. In no mood for an execution, he made his way around the crowd towards Ludgate Hill. On the corner of the hill, a man stood alone in the pillory, his ears nailed to the wood. His eyes were closed. He had passed out.

Christopher approached a constable standing close to the pillory and asked what the man had done to warrant the nailing. 'Spoke foully of his lordship the Earl of Leicester,' replied the constable.

'How so?'

'Said his lordship would rather be at swiving French ladies than fighting their menfolk.'

'A nailing for mere words?'

'Yes, sir. Since the news from France the justices are meting out harsher sentences. And quite right too, if you ask me.' The constable prodded the man's backside with his staff. 'I'll rouse him when the hanging's over. He's an hour still to go.'

When they had watched the hanging, his tormentors would be back to pelt him with mud and muck, and all for a few ill-chosen words, probably spoken in jest. What horrors would they see if the slaughter in Paris was repeated in London? Would the streets be piled with corpses, would the city burn from Woolwich to Westminster?

If the blow that sent him sprawling on to the cobbles on the corner of the alley that joined Ludgate Hill by the church of St Martin had been intended to kill, it was misdirected. It caught him on the side of the head and did not render him unconscious. He rolled on to his back to see the dim shape of his attacker standing over him, a heavy ballow in his hand. A mask covered all of the man's face but for his eyes. Christopher tried to focus. He fumbled for the poniard and as the man raised the ballow, he jerked it out. It slipped from his crooked fingers. Still unable to see his attacker clearly, he felt for it, found the handle and thrust it into a leg. His wrist jarred as the point hit a bone. The attacker screamed a foul oath and dropped his weapon. Christopher shouted for help. None came and the man hobbled off towards Blackfriars with blood soaking his breeches. Christopher shouted again. This time two filthy children appeared from a doorway, took a look at him and disappeared again. The alley was deserted.

He struggled to his feet, picked up the ballow and took a hesitant step. It was like stepping on to land after the crossing from France. The earth pitched and swayed, forcing him back to the ground. For several minutes he sat with his back to an ancient wall, alert to another attack but not able to stand without falling.

He tried again and found that he could walk slowly if he bent low and used the club to lean on. The street was quiet. A single beggar saw him and demanded a coin. Christopher ignored him.

He reached his house and hammered on the door with the ballow. Finding the key and pushing it into the lock without dropping it was impossible. His head was throbbing and his legs shook from the effort of walking. When Rose opened the door, he fell inside, almost knocking her over.

He was still on the floor inside the door when he came to his senses. Rose was mopping his brow with a damp cloth and clucking quietly. His mind slowly cleared and he remembered everything. Paris, Amiens and now London. The doctors' table at Pembroke Hall might as well have been a thousand miles away.

CHAPTER 20

Christopher sat waiting for John Berwick. Rose's ministrations with damp cloths and evil-smelling goose fat had almost removed the lump on his head although it was still sore to the touch.

He rubbed his hand and stared at the unlit fire in his study. Was his attacker a thief simply after his purse? The wretch had run off soon enough when Christopher stabbed him, as a thief would. Or had the blow to his head not come from a common criminal, at least not that manner of criminal? Had he been attacked on the orders of someone anxious to be rid of him? He might have been seen in London or word been sent from France. In either case, vipers had struck and would strike again. Did they want him dead as they had wanted Admiral Coligny dead?

Berwick arrived, as his message had said he would, at midday. Rose showed him into the study. 'Dr Radcliff,' he began, 'I am much relieved to find you safely home from Paris. Her Majesty is overcome with grief at events there and your safety has been a great concern to us all. I have prayed daily for you. Happily, God has heard me. By all accounts, the rivers of France are clogged with corpses and run with blood.' Berwick's voice had taken on a new tone — something akin to fear. 'How unfortunate that you should have been forced to witness the bloodshed. I trust you are unharmed.'

'Thank you, Mr Berwick. I returned quite unharmed although I find that London is also dangerous. Two days ago I was attacked in the street.' Christopher touched the lump on his head.

'Attacked? By whom, doctor? Did you see your attacker? He must be apprehended.'

'He was masked. He clubbed me from behind and would doubtless have killed me had I not managed to stab him in the leg.' He took the poniard from the table and held it up. 'Fortunately, I was carrying this.'

'Ah, your lock-picking dagger. Most wise, doctor. But are you badly hurt?'

'I shall mend.'

'Have you no inkling of the identity of this man or his purpose? Did he rob you?'

'He did not, and I wonder if it was my purse he was after. There are evil forces at work here — vipers, as the earl describes them — as there are in Paris. It seems that I might now be one of those they seek to devour.'

'That we will not allow to happen, doctor, and together we must discover their nest. The earl has instructed me to assist you as best I can. What is known and what suspected?'

So Berwick had wasted no time in currying more favour with Leicester. Now he was demanding intelligence. Christopher chose his words with care. 'The murder of Coligny by the duc de Guise, the possible involvement of the Scots and a plot named *Incendium*. Another attempt to free Mary Stuart is probable. There are scheming Scots in Paris. Some of them are known to Walsingham's agents.'

'The plot, *Incendium*, how is the name known?'

'An agent of Sir Francis Walsingham has heard it spoken.'

'*Incendium*. A fearful word, speaking of fire and death.'

'Exactly. And you, Mr Berwick, were you able to do as I requested?'

The look on Berwick's face suggested that he preferred asking questions to answering them. 'I did question James Kaye, Senior Warden of the Stationers, but discovered nothing. He could not account for Houseman's disappearance but suggested some transgression, from the possible consequences of which the man had fled. That would explain only money and valuables missing from his house. Houseman would have been compelled to leave everything else in his haste to flee.'

It would, thought Christopher, but such an action would not have been consistent with the character of the Houseman he knew. Nor would it have been consistent with his role as an intelligencer for the Crown. 'Did you examine the stain on the floor of his parlour?' he asked.

'I did. Again, I learned nothing, although I am hardly versed in the investigation of such matters. Blood, perhaps, but whose? I could not tell how long it had been there. Scant help, I fear.'

'What did you make of Kaye?'

Berwick hesitated. 'I found him courteous and straightforward, if a little wedded to his position. Dr Radcliff, I know that Houseman was a member of the Stationers' Company but is there any evidence of a connection between the company and his death? Is it not more likely that his disappearance is entirely unrelated to anything sinister?'

'And what, pray, about the lump on my head?'

'That too, doctor. Was it not the act of a vicious thief?'

Christopher pondered the question. It might have been the act of a vicious thief, but his instincts told him otherwise. 'You may be right, Mr Berwick, but let us not assume so.'

'Are we then to search Stationers' Hall and interrogate every member?'

'No, no. The stationers are well connected at court and I doubt we would discover anything but dusty volumes. Given their role in the printing of state papers they are almost an arm of the government. They would not take kindly to being interrogated. And, as you say, we have nothing of which to accuse any of their members.'

'And you, doctor, if you are a marked man you must take great care. The city is already filling with refugees from France and the streets are dangerous. You should venture out only when accompanied.'

'That is hardly practicable, Mr Berwick. But I thank you for your concern and I will take care.'

'Please, doctor, do.' Berwick doffed his cap. 'Now good day. I am sorry not to have been more help in your absence, but I shall continue to ponder our problem. Meanwhile, call on me at any time at Whitehall Palace.' He paused as if a thought had occurred to him. 'Would you care to walk in the queen's garden? The roses are still lovely and I should be delighted to accompany you.'

A stroll in the queen's garden to admire the roses or an opportunity to pick Christopher's brains? At least it would be a welcome break from city grime and he might find out more about the young man. 'Thank you, Mr Berwick, I should like that.'

Berwick beamed. 'Excellent. Let us do it when next you are at the palace. We will walk together.'

When he had left, Rose bustled in with a bowl of water and a linen cloth. 'Now, doctor,' she said firmly, 'you must not tire yourself with visitors. Let me attend to your head.'

'If you would leave the water and the cloth, Rose, I will attend to it myself.'

The old lady looked put out. 'Doctor, even you cannot see the side of your own head properly. Allow me to do it.'

She meant well and he should permit her this small task if that was what she wanted. 'Very well, Rose. But a few minutes will suffice.' He was due at the house of Thomas Heneage that afternoon – an appointment arranged by Wetherby.

'A few minutes only, doctor, and then I have a plate of beef for you. I had to pay extra but it will do you good. That was the young gentleman who called while you were away.'

'Are you sure, Rose?' Leicester must have sent Berwick to make sure the house was secure. Why had neither of them mentioned it?

'I am, doctor. That was him.'

Rose was as gentle as his own mother would have been and the beef was good. Refreshed, he set off for Thomas Heneage's house in the Strand. He passed a row of pillories at Temple Bar. The ears of one wretch had been hacked off and the severed hand of another testified to a second conviction for theft. The constable at Ludgate Hill had been right. The justices appeared to believe that the danger to England could be averted by mutilations.

Thomas Heneage had built for himself a mansion befitting his position as Treasurer of the Privy Chamber. It stood not far from the Savoy Hospital, built sixty years earlier for the alleviation of the suffering of the poor. Christopher had learned to pass on the north side of the street to avoid the miserable huddles of cripples, maunderers and street urchins who gathered outside the hospital demanding charity from any who came close.

The mansion looked over the river and across to the meadows beyond. A boat moored on his wharf below the house carried Heneage downriver to the city and upriver to Whitehall. He would seldom have need to mount a horse.

It was not the first time Christopher had met the Treasurer. They had more than once exchanged pleasantries in Whitehall Palace. But he knew little of the man other than that his father had served King Henry, he was reputed to be as ambitious as any of the queen's advisors and he was no friend of Leicester.

When Christopher arrived at exactly the time requested, Heneage was waiting for him in a library from whose windows he could see across the river to the bear garden on one side and Lambeth Palace on the other. It was an impressive room, a room in which a man might sit and contemplate his good fortune.

Heneage rose to greet his visitor. He instructed his steward that they were not to be disturbed and invited Christopher to sit. He was a thick-set man of middling height – several inches shorter than Christopher – with an unusually dense beard, heavy brows and narrow eyes. Most noticeable was the belligerent set to his neck and shoulders – thrust forward as if to intimidate.

'Dr Radcliff,' he began in a surprisingly soft voice, 'I thank you for coming. Does the Earl of Leicester know you are here?'

'If he does, sir, he did not learn of it from me,' replied Christopher. It was the response Leicester had suggested, covering all eventualities.

'That is as well, doctor. The earl and I have not always enjoyed each other's company. The circumstances of the death of his late wife did not sit comfortably with me, although I have much respect for his loyalty to the queen and to England. It is a loyalty that has at times bordered on jealousy.' Heneage laughed shortly. 'The earl did not care for my appointment to Her Majesty's privy chamber.' Christopher inclined his head in acknowledgement. That much he knew.

Heneage went on. 'You have been in London now for two years or more. How do you find it after Cambridge?'

'Bigger and busier and noisier, sir, but otherwise little different.' Christopher found that he was nervous and sat stretching his fingers.

'Was it the earl's charm that persuaded you here or the opportunity for advancement?'

Christopher hesitated, not knowing how much Heneage knew. 'The earl can certainly be persuasive and I hope one day to rise above my present station.'

'That is as I thought.' Heneage leaned forward in his chair. 'But if I may offer a word of advice, doctor, beware ambition too openly spoken. Better that your opponent should not know for certain which cards you hold.' Heneage smiled. 'But you do not need such advice from me. Forgive my presumption.'

'It is of no account, sir,' replied Christopher. 'And I am grateful for your thoughts.'

'I shall not ask about France. The reports have been fearful enough and you will be weary of having to describe them. In Toulouse and Orleans, I hear, it has been as monstrous as in Paris. You were fortunate to escape unscathed.'

'I was, sir, although not quite unscathed. In Amiens, I was attacked by a mob and saved only by the swift action of the bishop himself.'

'I am glad of it. There are stories of gallant bishops and priests elsewhere coming to the aid of the Huguenots. Not every Catholic drinks the blood of babes. But of course you know that. Mistress Allington's mother herself worshipped in the old way, did she not?'

Again Christopher tried to hide his surprise. Heneage was well informed. Best to pre-empt his questioning. 'Katherine too was brought up as a Catholic, Mr Heneage, but now follows a Protestant path. She believes that we all worship the same God and that it is our faith that matters, not the manner of its demonstration. Has the queen herself not expressed the same thought?'

'She has, although her belief was shaken by the *Regnans in Excelsis* and by Howard's plot. And none at court can come to terms with what is happening in France. A God of bloodshed and suffering is not the God I myself worship. Let us pray that such a God does not return to England. The terrible ways of Mary Tudor will live long in the memory.' Heneage shifted in his seat. 'Now, doctor, to the purpose of your visit. And, again, at the risk of sounding like a school-master, you are a man far too intelligent for me to speak other than frankly. You have served the Earl of Leicester well. He has spoken highly of you and it was you he chose to send to France. I shall not ask why because you will not tell me but he will have had good reason. Yet the earl's star is no longer in the ascendancy. The queen no longer confides in him or seeks his counsel as once she did. With Lord Burghley troubled by gout and in Paris, there are others now to whom she turns. I am sure you know to whom I refer — dancers and jousters and wits and sporting men they may be, but men also of intelligence and courage. Sir Francis Walsingham is one such.'

For a man noted for his brevity, it was a long speech. 'Are you not also one such, Mr Heneage?' asked Christopher with a slight smile.

Heneage laughed. 'I am a little old for jousting and I do not care for bear-baiting, of which Her Majesty is fond. However, I am her treasurer and she does confide in me. In that, I am much blessed.' He paused. 'Dr Radcliff, do not reply to my next remark but ponder on it, if you will, and bear it in mind for when the time comes. Our world is an uncertain place and change is inevitable. Should you feel it would serve your own purpose to good effect, there would be a place for you on my staff. I ask you to think on it, that is all.'

'Thank you, sir,' replied Christopher, 'I shall do so. For the present, however, I serve the Earl of Leicester as best I can.'

'Of course. I expected you to say nothing else. Your loyalty does you credit. I do not ask you to betray secrets. Merely to remember that there is more than one path through the forest.'

'I shall do so, sir.'

'Excellent.' Heneage rose and extended his hand. 'Call upon me whenever you wish.'

Christopher bowed his head. 'Thank you, sir. I shall.'

It had been much as Christopher had expected. Polite, cautious, straightforward. Heneage foresaw an opportunity and was building his strength to take advantage of it. Thomas Cromwell had once done it. Leicester and Burghley and Walsingham had done it. It was the way of the court.

CHAPTER 21

The next morning brought an early autumn chill to the air. Christopher put on his cloak to walk to Fleet Street where he bought a news sheet. The sheets could be a useful source of information but it was necessary to separate fact from the writer's opinions and his desire to sell his paper. Christopher sat in his study to read it.

This writer warned not only of murdering Catholics gathering to carry out the pope's instruction to rise up against their heretic queen but also of fire, plague, foul miasmas emanating from the Fleet ditch and an outbreak of smallpox around Aldgate. He wondered if anyone would buy a news sheet if it reported that the queen was in good health, there was no sign of plague or pox and the Spanish fleet had sunk.

But the queen's health had deteriorated. Leicester had spoken of Spanish vultures hovering over her, ready to fly to Madrid the moment her eyes closed for the last time. The shock of the slaughter in Paris had taken its toll and her physicians had urged her to remain in her apartments until she regained her strength.

The earl was also in low humour. The queen's malaise, word

from Spain of the taciturn King Philip dancing with glee at the news from Paris, word from Rome that Pope Gregory had celebrated the massacre, and the continuing threat of invasion: there was little to bring cheer to the heart. And *Incendium*. Still they knew not much more than the name.

Rose peeked around the open door to tell him that Mistress Allington was below. He was on his feet at once. 'Show her in, Rose.'

Even in distress, Katherine could not look other than lovely. Although her face was drawn, her green eyes still shone and her skin still glowed. Christopher took her hands in his and kissed her lightly. They sat, and for a few minutes neither spoke. Katherine was first to do so. 'I have struggled to come to terms with the knowledge that men and women who share the Catholic faith of my mother and her family before her have caused such atrocities to be committed. I have asked myself why a thousand times. Why? Why has God allowed it? And I have no answer.'

'The Catholic Church itself will suffer greatly from what has happened,' replied Christopher, gently. 'It will be for ever tainted with the blood of the slain. It should not have been so. If Coligny was plotting against the government, the king had reason to have him arrested. His murder was unnecessary and foolish.'

'And cruel and barbaric and an incitement to bloodshed and destruction. Ungodly and inhuman.' Katherine's voice rose. 'The actions of the mob had little to do with faith. They were driven by a lust for blood, and, for many, an opportunity to rob and steal. The Catholic Church will carry the blame not just for its own crimes but for the crimes of others.'

'Katherine, I saw women and children slaughtered like beasts and thrown on to fires. Wherever lies the fault, I shall never wipe those infernal images from my mind.'

'I know and I grieve for you. Please tell me what you discovered in Paris. I do not like being kept in ignorance.'

Christopher shook his head. 'You know that I cannot share such confidences with you. I am bound by my service to Leicester and the queen.'

Katherine leaned forward, her arms folded on the table. 'You must tell me. Why exactly were you sent to Paris and what intelligence have you brought back? Is England in danger? Is there another plot against the queen? Will violence erupt on the streets of London? Tell me. I wish to know.'

'I cannot.'

'You can. What can be so secret that I may not know? Tell me.'

Christopher sighed. He loved the determination of this woman as fiercely as he loved her beauty. She would not give up. 'Very well. I will tell you what is known, but with your word that you will discuss it with none but me. If it were known that I had confided in you, my career would be at an end. I could even be accused of treason.'

Katherine sat back in her chair, her arms folded in front of her. 'You have my word.'

He told her briefly of their suspicion that Coligny's murder was the first act in another plot to free the Queen of Scots and put her on the throne of England and that the plot was called *Incendium*. 'What is known to support such a suspicion?' she asked.

'Scottish agents have been seen in Paris. And the word *Incendium* has been spoken.' He did not tell her about the pistols or about the man who had attacked Sal in the stew or about the attack on himself.

'Is that all?'

'It is an accurate summary. Our task is to discover if there is a plot and to identify the plotters before they act.'

'How will you do this?'

'My agents are alerted. Walsingham's man Tomasso Sessetti is gathering what intelligence he can in Paris. It is likely that the queen's poor health has protected her from attack, both because her enemies might have been hoping that her death would spare them the trouble of killing her and because she has been confined and out of reach of an assassin's knife. That is no longer the case.'

'Then we must act quickly.'

'We, Katherine?'

'I will help.'

Christopher threw up his hands. 'Katherine, this is too much. First you demand that I tell you things I should not, now you think to help in investigating this plot. Much as I love you, I cannot agree to such a request. You must know that. Why do you force me to refuse you?'

'I wish to help. My conscience demands it of me.'

'How exactly would you help? Will you arm yourself with pistols and seek out Frenchmen on the streets?'

Katherine's face reddened in anger. 'That is unworthy.'

'Is it? Very well, tell me if you please how we might begin.'

'We shall begin by your telling me everything that you have omitted.'

He should have known. Katherine had realized at once that he had not told her everything. 'Very well. My agent Nicholas Houseman and his wife Sarah have disappeared. Houseman was a member of the Stationers' Company.' Katherine said nothing but held his gaze. 'I saw Roland Wetherby, Thomas Heneage's man, at the stationers' market. He was with a young Frenchman and, when he saw me, acted as if caught with his hand in another man's purse. And he is effeminate in his ways. Leicester does not trust him.'

'Is a man to be judged by the way in which he takes his pleasures? Would that not condemn half the court to a spell in Newgate?' Katherine knew, of course, that it would. She had little time for those she called popinjays and peacocks and even less for their 'pleasures' but that did not make them traitors. 'If this man Wetherby is a traitor,' she went on, 'would that not implicate Thomas Heneage?'

'Not necessarily. I have not mentioned my suspicions to Leicester because he resents Heneage's closeness to the queen and would not wish to give him cause to complain.'

'So evidence must be found.'

'That is what I am trying to do. Enough, Katherine, no more questions now. I have said far more than I should have. Let us speak of other matters.'

They had been apart too long. 'Or not speak at all if we are otherwise occupied,' replied Katherine. She stood up and held out her hands. 'Thank you. You have confided in me and I am grateful for it. I shall ask no more questions today.'

Christopher sniffed lightly. 'Roses. A deep scent.'

The autumn light was fading when she propped herself up on an elbow and traced the line of Christopher's cheekbone with a finger. '*Incendium*. Our enemies wish to see us burn. All of us — Catholic, Protestant and Puritan. It is power they crave.'

Christopher drew her to him and put his lips to her ear. 'Be silent, wench. '

They slept until the church bell rang out eight of the clock. When the eighth bell roused him, Christopher leapt from the bed and dressed hurriedly. He kissed Katherine and left her asleep.

Rose was in the kitchen. 'I did not like to disturb you, doctor,' she said with the hint of a grin. 'I have prepared breakfast for you both.'

'No time, Rose. I am late for the earl at Whitehall Palace. Mistress Allington will have it. How did you know she is here?'

'Her cape, doctor. It is in the study.'

'Ah, yes. Leave her to sleep, please, Rose. I will return later this morning.'

He almost ran down Fleet Street, his gown flapping behind him, along the Strand and up to the palace, where he was escorted immediately to the earl's apartments.

'Dr Radcliff,' said the earl, frowning, 'you have arrived. We await you.' John Berwick stood at his shoulder.

'My apologies, my lord—'

Leicester cut him off with a wave of the hand. 'Spare us your excuses, doctor. We have business to discuss. Lady Walsingham has returned from Paris – safely, thank God – and has delivered letters from Sir Francis. The city, he reports, is quiet, although the authorities cannot bury the bodies fast enough, and there is disease. Elsewhere there is still violence and he fears it will continue for some time yet. He confirms that the duc de Guise himself killed Admiral Coligny and he also has intelligence that Charles de Bourbon, Bishop of Beauvais, was involved in the massacre.' The bishop had conducted the wedding of the king's sister to Henry of Navarre. If he had been involved, it was hard to conceive of a more duplicitous act.

'Could Guise and Beauvais then also be involved in *Incendium*?' asked Christopher.

'Walsingham's agent, the Italian Sessetti, believes so. He continues to gather intelligence.' The earl paused. 'Have you yet met with Thomas Heneage?'

'I have, my lord. He suggested that I consider joining his staff.'

'That is no surprise. How did you respond?'

'I said little but that I serve you as best I can.'

Leicester nodded. 'That is as well. Berwick has spoken to me about Heneage's man Wetherby. You have reason to mistrust him, do you not?'

'I do, my lord,' replied Berwick. 'He has befriended a member of the duc de Montmorency's staff, a young man named Grégory Deschamps. I believe they are, er, two of a kind.'

'I saw Wetherby at the stationers' market,' added Christopher. 'He was with Deschamps and appeared unsettled when I spoke to him. Is there other reason to doubt him?'

'My father's advice was never to trust a man who prefers a boy's backside to a woman's,' said Leicester. 'Who knows what indiscretions such bedfellows might commit?'

'Wetherby a traitor?' asked Christopher. He could not see the effete young man as an agent for the French but then a good agent must be skilled at dissembling.

'I find it hard to contemplate,' replied Leicester. 'However, it would be as well to observe him. Or perhaps I should speak to Mr Heneage.'

'Would that be wise, my lord?' asked Berwick. 'Better, perhaps, that we keep a watch on Wetherby. If he is a traitor, there is a chance that he will incriminate himself. Then we shall have grounds to interrogate him.'

'Do you agree, doctor?'

Christopher inclined his head approvingly. 'Mr Berwick is right, my lord. If we jump too soon, we may learn nothing.' Damn Berwick. It was good advice.

'So be it. Mr Berwick will arrange for Wetherby to be watched.

But take care, Berwick. If the fellow senses danger, he will complain to Heneage or run. That would not help us. Let us hope that the queen's return to health is an auspicious sign and that a glimmer of light now shines on this matter. I shall not speak to Her Majesty of it until we are more certain. Good day, gentlemen.'

'Doctor,' said Berwick, 'we spoke of your accompanying me around the Great Garden and his lordship has kindly given his consent. Would you care to walk there now?'

It was scarcely the time for gardens but he did not wish to appear churlish. He glanced at the earl, who nodded. 'I would, Mr Berwick.'

They took their leave and walked along the new gallery that bordered the east side of the garden, separating it from the queen's own privy garden, and down a flight of stairs. The Great Garden had been designed in squares — sixteen parterres, each surrounded by a fringe of grass, connected by straight paths and laid out precisely within the square of the garden itself. Red and white roses had been planted in each bed. Christopher had seen the garden from above but never before set foot in it. And he had never experienced such a scent of roses. To the eye and the nose, the effect was overpowering.

Although the garden was much used by the royal household, they found it empty. They strolled between the beds, admiring the blooms and drinking in the scent, and again Christopher wondered at a place of such beauty so near the filth of the city. 'I doubt Wetherby presents a risk,' he said thoughtfully.

'I am inclined to agree, doctor,' replied Berwick, 'but let us not take a risk ourselves by ignoring the possibility. We will keep a watch on him.'

'Quite so. And you, Mr Berwick, how do you fare at court? Does the courtier's life suit you?'

'I do believe it does, doctor.' He waved away a bee that had settled on his sleeve. 'I would not serve Her Majesty well as a soldier, but perhaps one day I may do so as statesman or counsellor.'

'You may indeed. And your family? I know nothing of your background other than that your parents died in the uprising in the north.'

'My mother was a beautiful woman and devoted to my father. When she died, his brother sought a position at court for me and to my great good fortune the earl took me into his service. The queen has also been gracious enough to allow me into her presence.' Berwick paused. A small party was entering the garden from the west door. 'Ah. And, if I am not mistaken, here is Her Majesty.' Although the royal party was half the length of the garden away, he swept off his cap and bowed low. Taking his lead, Christopher did likewise. 'The queen prefers to be alone with her ladies. We will return the way we came.'

Christopher raised his head enough to see the queen take a small knife from one of her ladies with which to cut a single white bloom. When she held it against her heart, it stood out starkly against the black of her dress. She acknowledged Berwick with a smile, but did not speak. She continued along a path, clutching the rose. Her ladies followed silently behind.

'Her Majesty is still consumed by grief for events in France,' said Berwick when they had left the garden. 'I pray that she will soon recover her spirits.'

'As do I,' replied Christopher. 'I thank you for your kindness in showing me the garden, Mr Berwick, and now I must be back to my duties. Good day, and be sure to call upon me if I can be of any service to you.' The words did not come out easily.

'I shall, doctor. It is comforting to know that I have a wise friend nearby.'

Returning to the Holbein Gate, Christopher saw two figures walking towards him. One was Thomas Heneage, the other Roland Wetherby. He bowed his head as they passed. Wetherby doffed his cap. Heneage cast him a quizzical look. Neither spoke.

CHAPTER 22

He spent that night at Wood Street and set off for Ludgate Hill as dawn broke. Almost immediately he regretted it. It was the very worst hour for a man to be abroad in London. The night creatures who infested the dark streets — vagrants, thieves, whores, queer birds — still about their foul business as the creatures of the day emerged from their lairs and hovels in search of prey and food and a coin or two. Night-soil men, cutpurses, maunderers, gatherers of rags and crumbs and farthings fallen from a purse — the devil alone knew how many there were or where they hid. Cats and foxes by night, rats and crows by day. Hunters and hunted, carrion eaters, killers, the weak and the sick and the old. Christopher hastened back to Ludgate Hill and closed the door with a grunt of relief.

Berwick would watch Wetherby. Sessetti in Paris was gathering what intelligence he could. Ell and Isaac and others in London were watching and listening. Yet, somewhere, Leicester's vipers lurked unseen. He would have to pay another visit to Mr Kaye at Stationers' Hall.

An hour later, the warden, robed as ever in velvet and silk, bustled into the Stationers' grand reception room, scowling and red-faced. 'Dr Radcliff, I trust you will be brief. Our election has given rise to difficulties which it is my duty to resolve.' His bow was cursory. 'You do not call to ask about Nicholas Houseman again, I hope? My patience on that subject is exhausted.'

'I do, Mr Kaye, but I shall be brief. I believe that Houseman and his wife have been abducted. Do you know of anyone who bears him a grudge or has some reason to dispose of him?'

Kaye's eyebrows shot up. 'Really, doctor, and what, pray, would cause you to believe that?'

'If Nicholas had needed to leave London, he would have found a way to return my money to me. He is an honest man.'

Kaye bridled. 'As are all members of our company. But accidents and unforeseen events happen. Houseman would not be the first respectable man of business in London to disappear.'

'So you know of no one who might have wished Nicholas ill?'

'No, doctor, I do not. And now I must ask you to leave. I am entirely occupied with my work.'

'Thank you, Mr Kaye. I am grateful,' replied Christopher, relieved that at least Kaye had been so preoccupied with his election that he had not complained about John Berwick's visit to the Hall. A self-important, corpulent oaf of a man, probably nothing like as busy or competent as he would have one believe.

Since the attack near St Martin's church, Christopher had taken particular care to avoid dark doorways and alleys. He had been fortunate not to be more seriously wounded and might not be so fortunate next time. Keeping to the middle of the street, he walked briskly back down Ludgate Hill. As he reached the house, from somewhere along Fleet Street came the sounds of voices raised in anger. He passed the house and carried on towards the shouting.

On the corner of Whitefriars, a dozen figures had gathered to watch a fight. A young woman was hammering on the back of a smaller one who had turned away to protect herself, and shrieking that she was a papist witch. The smaller woman, older and frailer than her attacker, turned and lashed out with an arm. The younger woman ducked under the blow and reached for her face. The older screamed in pain and covered the bloody mess of an eye with her hand. Her attacker jammed the heel of her other hand into her nose and bellowed in triumph when she fell bleeding to the ground and curled up like a babe. The watchers stamped their feet and yelled their approval.

Christopher pushed through the throng and took hold of the younger woman's elbows from behind as she aimed a kick at her opponent's stomach. The crowd yelled at him to let her go but he held her fast. 'Hold, goodwife,' he shouted. 'The woman is down. If you kill her you will hang at Tyburn.'

She struggled in vain to free herself from Christopher's grip. 'Take your stinking hands off me,' she screeched. 'This is not your concern.'

Christopher ignored the shoves in his back. 'It is my concern,' he hissed into her ear. 'I am a doctor of law and you are causing an affray. I am saving you from the rope.'

'Pox doctor for all I care. Let me free. It's the hag should hang.' The crowd bellowed their agreement and for a moment Christopher thought he too would be attacked.

He was about to let her go when a woman in a long grey cloak stepped forward. He had not noticed her until then. Away from the stew, Ell never dressed as a whore. 'Best unhand her, Dr Rad,' she said quietly. 'This lot's in the mood to murder.' She turned to the crowd and spoke in a clear, firm voice. 'Enough. The fight is over. Take her home, Jeb.'

Christopher let the woman go. A man took her arm and dragged her away. The crowd dispersed, leaving the stricken old woman lying on the cobbles.

'Thank you, Ell. But what are you doing here?' he asked.

'Saving you from a beating, doctor. Why did you stick your nose in? You could have been hurt.'

Christopher laughed. He was close to a foot taller than Ell and probably twice as strong, but she was the one who had saved him, or so she said. 'What about the old woman?'

'Leave her be. A drink or two should see her right.'

Christopher doubted that any amount of drink would mend her eye. 'What had she done?'

'She has cats. They say she's a witch. Doll's baby died. She thinks it was the witch's doing.'

'And was it?'

'Who knows? Could have been.'

Christopher looked about, saw they were unobserved, took her arm and walked back to Ludgate Hill. 'Any word of House-man?'

'Nothing, doctor.'

'Keep trying, Ell. And I want the man who killed Sal. The Scotchman.'

'Grace says he was Irish. Don't know the difference, myself. Murdering bag of shit. I'll tell you if I see him.'

They had reached Ludgate. 'Have a care, Ell.'

'And you, Dr Rad. And stay out of fights that isn't yours. I might not be there next time.'

Rose was in the kitchen. 'Mr Berwick called, doctor,' she told him. 'Said you were to go to the palace at once.'

'Did he say why?'

'He didn't, doctor. Just said you must make haste.'

'God's teeth. This way and that. What now?'

When Christopher arrived, Berwick was with Leicester. They stood at a window, looking out at the palace garden. Both turned sharply when he was shown in. 'Where in God's name have you been, doctor?' demanded the earl. 'Once again you keep us waiting.'

Christopher started. The abruptness was unusual. 'I came as soon as I received your order, my lord. The streets are crowded.'

Leicester stood with his back to the window, fists clenched and head thrust forward. 'Crowded or not, Dr Radcliff, we have been waiting for more than an hour, have we not, Berwick?'

'We have, my lord,' replied Berwick with a sympathetic glance at Christopher. 'But I daresay Dr Radcliff hurried here as best he could.'

Leicester grunted. 'Be that as it may, you are needed here, doctor, not chasing around London looking for your lost bookseller.'

Christopher could not recall ever seeing him in such an ill temper. 'My lord, I—'

Leicester raised a hand. 'Spare me the excuses. We have more important matters before us. News has arrived from Sheffield that an attempt to free Mary Stuart has been prevented. A small force gained entry to the castle and attacked her guards. Fortunately the force was inadequate and was easily overcome. The leader of the rebels was injured and is being brought to London for interrogation.'

'Is the man's identity known?' asked Christopher.

'It is suspected that he is an Irishman, Patrick Wolf, whose family were properly deprived of their lands after the last uprising in Dublin. A vicious, dangerous man who bears a grudge. He has been fortunate so far to have escaped the gallows.'

'And there is more,' added Berwick. 'Sir Francis Walsingham has written again. The duc de Guise has been moving his forces north. It is possible that he intends to join the Spanish for an attempt on the south coast. Messages have been going back and forth between Guise and the Duke of Alba in Brussels. Some have been intercepted and decrypted. The Privy Council has been informed and Her Majesty has agreed to our defences being further strengthened. Unfortunately we do not know exactly where an invasion force might land—'

Leicester interrupted. 'When word gets out there will be greater risk of panic and anarchy on the streets. French agents will spread rumours. Agitators will stoke the flames. We must be doubly vigilant.' He coughed. 'At such a time Her Majesty believes that she must be seen by her people. She will ride in Richmond Park this afternoon and attend the bear-baiting at Paris Garden in Southwark tomorrow. Arrangements for her safety are being made and I shall accompany her.'

An attempt on Sheffield Castle and French forces gathering in the north. *Incendium?* And the ingratiating Berwick had known about both before Christopher had. 'How may I best serve?' he asked.

'You will mingle with the crowd in the bear garden. Observe faces and listen for words of disloyalty.'

Christopher disliked bear-baiting as much as the queen enjoyed it. He kept his face impassive. 'As you wish, my lord.'

Leicester fixed him with his dark eyes. 'Unless you have more pressing affairs to attend to, doctor. Intelligence of a plot, perhaps, and the names of the plotters?'

Christopher felt the blood rise to his face. 'I shall of course do as you order, my lord.'

Leicester scowled. 'Indeed you will. And you will waste no more valuable time on your lost bookseller. England is in danger. The traitor Wolf will be in the Tower within the week. You will assist in his interrogation, where your legal skills may be put to good use.'

'Surely there are others better skilled in such affairs?'

'As I order, doctor,' barked Leicester. 'In the interests of the state, the Privy Council has approved the use of harsh methods, but you will not be expected to turn the screws yourself. The man Wolf must be made to talk. If his futile attempt at Sheffield was part of some larger plan, we must know, and without delay. That is why force will be used if necessary. Is that clear, doctor?'

'It is.'

'He must speak, doctor. With or without the rack, find out what he knows. Do not fail me.' The black eyes burned. 'Mr Berwick will escort you out.'

Together they left the apartment and walked to the gate. 'When did the news from Sheffield arrive, Mr Berwick?' asked Christopher.

'Very early this morning, doctor.' He hesitated. 'I am sorry that the earl was in such ill humour. The progress, the queen's health, and now this. It is not surprising.'

'Did you suggest that I attend the bear-baiting?'

'I did not, doctor.' Berwick sounded aggrieved. 'Nor can I see any purpose in your doing so. The queen is pressing for an end to talk of another plot. She has even spoken of bringing Walsingham home from Paris. The earl is a man who is content only when he feels in control of events. When he feels otherwise he can be irrational, even vindictive.'

'No doubt you will skilfully guide him to recover a more even balance.' Berwick inclined his head in acknowledgement. 'Has Signor Sessetti sent any further word from Paris?'

'Nothing, doctor. I fear we must work alone.'

Christopher almost forgot. 'Oh, and I thank you for taking the trouble to visit my house while I was in France.' He looked for a reaction. There was none. 'Good day, Mr Berwick.'

Obsequious little toad. Always at Leicester's side, never saying the wrong thing, and now privy to intelligence before him. It was time the fellow slipped on a pile of horse dung and fell flat on his smug face.

CHAPTER 23

The Paris Garden had been built on the south side of the Thames, almost directly across from Temple Bar. Christopher clambered out of the wherry that had taken him over the river and joined the boisterous crowd making its way towards it.

Nothing was more popular in London than the bear-baiting and nothing less than Spaniards attacking Whitehall Palace would keep them from it. The queen loved it, her subjects loved it. At least, most of them. The Puritans spoke against it and Christopher hated it. As a child he had witnessed a baiting in a field outside Wisbech and had never attended one again. He saw no more justification for the cruel, purposeless death of an animal than that of a human. He had once said as much to Leicester. Had he remembered?

Outside the garden, a huge man played the bagpipes while his very small companion pulled faces, danced, pranced and collected coins. The small man had quite the ugliest face Christopher had ever seen. His nose was flat and his eyes unevenly set. Tufts of hair grew from every part of him except his head, which was large and round and almost bald. When he grinned, which he did often, he showed only a single tooth. His appearance was so odd that people stood and stared at him, which was exactly his purpose. His cap was full of coins.

Not far away a lutist had given up his struggle to be heard and was berating the crowd for their lack of appreciation. Another man, dressed in bishop's robes, was keeping them amused by baiting a monkey held on a chain. Every time he offered the creature food it would dart forward only to have the morsel lifted out of its reach. The more it howled the more the crowd laughed.

Christopher dragged himself away and into the garden. It was overflowing. Every one of the tiers built around the pit was full, almost every inch of space, other than that set aside for the queen's party, taken. There might be as many as a thousand people come for the entertainment. Lawyers and merchants, artisans and shop-keepers, soldiers and landowners — it was a sport for all and a good place for the queen to be seen. Word would quickly spread that she was in sound health and unafraid of those who would attack her realm and be rid of her.

Christopher squeezed into a seat on the highest tier, from which he had a good view of the pit and the circle of spectators around it. Awaiting the arrival of the queen, the audience were intent upon placing their wagers. It was said that more money passed from hand to hand in Paris Garden in a single afternoon of sport than at Smithfield Market in a week.

The bear, muzzled and hobbled, was led in by its keepers and chained to a post in the middle of the pit. One of the keepers pulled off the muzzle and stepped nimbly out of range of the animal's teeth. It reared on to its hind legs and clawed at the air, bellowing its fury and delighting the crowd. It was a miserable creature, its fur torn off in great clumps and its ribs clearly visible. It had been starved to increase its anger. The crowd cheered. Christopher wondered if he could slip away before the dogs were brought in.

The queen's entourage had yet to appear. In the faces around him he saw only lust and excitement. Did Leicester really suppose that a traitor would choose this place to show himself?

The space reserved for the queen was still empty when the dogs were brought in to be presented to the crowd. There were six — all terriers, snapping and snarling and straining to be free of the double chains held by two big men with ballows stuck into their belts. When the dogs saw the bear, it took strong men to hold them back. The dogs barked and snarled, the bear rose to its full height and bellowed, the crowd roared with delight.

To Christopher, as to the Puritans, it was neither entertainment nor butchery — there was nothing fit to eat when it was over. He could jab a sharp pitchfork into the thigh of a French farmer or his dagger into the eye of an attacker but he could not comfortably watch the unnecessary infliction of pain — even on an animal.

One dog, the biggest of them, was allowed close enough to the bear to snap at its legs. Blood flowed and the bear shrieked in pain. The dog jumped forward and sank its fangs into a flank. The bear shook it off and raked its claws down the dog's back. The dog screamed and backed away. It would be put to the bear again when the wretched beast had been weakened by the other dogs.

Christopher's stomach heaved. He saw women being hacked to shreds in front of their children and babes roasting in flames. He closed his eyes and pressed his fingers over them, trying to banish the fearful images. He sat very still, ignoring as best he could the cries of enjoyment from the crowd, and filled his lungs with each breath, until he was calm enough to stand. Then he slipped unsteadily out, head bowed and a hand to his face. Leicester or not, queen or not, he could stand this no longer.

Outside the pit, he hurried away from the clamour, intending to catch a wherry back across the river to Blackfriars stairs. The piper and his odd little friend had gone, so had the lutist and the bishop. They could not hope to gain much attention from a crowd sated with blood and anxious to get to the nearest tavern. If Leicester found out that Christopher had left early he would be displeased. More than displeased. Angry that his instructions had been disobeyed. Nothing made him angrier. Christopher quickened his pace.

'Give them bread and circuses, eh, Dr Radcliff?' asked a voice behind him. 'Juvenal, was it not?'

Christopher turned sharply. 'Mr Berwick, I had not thought to see you here. You too appear to be leaving.'

'I saw you do so, doctor, and followed you out. I understand that the queen has changed her mind and will not be coming. Such a disappointment. The people would have wished to see her.'

'I felt unwell. The heat, I think, and the noise.' The words came out in a rush. 'Do you know why Her Majesty has not come?'

'I do not. Perhaps she is unwell again. She so enjoys the bear-baiting. The noise does not appear to trouble her. I do not think she would have missed it otherwise.'

'We must pray for Her Majesty's return to good health.'

'Indeed we must.' Berwick paused. 'I had hoped to speak with you in confidence, doctor, and here is an opportunity. Shall we walk together to the stairs?'

'If you wish, Mr Berwick. It will be more agreeable than watching beasts rip each other to shreds. Or do you enjoy the spectacle?'

'I am indifferent to it.' Berwick spoke quietly, as if he might be overheard. 'Have you at last learned anything about your missing stationer?' he asked as they walked.

'I have not, although I continue to try. Is that what you wished to speak about?'

'Not really, doctor. It is Roland Wetherby about whom I would speak. As you know, I have had him watched. He was seen visiting a certain house at Woolchurch.'

'What manner of house? A stew? There are many in that ward.'

'A stew for gentlemen. No women would be found there. I am unsure what steps to take. Should I inform the earl? It is not the act itself but the foul and dangerous places in which he chooses to practise it. Monsieur Deschamps is one thing; this is quite another. I would be grateful for your counsel, doctor.'

Berwick was up to his ingratiating tricks again. 'Is there any evidence of the man being a traitor? Your suspicions were the reason the earl instructed you to watch him, were they not?'

'They were, and they are the stronger for knowing the company he keeps.'

They had almost reached the stairs before Christopher spoke. 'My counsel is to say nothing and keep watching, Mr Berwick.' Damned if he was going to help the man on his way. He must make up his own mind.

'Wise counsel, doctor, and I shall take it. In the meantime we must hope that Roland Wetherby does not himself come to harm. Those places are known to be the haunts of felons of every kind.'

'Do not fear, Mr Berwick. Bide your time and keep a close eye on Wetherby.'

'I am obliged, doctor. Now I must return to the entertainment. Rest assured that the earl will not hear from me about your indisposition in the bear garden.'

'Then I too am obliged, Mr Berwick. Good day.'

Christopher stepped into a waiting wherry and ordered the boatman to take him to Blackfriars stairs. Berwick had known he would be in Paris Garden. Surely he knew what he should do about Wetherby without asking Christopher's advice. It had simply been an attempt at flattery. The young man's ambition was his weakness. It might render his judgement flawed and one day present his rivals with the means to undermine him.

Katherine was waiting for him at Ludgate Hill. 'Where have you been?' she asked. 'I have been concerned.'

'The earl sent me to the bear-baiting in Southwark. I left early.'

Katherine embraced him. 'You are pale and shaking. Sit and I will fetch you wine.'

She returned from the kitchen with a beaker in each hand and held one out to Christopher. 'It is your strong Rhenish. You look as if you need it.' She sat opposite him and took a sip. 'Was the bear-baiting as foul as ever?' Katherine, too, hated the sport. 'In this one matter, I am a Puritan at heart. It is barbaric.'

'It is. And after Paris . . .' The words trailed off and he took a little wine.

Katherine leaned forward. 'Would it help to speak of it?'

Christopher put down his beaker and reached for her hand. 'I cannot, my dear. Perhaps when time has passed, but not yet. I could not bear it.' He took another mouthful of wine and changed the subject. 'John Berwick was there. He asked my advice about Roland Wetherby.'

'What about Wetherby?'

'He visits stews — male stews — and because of it Berwick thinks he is a danger. I told him to watch the man and wait for evidence of wrongdoing. And there has been an attempt to free Mary

Stuart. I am to observe the interrogation of a captured rebel in the Tower.'

Katherine crossed herself. 'The wretch will suffer greatly, may God have mercy upon him. And so, I fear, will you. Damn Leicester for forcing you to do this. It is cruel of him.'

'He does not know exactly what I saw in Paris, nor can he see the horrors that fill my mind.' He tried to smile. 'Perhaps the interrogation will be swift and easy.'

Katherine laughed lightly. 'Perhaps. But, Christopher, let me help you. Is there not something I can do to share your burden?'

Katherine would not rest until he had given her a task. 'By chance, there is. There is a Warden of the Stationers' Company, one James Kaye, whom I have mentioned to you. Berwick found nothing suspicious about him but I have doubts. He has been too ready to accept my explanation for wanting to find Nicholas Houseman and less than curious about my position. Almost as if he knows who I am without having to ask. I had intended to observe his movements myself, but now that I am to attend the interrogation, you would assist greatly by doing so in my stead.'

Katherine clapped her hands. 'Excellent. It is a start. The man does not know me and I am a good deal less conspicuous than you. What shall I be watching for?'

'Where he goes, to whom he speaks; if you are able, what he says. But take care. He will be alert to danger.'

'How shall I know him?'

'We will wait near Stationers' Hall and I will point him out when he appears.'

'Today?'

'If you wish.'

Katherine reached over and kissed him on the lips. 'Thank you,

Christopher. I grieve for your distress and pray it will soon pass. You must tell me if there is more I can do.'

They stood in the shadows outside St Paul's church. As afternoon turned to evening, James Kaye left the Hall. He wore a soft cap the colour of a plum and a long black cloak. Christopher pointed him out. 'That is Kaye,' he whispered to Katherine. 'Mark him well and do not approach too close unless there is good reason. Observe where he goes when he leaves the Hall and, if you can, find out where he lives.'

'I will change my appearance each day,' said Katherine, 'and keep well hidden.'

'Good. Now let us take supper together. Your work will start tomorrow.'

CHAPTER 24

The earl's order arrived the morning after next. The traitor Wolf was in the Tower where his interrogator awaited Christopher's arrival. Within a few minutes he had locked the house, walked to Blackfriars and taken a wherry to the Tower steps, glad that he wore an extra undershirt against the early autumn chill.

The earl had promised that he would not have to turn the screws with his own hand. He would, however, be in a prison for the first time since he had left Norwich and could not be sure how he would cope. Any sign of weakness would surely reach Leicester's ears.

With a passing thought for the Duke of Norfolk, he walked up the hill, entered by the Postern Gate and was escorted by a guard to the White Tower. There he was led down a flight of stone steps to the basement. Wall lanterns lit the gloom but could not dispel the chill. He shivered and pulled his gown more tightly around his shoulders. The guard produced a ring of keys from which he selected one, opened the middle of three oak doors facing them and ushered Christopher in.

Inside, there were fewer lanterns but evil-smelling tallow candles had been set on a low table at one end of the chamber. A fire had been lit, over which hung a simmering cauldron. A pail and a strange instrument with a long spout and wooden handle attached to a circular container stood beside the fire. Christopher blinked his eyes to accustom them to the gloom and tried not to gag on the foetid air. There were three men there — a small, sharp-faced man in a lawyer's gown, whom he took to be the interrogator, a much taller, broader man in a leather apron and leather breeches, and the prisoner, who was chained by his ankles and left wrist to an iron chair, itself fixed to the stone floor. His right arm was twisted at the elbow, so that it stuck out away from his body.

The smaller man spoke first. 'Dr Radcliff?' Christopher nodded. 'We await you, sir. This man is believed to be one Patrick Wolf. He was taken during an ill-advised attempt to secure the release of Mary Stuart from Sheffield Castle. Wolf and his family are known to us and we would be justified in hanging him without further ado. However, we believe him to be involved in a wider and even more heinous conspiracy to assassinate our queen. I shall be encouraging him to name his fellow conspirators to save himself a traitor's death.' He glanced at Wolf, who sat head down and apparently uninterested. 'Drawing and quartering is the most extreme punishment available to us. If this man does not cooperate, he will suffer it.' The interrogator had not bothered to give his name or that of his colleague.

Christopher looked at Wolf. Even sitting, he was a large man, broad in the shoulder and well muscled. His hair, once red, now streaked with grey, hung in twisted knots to his shoulders. His face was caked in dirt and scarred from temple to chin. As if sensing Christopher's eyes on him, he raised his head and looked up. He did not have to speak. The hatred in his eyes cut through the gloom. There was no sign of fear. Just deep, all-consuming loathing. Christopher wiped sweat from his hands and with difficulty resisted the urge to run from this hellish place. He had no experience of interrogation but did not think that this man would be easy to encourage. He found a stool in the corner and sat down to watch and listen.

The interrogator did not hurry. He cleared his throat and stretched his hands to crack the knuckles. Only after a long pause did he begin. No attorney in the Court of Requests could have spoken more clearly or asked more penetrating questions. He asked about Wolf's family, where he had been born, his age, his opinions, his beliefs, his hopes. His voice was never raised and he never faltered in his questioning. He did not mention Mary Stuart or Sheffield Castle again. It was almost as if he were simply being polite to a new acquaintance. Twice he told the larger man to give the prisoner water. Twice the proffered cup was ignored.

After an hour of persistent, unrelenting interrogation, the prisoner had spoken not a word. The interrogator rose and signalled Christopher to follow him out of the chamber. They climbed the stairs and entered a small parlour, where wine and cakes had been set on a table. The interrogator helped himself. 'I did not mention my name, doctor, because I do not care for it to be widely known,' he said after a sip of wine. 'If this man goes to the gallows, as I am sure he will, I would prefer his family not to have any inkling of who sent him there. I am Fulke Griffyn, in the service of Her Majesty. My assistant is Pygot.'

Christopher bowed his head. 'Mr Griffyn. I much admired your skill, yet the prisoner has not spoken.'

'With his tongue he has not spoken but with his eyes he has. He is Patrick Wolf, he is an enemy of England, and he will die for his beliefs. I am confident that we shall learn more in due course.'

'Do you anticipate the use of torture, Mr Griffyn?'

'Almost certainly, doctor. However, I shall delay that for as long as I can. The man is injured and will not long tolerate the rack. If he dies before we have extracted from him what he knows, we shall have failed. Now, let us return to our work.' Christopher, only a little less disquieted for the food and wine, followed him back into the interrogation cell.

Wolf still sat head down in the iron chair. Pygot stood behind him. Griffyn strode up to the prisoner and spoke briskly. His tone had changed. Now the menace was unmistakable. 'Why were you at Sheffield Castle, Wolf?' he demanded. 'What was your purpose in a futile attempt to release the Scotch queen from her just imprisonment? You were not acting alone. With whom did you conspire to commit this treachery? I want names or you will suffer.'

When Wolf did not reply, Griffyn tried again. 'We know there is a plot against the Queen of England. We know that you were involved in it. We know that it is connected to the recent ungodly bloodshed in France. There is nothing to be gained by silence. Tell us what we wish to know and save yourself the agonies of hell.' Wolf lifted his head and spat at Griffyn's feet.

'Very well,' said the interrogator, ignoring the spittle on his shoe, 'we shall do it your way.' He turned to Christopher. 'Observe, doctor, that it is the prisoner who has chosen this path, not we who have forced it upon him.' He nodded to Pygot who dipped the pouring device into the cauldron and, with a hiss of steam, filled it with boiling water. He stood beside the prisoner and, on Griffyn's word, dripped the water on to Wolf's hands. Wolf's back arched but he did not speak or cry out. The water was applied to his hands and then to his head. It dribbled down his face causing him to shake his head violently. Pygot glanced at Griffyn, who nodded. He took a thick cloth from around his neck and tied it around Wolf's eyes. He filled the bucket from the cauldron, stood before Wolf and threw the water over him. Steam rose and the skin of his face and arms melted.

And Wolf screamed — a scream that erupted from deep in his chest to explode through his mouth and into the chamber. It went on and on, bouncing off the walls and bludgeoning Christopher's mind. It is not the torture of a helpless animal, he reminded himself, nor is it the senseless massacre of innocent children. It is the necessary extraction of intelligence relating to the safety of our queen and our country, just as disabling that French farmer with a pitchfork was necessary.

'There,' said Griffyn with a tiny smile when at last the scream became a whimper. 'At last the prisoner has spoken. Or at least made a noise.' Wolf's head had slumped forward. Pygot untied the cloth. Griffyn lifted the head by the hair and crouched to put his face very close. He spoke in a whisper. 'Good. You can see well enough. That was but nothing, Wolf. You will speak or you will suffer the rack.'

Griffyn straightened up. 'Come, doctor, let us leave the prisoner to think on what is to come if he continues to obstruct us. We will return after dinner.'

They sat at the table in the parlour, where cold mutton, manchet bread and a large cheese had been laid out for them. Christopher looked at it and doubted if he could keep even a mouthful down. Griffyn helped himself to meat and bread and set about them with relish. 'One becomes accustomed to it, doctor,' he said, wiping his mouth with a linen napkin. 'I much prefer to find out what I am instructed to discover by persuasion rather than by the infliction of pain but sometimes there is no alternative. Wolf is a brave man but a foolish one. I will make a final attempt to persuade him of this and then, I fear, he will be set to the rack.'

Christopher put a morsel of bread into his mouth and chewed

carefully. 'If we could discover some names, Mr Griffyn, that would be sufficient. Others may not be as brave.'

'Few are. Is there a name I might tempt him with?'

Christopher pursed his lips. 'Offer him the names of Roland Wetherby and James Kaye.'

'Roland Wetherby and James Kaye. I will observe his reaction to them.'

In the basement, a rack had been brought in and placed where Wolf could see it. A wooden frame with rollers and ratchets at both ends, it was designed to separate muscle from bone and limbs from bodies. On the frame lay a dead sheep.

'Now, Wolf,' said Griffyn as they entered, 'I will show you how the device works and then we will converse again. Observe carefully. If your eyes should close, we have a way of opening them. I do not advise you to test it.'

The sheep lay belly down, its legs chained to the rollers. Pygot took hold of the handle at one end and began to turn it. Griffyn did the same at the other end. The rollers turned slowly, stretching the animal until a series of noises like corks being pulled from bottles told them that its legs had been dislocated from its body. They continued to turn the handles, tearing the animal's sinews apart, until eventually the limbs were ripped entirely off, leaving the carcass of the animal lying, bloody and dismembered, on the bed of the frame. Christopher swallowed hard and stretched his fingers.

Griffyn left the rack and stood in front of Wolf. 'Exactly the same result is achieved with a man's body, Wolf,' he said. 'It simply takes a little longer. However, you can avoid suffering this fate if you give us the names of your fellow traitors.' His voice rose to a shout. 'Names, Wolf, now!' Wolf's eyes, red and encrusted with filth, glared back at his tormentor. He did not speak. 'Allow me to help you,' went on Griffyn. 'We know that Roland Wetherby is a traitor. What can you tell us of him?' Christopher had recovered his poise and was watching carefully. At the mention of Wetherby, Wolf blinked but his expression did not change. 'And there is another of whom you will be aware. James Kaye.'

Was there a flicker of surprise? 'With your permission, sir,' Christopher said, 'I will put the names to the prisoner again.' Griffyn indicated his consent. 'Roland Wetherby, a young man in Thomas Heneage's service, and James Kaye, a warden of the Stationers' Company. Do you know them?' Wolf's eyes closed and his head dropped to his chest. There had been no more hint of recognition. Christopher tried another path. 'The whore you attacked in the brothel near Cheapside. She is dead.' Wolf did not stir. 'She heard you speak of blood and fire. *Incendium.*' Wolf's shoulders twitched. '*Incendium*, Wolf. The plot has been discovered. The plotters are known to us. Spare yourself more pain. Tell us exactly what has been planned.' There was no response.

'We will leave the prisoner to gather himself for the morning,' said Griffyn. 'I find that the night can be a useful ally. Eleventh-hour changes of heart are quite common.'

'Should we not press ahead?' asked Christopher, once they were outside the chamber. He wanted this over.

Griffyn shook his head. 'No, doctor, the man is too far gone. He will last not a minute on the rack. We will give him food and water so that he recovers a little strength. Thus we will be more likely to break him before he dies.'

Christopher stood outside the Postern Gate, filled his lungs with air and tried to banish the image of the sheep from his mind. His hand, which had scarcely troubled him since his return from Paris, had started to throb. He rubbed the palm. A welcome chill was still in the air. He would walk to Wood Street.

In Bishopsgate he bought a twist of sugared almonds and some marchpane biscuits — Katherine had the sweetest of teeth — and shook the horror of the morning from his head. Had Wolf known the names or had Christopher imagined it? He stepped carefully around a pile of dung and tried a biscuit. It was too sweet for his taste. He threw it down. A child covered only by a piece of sacking skipped forward to pick it up and held out his hand for more. Christopher ignored him. There were hundreds like him in the city. No man could favour them all.

At the house in Wood Street, Katherine took the almonds and the biscuits with a grin. 'You know where my heart lies, Christopher. What is it you seek in return?'

'Your company only, Katherine, and a bottle of your good Spanish wine. That will suffice for now.'

Katherine brought the wine to the parlour and set about the biscuits while he sipped from a glass beaker. 'Your face is strained,' she said. 'Have you been at the palace?'

'I have been at the Tower. It was not a pleasant experience, nor an informative one. All prisons bring Norwich to my mind. The prisoner, Patrick Wolf, told us nothing. Tomorrow he will be put to the rack. I am not looking forward to it.'

'Are you required to be there?'

'Unless Leicester sends for me, I am. And what of Kaye? Have you observed him?'

'I went early to St Paul's and waited until he arrived. I wanted to be certain that I knew his look and demeanour. I shall return later to observe his departure and will follow at a distance.' Katherine rose. 'The wine has not improved your look,

Christopher. You are much distressed. Will you rest here or at Ludgate?'

'I would be a poor bedfellow. I shall return to Ludgate.' He too rose and kissed her lightly. 'Take care. Bring me news when you have it.'

CHAPTER 25

Christopher spent much of the night at his writing table, reading reports and thinking about the ordeal that was to come. He might be able, unnoticed, to close his eyes but he would not be able to close his ears. Tomorrow the streets of Paris would come back to him. But they needed Wolf to speak and to speak quickly. As Griffyn had said, he would not survive the rack for long even though the interrogators would be adept at keeping a man alive on that fearful device. Wolf had not the strength.

When he arrived at the Tower, Griffyn was waiting for him. 'Come, doctor,' the inquisitor greeted him with a pat on the shoulder. 'Let us see how our prisoner fares this morning.' They descended the steps to the basement and found Pygot lighting the fire in the chamber. 'We are ready, Pygot. Fetch Wolf and we will begin,' ordered Griffyn.

Pygot left the chamber and they heard the sound of a key being turned in a lock. It was followed by a foul oath and another yet fouler. Griffyn almost ran out of the chamber. Christopher followed him.

The cell was barely wide enough for a man to lie down, no larger than a closet. Water dripped down the walls to form pools on the stone floor. There was not a stick of furniture. The stench was vile. Wolf lay face up, his arms and legs spread as if he were on the cross. Griffyn stepped forward. The dead man's eyes stared unseeing at the world he had left. The blood on his fleshless face and arms had congealed. His lips were bitten through and twisted in the agony of death. Griffyn turned to Pygot and struck his face with the back of a gloved hand. 'It was your job to keep him alive, man,' he hissed. 'How in the name of God has this happened?'

Pygot thrust forward his chin. 'He was alive when I brought his food, not two hours ago.'

'Did he eat?'

'He did not.'

'You did not admit a visitor?'

'No, sir. You forbad it.'

Griffyn knelt beside the body. 'I see no marks but those inflicted when he was taken and yesterday during our questioning, yet his lips are bitten.' He prised open the mouth. 'And so is his tongue, as if he had suffered a fit. Can you swear that he could not have been poisoned by his own hand or another's, Pygot?'

'I swear it, Mr Griffyn.'

Griffyn stared at him. 'If I find otherwise, your position will be forfeit and you will undergo examination yourself.'

'It cannot have been otherwise, sir. The prisoner has suffered a fit causing his heart to fail. The scalding was more than it could bear.'

'Then why in God's name did you allow it, man?'

'I merely carried out your instructions, Mr Griffyn, as well you know. The doctor will attest to it.' There was fear in Pygot's voice.

'The doctor will attest that I gave no instructions as to the quantity or heat of the water. I depend upon your experience in such matters. The fault was yours, Pygot, and it is you who will pay for it. Come, Dr Radcliff, we have no more business here.' Griffyn swept out of the cell and up the stairs to the parlour. Christopher followed.

'The Earl of Leicester must be told at once,' said Christopher. 'He will not be pleased.'

'I trust you will describe events exactly as they happened, doctor. The fool Pygot should have known better than to use water so hot and in such an amount.' Griffyn reached into a purse hanging at his waist. 'I would be pleased to offer a small sum in return for an accurate account.'

Christopher shook his head. 'There is no need, Mr Griffyn. My account will be accurate. I will go directly to Whitehall to give it. Good day.'

For all his airs, Griffyn had proved incompetent. His paymaster would certainly not be pleased. Better to deliver the news without delay.

The earl was with the queen. When Christopher told the guard that his business was urgent, he was shown into the antechamber and asked to wait. This time the room did not remind him of waiting for his trial in Norwich. His mind was too full of what he had witnessed at the Tower for that. He found that he could not sit but paced up and down, stretching his fingers, half glad that he did not have to see Wolf on the rack, half dreading being the one to give Leicester the news.

It was a long wait — an hour or more — before Leicester appeared. 'Dr Radcliff, I have been attending Her Majesty, who insists that we name the traitors behind the attack on Sheffield Castle without delay. You bring good news, I hope.'

'Alas, my lord, I do not. The traitor Wolf is dead. We learned nothing from him.'

Leicester slumped on to a chair. 'God in heaven. The queen unwell but insisting on showing herself to her people and now you tell me our chance of at last discovering something certain has gone. How did it happen?'

'The interrogation was too severe. His heart was not strong enough.'

Leicester swore and thumped his fist on the arm of the chair. 'Griffyn. It is not the first time. Did we learn nothing at all?'

'Only that his refusal to speak even under extreme pressure might be taken as evidence of his guilt. A lesser man would have offered names in return for a swift end.'

'Was the rack used?'

Christopher shook his head. 'No, my lord, except to show the prisoner what it can do.'

'Ah, yes. One of Griffyn's tricks. It often works. Sheep or goat?'

'A sheep.'

'Damn the man. So we know no more than we did, not even if the attempt to release the Queen of Scots formed part of a larger plot or not.'

'If it was, my lord, its failure will have been a blow to the plotters. The flames might have been extinguished.'

'The queen doubts that such a plot exists and I have little with which to convince her. What do we have? A two-barrelled pistol, of which it is said there is a pair, a Scotsman who has disappeared in France, and your suspicions of the stationers.'

'And the disappearance of Nicholas Houseman, my lord. And the murder of Admiral Coligny and the massacre in France, and John

Berwick's suspicions of Roland Wetherby and the recent attempt to free Mary Stuart.'

'Yes, yes. We have been over this before. My instincts were that there was more than the usual rumour and conjecture about it all. Now, well, surely we would have discovered more by now if this plot did exist.'

'Had Wolf not died, my lord, we would have discovered more. The threat cannot be dismissed.'

'If there is a threat. Her Majesty is determined to ride tomorrow. Unless I can show her proof that her life is in danger, I shall not be able to dissuade her. Even then, I daresay she would call me a feeble old woman.' He sighed. 'Compared to her, most of us are. Go now, doctor, and discover the truth however you must.'

Christopher left the palace and walked briskly back along Fleet Street. 'However you must' — but how must he? Interrogate Wetherby, arrest Kaye — for what and on what evidence? He swept past an urchin demanding a penny, pushed his way through the stalls on the corner of Ludgate Hill and almost ran up to the house. He fumbled for his key, threw open the door and slammed it closed behind him.

Rose came out of the kitchen and handed him a small scrap of rough paper of the sort used by vendors to wrap their goods. 'It was pushed under the door, doctor,' she said. 'I nearly swept it up. There are marks on it. Is it important?'

Christopher held the paper up to the light. A single word had been scratched on it in the hand of a child. *Ell.* 'It might be, Rose. Thank you.'

'Waiting for you, she is,' gasped Grace, letting Christopher into the stew. 'You've cost me a few shillings and I'll want it made up. Wouldn't take no other gentlemen in case you came. A pound and you can go up.' Christopher was in no mood to haggle. He handed over a pound.

This time Ell was fully clothed and sitting on the side of the bed. 'You got the message then, doctor. How were my letters?'

'Good enough, Ell. Do you have something?'

'It might be something, doctor, or it might be nothing. I was in the Boar in Bishopsgate last night. Don't often go there, only when I'm not working. Busy it was but just one of the drinkers seemed to be paying for the ale. Paying and paying he was as if he was made of silver shillings. He was a foul-mouthed beggar but if he had money to spend I thought he might be a good customer and Grace none the wiser, so I asked him if he'd like a lady's company. He'd drunk six tankards of ale since I'd been there and I reckoned he wouldn't be upright for much longer. He asked how much. I told him a lady's company would cost him a pound. He fished into a purse and handed me the coins. "There you are, my lovely," he said. "There's another one if you serve me well."

'His words were coming out like eels — slipping around so you couldn't tell one from another. Just to keep him sweet, I told him he must be good at his work and asked him what it was. He didn't exactly say but he did say he'd had a job clearing out a house at Cripplegate and had just been paid well for it. Then he laughed. "The owners have no more need of it." It was the way he said it that pulled me up, doctor. I would have pressed him but he knew he'd said too much. He hissed at me to keep my mouth shut or he'd slice out my tongue.'

'What did you do, Ell?' asked Christopher, reluctant to allow his spirits to rise.

'I buggered off sharp when his back was turned, with a pound in my hand, and left the pig to his ale.'

'He didn't mention a name?'

'Not that I heard. But he did mention Cripplegate. I thought you should know.'

Cripplegate. 'You were right, Ell. Would you know his face?'

''Course I would.'

'Tonight, Ell. The Boar. Be there to point him out, please.'

'I will, doctor, if he's there. Be a treat to see him taken away. Nasty beggar he was.' Ell laughed. 'A mercy I got his money without having to do no work for it.'

It took four pounds to persuade two dockers to act as constables. They were to be in the Boar by six and to watch for Christopher's signal. He told them that the man they sought was a thief and a murderer and the Earl of Leicester wanted him in Newgate that day.

The tavern was quiet when Christopher arrived — a handful of drinkers, his two constables sitting quietly in a corner, a serving girl and the landlord. The coarse smell of tobacco smoke hovered in the air. There was no sign of Ell. He bought a blackjack of ale and found a stool near the door.

The tavern slowly filled up until all the tables were occupied. The serving girl went from one to another sloshing ale into wooden tankards and collecting the price from her customers. For an hour Christopher sat patiently, keeping an eye on his two constables in case they slipped off and listening for any tell-tale word from the drinkers. There was none. He was beginning to fear that neither Ell nor the man they sought would arrive when a weaselly black-haired fellow strode in and demanded ale. He took a blackjack from the serving girl and looked around the room. He spoke loudly enough for every man in the room to hear. 'There was a whore yesterday, took my money and didn't so much as look at my prick.'

When a voice asked if the wench would have been able to see it if she had looked, the black-haired man spat on the boards of the floor. 'If I see the bitch, I'll cut her so she'll not whore again.'

Here was the man he wanted. Christopher rose from his stool. He glanced around. Ell had come quietly in. 'That's him,' she shouted, pointing a finger at the fellow. 'He's the thief who knocked me down and stole my purse. Should be in Newgate, the thieving pig.'

Christopher signalled with his hand to the constables, who stepped forward and grabbed the man's arms before he could react. 'The woman tells the truth,' he said. 'I saw this man attack her. I am an officer of the law and will see he is taken to Newgate.' He used his height to advantage, standing as tall as he could and throwing his voice across the room. There was no protest except from the accused man who spluttered that Christopher was lying and the wench was the thief. The constables dragged him out, leaving the drinkers to their ale. Christopher and Ell followed.

'Easy enough, Dr Rad,' said Ell as they marched the man along Bishopsgate. 'This is him.'

'Bitch,' snarled the prisoner, held fast by either arm. 'What is this trick? The woman's a foul whore.' He struggled in vain to free an arm. 'I'll get the truth from her.'

'You will find out soon enough,' replied Christopher from behind. 'Hold your tongue and save your breath for when you need it. You have questions to answer.'

'What questions?'

Christopher stepped around a constable and slapped the man hard. 'Hold your tongue or you'll lose it.'

'Don't think you'll need me any more, doctor, will you?' asked Ell. 'I'll be back to work now.'

'Thank you, Ell. You've done good service.'

'Hope he's the man you want, doctor.'

They marched the man up to Moorgate and along the old wall to Cripplegate, ignoring the stares of passers-by and his demands to be set free. Christopher pointed at the house beside the cobbler's shop. 'Is this the house you stole from?' he asked.

'That whore has been talking. I warned her. I'll cut off her tits and feed them to the dogs.'

Christopher felt his temper rise. He grabbed the man by the hair and pulled his head backwards. 'And I am warning you, churl. Answer my questions or you'll feel the rack. Is it the house?'

'How should I know? It was dark.'

'It's dark now. Is it the house?'

'Might be.'

'What is your name?'

'Elias Smith. And who are you to be asking questions?'

'Who told you to come here, Smith?' Smith shrugged. Christopher pulled the poniard from his belt and held the point to Smith's eye. 'Who?'

'Didn't know his name.' The bravado had gone and Smith's voice cracked. Christopher lowered the dagger.

'How many of you were there?'

'Two. The other's gone.'

'Gone where?'

'Don't know. Hell, for all I care.'

'What was his name?'

'He didn't give it.'

'Did you kill Nicholas Houseman and his wife?'

'No, no. It was him. I tried to stop him. He wouldn't have it. He cut their throats. It wasn't me.'

'Why did they die?' Christopher raised the dagger again and touched the point to an eyelid.

'It was a word. We had to find out if he knew about it.'

'Was the word *Incendium*?'

'A word like it.'

'Did Houseman know about it?'

'I don't think so.'

'Yet you killed him and his wife.'

'It wasn't me. He killed them. I did only what he said.'

'Who was he working for?'

'How should I know?'

Christopher withdrew the poniard. 'We'll see if a stay in Newgate improves your memory.'

They marched him to the prison, sullen and protesting. Outside the walls, queer-birds and beggars watched as the four figures passed in the gloom but said nothing. It was a common enough sight.

At the gate, Christopher gave his name to a guard and told him he was acting on the orders of the Earl of Leicester. The guard summoned two gaolers to take the prisoner in charge. When he was secure, Christopher ordered them to take the prisoner's money and to give him no food or ale.

He gave the dockers another pound each. 'Is he a murderer?' asked one.

'He is,' replied Christopher. 'And London is a safer place for his being in there.' From inside the walls came a long, despairing cry, followed by voices raised in anger and screams of agony. There were no prisoners in Newgate more vicious than their gaolers, and Christopher had told the guard that Smith had murdered two innocent people and had been arrested on the orders of the Earl of Leicester.

CHAPTER 26

Christopher was back at Newgate early the next morning. He was admitted by the guards and escorted to a narrow flight of stone steps that led down to the cavern known as Limbo — a black, foetid, verminous hole under the prison gate. The stench of filth and corruption from an open sewer that ran through it and the anguished wailing of men and women tight-packed into the cells rose from below as if to warn a visitor that he was about to enter hell.

A gaoler, grown fat on the rich pickings to be had from the families of prisoners with the means to pay for food, led Christopher by the meagre light of a cheap rush torch down the steps and along a dark passage, lined on either side by barred cells from which arms reached out and despairing voices pleaded for food or water. If a prisoner in Newgate had not the money to pay, he would go hungry and his stay would be brief. Christopher put the wretches from his mind.

He had ordered Smith to be kept down there for the night and not to be given food. In the final cell, furthest from the steps and from the tiny glimmer of light that penetrated the blackness, shadowy figures lined the walls and lay on the floor, legs and arms entangled.

The fat gaoler pointed to Smith. He sat with his back to the wall, knees drawn up to his chin, in a pool of blood and piss, his ankles chained to a ring set into the stone floor. 'There he is, sir,' said the gaoler. 'Shall I bring him up or will you speak to him here?'

Christopher called through the bars, 'Are you ready to speak, Smith, or will it be another day and a night down here?'

Smith raised his head. His eyes were red and his face streaked with filth. 'I will tell you what I can.' His voice was a hoarse whisper. A single night in Limbo had much diminished the man.

'Very well, gaoler,' ordered Christopher, 'bring him up and give him bread and a beaker of ale.' He left the gaoler to carry out his instructions and found his way back along the passage and up the steps. Above ground, he took a deep breath and shook his head clear of the foul air below.

They sat on stools in the main yard of the prison while Christopher watched Smith eat and drink. A taste of food and ale and cleaner air to breathe might persuade the man to avoid returning to Limbo.

When Smith had finished, Christopher began. 'Why did you kill Nicholas Houseman and his wife?'

'I did not. It was the other.'

'The man whose name you say you do not know.' Smith nodded. 'Yet you were his accomplice.'

'I did only what I was told.'

'You have said this before. Why was Houseman killed?'

'He knew the word. *Incendium*.'

'What does it mean?'

'I do not know.'

'Who were you working for?'

'He spoke of powerful men, wealthy men who reward loyalty.'

'Did you hear a name? Roland Wetherby, James Kaye?'

Smith shook his head. 'No.'

Christopher summoned the gaoler. 'Take him down again. No food, no ale. I will have him moved to the Tower.'

Smith shrieked, 'I've told you what I know.'

'Do you wish to live?'

'There is nothing else to tell.'

'Where are the bodies?'

'Smithfield. The graveyard of St Bartholomew's Church. Under a yew tree in the north corner.'

'If you are lying, Smith, the rack will soon draw the truth from you. Take him down, gaoler. I will return to make sure you are not treating him too kindly.'

It was not easy to persuade the coroner to provide two men and a handcart nor to persuade the priest to permit them to dig in the graveyard of his church. Both succumbed eventually to the weight of the Earl of Leicester's name.

Christopher stood a little apart and watched the men dig. Once started, it did not take long. Under the yew tree, two bodies had been buried in a shallow trench, barely deep enough to protect them from scavenging animals, but safe from accidental discovery. What better place to bury two bodies than in a graveyard?

When they were exposed, the stench of putrefaction rose in a wave from their grave. Christopher stepped back and held a sleeve to his nose. Both wore the remains of their night clothes, one a man, the other a woman whose nightgown had been cut to reveal her stomach and breasts. Both throats had been cut. Although their flesh had long since begun to weep, their faces were dissolving and insects devoured the seeping fluids, there was no doubt. His friends, Nicholas and

Sarah Houseman, had been murdered and hidden among the bodies in this graveyard. In this at least Elias Smith had told the truth. Christopher would find the other murderer and together they would hang.

The coroner's men, seemingly impervious to the smell, loaded the bodies on to their cart, covered them with old blankets and wheeled them off to the deadhouse. Christopher told them that he would attend later that day to identify the bodies formally. Sad and angry as he was, at least now Nicholas and Sarah could be given proper burial.

He hurried to Wood Street, where they sat, as usual, in Isabel's little parlour. Two glasses of yellow wine stood on the coffer between them. Avoiding mention of Ell, Christopher explained that an agent had reported hearing a drinker in the Boar boasting of emptying a house at Cripplegate and that they had set a trap for the man, who was now in Newgate. The bodies of Nicholas and Sarah had been found and were in the coroner's deadhouse.

Katherine leaned forward and took his hands in hers. 'I am sorry for it. They were your friends. May they rest in peace. I too have news. Last night I followed James Kaye from Stationers' Hall. He wore a long cloak and a cap low over his face. He walked to the churchyard of St Ann's church at Blackfriars. I did not venture into the yard as I knew it to be small and with but one entrance, but waited outside in the street. He was there for perhaps half an hour. It is certain that he was meeting someone. Why else would he go alone to that place?'

'Did you see anyone else?'

'I did not. I should perhaps have stayed longer but I chose to follow Kaye. His house is close by in Blackfriars Lane. If he goes to St Ann's again, I will watch for the one he is meeting.'

'There is a small church in the yard. Queen Mary insisted it be provided when she came to the throne. It is reached by a narrow flight of steps. He could have gone there, although I know not why. I believe it to be no more than a shabby chamber, long disused.'

'I will go there.'

'I am sure that Kaye is not what he appears. He showed little concern for Nicholas Houseman who we now know was cruelly murdered; my questions did not surprise him; he did not press me for my purpose and now you have observed him attending a secret meeting. I am inclined to ask the earl for his permission to arrest the man and put him in Griffyn's hands.'

'Who is Griffyn?'

'Griffyn was the interrogator entrusted with extracting information from the traitor Wolf, who led the attack on Sheffield Castle. Wolf died before he could tell us anything.'

'Then why not ask the earl? Surely the gravity of the threat warrants it.'

'In the Tower there is always a risk of early death. Wolf's fate might also be Kaye's. It would be better by far to discover the identity of the one he was meeting at St Ann's. And I may yet get something more from Smith, although I doubt he is hiding much. The man is too craven to resist.'

'Christopher,' said Katherine, 'have you given consideration to the nature of the word *Incendium*? Why that word, do you suppose?'

'I have. I had thought it to embrace the slaughter in France and the burning of English Protestants as in the time of Queen Mary. Now, however, I fear it might suggest a still greater evil — a conflagration, an immense destruction by fire, a catastrophe in the guise of a sign from God? It preys on my mind.'

'How could such a thing be accomplished? Spanish fire ships on the Thames? An explosion in the crypt of St Paul's? A well-placed spark in Smithfield?' Katherine sounded incredulous.

'Perhaps. The word was not chosen at random. There is meaning in it beyond the French tragedy. Still, our most pressing task is to find the plotters. From them we shall discover the true nature of their scheming and the significance of the word. Find out who Kaye is meeting and I will speak again to Smith. Perhaps also John Berwick has learned more of Wetherby. Now I must go to the coroner to inspect the bodies. He will need confirmation of their identities.'

They rose. Christopher put his arms around Katherine and kissed her on the forehead. 'The earl must not know of it, but I am glad of your help,' he said quietly. 'Thank you.'

The deadhouse was close by the coroner's house and St Bartholomew's church. It was a low, windowless brick building, in which bodies awaiting burial were kept, lit by cheap tallow candles and rush torches on the walls. Christopher was admitted by the keeper of the house and shown to a room in which half a dozen shrouded corpses had been laid out on a long table. One was much smaller than the others. The sweet stench of corruption hung in the air. The coroner, a sharp-faced, mean-mouthed little man, looked up from searching a body for money or items that could be easily sold. Many coroners made a living by such means — 'basket coroners' who stole from the dead and took bribes to give the opinion required. This one was no different and he smelled like a privy.

The two bodies at one end of the table were still covered by the blankets, which the coroner removed. Their faces had been wiped clean of earth and their night clothes, such as they were, had been removed. Both lay, obscenely exposed, their flesh falling away and showing signs of the insects that had infested them. Christopher wasted no time. He barely looked at them. 'They are the bodies of Nicholas Houseman and his wife, Sarah. Was anything found with them or nearby?'

'If it had been, it would have been placed with the bodies, as is proper,' snapped the coroner.

'Then you will doubtless bury them properly. Have you sent for a searcher of the dead?'

The coroner snorted. 'Where is the purpose in that? Searchers cost money and any man can see that the woman suffered a long cut to her chest and both throats were cut. There are no signs of a struggle, no bruising, no broken bones. They were wilfully murdered.' The coroner looked down his long nose. 'Are you able to suggest a murderer or a motive?'

Christopher ignored the question. 'Was the same weapon used in both cases?' he asked.

'It is reasonable to assume so,' replied the coroner, as if the question was an absurd one.

Christopher bent to examine the cuts. To his surprise, he found that, unlike in Paris, here, where he had a task to perform, he could put thoughts of the violence his friends had suffered from his mind.

Both cuts had been cleanly made with a sharp knife or dagger, probably the same one, but there was a difference. The direction of the cuts and the uneven depths of penetration suggested that Sarah had been murdered by a man standing behind her while Nicholas had been facing his murderer. That was consistent with what Smith had told him. Two men, one murder weapon; Sarah cut to make Nicholas speak. The question was, what had Nicholas said?

He walked around the table, holding a corner of his gown to his face and examining the bodies from different angles. They had no more to tell him. 'Speak to the priest,' he ordered. 'I want them buried in Christian graves by this hour tomorrow.'

'Who will pay the price?'

'If it hastens the task, I shall.' Christopher handed the man five silver shillings from his purse. Yet another expense to be reclaimed from the earl's coffers.

The coroner bit the coins and pocketed them with a thin smile. 'It will be done.'

Elias Smith was plainly terrified. He sat with his back to the wall, knees drawn up, and eyes darting left and right as if expecting to be attacked. He was filthy and stank of human muck. Christopher peered into the gloom of the cell and barked at him: 'On your feet, Smith. Bring him up, gaoler. I want information. No food until I have it.'

Smith was led clanking up the steps, his ankles still shackled. He screwed up his eyes and tried to cover them from the light. The gaoler stood behind him. 'You told me that the bodies were buried in the graveyard at St Bartholomew's, Smith. We dug under the yew tree. No bodies. You lied. What else have you lied about?' Better that Christopher should lie than the pitiful Smith, if his lie revealed the truth more quickly.

Smith opened his eyes in surprise. 'We buried them under the tree, just as I told you. I told the truth. You dug in the wrong place.' The panic in his voice was unmistakable.

'There is only one yew tree in that graveyard. One tree, no bodies. Why did you lie?'

'I did not lie. Someone has moved them. That is where we buried them.' Now the voice was shrill.

'We? Who was the other?'

'I have told you. I do not know his name.'

'We have arrested the man you acted with. He says that it was you who gave the orders and you who murdered the Housemans.'

'He lies. It was he who killed them. He cut their throats.'

'Why?'

'I have told you. Houseman knew the word.'

'What word?'

'*Incendium*. He said we were to find out if the bookseller knew it.'

'It is a word we know. You are involved in a treasonous plot, Smith. If you survive the rack you will be executed as a traitor. You will be hung and drawn and your body quartered. Your head will be impaled on a spike for all to see. Your family will be as lepers.'

Smith shook his head in confusion. A night in Limbo, a single crust of bread and threats of a traitor's death. Christopher knew that the pretence was having the effect he sought. The man did not understand what was happening to him. 'I did not kill them. We buried the bodies. That is all I know,' muttered Smith, scratching at a livid sore on his face.

'Give me a name, Smith, and you will not go back to Limbo. Did he mention a name? Who employed him? Who paid him?'

Smith screamed, 'I do not know!'

Christopher moved closer. 'How then do you know that Nicholas Houseman was a bookseller?'

'The other knew. He called the man "the bookseller".'

'How did you gain entry to the house?'

Smith's last scrap of resistance had crumbled. 'He said we carried an urgent message from the Stationers' Company.' It was almost a sob. 'He killed them. We buried them under the yew tree. That is all I know.'

'What else did Houseman say?'

'Only that he had heard the word but he did not know what it signified.'

'There was no name mentioned?'

'None.'

'Did the other man believe him?'

'He did. He was sure the bookseller knew no more. So he killed them both.'

No name but it was enough. Nicholas's death had been ordered by someone at Stationers' Hall. 'Take him away, gaoler. The man is a murderer. Put him with his fellows.'

'It was not I—'

'Hold your tongue,' growled the gaoler. 'Just pray that the fever takes you first.'

Christopher almost ran out of the gaol. He hurried past the Newgate beggars, narrowly avoided a rider and a baker's cart and tore up Wood Street. He was panting when Katherine opened the door. 'The murderers gained entry by claiming to have a message for Nicholas from the Stationers' Company,' he gasped. 'Smith has admitted as much. There is a connection. There are traitors in Stationers' Hall.'

'Do you know more about the plot?'

'Not yet, but I shall. It is time to call again on Warden Kaye.'

'Come and sit. Let us consider more carefully before you act.'

'Katherine—'

'Lemon water or wine?'

Christopher shrugged.

'I will bring the sack.' Katherine fetched the bottle and they sat in the little parlour before the fire. It was not yet cold enough for it to have been lit. 'Now,' she began, 'let us think a moment. You have evidence that the murders of the Housemans were ordered by a member of the Stationers' Company—'

Christopher interrupted. 'James Kaye, unless I am much mistaken.'

'I have been to St Ann's churchyard. The door to the church was locked. Kaye must have been attending a meeting when I saw him. You have interrogated the traitor Wolf but learned nothing. However, he is unlikely to have been acting alone. Were any of his men captured?'

'I believe not. All were killed or escaped. Katherine, I do not know why we are examining this again. We have reason enough now to have Stationers' Hall searched and the members interrogated.'

'If you were to do such a thing, you might as well have every church bell in London rung to warn the plotters that their scheming has been discovered. Would they not flee at once?'

'Yet if Kaye could be made to speak . . . Smith has sung like a thrush.'

'Smith is no more than a common criminal trying to avoid a traitor's death. Wolf was a man of conviction. He did not speak. Would Kaye do so? If he is driven by faith to betray his country, I cannot suppose that he would. His conscience would not permit it. Again, the plotters would simply disappear to await another opportunity. We would never know their names.'

'It is often hard to believe that you shared their faith.'

'Yet I did. What I do not share is the desire to impose it by force on others. Nor to use it as justification for the pursuit of power by means of violence.'

'But as to Kaye, few men remain silent on the rack.'

'So are we to take him, rack him and force the truth from him, while his fellows slink away in the night? Let us find out who Kaye was meeting before we act.' Katherine's green eyes shone with determination.

'Katherine, these are dangerous words. For the country, for the queen, for us. If Leicester knew that we had stood by and watched as a suspected traitor walked free on the streets, it would go badly for us. The more so if the queen's life was directly threatened. Our own would surely be forfeit.'

'Tush. We would simply be using the vixen to catch the dog. If we sense danger we will act at once to take Kaye.'

'Still, Katherine, I am unsure.'

'Two days. Let me observe Kaye for two days more. If we have learned nothing by then you will speak to the earl and arrange for his arrest and a search of Stationers' Hall to be carried out.'

'Two days. Not an hour more. I cannot keep this from the earl for longer.'

Katherine rose and kissed him. 'You will see that I am right.'

CHAPTER 27

Katherine came late to his house. She had seen Kaye arrive at the Hall and leave it. He had not gone to St Ann's and had spoken to no one in the street.

'And you did the same yesterday,' said Christopher. 'He has not led us to our quarry and the hunt is over. Did you enter the church?'

'The doors were locked, as before.'

'Tomorrow I shall speak to the earl. That was our agreement.'

Katherine took his hand. 'One more day, please. Just one more and if that reveals nothing, it is over.'

'No, Katherine. I am not prepared to put my career in further jeopardy. I should not have been persuaded by you in the first place. I shall go to Whitehall tomorrow afternoon. The earl is invariably at his desk after he has dined.'

'Christopher—'

'Enough, Katherine. Let there be no more talk of this.' He had given her two days. He would give her no more. She stormed out of the house in bad humour, barely wishing him good evening.

Christopher left Rose to prepare his meal and walked to the gaol. There was no good time to be in Newgate, so he had decided to get it over with. The guard at the entrance let him in and left him to find his own way down to Limbo, where the gaoler was sitting at his table chewing a leg of chicken. He recognized Christopher but continued his chewing. 'If you've come for Smith, you are too late,' he growled. 'Found him dead this morning.'

Christopher swore under his breath. Another dead prisoner? First Wolf, now Smith. He had known the risk of leaving Smith in Limbo well enough but had hoped for one more try at him. It was a blow, a bad blow, and would not be easy to explain to Leicester. 'How did he die?'

'Who knows? Gaol fever, hunger, what does it matter? The man's dead and not a tear will be shed.'

'I wish to see the body.'

The gaoler laughed. 'It'd be a miracle if you did. We burned him, same as the others. We always get rid of the bodies quick. Quicklime or fire, either does the job. No chance to rot and makes space for others.'

'Had he any other visitors?'

'Visitors? None, sir. Not many down here gets visitors.' Christopher did not know why he had asked the question. The gaoler would never have told him even if Smith had had a troupe of visitors. He would have been paid not to.

Cursing himself for leaving Smith in the prison — few lasted more than a day or two in Limbo — Christopher went to Cheapside. He of all people should not have underestimated the risk of leaving the miserable wretch there. Perhaps Ell would have heard something more.

'Ell's not here,' spluttered Grace, opening the door. She was munching a slice of pie and reeked of drink. 'Gone to see her old father, she said. Lives in Shoreditch, don't know where. I've given her room to a new girl until she's back. Fancy going up?'

It had never occurred to Christopher that Ell might have a family. Parents, siblings, a life like any other — the thought was strangely unsettling. 'When did Ell leave?'

'Three days since. Can't have the room empty. Rooms have to earn a shilling, same as the girls.'

It was three days since they had caught Smith in the Boar. A cold finger ran down his spine. He needed Ell. 'When she returns, tell her to send word. She knows where.' Christopher handed the woman a coin, which disappeared into her kirtle.

'She won't return. They never do. Run off with a fat merchant with a few pounds to spend on her or floating in the river, she is.' Grace closed the door and left him standing in the lane. One girl or another for the fat stew-keeper. It made no difference to her as long as they worked hard to fill her purse.

He would miss Ell if she did not return and not just because of her use as an agent. He knew no one — man or woman — so incapable of envy or dissembling. Ell Cole said exactly what she thought and to hell with anyone who did not like it. A little like Katherine, but in a manner rather less polite. Come back soon, Ell, he said quietly to himself. Help me find the traitors and make me laugh.

He sat in an inn at the river end of Blackfriars Lane with a black-jack of ale before him. He had chosen the place because he knew a man might sit and drink there unmolested by poxed whores or limb-less beggars or scarred soldiers with long tales of woe to tell. The innkeeper had a reputation for tolerating none but peaceful customers. To those he was a gracious host. To anyone else, a firebrand.

In France: the open slaughter of thousands, the murder of Admiral Coligny and the duc de Guise's army gathered in the north. In the Low Countries: a Spanish army making ready to embark. Nothing hidden, nothing denied. Open hostility.

In England: an attempt to free the Queen of Scots and its leader dead having revealed nothing. The Housemans murdered by the dead Smith and another, by means of a ruse involving Stationers' Hall and, Christopher would wager, James Kaye, but no proof of either. Kaye's meeting in St Ann's with a man unknown. Berwick's suspicion of Wetherby. One of two unusual pistols. Secrets, deaths, a plot. And now Ell disappeared.

For an hour he sat with his ale, barely noticing the other drinkers and speaking to no one. Since coming to London, he had seen and done things he could never have imagined while he quietly taught civil law to pupils at Pembroke Hall. He had travelled to France, been attacked twice, seen women and children slaughtered like sheep, stabbed a farmer with his own pitchfork, lied and threatened.

Yet the threat of *Incendium* remained. It was time to face Leicester again.

'Dr Radcliff, I hardly know what to make of this. You bring me little upon which to form a judgement. Two men have died in prison. Still you have found no proof of a plot other than a word, no names of those behind it. I need names if I am to bring them to justice. Her Majesty has lost patience and will go riding again tomorrow. What is it you advise me to do?' The earl tapped a finger impatiently on the desk. His manner reminded Christopher of the time he had brought news of the Housemans' disappearance. Stern and unforgiving.

'My lord, I believe that James Kaye should be arrested and questioned. Under the threat of the rack he might reveal names. That there is a plot I have no doubt.' Christopher could hear the nerves in his own voice.

Leicester sighed. 'Walsingham too believes so. I myself thought so. But we have no evidence. If only Wolf had been made to speak.'

'There is another matter. The word itself — *Incendium* — suggests fire. I thought that this referred to the massacre in France and the burnings in England fifteen years ago but now I am sure that the word implies something more. The destruction by fire of the Guildhall, perhaps, or even of the palace in which we now stand. And the deaths of every man and woman in them.'

'The Guildhall or Whitehall Palace burned down? It sounds fanciful. How would such a thing be achieved?'

'That is what we must discover, my lord.'

'If it is true. What has made the idea suddenly come into your mind, doctor?'

'I am not sure, my lord. Perhaps in discussion with Mistress Allington.' No sooner were the words out than Christopher regretted them. Mention of Katherine was foolish.

Leicester raised a dark eyebrow. 'Ah, Mistress Allington. And what, pray, does Mistress Allington make of recent events in France? Does she excuse them?'

'She does not, my lord. She wholly condemns them, just as she is wholly loyal to Her Majesty and to England. She believes, as do I, that the massacres were driven by politics as much as religion. The Catholics, led by the duc de Guise, saw Admiral Coligny and the Huguenots as a threat. That is why they acted against them. The violence spread so rapidly that it could not be stopped. Like a forest fire, it had to burn itself out.'

'Hm. Fine words, doctor, but how much truth is in them I am unsure. And it seems that you have taken it upon yourself to discuss our affairs with the lady. A breach of confidence, to say the least.'

'Mistress Allington has rendered valuable assistance in my work, my lord. She has been observing the movements of the Stationers' warden, James Kaye.' Christopher found himself rubbing his hand. He stopped and clasped his hands behind his back.

'And for how long has she been observing this man?'

'Two days, my lord.'

Leicester scratched at his beard. 'Forgive me, doctor. I am finding this difficult to comprehend. You have taken Mistress Allington into your confidence and she has been assisting you. You fear the destruction by fire of this palace and all who live and work in it, yet you have allowed a man you suspect of involvement in the plot to walk free for two days. Did Mistress Allington persuade you to this?'

'No, my lord, she did not. I hoped that Kaye would lead us to others.' Even to Christopher, it sounded hollow.

'But he did not. It was a rash act, Dr Radcliff, and untypical of you. It is hard to understand why your lawyer's caution deserted you at such a time.'

'It is I who must take the responsibility. No fault attaches to Katherine Allington.'

'That is for me to decide. Once again, doctor, you disappoint me. Fortunately, Mr Berwick has had rather more success. Kindly order the guard to send for him.'

While they waited, Christopher tried once more. 'My lord, I urge you to take the threat of fire most earnestly. Such an event would—'

Leicester held up a hand. 'Enough. Let us hear what Mr Berwick has to say.'

John Berwick was shown in by the guard and bowed to the earl and to Christopher.

'Mr Berwick, please tell us what you have discovered. I wish Dr Radcliff to hear it.'

'As instructed, my lord, I have had Roland Wetherby closely observed, and, at times, have observed him myself. In the area around Cheapside there are houses which cater for tastes such as his. He frequents them regularly.' He paused. 'He has also been observed in a low tavern in Bishopsgate, the Boar. He meets another man there. The man's name is Smith, Elias Smith. By all accounts, a common thief. Why would Wetherby meet such a man in such a place, I wonder?'

Christopher looked up sharply. Elias Smith and Wetherby in the Boar in Bishopsgate. How was it that Smith had not confessed to this? The man had been willing enough to speak. Or had he more courage than Christopher had given him credit for? 'I know of this man. He was one of the two who murdered Nicholas Houseman and his wife. I had him taken to Newgate for questioning.'

'I was unaware of this, doctor,' replied Berwick, plainly a little taken aback. 'Did you learn anything from him?'

'Only that he and another whose name he did not know were paid to find out if Nicholas recognized the word *Incendium*, and, if he did, to kill them both. Smith died in Newgate before I could question him further.'

Berwick smiled. 'Unfortunate. Not perhaps the wisest choice of prison for a man with questions to answer, doctor. Gaol fever, starvation, plague . . . one of them ready to do the hangman's job. May I inquire how you knew of Smith's involvement?'

'He was a man given to boasting. An agent overheard him.'

'Could this agent provide more intelligence?'

'She has disappeared.'

'She? Mistress Allington?' demanded Leicester.

'No, my lord. The whore Ell Cole.'

'Ah, yes. I recall her. Disappeared? Also unfortunate. However, the fact that Wetherby and Smith were observed together is alarming, and Mr Heneage must be told. What of the stationers, Mr Berwick? Can you shed light upon them?'

'None, my lord. I have found not a scrap of evidence to suggest that any member of the company is a traitor or a hostile agent. Nor has there been word of a pistol matching the descripton of that Dr Radcliff brought back from Paris. If it exists, I believe it is still in France.'

'Before he died, Smith spoke of the stationers. They were used as a ruse to gain entry to Houseman's dwelling.'

Berwick snorted. 'Or so he might have said, doctor. But a man under threat of death will say whatever comes into his head if he thinks it will save him, will he not? A pity we cannot question Smith further.'

'And what of the plot?' asked Leicester. 'Dr Radcliff, or perhaps more accurately Dr Radcliff's confidante, believes that its name signifies the burning of London.'

'Not all of London, my lord,' said Christopher, 'but possibly the Tower or the Guildhall or this palace.'

'Both Whitehall and the Tower are large,' said Berwick, 'but they are well guarded and defended on one side by the river. How would an enemy set fire to either? Surely not fire ships?'

'No, Mr Berwick, not fire ships, but if there were traitors within, such a thing might be possible.' Berwick was milking this for every drop.

'I do not see how, doctor,' said Leicester. 'What do you say, Mr Berwick?'

Berwick hesitated. 'It seems to me a far-fetched notion, but Dr Radcliff is more experienced than I in reading the minds of traitors. If he believes there is a danger, I suggest a search of Westminster

Hall and an interrogation of all who work there. The Hall is less well guarded and I suppose could possibly be a target. It is the place I would choose for an act of destruction.'

Leicester nodded. 'Arrange it, if you please, Mr Berwick. Use as many men as you need. And I shall speak to Mr Heneage about Wetherby. He should be held securely while we continue with your search of the Hall. Heneage will be unhappy but that cannot be helped. I thank God that we have at last made a little progress.' With another bow, Berwick departed.

Why did Christopher invariably feel at a disadvantage in Berwick's presence? The man seemed always to be a step ahead of him. And what poison had he been dripping into Leicester's ear? 'And I, my lord?' he asked with as much resolve as he could muster. 'What would you have me do?'

Leicester sat back and stroked his beard. 'I would have you consider whether the life of an intelligencer is really the life for you, Dr Radcliff. In the meantime, the queen will ride tomorrow morning in the fields at Holborn. We must pray that she will be safe from an assassin's pistol. I need not trouble you further for the present.'

Berwick was waiting at the Holbein Gate. 'I must apologize again, doctor. I had not meant to embarrass you.'

'It hardly appeared that way, Mr Berwick,' replied Christopher. 'If you will permit a word of advice, do not allow your ambition to cloud your judgement. The earl is a man of perception. Now, good day.' As he left through the gate, he felt Berwick's eyes on his back.

He walked down to the stairs at the river but instead of taking one of the waiting wherries turned to follow the stony bank. He picked his way over the pebbles and around the daily debris washed up on the tide. It would not greatly pain him to leave London. It was knowing that he had failed in his task that would eat away at him like worm in wood.

What would make a young man like Wetherby seek to destroy the country of his birth? Conviction? Guilt? Coercion? If he had consorted with Elias Smith, he had connived at the cruel murders of Nicholas and Sarah. How could Thomas Heneage, Treasurer of the Privy Chamber, not have been aware of his duplicity? Or could Heneage himself have been involved? If the Duke of Norfolk, a cousin of the queen and the only duke in England, could be executed for treason, so could a mere courtier.

As for the peacock James Kaye, was it his unfailing courtesy that struck a false note or was Christopher imagining it? The warden had shown a strange lack of concern about the fate of one of his members and had not questioned Christopher's interest as he might have been expected to. Smith had implicated the stationers. Kaye was involved in the plot. Whatever it was.

The stench from a dung barge, carried on a fluke of wind, roused Christopher from his thoughts. He stepped over the remains of a swan and around a broken barrel. Ahead of him a group of scavengers searched among the pebbles for a stranded fish or a coin or a bottle disgorged by the river — anything that might be eaten or sold. The scavengers would most likely be homeless vagrants, liable to be arrested if caught but without other means of staying alive. It would be wise to avoid them. He left the river by the stairs at the Temple and carried on through the streets to Ludgate Hill. Today the Thames had provided neither cheer nor answer. The earl had made plain his opinion.

CHAPTER 28

A week later, a long, frustrating week, there had been no sign of the Spanish galleons rumoured to be collecting in the narrow sea but arriving Huguenots still brought tales of killing and maiming and the news sheets and criers were still warning Londoners to be wary of foreigners and alert to hints of treason. And the fear of invasion had not diminished. Christopher had watched a sad procession of carts and wagons leaving through the Cripplegate, each one loaded with crates and chests of possessions as if the owners were fleeing the plague. While merchants and lawyers left the city with what they could carry, vagrants and vagabonds poured in, some seeking shelter and employment, most on the look-out for easy pickings. Deserted houses, abandoned animals, the old and the sick — each a lure to the unscrupulous.

Yet for all that, Billingsgate fish-sellers and Smithfield butchers carried on trading and the cluster of markets in Cheapside from somewhere found food and drink to sell and customers to buy them. Even with storm clouds over the city, the people had to eat. A visitor might have noticed nothing untoward, but Londoners saw and heard and sensed the mood.

The earl's letter confirmed that John Berwick was conducting a search of Westminster Hall and that Wetherby would be interrogated and held. As there was no evidence against the warden James Kaye, he would not be inconvenienced. Christopher threw the letter on to his table. He should not have spoken of Katherine. Leicester was angry. He left the house and set off for Wood Street, intending to be there before dark.

He heard the flames before he saw the smoke. From the direction of Cheapside Cross came the sounds and smells of fire. He ran towards them. At the Cross a crowd had gathered around a burning heap of timber, dry dung and old rags. Three figures in plague masks, long leather coats and leather gloves brandished torches to keep back the onlookers. The figures were all in black, their faces hidden by the ghoulish masks. The beaks of the masks were thick at the base to hold fragrant herbs, tapering to a sharp point and curved downwards like a carrion crow's. They were held in place by leather straps. Circles of glass covered the eye holes. The figures could as easily be old or young, fair or dark, man or woman. In the evening light, they could have been figures from hell.

'Is there plague here?' Christopher shouted over the flames. The three masks turned silently towards him. He tried again. 'Is there plague here, I say?' Still none of them spoke. 'Why do you not douse the fire?' He ran forward and made to grab a figure's arm. A gloved fist slammed into his shoulder and he stumbled. He struggled to his feet and tried to focus his eyes. The smoke was becoming denser. 'For the love of God, why do you not find water? The fire might spread . . .'

The words died on his lips. Two more masked figures appeared from an alley, dragging a limp body by its arms. Before anyone could stop them, they heaved the body on to the flames and watched it catch light. The air was filled with the awful, sickly stench of burning flesh. Christopher shouted for help but the watchers stood silent and unmoving, as if caught in some terrible nightmare. He shouted again and dashed forward to grab a mask. His hands were on the beak when his elbows were pinioned from behind and he was hauled aside. He jerked himself free only to be forced to his knees and held there by his hair.

Still the crowd stood silently as if mesmerized by what they were seeing. Another figure addressed them in a voice only a little muffled by the mask and powerful enough to be heard over the flames. 'This is a warning of what is to come. London will burn and every heretic will burn with it.' He swept an arm over the crowd. Not one person moved. 'Every one of you who insults God by your Protestant ways will burn. What, with God's blessing, has happened in France will happen tenfold in England. The witch-queen will die and her heretic subjects with her. His Holiness the Pope has commanded it. Mark this and return to the true religion before it is too late.'

The crowd stood and stared. Christopher tried once more to reach a mask. A torch thrust at his face forced him back. The figure spoke again. 'Mark my words, people of London. Your city will burn and with it every man, woman and child who denies the true faith. All heretics will die.'

Behind them there was a commotion. Six militiamen armed with halberds pushed their way through. The masked figures hurled their torches at them and disappeared up the alley from which the body had been dragged. No one followed them.

The militia captain called for water while his men tried to drag the burning body clear of the flames with their weapons. It rolled off the heap and lay, black and smouldering, on the cobbles. They struggled to prevent the fire from spreading until barrels of water arrived on hand carts and slowly the flames were extinguished. What was left of the body was drenched in water, wrapped in a cloak and carried away by the militia.

Christopher asked the captain if such a thing had happened before. 'In the name of God, I hope not,' replied the captain, mopping his brow with a sleeve. 'Did you hear the man speak?'

'I did,' replied Christopher and recounted his words. 'If his aim was to spread terror, I daresay he succeeded. Threats, plague masks and fire.'

'Are we to see more of this, sir?'

'We are, captain. It is a surprise that it has not happened before. You will of course report what we have seen, as will I.'

'I shall, sir. And may God protect us,' muttered the captain.

They sat in the parlour drinking lemon water. 'Plague masks and torches?' asked Katherine. 'Was there no glimpse of their faces?'

Christopher stretched his fingers. 'None. Plague doctors take care to hide every inch of their skin. Their leader did speak but there was nothing to be learned from his voice other than that he was a man. He spoke of our witch-queen and the terror coming to London.'

'Is this the beginning, Christopher?' Katherine reached out for his hand.

'I fear that it is.'

'May God protect us.'

'Those were exactly the words of the militia captain.'

When Katherine inquired about Wetherby and Kaye, Christopher recounted his meeting with Leicester. 'So John Berwick, who is little more than a boy,' she said, 'is conducting a search of

Westminster Hall for we know not what, Wetherby is to be interrogated, Kaye is free to do as he pleases and you are not required. How has this happened?' she asked.

'The earl is angry that I used you to watch Kaye.'

'You did not use me. I was pleased to help.'

'He does not realize this, or chooses not to. He can be a difficult man to understand but above all, he values loyalty. John Berwick, I think, is adept at profiting from this. He is clever and ambitious.'

'Should you not then encourage Berwick's friendship? Flatter him, seek out his opinion, treat him as more experienced in the ways of the court than he is, ask his help.'

'Katherine, you know I am a poor hand at such things.'

'Try, Christopher. And as for Leicester, it is my guess that he is testing you. He valued you enough to bring you to London and to send you to Paris and has always expressed himself content with your work, yet now he is making your life unpleasant. To be sure, he is testing you.'

'Testing me for what?'

'For your commitment. He wishes to know whether you will persevere in his service or scurry off when things do not go as you would like them. Remember that he has John Berwick now, who could replace you.'

'And would no doubt like to. Very well, Katherine, I shall try. But do not expect me suddenly to become the earl's spaniel.'

'Never. And this is no time to be weak. What you saw and heard today must not be allowed to spread. Whatever Leicester's opinion, you are needed.'

John Berwick was right. If there was a single building in London that combined magnificence and tradition with the practical business of governance it was not the Tower or the Guildhall or even Whitehall Palace. It was Westminster Hall. There sat the courts of the Queen's Bench and the Chancery and there worked the army of tax officials, clerks, administrators and lawyers whose task it was to carry out the decisions of the judges and the wishes of the queen's ministers. There stood the King's Table, symbol of the power of the monarch, and there the queen had been crowned. Berwick was right in thinking that its destruction would be more than just the death of a building. It would threaten the entire system of government, built up brick by brick since King John and his barons had signed the Great Charter more than three and a half centuries earlier. If Christopher were an enemy of England, he would delight in burning it to the ground.

The next morning Christopher entered the great hall through the grand entrance. In the huge space under the mighty oak beams of the arched roof, gowned clerks scurried about carrying bundles of paper, lawyers spoke quietly to their clients and officials sat at their tables, writing or reading or busy in earnest discussion.

He found a guard and asked for Mr Berwick. 'You'll likely find him in the cellars,' replied the guard, 'him and his searchers. If I knew what they were searching for I might be able to help them. But they're tight-lipped, as tight as my wife with a bottle. Happy to let me go thirsty, the bitch.' Christopher asked how to get to the cellars. The guard pointed to the other end of the hall. 'Steps through the door in the far corner.'

In the cellars, lit by burning lanterns along each wall, Christopher counted twenty of them. Twenty men opening boxes, poking in corners and tapping on walls for signs of secret places. No one could say that John Berwick was not carrying out his task with proper diligence.

Berwick was in one of the stone alcoves that lined the walls of the cellar, supervising the opening and reclosing of a stack of wooden crates. He looked up in surprise when Christopher addressed him.

'Dr Radcliff, I had not thought to see you here. I understood from the earl that I was to conduct the search.'

'Indeed, Mr Berwick, and so you are. I merely thought to see how you are faring. It is a task to test Hercules.'

Berwick straightened up. 'It is, and we have not yet attempted the hall above. There is so much down here that we will be busy for some days yet. Do you bring news?'

'No, Mr Berwick, except that last evening I witnessed a foul and frightening incident at Cheapside Cross. A corpse thrown on to a fire by figures in plague masks amid threats of all London and its people burning on heretic fires.'

'Plague masks? Were these men apprehended?'

'They ran off when the militia arrived. I fear we shall see more of them in the days to come.'

'*Incendium* was the word you heard, was it not, doctor? Could what you saw have been part of it?'

'I do not doubt it, Mr Berwick, and I should appreciate your advice on a matter related to it. Does your labour permit dinner and a beaker or two of ale? There is a respectable inn nearby.'

'My advice, doctor? I cannot think how I might be able to advise you, but as I am weary and thirsty, I should be pleased to accept your offer.'

The inn was agreeable enough. A very few drinkers sat with their ale and long-stemmed pipes of tobacco. It was a habit Christopher had never acquired but, unlike some, he did not find the smell unpleasant. They ordered bread and meat and beer and found a quiet corner. 'So your diligence has revealed nothing yet?' asked Christopher.

'Not for want of trying, doctor, as you saw.' Berwick's tone had become a little sharper.

'How long will it take to search the entire building?'

'That I cannot say, doctor. Now, you were kind enough to advise me on the matter of Roland Wetherby; how may I now advise you?'

'You found no evidence to suggest that Nicholas Houseman and his wife were murdered but their bodies have now been found. Why do you think they were killed?'

'That is surely more for you to ascertain, doctor. I merely carried out the earl's instructions while you were in Paris. The same might be said about Stationers' Hall. I could find nothing to implicate the company in any plot.'

'Did you speak to the Senior Warden, James Kaye?'

'Of course. And to the other wardens. Really, doctor, is this why you have taken me from my work?'

Christopher spoke severely. 'England is in danger, Mr Berwick. This is no time for argument amongst ourselves. No, it is about the earl that I seek your opinion.'

'In what manner?'

'I am distressed that he has turned his face against me. Would you ask the earl to receive me so that I might put my case to him?' The words did not come easily.

Berwick scratched his neck. 'I am new to court, doctor, as you are aware. I believe I enjoy the trust of the earl and would not wish to jeopardize it. I doubt he would give much weight to the opinion of a newcomer such as I.'

'You undervalue yourself, sir. The earl clearly holds you in high esteem.' He paused. 'And I would wish to be your ally at Whitehall.'

Berwick frowned. 'I will consider what you have requested of me.'

'I am grateful,' said Christopher, draining his beaker. 'And now I must allow you to return to your labours. Let us hope that they are soon over. Ah, I almost forgot. What of Roland Wetherby? Has he revealed anything?'

'It is but a matter of time. I am sure that he is involved in something evil, as is the earl convinced. He spoke to Mr Heneage and has had Wetherby sent to the Gate House prison.'

'It cannot have been an easy discussion with Heneage.'

'It was not. The earl came close, so he told me, to losing his temper. Now, if you will forgive me, I must resume my labours. Good day, Dr Radcliff.'

'Do consider my request, Mr Berwick. I should be indebted to you.'

'I shall, doctor.'

CHAPTER 29

St Martin's church was cool and quiet — an isle of calm in a sea of tumult. At the back of the nave, Christopher rose from prayer and left quietly. Compared to the great cathedral at Amiens, whose magnificence he could admire only for its own sake, St Martin's was simply a place of worship. A plain altar, plain windows and walls, plain seats, plain words. A place where a man could try to speak to God without the need for a priest or the trappings of the priesthood, a place where thoughts and prayers were enough. He had felt the need to go there. It was a need he had rarely felt since coming to London.

In the three days since his visit to Westminster Hall he had heard nothing from Berwick but there had been more fires — at Charterhouse, Shoreditch, Holborn and in other wards outside the city wall. Like plague, they had appeared without warning and for no apparent reason. At Aldgate a child had died; horses stabled at Lincoln's Inn Fields had bolted leaving their owners to bear the loss; and on street corners and in churches and inns the people asked themselves why.

For all their apparent randomness, there was planning and skill behind them. Figures in plague masks had been seen running from the fires but none had been caught, their devilish appearance adding to the common fear. The ghostly figures knew their business — light the fire, run, light another. Faces hidden, spreading terror, destroying. If this was not *Incendium*, what was it? And if it was *Incendium*, what was coming next? Militia walked the streets and the watch had been doubled. To no avail. The fires had continued.

A slim figure, her face half hidden by a shawl, stood outside his door. It was Ell. 'Grace said you were looking for me, doctor,' she explained when she saw him. 'Changed your mind, have you? About time, I'd say. Ready for me at last?'

Christopher could not help himself grinning. He glanced up and down the hill. He saw no one watching. 'Better come in, Ell,' he said. 'We don't want you seen here.'

'Too grand for you, am I, doctor?' she laughed as she entered. 'Too much the lady for Ludgate?'

They went into the study. 'Sit down, Ell. Grace told me you had gone to Shoreditch. She thought you had left for good.'

'Stupid cow. Where would I go? What would I do? I told her I'd be back but she gave my room to a new girl. Soon put her back on the street. It's my room, where I entertain my customers and conduct my business. Can't have any scabby old doxy using it. Why did you want to see me, doctor, if it wasn't for my charms?'

'The Irishman who murdered Sal is dead. His name was Wolf. So is Elias Smith, the man in the Boar. I thought you'd like to know.'

'Hope they're rotting in hell. Nasty pair of weasels. Was there anything else?'

'The fires, Ell, and the men in masks. Have you seen them?'

'I haven't, doctor, but plenty have.'

'We need to know who's doing it. Have you heard anything?'

'Not much, doctor. Is it about that word you told me to listen for? You said it meant fire.'

'*Incendium*, Ell. It does mean fire. Have you heard it spoken?'

'It's not the sort of word you hear around Cheapside. But I'll keep listening out for you.'

'Do that, Ell. There are bad things happening. Fires and plots and killing. They must be stopped.' Christopher was stretching his fingers and rubbing his hand.

'I can see you're in a state, doctor. I'll keep my ears open. Open arms, open legs, open ears — that's my secret.' Ell's laugh was like a fingernail scraping on a slate.

'I shall be here if you hear anything. Anything at all.'

She touched his sleeve. 'I will, Dr Rad, and pay no mind to me. I can be a silly bitch when I'm frightened. You mind out for yourself, now.'

Ell had barely left when there was another knock on the door. Three men stood outside. One was John Berwick, the other two palace guards. 'Mr Berwick, good day to you,' Christopher greeted him. 'Guards?'

Berwick did not respond. 'If you would admit me, Dr Radcliff, I will explain why we are here.' Not a hint of reticence in his tone, but brisk and businesslike. A little taken aback, Christopher stepped aside to allow him in. The guards remained on the street.

'Well, Mr Berwick, what is this about? Have you spoken to the earl?' he asked.

'Dr Radcliff, I am sent by the earl to inform you that from this hour you are confined to this house. You may not leave it or receive visitors without his express authority.'

Christopher stared at him. 'What? If this is a jest, Mr Berwick, it is in poor taste. England is in danger.'

'There is no jest, doctor. The earl believes that it would be best for all if you stand aside and allow others to discover the nature of the danger. I am merely his reluctant messenger.'

'Best for all? How so, exactly?' His temper was rising. He clasped his hands behind his back, lest he should strike out in fury as he once had in a Wisbech tavern.

'You were attacked in the street. He is anxious for your safety.'

'It was nothing. Doubtless you were right. An incompetent thief, no more.'

'The earl is disappointed that you questioned Smith yet did not extract from him a vital name. As you did not from the traitor Wolf.'

Christopher swallowed hard. 'I hardly think that blame for Wolf's silence can be placed at my door. The interrogator Griffyn and his assistant Pygot were responsible for his treatment. I was merely an observer. He is aware of this.'

'Griffyn has assured the earl otherwise. He says that you insisted on boiling water when the prisoner was plainly beyond resistance.'

'That is a lie. Griffyn himself—'

Berwick held up his hands. 'Dr Radcliff, it is not I who has made this decision. The earl is worried. Two prisoners unexpectedly dead and it was you who suggested that the word *Incendium* might mean the burning of Westminster Hall or the Guildhall. Yet now we find fires being lit all over London save for these very places. Figures in plague masks have been seen at the scenes of the fires. There have been threats of burning and killing.'

Christopher reached out to steady himself against the wall. 'This is outrageous. I wonder that you do not also accuse me of lighting the fires with my own hand.'

'No, no, doctor. The earl does not doubt your loyalty. It is your judgement that concerns him. You have found no proof of a plot and the earl believes that your safety and that of our queen will be better served by your temporary confinement while we discover the truth.'

'Proof? The massacres in France, intelligence that an army is gathering in the north, the pistol, Houseman, Smith, Wolf, the fires. I was fortunate to leave France with my life and I brought back the pistol and intelligence of *Incendium*.'

'A pistol, of which there may or may not be another. And even if there is, is it not more likely left in France?'

'I believe that the Stationers' Warden, James Kaye, is involved in the plot.'

'Yet the fact remains that we have discovered next to nothing about a plot. Or the name of a single plotter. All we have is assumption and conjecture. Please understand that I spoke for you. The earl was inclined to imprison you in the Gate House with Wetherby. I persuaded him otherwise.' Christopher saw the smugness on Berwick's face and longed to smash a fist into it. The man's ambition was writ all over it. 'It would be unwise to resist, doctor.'

'My housekeeper, Rose Crouch. Is she permitted to attend to her duties? I should be at a loss without her.'

'She will be admitted for one hour each day. Your door will be locked from the outside and a guard will be stationed there at all times. And I will take your dagger.'

This time his temper snapped. 'Go, then, Berwick,' he shouted. 'Go, and inform the earl that I will obey his command, absurd though it is. And do not return to this house until the danger to our country has abated.' He drew the poniard from his belt and passed it, point first, to Berwick, who took it carefully but said nothing.

Christopher watched him leave and listened for the sound of the key turning in the lock before going to his study. Anger, disbelief, frustration — for some time he could not order his thoughts. He stretched his fingers and sat seething. Berwick had dripped poison into the earl's ear. For all his protestations, driven by selfish ambition, he had lied and dissembled and found ways to cast blame on two rivals. Both were now imprisoned. At a time of great danger to the country, the man had played skilfully on the earl's doubts and used events to further his own aims. Leicester had been gulled by a fresh-faced youth newly come to court. If advancement in the service of the Crown required such duplicity, Christopher would do well to leave London the moment the earl gave his consent.

For the rest of the day he could not read, he could not write. Rose was not due until the next morning. He scraped together a simple plate of manchet bread and cold beef and washed it down with a bottle of hock. He thought of feigning sickness, of climbing through a window, even of setting fire to the house and escaping in the confusion. Eventually the wine did its work and he fell asleep in his chair. Sometime in the night he struggled to his bed chamber and fell, fully clothed, on to the bed.

He woke with the devil's blacksmiths hammering away inside his head and a mouth full of dust. For as long as his bladder would let him he hid his face under a pillow and tried not to think of what had happened. Only when the urge to empty it could be resisted no longer did he rise and stumble down the stairs. He swallowed a beaker of ale and chewed on what was left of the bread. Thank God Rose was due that morning. He would send her out for food. The guards would have to be explained away but he would tell her no more than that he felt a little unwell and would be remaining in the house that day. He doubted there would be any visitors.

He sat at his desk and carefully sharpened a duck-feather pen. He dipped it into a fresh pot of ink and tested it on a scrap of paper. Satisfied, he began the first of two letters. It was brief. He told Katherine that he was unable to leave the house and that she would not be admitted by the guards and asked, if she learned anything more about Kaye, to send word through Rose. It also asked her to deliver the second letter – addressed to the earl at Whitehall Palace.

When Rose arrived, she was untroubled by the guards. 'Glad to see the earl is looking after you, doctor,' she whispered. 'Are you unwell?'

'My head is a little sore again, Rose, and I am advised not to venture out for the present.' She appeared to accept the untruth. He handed her the letters. 'Please put these somewhere safe and take them to Mistress Allington on your way to the market. Do you know her house?'

Rose nodded. 'I do, doctor.' She tucked the letters down under her smock and grinned. 'Should be safe. No one's looked there for years.'

'Excellent. If there is a reply please bring it back with you. Best go now before the market is too busy.'

Rose was back within the hour, her basket laden with meat and cheese, bread and vegetables. 'Did you see Mistress Allington?' asked Christopher, showing no interest in the food or from where Rose had managed to acquire it.

'I did not, doctor. The mistress was not at home, so I pushed the letters under the door. Did I do right?'

Isabel had probably been resting. A pity. It would have been a relief to be sure that Katherine had received them. 'You did right,

Rose. Thank you.' He took an apple from the basket and bit into it. 'Now will you make one of your pottages? I am hungry.'

When he had eaten and Rose had left, he sat and thought for an hour. Only Berwick had saved him from joining Wetherby in the Gate House. What was really going through the earl's mind? More than Christopher's own safety to be sure.

Berwick was back again that evening. In his hand he held Christopher's letter addressed to the earl. 'Delivered by a woman — Mistress Allington, no doubt — to a guard at Whitehall Palace and quite properly passed to me.' He unrolled the letter and began to read. Christopher stood and glared at him. '"Be assured, my lord, of my loyalty to you and to our queen. I beg you to lift this ban on my movements so that I may continue to serve you. I can do nothing while confined to this house." The earl would have been displeased to know that you were questioning his orders. Fortunately, he has not seen it. Did you suppose it would find its way to him without coming to my attention?'

With an effort, Christopher controlled himself. 'I gave the matter no thought, Mr Berwick. I merely wish to continue my work. My being imprisoned here serves no purpose.' He paused. 'Have you completed your search of Westminster Hall?'

'The search has been called off. It was a foolish idea and proved fruitless.'

'But was it not you who—?'

'Enough, Dr Radcliff. The earl has instructed me not to communicate with you while you are here. In future, your house-keeper — I assume it was she who took the letter to Mistress Allington — will no longer be permitted to call. Food will be brought to you. And, beware, doctor, the earl will certainly be informed of any further transgression. Mistress Allington will also be informed of the earl's wishes.' Berwick swept out and was gone. Christopher stood and stared at the door.

This was indeed a new John Berwick. No hesitancy and no deference. A man set upon his course and determined to take his opportunity. In a perverse way, Christopher rather admired his spirit.

Back in his study, he tried to think clearly. No Rose, no Katherine and no means of contacting Ell or Isaac. So much for Paris, Amiens and being attacked on a London street. All of little account in the world of the court. He had not thought the earl could be as heartless, or as fickle.

He had found himself to be braver than he would have expected in the face of danger, and unexpectedly willing to use violence to defend himself. He had stabbed two men. And he had managed to return alive to London. By hard work he had risen from lowly commoner pupil at Pembroke Hall to Tutor and Doctor of Law. Yet the trained lawyer's mind upon which he depended had failed him. He could not see through the mist to what lay beyond. He was not as clever as he thought.

It came to him not in a blinding flash of light but gradually. One of Pythagoras's principles — the fewer the assumptions the more likely the proposition. Once rid of what he had taken to be true, his mind cleared and the real truth emerged. He must find a way to reach the earl.

Chapter 30

He sat in the darkness, searching for a way to make contact with the earl and persuade him to listen. He found none. Sometime in the night his eyes closed and he dozed.

He was roused by a gentle tapping on the narrow window. At first he thought he was imagining it, but the knocking was persistent. He lit a candle and opened it. 'I feared you would be in your bed, Christopher,' whispered Katherine. By the light of a rush lantern she had squeezed down the foul alley between the house and the old city wall and found his window. 'Tell me quickly what in the name of God has happened. This alley is dark and nasty and I am up to my ankles in filth. I have been ordered not to try to contact you.'

'The letter you took to Whitehall was intercepted. John Berwick has poisoned the earl's mind. The man is a traitor. The earl must be warned.' The words came out in a rush.

Katherine's voice rose in astonishment. 'Berwick a traitor? How do you know this?'

'Ssh. Speak quietly lest the guards hear us. It explains all that I could not make sense of. He lied about Heneage's man, Wetherby, and about me. He suggested the search of Westminster Hall because he knew there was nothing to be found there. He did not question James Kaye, the Stationers' Warden, as I asked him to. He might have had the Housemans murdered. You must get word to the earl.'

'How? If Berwick is clever enough to have deceived the earl and the queen herself, he is dangerous,' she said. 'To accuse him of treason without proof absolute would be fatal. He would find a way to turn the accusation against the accuser. And why would the earl listen to me?'

Christopher reached through the window to take her hand. 'Katherine, you must find a way. *Incendium* exists and Berwick is part of it. Tell the earl I have proof, but take great care to avoid Berwick. He is more than clever. We will both be for the Tower if you are discovered.'

'I have no idea how to do this, Christopher, but I will try.'

'Thank you. Go now before you are found. Come again only if you have to.'

Katherine squeezed his hand. 'Pray hard.'

He closed the window and held his breath, listening for sounds from the guards at the front of the house. There were none.

For two days Christopher waited for news. Reading, sleeping, even eating were well nigh impossible. He picked at crusts of bread and morsels of cheese, sipped small beer and dozed in his chair. He did not go to his bed chamber in case Katherine came again to the window. Twice he was overcome by a premonition of doom and wished he could reach out to her. He had been unable to think of a way for her to approach the earl. How could he suppose that she would do any better? His spirit was failing. He could not leave the house, he had no one with whom to speak, he knew nothing of what was happening outside.

When the door was thrown open and the guards came in, he was in the kitchen. They ordered him to put on a coat and come with them. He feared they were taking him to the Tower, but they turned into Fleet Street and marched him along the Strand to Whitehall Palace. It was dusk and there were few people on the streets but he was conscious of heads turning and eyes following. He breathed deeply and tried to stay calm.

At Whitehall he was escorted to the earl's apartments. A guard knocked loudly on the earl's door and they were summoned in. Christopher squared his shoulders and looked straight ahead.

The room was well lit by tall wax candles and by the flames of a fire in the grate. The earl sat, unsmiling, before it, opposite him another figure, her hands clasped protectively over her stomach. The earl wasted no words. 'Dr Radcliff, Lady Walsingham requested that I have you brought here. She wishes me to hear what you have to say. First, however, explain why you employed Mistress Allington to observe the Stationers' Warden, James Kaye.'

'She wished to do so and, being unknown to him, would not arouse his suspicion. I believe he is involved in *Incendium*.'

'Is Mistress Allington always permitted to do as she wishes?' The earl's tone was sharp.

After three days' confinement, Christopher's temper was short. 'Have I been brought here to be admonished like an errant child, my lord? If so, I would wish to return to my prison.'

'Take care, doctor. You are here only because Lady Walsingham is a dear friend and I trust her judgement entirely. Tell me what it is you wish me to know.'

Another deep breath and Christopher explained, carefully and without rushing, why he had realized that John Berwick must be a traitor. The murder of Nicholas Houseman, the attack on him in the street, the connection to the Stationers' Company, the story of Wetherby's meeting in the Boar with Smith, Smith's death, Wolf's death in the Tower, the pointless search of Westminster Hall while fires burned in the city, and his own confinement at Ludgate Hill. All made sense if Berwick was behind them.

'So you believe John Berwick and the warden Kaye to be behind this *Incendium*, doctor, is that so?' asked Leicester.

'It is, my lord. Kaye is a murderer and a traitor and so is Berwick.' Christopher glanced at Ursula Walsingham. Her face was impassive.

'Dangerous words, doctor,' said Leicester. 'The queen would not tolerate a false accusation against a young man whom she trusts entirely and I could, perhaps should, lock you up for them. It seems to me that that which you call proof is little more than opinion. Hardly convincing, doctor, hardly the felon caught with blood on his hands.'

'Berwick claimed that he persuaded you not to put me in the Gate House, my lord. Is that true?'

Leicester steepled his fingers in front of his chin, as he often did when thinking. 'It is not. On the contrary, he advised me to have you imprisoned. For your own safety, he said. I decided you should be confined to your house. But answer me this. John Berwick's father was killed during the rebellion in the northern counties. He was a brave man and a loyal one. Why would the son turn with such hatred against that which the father held most dear?'

'I have asked myself that question and do not have an answer, although there must be one. You spoke once of vipers lurking. John Berwick is a viper.'

Leicester sighed. 'I still do not believe it. The queen herself wished me to take Berwick under my wing. How could he have deceived her so easily? It is not credible. If it is, one wonders from what nest the next viper will slither. Am I to fill every prison in London in the hope of snaring the right one?'

'Do you really believe me capable of treachery, my lord?' asked Christopher.

Leicester shook his head. 'I do not. It is your judgement that can fail you. You employed Mistress Allington without my permission. I do not care for my authority to be flouted. But no, doctor, I do not think you a traitor and I remain to be convinced that Berwick is.'

'And Wetherby — may I speak to him, my lord?'

'In the circumstances I can hardly refuse such a request, but be discreet. Wardens and gaolers have ears.'

There was a silence. Christopher turned to Lady Walsingham and asked quietly, 'Does Sir Francis fare well, madam?'

Lady Walsingham smiled. 'I believe that he does, for all the horrors in France. He hopes to return to London for the birth of our child in January. You are a fortunate man, doctor. I would never have thought that I could be persuaded by a person I had never before met to intercede with the earl on another's behalf. Mistress Allington is a most resourceful and persuasive woman and you are blessed to have her as a friend. I hope you are aware of that.'

'I am, my lady. And I thank you for your trust in her.'

'Your own resourcefulness in France did no harm to her argument, doctor.' Christopher inclined his head in gratitude.

'Now,' said Leicester, 'the question is, what is to be done? The days pass and the danger presses ever closer, yet still we do not know exactly what *Incendium* is, or what form it will take.'

'My lord,' said Christopher, 'we believe that it involves the French and the Spanish and probably the Scots. The treaty signed at Blois will be of little account if the duc de Guise is behind the plot. And remember, please, that the French king sent the admiral's head to Rome. Is that not evidence of his true feelings? Queen Catherine can surely harbour no more hopes of the marriage of her son to our gracious queen. The plot is not the deluded idea of some deranged Bedlamite. It involves murder and fire not only in France but also in England. We have seen fires all over London. *Incendium* threatens our country and our queen. We are fortunate that it has not already struck with its full force. Let us act at once. Arrest Berwick and Kaye and have them interrogated.'

'On what grounds might Berwick be arrested, doctor? The queen was reluctant to believe in her cousin Norfolk's treachery. She will not countenance the arrest and interrogation of a young courtier whom she favours, without proof of his guilt. We hardly have that. And if two are arrested, will a hundred more not disappear under rocks and bushes to bide their time in the hope of another chance to bare their fangs? These too we must trap.'

'Yet if they remain at large,' said Lady Walsingham, 'the danger is undiminished. I ask myself what Francis would do.'

Christopher spoke hesitantly. 'Perhaps there is a middle way.'

'And what is that?' asked Leicester.

'You could order a search of Kaye's house and have him alone arrested. Berwick's reaction would be instructive.'

'Arrested for what?'

'Surely, my lord, the searchers could find something — a letter, a document — which incriminates him.'

'Do you suggest that evidence is fabricated?'

'The country is in danger, my lord. Would it be such a crime?' Christopher found that he had no qualms about such an action.

'And if we do this, what then?'

'Berwick is observed and Kaye is interrogated.'

'Dr Radcliff,' said Lady Walsingham with the hint of a grin, 'I am surprised that this is what a student of law learns at Cambridge. It is an excellent idea, of which my husband would approve. What do you say, Robert?'

'What is to be done with Wetherby and Dr Radcliff? If they are released, Berwick will want to know why.'

'Then they must stay where they are.'

'No, I have a better idea. Dr Radcliff will join Wetherby in the Gate House. Berwick will be told that they are both under suspicion and may not be visited. I take it you have no objection, doctor?'

The Gate House. Another prison. He had a dozen objections. 'If Katherine is permitted to bring me food and wine, I will do as you ask. But is it necessary for Roland Wetherby to be detained longer? Can Berwick not be told that the evidence is not strong enough to hold him?'

'No, doctor, Wetherby must stay where he is. The gaolers will be told nothing. Only the prison warden will know the truth of the matter. For all that I trust Lady Walsingham's judgement, should your suspicions prove groundless, you will both remain confined until I deem it safe to release you. Meanwhile, the arrangements you request will be made. We must hope that Berwick does not learn of your visit here tonight and I will find other work to keep him occupied. Mistress Allington must understand that she is not employed as an intelligencer and that any interference by her will not be tolerated.'

'Rest assured that I shall make certain that she knows this,' replied Christopher. Although whether or not she would take any notice, he could not say.

'And I will authorize visits by Mistress Allington,' said Leicester. 'You will be escorted now to the Gate House.'

'My housekeeper, my lord, will you authorize her return?'

'Very well, but ask for no more favours. Go now and pray that *Incendium* is extinguished.'

The Gate House prison, built as a gatehouse to Westminster Abbey some two hundred years earlier, was used for minor felons awaiting trial and, occasionally, for political prisoners. It lacked the reputation of Newgate or the Clink but it was foul enough. Christopher was handed over to the warden — a scrawny, evil-smelling man — and led down a flight of stone steps to a dark passageway, lined by cells. Rush lanterns burned feebly on the walls. In the door of each cell was a tiny window through which the prisoners might be observed.

The warden took a key from a large bunch attached to his belt and ushered Christopher into a small cell, containing only a thin palliasse laid out on the floor, a blanket, a single chair and a bucket. 'There you are, sir, the very best we can offer,' said the warden with a lop-sided grin. 'My orders are to admit no visitors but one lady and to allow you to speak with the prisoner in the next cell. The lady will bring your victuals.'

The cell was dark and foul and damp. Christopher thrust memories of eight weeks in Norwich gaol from his mind. At least here he had reason to hope for an early release. For all the wretched Wetherby knew, he would spend the rest of his life in prison. The warden closed the door and locked it. Christopher felt his way to the palliasse and lay down under the blanket. He had traded a comfortable room on Ludgate Hill for this. He had risked his life in France, been accused of faulty judgement and disloyalty, and angered Katherine. He rubbed his hand and wondered what was coming next.

The earl was as good as his word. Katherine arrived the next morning and was admitted by the guards. She put a basket of food and a bottle of Rhenish wine on the chair. Christopher wrapped her in his arms. 'Do not tell me what made you think of Lady Walsingham or how you persuaded her. I am content to know that you are brave, beautiful and brilliant.'

'I understand barely half of what is happening, Christopher,' she said, 'but at least I find you unharmed.' She gently disengaged herself and started to unpack the basket, while Christopher opened the bottle.

An hour later, she knew as much as did Christopher. 'The search of Kaye's house might already be under way,' he said, 'and Kaye should soon be in the Tower. Then we shall learn what Berwick has to say.'

'Have you any notion of the time left to us?' asked Katherine.

'None. But I have thought about the fires. My suspicion is that they were not only designed to spread fear but also to send a signal that *Incendium* is imminent. We must assume that there are those in London waiting for the word.'

'Catholics all?'

'Not necessarily. As in Paris, there will be others tempted by money and promises rather than driven by faith.'

'It is a wonder that they have not been discovered.'

'It is. And all the more frightening for that. In a manner not dissimilar, events in France were as sudden and as unexpected. If the massacres there were part of a wider and yet more terrible scheme, we must expect nothing less here. The advantage in numbers of the French Catholics will be replaced in England by men of grasping ambition at the head of armies of paupers and criminals. The Englishman who cannot feed his family will act with just as much violent intent, when the opportunity comes, as did the Frenchman.'

'But why have they not yet acted?' asked Katherine, almost to herself.

'I can only think that the plotters have experienced some problem, some delay to their plans. Wolf's attempt at Sheffield failed. The extent of the killings in France might have been unforeseen and have set them back. The bloodshed was so terrible that some will have turned away from the risk of more. Even some of the bishops were aghast, as I found in Amiens. However, we must assume the need for urgency.'

'What can I do?'

Christopher held up his hand. 'The earl has expressly commanded you to do nothing, Katherine. If you try to interfere, you risk Newgate.'

She waved a hand dismissively. 'Tush. I cannot sit idly by, merely acting as your messenger.'

'You can, Katherine, and you will. For all that I love you, I have given my word to the earl.'

'Then I shall join one of the miserable bands leaving the city and return to Cambridge.'

'I do hope you will not but, if that is what you wish, I cannot stop you.' He did not know whether to believe her or not.

Katherine stared at him. Her voice was icy. 'You have suffered much, Christopher, but there are times when you are a cold fish. Could you not make some effort to persuade me to stay in London?'

'How would I do that? You are at liberty while I am confined here.'

'Nonetheless, an attempt would have been welcome. Just an attempt.' She sighed and stood up. 'Ah well, you are safe here, I suppose.'

Christopher rose to take her hands. 'Take no risks, Katherine, for my sake as well as your own. The earl's anger is not what we need at this time. Leave them to question Kaye and I will speak to Wetherby.'

'If I must, Christopher, but my patience will not last for ever. You can tell me what Wetherby has to say tomorrow.' She kissed him briefly and called for the gaoler to open the door. 'There is a copy of *The Prince* in the basket. Signor Machiavelli will help pass the time.'

Roland Wetherby was lying on a narrow cot, his face to the wall. 'Mr Wetherby,' said the warden, 'you have a visitor.'

Wetherby rolled over, saw Christopher and sprang from the cot. He hurled himself forward and knocked Christopher backwards. Taken entirely by surprise, Christopher, despite his advantage in height and strength, stumbled and slipped to the floor. Wetherby sat astride him, thumped a fist into his chest and bellowed. Christopher pushed him off and was on his feet when the warden threw a blanket over Wetherby's head and wrestled him back to the cot. They held him there squirming like a fish and panting for breath.

'Be calm, Mr Wetherby,' said the warden, 'or it will be the worse for you. I could have you taken down to the cells below for attacking a visitor, never mind me. Dr Radcliff has asked to speak to you and the earl has agreed. Count yourself fortunate and lie still.'

'I mean you no harm, Mr Wetherby,' added Christopher. 'There are questions I must ask you, that is all.' From under the blanket came a muffled obscenity and a violent shake of the head. 'I will remove the blanket while the warden stands guard. Please do not resist. I am here to help you, not cause you to suffer further.' He nodded to the warden and pulled off the blanket.

The look of hatred in Wetherby's eyes made him start. 'Why

am I here?' Wetherby demanded in a hoarse croak. 'Why have you sent me here to die? I have done nothing.' A twitch had appeared by his eye.

Christopher backed away from the cot, leaving Wetherby to sit up. The warden stood at the door. 'It was not I who had you sent here, Mr Wetherby. There are others who mean you harm. I would speak to you in private. If we are left alone, will you be calm?' Wetherby's eyes narrowed as if he were on the point of attacking again. 'I do not advise more violence, Mr Wetherby. It can do you no good.'

For a few seconds, Wetherby held his gaze, then shrugged and swung his legs round to sit on the cot. 'Why did you send me here?'

'Mr Wetherby, it was not I. Would I be here if it were? May I ask the warden to leave?' Wetherby nodded. His eyes burned with anger. 'Good. I will call him when we are finished.' The warden closed the door behind him and turned the key in the lock. 'Now, Mr Wetherby, let us speak as civilized men. Have you had word from Mr Heneage?'

'I have not. He too has abandoned me for the crimes of others. The Earl of Leicester has persuaded him of my guilt, just as you persuaded the earl. Guilt of what I know not.'

'That is untrue, Mr Wetherby. It was John Berwick who accused you, not I.'

'Of what exactly am I accused by Berwick?' There was no sign of fear in the young man, just fury.

'He claims that you were seen in the Boar in Bishopsgate with a man known to be a traitor and in a street of stews and unnatural houses.'

Wetherby shrugged. 'There is no crime in such places.'

'But there is risk. A man might be forced to act against his will for fear of his habits being exposed.'

'That is still no crime and I have never frequented a tavern as mean as the Boar. Never set foot in it, never met any man there. Who is this traitor? Has he been questioned?'

'His name was Elias Smith. He was a traitor and a murderer. He is dead.'

'I know of no such man. Who claims otherwise? Berwick?' Wetherby's confidence was growing. His voice was firmer.

'Perhaps. Do you know James Kaye, a warden of the Stationers' Company?'

'No.'

'Yet I myself have seen you at the stationers' market.'

'That is absurd. I have also seen you, yet I do not accuse you of being a traitor.'

'You appeared discomfited to have been seen there.'

Now Wetherby looked vulnerable again. He did not meet Christopher's eyes when he replied. 'There are certain books, unusual books, which I obtain there.'

'And that is why you go there?'

'It is. You claimed to be here to offer help, yet your questioning is hostile. I am what I am, Dr Radcliff, but I am not a felon or a traitor.'

'And Monsieur Deschamps?'

'Grégory has returned to France. He was concerned for his parents.'

'Have I your word that you told him nothing of use to our enemies?'

Wetherby threw up his hands. 'Ha! I do not know anything of use to our enemies.'

'Then you will permit my questions without fear. Do you know of an Irishman named Patrick Wolf?'

'Wolf? No. Nor Lamb nor Fox. How many must I deny knowing before you are satisfied?'

'No more names, Mr Wetherby, but one word. *Incendium*. What does it mean to you?'

'The same as it does to you. Fire. What of it?' Christopher watched his face and caught his tone. Roland Wetherby was telling the truth.

'I would tell you if I could, Mr Wetherby. Suffice it to say that there are fires in London, lit by our enemies to cause panic among the people and, we fear, to signal the coming of bloodshed.'

'I am of course aware of the fires. As there have been in France.'

'Exactly.'

'Bloodshed. A plot? Am I thought a plotter? Is that why I am here?'

'It is. And here, I fear, you must remain for your own safety until the plot is exposed and the plotters dead or captured. If it is of any comfort, I am in the cell next to you. And be assured that my hatred of prisons is at least as great as your own.'

'So you believe me innocent?'

'I do, sir, but the earl must also be persuaded.'

'That is some relief,' replied Wetherby, with a sigh, 'although I shall rejoice only when I am a free man again and suspected of no crime.'

'John Berwick. Tell me what you know of him.'

'No more than you, I daresay. I know that his father died during the rebellion in the north and that the queen found his son a position with the earl. Sir Philip Berwick was, by all accounts, a brave and loyal man.'

'There is more to Berwick. I believe him a traitor. The earl remains to be convinced and is naturally wary of the queen's reaction to such a suggestion. That is why he has not yet had Berwick arrested and is proceeding with great caution. He does not understand how the son can have betrayed a father's memory so.'

Wetherby's voice rose in astonishment. 'Is there nothing in the man's background to explain it? What of his mother?'

'I believe that she died soon after his father. I know no more about her.'

Wetherby leaned forward on the narrow cot, making it creak. 'Then may I suggest that inquiries are made? There must be something.'

'I will speak to the earl. Now, you must eat and drink.' Christopher rose and hammered on the door. 'There is food and drink in my cell, warden. Please have it brought to Mr Wetherby.'

'I can make no sense of this, doctor. Why are you too in a cell?'

'I am here to test Berwick, just as you are.'

'Then be quick, doctor,' replied Wetherby. 'I am no hero.'

'Be resolute, Mr Wetherby. Berwick and his murdering friends shall not succeed.' Christopher returned to his own cell. Wetherby was no traitor. He was a victim and a very angry one. If he'd had any doubts remaining about Berwick's guilt, they had gone.

Katherine came again to the Gate House that afternoon, wrapped in a thick woollen shawl, and carrying another basket. The weather had turned colder. She kissed Christopher and sat on his cot. 'James Kaye's house has been searched. A letter was found. He has been arrested and taken to the Tower.'

Christopher could not suppress a smile. Kaye must be exploding with fury. 'And what of Berwick?'

'I do not know. My information comes from Ursula Walsingham.'

'I have spoken with Roland Wetherby. He is no traitor and suggests that the earl find out more of Berwick's family. The earl should speak to the queen.'

She shook her head. 'He will not like the suggestion.'

'He must be persuaded to suffer it.'

'Very well. I will speak again to Lady Walsingham. She is a formidable advocate. What else should I pass on?'

'That I could do more if I were not confined.'

'Perhaps you could, Christopher. You might also stir up a hive of angry bees.'

'Give half the food to Wetherby. He is in a sorry state.'

'As you wish. How is Signor Machiavelli?'

'I have not yet opened him. A pleasure in store, no doubt.'

Katherine did not stay long. She said that she was anxious to learn more news. If there were any.

CHAPTER 31

The guards came that night. Christopher was roused and told to dress. 'Where am I to be taken?' he asked, rubbing sleep from his eyes.

'The Tower,' replied one of the guards. 'The Earl of Leicester has commanded it.' Christopher swore. Had the earl changed his mind again?

They travelled by barge to the Tower stairs. Christopher huddled into his cloak against the night cold. To their left, glimmers of light from watchmen's lanterns flickered in the blackness; to their right the marshes and meadows were black as pitch. At night, the river was a strange, ghostly place and, especially under London Bridge where the currents sucked and swirled, a place of danger. Was he to meet James Kaye or had the viperous Berwick somehow contrived to drip more poison in the earl's ear?

The Warden of the Tower met them inside the Postern Gate and conducted Christopher to a bare room in the White Tower. 'Dr Radcliff,' he said, 'the Earl of Leicester wishes you to interrogate the prisoner.'

'Kaye?'

'James Kaye.'

Thank God. Interrogator, not prisoner. 'What of Mr Griffyn?'

'The earl wishes you to conduct the interrogation. That is all I know.'

'I need time to think. Bring him in twenty minutes.'

When James Kaye was escorted in, his hands and feet were chained and his face streaked with grime. Still, however, his look was arrogant and defiant. If he was surprised to see Christopher, he did not show it. 'Let the prisoner sit,' ordered Christopher.

Kaye shook his head. 'I shall stand.'

'As you wish, Mr Kaye. You have been arrested on suspicion of treason and murder. Do you deny these charges?'

'I have never killed a man and I deny that wishing for a just and godly society is a crime. A man must follow where his conscience leads him.' In his manner and voice Christopher detected only defiance and determination. James Kaye would not be an easy nut to crack.

'And whither does your conscience lead you, Mr Kaye? To order-ing the deaths of an innocent bookseller and his wife, to plotting to kill the queen of England, to ordering fire and destruction?' Kaye said nothing. 'You would do well to cooperate, sir. There are less gentle interrogators than I.' Still Kaye remained silent. 'Very well. Tell me what you know of *Incendium*.' There! In Kaye's eyes there was a flicker of recognition. 'What part have you played in it?'

'I have no notion of what you mean by this. What is this *Incendium*?' Still no hint of fear.

'Fire, Mr Kaye, as well you know. Fire, the like of which we have already seen on the streets of the city and in France.'

'Then you know what it is, Dr Radcliff, without my having to enlighten you. Fire, conflagration, flames. Think of the poet Virgil's account of the sacking of Troy, the city ablaze, the Trojans dying in their hundreds, the triumphant Greeks rampant. That was *Incendium*.'

'As it was in Paris. Do you say that such fury will come to London? Is our city to suffer as Paris has suffered? Are women and babes to be slaughtered and burned in the name of some satanic principle?'

'Satanic? No, sir. Just and godly. A fury that might visit any city that rejects the true ways of the Church.'

'And fire that would destroy the homes of its people.'

'Were the monasteries not destroyed by the adulterer Henry?'

'You are a Catholic, Mr Kaye.'

'That is not yet a crime.'

Christopher changed direction. 'What is it that takes you to St Ann's churchyard?'

'St Ann's? May a man not simply enjoy the peace of a place?'

In Kaye's eyes did he see the tiniest look of alarm? 'Your own house is nearby.'

'It is. That is why I choose St Ann's churchyard to sit and think. Sometimes I pray there. The solitude is uplifting.' Kaye had quickly recovered his poise.

For several minutes, Christopher sat and stared at Kaye. He had at least prised from him some intelligence. Eventually he stood and said, 'You have spoken with conviction, Mr Kaye, yet I am unconvinced. You are as likely to be driven by the prospect of power and wealth as by your beliefs. And there is much you have not told me. You will stay here. I shall return at dawn.' He swept out of the room, leaving Kaye in the charge of the guards. He would ask the Warden for a place to rest and think before resuming the questioning.

Three hours later, Christopher returned to the room where Kaye was still standing, chained and guarded. He had half expected the prisoner to be frightened and compliant but it was clear at once that standing for three hours with little but death to think on had done nothing to dampen the man's spirit. He held his head high and his shoulders square. The velvet-clad peacock had unexpected courage. 'I have more questions, Mr Kaye,' said Christopher. 'Would you care to sit?'

'No, sir,' replied Kaye, 'and it is I who have questions. What proof have you of my guilt of any crime? You accuse me of murder and treason. I am told a letter was found in my house. What letter and how has it sent me here? It is fraudulent. Have you real evidence? Have you witnesses? I demand to know.'

'You showed no surprise when you saw me. So you knew already that I am employed by the Earl of Leicester and at our previous meetings you therefore dissembled. Did you deduce that Nicholas Houseman was my intelligencer? Is that why you had him murdered?'

'Mere conjecture.'

'Elias Smith was questioned before he died. We know that his accomplice tricked Houseman into opening his door by mentioning the Stationers' Company. Why would he do that if there was no such connection?' At the mention of Smith, Kaye showed no emotion. Christopher continued. 'Patrick Wolf was also questioned after his capture at Sheffield Castle. *Incendium* is a plot to replace the queen with the Queen of Scots and to return England to Catholicism. That it comes so soon after the execution of the Duke of Norfolk for his part in a similar plot is no great surprise. Every month we learn of yet another piece of insidious treachery. Very little of it survives being crushed at birth. *Incendium*, it seems, is an exception. Perhaps that is because it was hatched in France and the murder of Admiral Coligny was its first bloody step. The duc de Guise is a formidable man with a consuming hatred of Protestants. How many other members of the Stationers' Company are involved in the plot?'

'Your conjectures become ever more fanciful. I know of neither Smith nor Wolf. The duc de Guise is but a name to me. I am Senior Warden of the Stationers' Company, unlawfully kept prisoner. I do not hold public office and am not required to take an oath denying the pope's supremacy of the Church. You are detaining me here against the law.' Kaye's voice was firm. Whatever he was driven by, it was a powerful force.

'Your religious beliefs are of little interest to me except insofar as they influence your loyalty to the Crown. You are not held here for your faith but for your treason.'

'I do not recognize the crime of treason. A man must be loyal to his beliefs and to God.'

Christopher's patience snapped. 'Be assured, Mr Kaye, that the hangman who keeps you barely alive on the scaffold and the butcher who slices open your stomach, slowly draws out your intestines, cuts off your manhood and burns your organs before your very eyes, they do recognize it. As will the cheering crowd who witness your humiliation. They will have no interest in your sophistry, only in seeing you die slowly and in agony.' He paused to let his words sink in. 'And John Berwick will die beside you. We shall meet again soon, Mr Kaye. Take him away, guards, and leave him to think on what awaits him.'

Christopher's outburst surprised even himself. Before Paris, he would not have believed himself capable of using such words. It was Kaye's insufferable arrogance that had caused it. He must find a way to break the carapace.

CHAPTER 32

Paris

'The time draws near, my dear Charles,' said Guise, raising a glass of wine the colour of blood. He sat with his scarred cheek towards the blazing fire, the bishop opposite him.

The bishop raised his own glass, placed it on the table between them and put his palms together in the manner of prayer. 'It does and I thank God for guiding us. I hear that King Philip laughed at the news of the deaths of so many Huguenots and our new pope was delighted to receive Coligny's head. It is reassuring to know that our allies are firm in their resolve.'

'And the king?'

'Now that we have come this far, the king urges us on. Are we now ready?'

The duc de Guise laughed. 'You have asked me that a dozen times, Charles. We are ready. Within a day of the news of the Protestant whore's death, we will take ship from Calais and join Alba's fleet ten miles east of the English coast. I have persuaded him that a show of force would not go amiss. He will sail soon and show himself to the English in the hope of luring them out of their harbours. My agents report that their ships are few and their defences along the south coast still pitiful. Now that autumn is here, the town officials believe it too late for an invasion and will resume work on their defences in the spring. How wrong they are they will soon discover. Has there been word from London?'

'None since the doomed affair at Sheffield Castle. Our friends were right to be worried about Wolf. The Irish were never willing followers of orders. No matter, he died without speaking and the Queen of Scots will be freed soon enough.'

'Our friends, are they still firm?'

'I have no reason to think otherwise. From elsewhere I hear that the first fires have been lit and the people are ready.'

'When the whore's palace is shooting flames high into the night sky, they will see a fire the like of which few have witnessed. Whitehall will be consumed and everything within it. The whore will die and her heathen counsellors with her. Our army will march on London and take the city unopposed. England will be restored to the godly ways of Queen Mary.'

'There will be obstacles. There always are.'

'They will be crushed. The people of England will gladly follow wherever their new queen, my blessed cousin, leads them. *Cuius regio, eius religio.* It was ever thus.' Guise raised his glass again. 'To God and victory.'

'God and victory.'

Chapter 33

London

Christopher had come straight to the palace from the Tower. On the river it had been cold but cold of a sort that a man who has been locked up in his own home and in a prison below ground could enjoy. He held his face up to the milky sun and filled his lungs.

He did not have long to wait in the antechamber. The earl soon came in, as always immaculately attired in a high-necked doublet, white hose and a short blue velvet jacket. Christopher wondered fleetingly if the Master of the Queen's Horse would manage to appear as elegant if half of London was in flames.

'Dr Radcliff,' said the earl. 'Have you been at the Tower?' He did not enter his study but stood facing Christopher in the antechamber.

'I have, my lord. You had Kaye arrested but did not order him to be interrogated by Mr Griffyn. May I ask why?'

'There is still no proper evidence against Kaye and Griffyn can be heavy-handed. I thought your approach would be more subtle and thus more likely to succeed. Did it?'

'Would that I could claim so but Kaye is proving stubborn.'

Leicester shook his head. 'Have you learned nothing, doctor?'

'On the contrary, I have learned that Kaye is an avowed Catholic as well as a man of business. He denies involvement in a plot but spoke of fire and flames and the destruction of our foundations. He also denies the crime of treason on the grounds that a man owes his first loyalty to his conscience not to the country of his birth. In his case, ambition might be a word more apt than conscience. If I am not mistaken he craves above all power and wealth.'

'Is he a traitor?'

'He is, and he has much to tell us about *Incendium*.'

'Then you must hasten to make him do so. Show him the rack if you must.' A beringed finger was jabbed at Christopher's chest.

'I have yet to question him about John Berwick or the pistols, my lord. Allow me to do so first.'

Leicester turned his head to one side and scratched at his beard. Never before had Christopher seen him embarrassed. 'Berwick's whereabouts are unknown. I have ordered him found.'

Before Christopher could speak, there was a knock on the door and a guard entered. 'A visitor has arrived for you, my lord. He claims that his business is urgent and gives his name as Signor Sessetti. He has travelled from Tilbury.'

'Walsingham's man,' said Leicester. 'Bring him in immediately. I did not know he was travelling to England, but his arrival is opportune. We will take breakfast together.' The guard bowed and left.

Tomasso Sessetti had made little effort to rid himself of the effects of his journey. His black hair was dishevelled, his eyes red and his thin lips dry and cracked. His cloak and doublet were creased and stained and his shoes dirty. He bowed to the earl. 'My lord, doctor, please excuse my arrival at such an hour and without warning. I have ridden hard from Tilbury and could not delay.'

'You are welcome, Signor Sessetti,' replied Leicester. 'Dr Radcliff's presence here is a happy coincidence. We will speak while we eat. I have ordered food to be brought.'

'My thanks, my noble lord. And you, doctor, how do you fare? I was much relieved to learn of your safe return to England.' He took Christopher's hand in both of his. 'In all truth, I did not think that you would escape France unscathed.'

'It was not without mishap but I fare well now that I am home. As I hope do you. And I have you to thank for saving my life.'

'Oh, how so?'

'In Paris. The slaughter we witnessed.'

'Ah, yes. You would have interfered.'

'I believe that I would. And swiftly regretted it.'

Leicester interrupted. 'I know not exactly what you might have regretted, doctor, and you may tell me another time. Now I must know what news our visitor brings with such urgency.'

'First, my lord,' said Sessetti, 'there is now not a grain of doubt about the intentions of the French. Guise's men have been quietly assembling outside Calais while ships are prepared for the crossing. In the ports of the Low Countries, Alba's ships are being provisioned. An attack is not far away despite the lateness of the season. We believe that it will happen in not more than a month, before the end of October.'

While he was speaking, a servant brought a silver bowl of water and three linen towels for their hands. He was followed by two guards carrying a round table which they placed in the middle of the antechamber. They returned with three chairs and silver dishes of fruit and fish, manchet bread, butter and a large cheese tart. 'Sit, gentlemen,' said the earl, 'let us eat while we speak. Today is

Wednesday, so no meat on our table. Do proceed, Signor Sessetti. From where does this intelligence come? Is it to be trusted?'

'Like all good intelligence, sir, it comes from good sources, corroborated by other good sources. I myself can vouch for it.' Tomasso, who had been travelling all night and must have been ravenous, took a bite out of an apple and wiped a dribble of juice from his chin with a napkin.

'And Sir Francis?'

'Sir Francis, too, is sure of its accuracy.'

'Has the plan the backing of the king and his mother?' asked Christopher.

Sessetti nodded. 'The king sent Coligny's head to Rome, so we must assume that he approved of it from the outset. As for Queen Catherine, we think not. It was she who arranged the marriage of her daughter to the Protestant Henry of Navarre and sent Montmorency to London, and she who visited Coligny after the shooting. Her son does not always confide in her. It is Guise whom we should fear most. A cousin of the Queen of Scots, a passionate hater of all Protestants and the brutal murderer with his own hand of Coligny. The Bishop of Beauvais is also involved. He, too, is a man of great influence. An attack will come. Is England prepared to defend itself?'

'With rusty cannon, leaking hulks, ancient muskets, pitchforks and ballows, it is,' replied Leicester. 'With modern weapons, fighting ships and trained soldiers, it is not. The invasion must be stopped before it starts.'

'The very words that Sir Francis used. What more is known about *Incendium*?'

'We know that it exists and the word suggests fire,' replied Christopher. 'We have already seen fires in the city and expect more. The attempt on Sheffield Castle is proof of the involvement of the

Scots. The pistol fired at Admiral Coligny and its twin suggest an assassination attempt. We must assume that this will be an attempt on the queen. We have identified one plotter and suspect another. Is there anything to add, my lord?'

'Only that we do not know where or when an assassination attempt will be made. The queen does not care to be confined. She insists on showing herself to her people. It is not possible to guard her at all times.'

'What of the plotters themselves?' asked Sessetti.

'One is held in the Tower — a warden of the Stationers' Company, James Kaye — the other is one John Berwick.'

'I recall your interest in the stationers, doctor. I could find no connection to them in Paris. Who is John Berwick?'

Leicester rose from his chair and walked to a window. 'He is a young man in my employ. I trusted him, as indeed did the queen herself, but it seems now that I was foolish to do so. I should have had him arrested with Kaye. Now he has disappeared.'

There was an uncomfortable silence before Christopher spoke. 'My lord, I suggest that while Berwick is absent from the palace, Signor Sessetti and I search his apartments and Kaye's house again. There may be clues as to where he is and we still do not know the whereabouts of Monsieur Caron's other pistol. Then I will question Kaye again.'

'I will arrange for both keys to be given to you,' replied Leicester, plainly relieved to have received a clear proposal. 'If Berwick returns, no harm, hopefully, will have been done. If not, we must assume you were right, Dr Radcliff. Let us hope Kaye can be made to speak. Now, you will want to refresh yourself after your journey, Signor Sessetti. I will have a room made ready for you. Dr Radcliff will meet you there in one hour.'

Sessetti rose from the table and bowed. 'I am obliged, my lord. One hour, Dr Radcliff.'

John Berwick's apartment was one of a row set aside for junior officials, overlooking the north end of the queen's privy garden. It was small but adequately provided with oak furniture. The walls were bare of paintings or hangings, the bed was wide and boxed. A bookcase housed a few volumes and papers covered the tables.

'If you take the bed chamber, I will attend to this room,' suggested Christopher.

'Do we have any notion of what we are looking for?' asked Sessetti.

'A twin of the pistol would be as gold. Failing that, anything to incriminate the man in the plot — documents, a letter, just the word itself, anything. I will start with the books.'

It was tedious work. They opened every book, emptied Berwick's clothes chest, heaved the heavy mattress off the bed to peer under it, tapped on the floor in search of a loose board, examined every scrap of paper. And, at the end of it, had found nothing. 'We should not be surprised,' said Sessetti. 'If I were a traitor I would not leave evidence in the queen's own palace. I would certainly hide it elsewhere.'

'As would I,' agreed Christopher. 'But we had to be sure.' He held up his poniard. 'And at least I have recovered this. It was behind a book. I doubt Berwick will notice that it has gone. Everything else we must put back as we found it in case he returns. Let us hope that James Kaye's house proves more fruitful.'

When they had put the room back together, Christopher asked, 'My legs are in need of stretching. Would you care to walk to Blackfriars? Kaye's house is there.'

'Your legs are longer than mine, doctor,' replied the Italian, 'but as long as Blackfriars is not too far distant. I do not know London well.'

'Then you will have the chance to see a little of it. Hold your purse close and walk beside me. And if we are to work together, I should prefer you to use my given name – Christopher.'

'And I am Tomasso.'

In the Strand they passed chestnut-sellers roasting their wares over charcoal braziers and butchers offering slabs of salted pork for the winter. 'One would not see this in Florence,' said Tomasso. 'Happily the Italian winters are milder than in England.'

In Fleet Street, a squealing pig galloped towards them, pursued by its furious owner. 'Are these animals permitted in the city?' he asked. 'To keep the Jews at home, perhaps?' Christopher looked sharply at him. There was a twinkle in the Florentine's eye.

'They are not. But pigs are clever animals. They often escape and when they do, nothing is safe. They will eat anything, even the clothes drying on a line. The people, too, have been escaping the city. The news from France has driven them out just as the Huguenots have been driven here. It is as well that the plot has not become known to the printers of news sheet or on the streets. London would have been left to rats and ne'er-do-wells.'

The land on which James Kaye's house stood, like the church-yard of St Ann's, had once been owned by the black-robed Dominicans. After the dissolution, almost all of the friary buildings had been demolished and new dwellings fit for the members of the nearby guilds – stationers and apothecaries among them – erected. They were brick-built and tiled and their windows glazed. Kaye's house in Blackfriars Lane backed on to what would once have been a section of the friary wall.

Christopher used the key to let them in. They stood in the entrance hall. 'He has no family, I assume,' said Tomasso.

'No family. He lived alone. A grand mansion for a single man.'

'If Kaye is in the Tower, has it not already been searched?'

'It has, and a letter was found. Enough to hold him. But the search was less than thorough. Let us start in his study.' There was no reason to tell Tomasso where the letter had come from.

It was a cluttered room, the tables heaped with books and documents, the desk a mess of inkpots, pens, sharpening knives and sand-shakers. They worked their way steadily through every book and paper, looking for any hint, any trace of Kaye's guilt. They looked behind paintings and in drawers. There was nothing. It was the same in the sitting room and the kitchen, where Tomasso stepped into the hearth and peered up the chimney. It was black and dirty and hid nothing but soot. They stamped on floorboards and tapped on walls. Nothing.

Up a narrow flight of stairs there were two bed chambers. The first contained a large boxed bed, a chest and a small table and chair. They tipped the mattress off the bed and peered under it. They emptied the chest of clothes and checked the walls for hidden alcoves. Nothing.

They tried the second chamber. Here there was just a bed and a leather-covered coffer, large enough to hold clothes or other possessions. They found nothing hidden in or under the bed and turned their attention to the coffer. It was locked. The only key they had was the one with which they had opened the door. Christopher took out his poniard. 'This has opened a lock before,' he said. 'Hold the chest steady and I will try it.' He slipped the point into the lock and twisted gently. Nothing happened. He twisted a little more firmly and they heard a faint click as the bar moved in its housing.

Another push and the lid sprang open. Christopher withdrew the poniard and tucked it back under his belt. 'Were your family lock-smiths as mine were gunsmiths, Christopher?' asked Tomasso.

Inside were several dozen rolls of paper, each tied with a blue ribbon and marked on the outside with a month and the year. 'Orderly, as befits a stationer,' said Tomasso.

Christopher took a roll from the top layer. 'This is dated August of this year.' He untied the ribbon and laid the papers on the bed. They were accounting records for the purchase of stock from paper mills in Guildford and Winchester and its delivery to various custom-ers, marked as received and paid and signed *J. Kaye.* Among his customers were two Fleet Street printers, the Corporation of London and St Paul's School. James Kaye was well-connected.

The second roll, dated September, revealed nothing more, but the third, also dated August, included an account for two hundred quires of fine paper delivered to Whitehall Palace. The signature of the recipient was illegible but James Kaye had again written his ini-tials to confirm receipt of payment. 'Two hundred quires, if I am not mistaken, is five thousand single sheets,' said Tomasso. 'The palace clerks do much writing.'

One by one they checked every roll on the top layer back to January. In each of the months April to August, James Kaye had supplied to Whitehall Palace at least two hundred quires and in some months as many as five hundred quires of good-quality rag paper. It was a mountain of paper, even for the royal household and its Privy Council.

'There is some deceit here,' said Tomasso, 'some fraud or theft.'

Christopher stretched out his bent fingers and scratched his chin. 'If you wished to smuggle guns or powder into the palace how would you set about it, Tomasso? Would you not disguise it as something else, something harmless and unlikely to be noticed?'

'Would I not need an accomplice to place orders and accept the goods?'

'You would.'

'Why would I not destroy the records of the transactions?'

'To prove that the deliveries had been made perhaps, or simply because, as an orderly man, you do not care to destroy your records.'

'I would risk attracting the attention of a clerk in the office of the Master of the Household.'

'In the labyrinth of offices and the grind of daily work, you would as likely go unnoticed.'

'God in heaven.'

'Come, Tomasso, the streets are crowded. We will travel to the palace by wherry.'

The hundreds of items needed to run Whitehall Palace without inconvenience to the queen or her courtiers — furniture and hangings, empty barrels, fabrics, cloth, and tools and instruments for mending, cleaning and carpentry — were stored in the palace's huge cellars. A carter making a delivery would wait outside one of the gates while an army of servants carried his boxes and crates down a flight of steps behind the chapel to the cellars. There a storeman would count them off and take both copies of the note of delivery to the store master who would sign them as complete or part-complete. The signed notes were sent each day up to the household office where they were recorded and filed for payment. The carter returned the second note to the supplier. Only rarely would a storeman bother to look inside a crate or box or barrel to check that the contents were as the note of delivery said they were. Only members of the appropriate guild, and thus vouched for by their company, were permitted to supply the queen's households. Any man found to have acted in any way fraudulently risked his guild losing its privileged status as a royal supplier. Such a thing was unheard of.

Christopher and Tomasso leapt off the wherry at Whitehall stairs and ran up to the chapel. They descended the steps to the cellar and waited at the foot to allow their eyes to adjust to the gloom. The light from the torches flickering on the walls was meagre and shadowy. A storeman saw them and asked what their business was. 'We must speak with the store master on an urgent matter,' replied Christopher.

'And who might you be?' growled the storeman. 'The master is busy.'

Christopher stepped forward and towered over the man. 'I am Dr Christopher Radcliff, a member of the staff of the Earl of Leicester. This is Signor Tomasso Sessetti who is assisting me, and your master is not too busy to speak to us immediately.' The storeman shook his head, muttered something about the earl and slouched off to find the man they sought.

The master was a short, stout man, displeased at the inter-ruption. 'What is it you want, sirs?' he waddled up and demanded without greeting. 'I am occupied in my work and can spare little time.'

'We wish to examine the deliveries of paper made since April. I understand there have been a good many of them.'

'Indeed there have and causing me much inconvenience. The crates take up space intended for other items. I have been forced to open up an old part of the cellar no longer in use. Mr Berwick instructed me to ensure that the paper is kept dry. It is of very fine quality.'

Christopher and Tomasso exchanged a look. 'Mr Berwick,

who is employed by the Earl of Leicester?' asked Christopher.

'I know of no other in Whitehall. He was most insistent.'

'Did he explain why so much paper has been delivered this year? Surely the quantity is greater than usual?'

'Mr Berwick told me that the price of paper is set to rise and that he had been able to secure a large quantity at a good price. I gathered that he has connections at Stationers' Hall.'

'Were the crates checked? Have any been opened?'

'Not yet. There has been no need.'

'We will see them at once. They must be opened.'

The store master scratched his head. 'I cannot see how that might be done. Mr Berwick was most insistent that the crates be secure until he order them opened. The quality of the paper would suffer from exposure to light or damp, he said.'

'In this case, store master, I must overrule Mr Berwick. Kindly take us to the crates immediately.'

'I can show you the crates, sirs, but I cannot allow them opened.'

Christopher stared at the little man. 'We have wasted enough time. You would do well to do as I ask. This is not a matter for argument.'

'I cannot, sir. Mr Berwick's orders were clear.'

'And did Mr Berwick offer you a reward for your services?' asked Tomasso.

The store master shuffled his feet and looked embarrassed. 'I take only what is due to me.'

Christopher turned his back on the man. 'Enough of this, Tomasso. We will see what the earl has to say.' Tomasso followed him up the steps and into the palace grounds. A guard stood at one corner of the chapel. 'We must see the Earl of Leicester at once,' said

Christopher. 'The queen is in danger. Escort us to his apartments.'

The guard recognized Christopher and caught the urgency in his voice. 'Follow me, doctor, although I know not if the earl is there.'

They were admitted by the guards at the earl's door and asked to wait in the antechamber. They did not wait long. Leicester strode in and demanded to know what new danger the queen was in. 'You must accompany us to the cellars, my lord,' replied Christopher. 'There I believe you will see the danger for yourself.'

Leicester sighed. 'Very well, doctor. I shall not misjudge you again. To the cellars it is.'

At the steps to the cellar they were greeted by the store master. Seeing the earl, the little man swept off his cap and bowed as low as his stomach would allow.

'What is it you wish me to see, doctor?' asked Leicester.

'The crates containing deliveries of paper since April, my lord. There are many.'

The store master led them into the cellar to the place where the paper had been stored. Stacked up against a wall towards the back of the cellar, where there was little light, were dozens of crates, all sealed and stamped with the crest of the Stationers' Company. 'Am I to understand that these all contain paper?' asked Leicester in disbelief. 'How can we possibly require so much to be held in store?'

'I suggest that one crate is carried outside,' said Tomasso. 'We would be unwise to open it near the flames of the torches.'

'Have it brought up,' ordered Leicester. 'Let us see what has so exercised you.'

Outside, they waited for the crate to be carried up the steps. One of the storemen had a short iron bar, with which he began to prise open the lid. 'Take care, man,' said Christopher. 'We do not want a spark.'

The lid came off and they peered inside.

'I see only paper, doctor,' said Leicester.

Christopher leaned over and carefully removed several bundles of dusty paper. Under them was a grain sack, lying on its side to fit into the crate. He lifted it out gently. 'My lord, I suggest you stand back,' he said, taking out his poniard and slowly slicing the cloth. A handful of grey powder fell from the cut. He took a pinch in his fingers and sniffed. 'Gunpowder. And stored in sacks for ease of transport. A single spark and it could have exploded. There are dozens of crates down there. If they all contain powder, the palace would have been destroyed and everyone in it. Her Majesty would not have escaped.'

'In the name of God,' said Leicester. When he wiped a bead of sweat from his brow, Christopher noticed that his hand was shaking. 'How has this happened and by whose authority?'

The store master struggled to speak. 'Mr Berwick ordered the paper and gave us instructions to keep it in a dry place.' The words caught in his throat and he was trembling.

'Berwick. So your suspicions are now certainly confirmed, doctor.'

'My lord, let every crate be brought up from the cellar and held in a safe place.'

'Order it done, store master. And do not leave the palace grounds without my express authority. If you do so, it will be taken as an act of treason. Do you understand?' The man mumbled that he did. 'Have every crate up here within the hour.' He turned on his heel and strode off to his apartment. Unbidden, Christopher and Tomasso followed.

They sat in Leicester's study. A servant had poured wine for each of them. The earl's face was ashen. 'It would have been simple,' he said. 'A single open crate, a flame placed nearby and Whitehall would have exploded.'

'Conflagration, my lord,' replied Christopher quietly. '*Incendium*.'

Leicester tapped his temple with a finger. 'It would have been done at night.'

'Or when the Privy Council was meeting. The consequences are too dire to imagine.'

'They are. How did you discover the plan?'

Christopher explained what they had found in Kaye's house and how it had led them to the Whitehall cellars. Leicester took a gulp of wine. 'It is beyond belief: the queen's palace shown so abjectly vulnerable to attack and, for all her bodyguards, the queen herself in grave danger. It makes a mockery of her loyal servants and I myself feel responsible.'

'To succeed, the plan required an enemy within, my lord,' said Tomasso, 'and a clever one.'

'Berwick must be found and interrogated, and without delay.' The wine had brought a touch of colour to Leicester's face but his voice was still shaky.

'We must not forget that there is a pistol unaccounted for,' said Christopher. 'An assassin's weapon identical to the one you have, my lord. It has a purpose. We must discover what and how before it is too late.'

'I take it there was no trace of it in Berwick's apartment?'

'None.'

'Very well. Dr Radcliff, you will again question James Kaye. I shall speak to the queen and to Heneage. You and I will question Berwick when he is safely in the Tower with Kaye. The pistol and its keeper must be found.'

'Stationers' Hall must also be searched and every member questioned.'

'I shall arrange it. Mr Heneage will doubtless assist by providing men for the task.'

'And Roland Wetherby, my lord? He is surely innocent of any involvement in this plot.'

'Ah, Wetherby. I had quite forgotten him. He will be released, as are you, doctor.'

Christopher inclined his head. 'I am grateful, my lord. '

'Go at once to the Tower. I will have a guard accompany you and a barge ready at the stairs in ten minutes. Signor Sessetti will remain here. I would hear more of Paris.'

CHAPTER 34

If Christopher had expected the threat of being half-hanged, drawn and quartered to have penetrated Kaye's carapace of arrogance, he was mistaken. For all that he needed the attention of a barber and a clean set of clothes, the man was every bit as haughty as he had been at their last meeting.

'I trust you have thought on the fate that awaits you if you do not assist me in my inquiries,' he began. Kaye simply stood and stared at him. 'We now have proof absolute of the guilt of John Berwick and the plot to blow up Whitehall Palace. The gunpowder has been found and rendered harmless. Stationers' Hall is at this moment being searched from cellar to roof and every member of the company questioned. Any man thought to be connected to *Incendium* will be arrested and interrogated, under duress if necessary. It was an evil plot and they will pay with their lives.'

Kaye smirked. 'Then you have no need of anything further from me.'

Christopher ignored the remark. 'Berwick will be arrested within hours. Meanwhile, you will tell me where the assassin's pistol is hidden.'

A fleeting look of surprise crossed Kaye's face. He recovered quickly. 'I know of no pistol, as I know of no plot to blow up Whitehall Palace. This is all a fabrication, no doubt devised by the wife-killer Leicester, whose yapping pup you are, to hide his own ambitions.'

'Those are treasonous words, Kaye. You could hang just for them.'

'As you have already told me I shall. What else have you in store for me? The rack, amputation of my hands, removal of my ears? I am immune to such threats, as by now you should have realized. My faith makes light of worldly suffering.'

Christopher tried a different tack. 'You accuse me of being a yapping pup, yet are you not the pup of the duc de Guise and, through him, of the French king? Is it not them from whom you have taken your orders?'

'My orders come only from God. It is him whom I obey.'

Christopher jabbed a finger at him. 'You try my patience, Kaye. We all serve God. You are no different and your empty sanctity rings hollow in my ears. Where is the pistol?' Kaye remained silent. Christopher was tempted to take him by the neck and shake the truth from him. Instead, he lowered his voice and whispered. 'Where is the pistol?'

'I know of no pistol.'

Christopher exhaled. 'As you wish. The pistol will be found and with it the would-be assassin. The intentions of the duc de Guise are known to us. Go to your God knowing that no Spanish ship will drop anchor in English waters or French foot walk on English soil. The slaughter in France will not come to England, however many child-killing vipers slither from their nests. England will remain at peace and governed by its rightful queen.'

'A pretty speech, doctor. And quite mistaken.'

'Take the prisoner away, guard. I can listen to no more of this.'

It was as if London was holding its breath. News, both true and false, had spread from house to house and market to market. Knots of artisans and tradesmen were gathered on street corners to share gossip and opinion. On his way home from the Tower, Christopher could not but sense the fear. The plot to blow up Whitehall would soon be widely known. The storemen had wives and the wives had friends and the story would spread in days. Then the streets would be deserted, the taverns and churches full.

He should have returned directly to Whitehall, where the earl would be waiting for his report of Kaye's interrogation, but he craved rest and he had no real news to deliver. He would sleep awhile and go later.

Rose's wrinkled face split into a toothless grin when he walked into the house. 'There you are, doctor. Home safe, thank the Lord.'

'Here I am, Rose, and I too thank the Lord for it. Can you manage a little food before I retire to my bed chamber? I must go to Whitehall later.'

'I can, doctor. You look as if you need it. I will bring it to your study.'

'Thank you, Rose. Have there been any callers?'

'Only one, doctor. A woman who gave her name as Ell. A common sort, although she claimed to know you. I told her you were away.'

'She did not say what her purpose in calling was?'

'No, doctor. I was surprised that you knew such a woman.' Rose was fishing.

'I meet all sorts in my work, Rose. If she calls again I wish to see her.'

'Very well, doctor. Sit down now and I will bring your food.'

An hour later, Christopher was woken by a hammering on the door of his bed chamber. 'Doctor, doctor, the woman Ell is here again. You said you wished to see her.' Rose struggled to make herself heard through the door. Christopher dragged himself from sleep and stumbled to open it.

'Ell, did you say, Rose? Show her in and tell her I shall be down directly.'

'Doctor, are you sure that would be proper?' Rose sounded horrified.

'Entirely proper, Rose. Please do as I say.'

He pulled on trousers, covered himself with his gown and went down the stairs. When she saw him, Ell giggled. 'This is a new affair, Dr Rad. Me dressed proper and you in no more than your gown.'

'It saved me dressing, Ell. I have been at the Tower and at the earl's beck and call. I need sleep. Take that chair. What news do you bring?'

'The Tower, eh? Better than Newgate, they do say. What were you doing there?'

'It's a tale too long to tell. News, Ell?'

'Not really news, doctor, but you told me to keep my ears open. I heard that word spoken. *Incense*, wasn't it?'

'It was, near enough. Where did you hear it?'

'A gentleman. He was counting out the price when he suddenly said it. He said after the *Incense* women like me would be grateful to men like him. Thought at first I hadn't heard right but now I'm sure I did.'

'Who was he, Ell? Did he tell you his name?'

'No name, doctor, but from the way he talked I took him for a bookseller or a writer. Went on about books and reading and suchlike.'

'Can you describe him?'

'Short and plump. Not much hair. Smell of old turnips about him.'

'There's a lot like that, Ell, but you were right to tell me. Next time—' There was a thump on the door and Rose poked her head in.

'Sorry to disturb you again, doctor. Mistress Allington is here. What shall I tell her?'

'One moment, Rose. Is there anything else, Ell?'

'No, doctor. Should I go?'

'Rose, tell Mistress Allington that I have been asleep and would be grateful if she would return in an hour or so. Tell me when she has left.'

'An hour or so. Very well, doctor.'

'Give her a few minutes, Ell, then slip away. She would never believe the truth. Thank you for coming.'

Ell grinned. 'My pleasure, doctor. Or it would be if only you'd allow it. Whatever this *Incense* is, I hope you get rid of it soon. It's making me nervous just knowing the word. Plague is like that.'

There was another knock on the door and it was opened an inch. 'The mistress has left, doctor,' whispered Rose.

'Off you go then, Ell. Better if I call on you next time. Just write your name on a bit of paper and push it under my door, as you did before. I'll come to Cheapside.'

'I will, doctor. Sorry to have woken you.' Rose shut the door behind her and Christopher returned to his bed. An hour would give him time for a short sleep.

It was a forlorn hope. Rose had barely left when the

bed-chamber door was thrown open and Katherine strode in. The green eyes flashed with anger. 'And is she your whore?' she demanded.

'Who?' Christopher could not think clearly.

'Do not dissemble, Christopher. I knew at once something was amiss or you would not have sent me away. I saw the woman leave. Your whore, is she not?'

'Calm yourself, Katherine. She is a whore, although that is not the reason she was here. She is an intelligencer, as I have often told you.'

Katherine's voice had become almost shrill. 'Am I expected to believe that? I risk my life by creeping down a foul alley, speak for you to Ursula Walsingham, visit you in gaol, and all so that you can bed a common whore. How dare you so insult me?'

Christopher sat up. 'Katherine, it is not how it appears to you and I cannot help your feeling insulted. I am engaged in the most serious work and will speak to whomever I choose.' He glared at her. 'And I am tired. Let me sleep and we will speak of it later.'

Katherine was not to be put off. 'No, Christopher, we will not speak of it later. We will speak of nothing later. Or ever again.' With a withering look, she slammed the door behind her so hard that the window rattled in its frame.

Christopher clutched at a pain in his stomach. He had no strength left for another fight. He laid his head back on the pillow and closed his eyes.

CHAPTER 35

October

It was dark as pitch when he woke. For a while he lay ordering a jumble of thoughts, then groped around for his candle and the tinder and flint he kept beside it. It took several attempts but eventually he made a spark, the tinder caught and the candle flickered into life.

Why had he been so foolish as to allow Ell into his house? It would be weeks before Katherine spoke to him again and even when she did, she would not believe what he told her. Perhaps he should just claim that he felt the need for a rough whore. She would believe that, although she might not forgive it.

If Tomasso's intelligence was right and if there was indeed more of *Incendium* to come, the assassin's pistol and with it the assassin must be found before Alba's fleet set sail. A thought occurred to him. Was the assumption that the queen was the assassin's target a fair one or might he be planning to point his two barrels at Burghley or Walsingham in Paris or even Leicester himself? Or another member of the queen's council? Or all of them? No, the gunpowder would have been aimed at all of them — ignited when the council was meeting in its Star Chamber. If Burghley or Walsingham were at risk, there was nothing to be done now to protect them. If Leicester, the earl would say simply that his task was to preserve the life of the queen, if necessary by sacrificing his own.

Whitehall Palace destroyed, the deaths of important men, men who governed the country at the will of the queen, an invasion by an alliance of the duplicitous French and the bloodthirsty Spanish . . . the assassin's target could only be the queen. Elizabeth dead, no heir, the Scots determined to put their queen on the English throne. It could only be the queen.

It was not yet light when Christopher left the house for Whitehall. He had eaten a hasty breakfast and walked to Blackfriars stairs, where he found a wherryman wrapped up against the chill and dozing in his boat, awaiting his first customer of the day. Christopher gave him a nudge with his foot and asked to be taken to Whitehall with all speed. The wherryman shook himself awake and motioned to Christopher to step in.

'Spanish ships off Tilbury, they say,' he growled as he took hold of his oars and began to heave. 'Won't be long before we're Romish again.'

'Spanish ships? Where did you hear this?'

'Talk of the wharves. Big ships with tall masts and thousands of Spanish soldiers in the holds. Some say they have pricks as long as their arms. My woman says if they do they're welcome here.' His laugh brought on a fit of coughing and brought the wherry to a halt.

'Save your breath for the journey,' ordered Christopher, not wishing to be drawn into conversation. 'It is idle chatter, no more.'

It was fully light when Christopher handed the wherryman a

coin and walked up to the palace gate. He found Leicester at his breakfast.

'Dr Radcliff, I had expected you yesterday. Were you delayed?' Leicester bit into a chicken leg.

'I was, my lord, but by nothing more than fatigue.'

'I have spoken to Her Majesty. She is horrified at Berwick's treachery and has ordered his late father's brother arrested. It was he who presented Berwick to her. More than that we do not know.'

'If Berwick swore the oath, Her Majesty would reasonably have assumed his loyalty to her.'

'He did swear it but to such a traitor an oath is no more than words. It has no substance or meaning. What of Kaye?'

'I have learned nothing of importance. Even the threat of being drawn and quartered did not make him speak. Nor, I fear, would the rack.'

'Nor did the search of Stationers' Hall reveal anything. What is more, I have this morning received a report from Dover that Spanish ships have been seen not ten miles off the coast.' So the wherryman's rumours had some truth in them. 'It can be only a matter of time before their cannon open fire on our ports and although we have done what we can with our defences I doubt we will be able to withstand a sustained attack. Our best hope is an autumn storm sweeping down from the North Sea and forcing them to seek safe haven in the harbours of the Low Countries. At present there are no signs of that.'

'My lord, we have prevented the destruction of this palace. Once the queen is known to be safe, will the Spanish and the French not abandon their plans?'

'The Privy Council believes that they will and are pressing me to find Berwick and drag the truth from him. The discovery of gunpowder under their noses has alarmed them, as it has me. The queen herself is sanguine. She believes that the plot to blow up Whitehall could never have worked — why, I am not entirely sure — and has faith in our ability to discover and prevent any attempt on her life. She points out that there have been several attempts already and all have failed. She told me that she would die when she was ready and that she was not yet ready.'

'Does the queen know of the pistol?'

'She does. I showed her the one we have. She thought it most ingenious and suggested that we have some made. When I informed her of the likely cost, however, she felt that we could do without them.'

'Her Majesty has more courage than I.'

'Or I. And she is insisting on worshipping at St Andrew's church in Aldgate. She has chosen the fourth day of this month.'

Only three days hence. 'So soon? Can Her Majesty not be persuaded otherwise?' asked Christopher.

Leicester shook his head. 'She is unshakeable. She has often worshipped at St Andrew's and she wishes to be seen, well and unafraid, by her people. There is a determination in the royal heart that I know only too well.'

'She will be vulnerable.'

'Her Majesty is perfectly aware of this.' Leicester pushed aside his unfinished breakfast. 'I find it difficult to eat and sleep is elusive. This is the most troubling time since dear Amy died.'

Christopher gave the earl time to recover himself before asking, 'Does the palace employ a skilled locksmith, my lord?'

'A locksmith? Why?'

'Kaye was seen entering St Ann's churchyard and remaining there for half an hour, although his house is close by. We had thought he was meeting another in secret, although no other was seen. The little church of St Ann was locked. It is no longer used but perhaps we should examine it.'

'If it is no longer used, why— Oh, as you wish, for want of any other idea, let us examine it. I will find you a locksmith to open the church door. What do you expect to find there, doctor?'

'I know not, my lord. Guidance, perhaps.'

'A jest, doctor? That is unlike you. You too must be suffering from the strain of uncertainty. Wait in the churchyard and I will send the locksmith to you. And take Sessetti with you. He lacks work.'

They stood together under the plane tree in the churchyard waiting for the locksmith. 'It is better to be doing something than nothing,' said Tomasso, rubbing his gloved hands together, 'though I would wish for Italian sunshine.'

Christopher stamped his feet. 'There are Spanish ships off Dover. Let us hope that the Spanish soldiers are freezing in their holds.'

'Either they are simply testing your defences or they are preparing their attack. A fast ship from Dover could bring them orders in a few hours. It would be tempting to send a false message ordering them to return home, but I doubt they would believe it without proof. Ah, here is our man.'

The locksmith was a large fellow, as tall as Christopher and half again as heavy. He was ruddy-faced and clean-shaven and when he removed his cap, had not a hair on his head. Over his shoulder he carried a sack. He spoke in the voice of a man of Kent. 'Dr Radcliff, sir, I am Oxnard, locksmith to Her Majesty at Whitehall. I am sent here to assist you. What is to be done, if you please?'

'Goodman Oxnard, Signor Sessetti and I must enter the church.'

Christopher pointed to the church door at the top of the wooden steps. 'Be so good as to open the door for us.' Oxnard peered at Tomasso and frowned. 'Signor Sessetti is from Florence. He is Italian and a true friend to England.'

Oxnard's face relaxed. 'Of course, sir. I meant no offence. It is just that—'

'We know, goodman. Open the door if you please.'

Oxnard clambered up the steps and put down his sack. He bent to put his face close to the lock and peered at it. Apparently satisfied, he fished into the sack and brought out a tool that resembled a long sewing needle. This he inserted into the keyhole and jiggled about before withdrawing it and pulling from his sack a heavy key of the sort carried by prison gaolers. He turned this in the lock and almost immediately there was the sound of it opening.

Oxnard straightened his back and grinned. 'No trouble, sirs. These old locks present few problems and this one has been recently used.' Tomasso and Christopher exchanged a look. 'Anything else I can do for you?'

'Thank you, Mr Oxnard. The door must be locked again when we have finished so please wait here until we come out.' Oxnard picked up his sack and heaved it down the steps. Christopher and Tomasso climbed up and entered the church. The open door allowed in sufficient light for them to see.

It was small, no more than the size of Leicester's antechamber, and bare of any furniture or decoration, save for a single faded screen behind which a priest might have sat. The room lacked any form of window and had been cheaply constructed of overlapping timbers. There was no evidence of recent use but also no smell of damp. 'Air has reached the room from somewhere,' said Tomasso. 'Probably from the door being opened. Still, let us check the floor and walls.'

They walked around the room, tapping the walls and floor timbers. There was nothing. They walked around again, this time
feeling the joints of the timbers with their fingers. In one corner of
the recess in which would have stood the altar, Christopher noticed a
slight gap between the timbers on either side of it. He ran his finger
down one side of the corner and felt, at the level of his eyes, a hole in
the timber about the size of an inkpot. He hooked the fingers of his
left hand around it and pulled. A hidden panel moved on its hinges
and creaked open.

Tomasso had been watching. 'Effective enough for most
purposes,' he said. 'What can you see?'

'Little. I would guess at a small, dark room. We need a candle.
Ask Oxnard if he's got one in his sack.'

Oxnard had not only a tallow candle but also a means of lighting
it. Tomasso returned with the flame shielded by his hand. He held it
out in front of them and they peered into the narrow space behind
the panel. On a bench, neatly laid out, were a crucifix, two sets of
rosary beads, a priest's vestments and a rolled-up altar cloth.

'So this is why Katherine saw Kaye entering the churchyard. It
was not for a secret meeting but for this. He is preparing for a mass
to celebrate the success of *Incendium*.'

'Do you suppose that Kaye himself is ordained?' asked Tomasso.

'A priest in disguise awaiting the glorious day? Stranger things
have happened.' Christopher took a step into the room and reached
out for the altar cloth. It was heavy. There was something inside it.
He dragged it into the church and together they unrolled it. And
there it was — an exact match for the pistol safely in Leicester's
possession and another example of the craftsmanship of Monsieur
Caron of Paris. Christopher picked it up and hefted it in his hand. 'A
beautiful piece of work.' He handed it to Tomasso.

'Just like its twin, weighted to balance the length of the barrels.'
He squinted along them. 'A masterpiece of the gunsmith's art. The
net closes around Mr Kaye and Mr Berwick.'

'So it does. And they shall not escape.'

They carefully closed the hidden panel and had Oxnard lock the
door before hastening back to Whitehall. Christopher wrapped the
pistol back in the altar cloth and put it in the locksmith's sack for
safety. He and Tomasso walked either side of the locksmith, as if
they were guarding him. They kept to the middle of the street away
from dark doorways and filthy alleys but still Christopher found himself glancing nervously around as they hurried down Fleet Street.

At the palace gate he retrieved the pistol in its wrappings,
instructed Oxnard to say nothing of his morning's work, and asked to
be taken immediately to Leicester. The guard knew Christopher by
sight and must have caught the urgency in his tone because he did
not ask what it was they carried but escorted them directly to the
earl's apartments.

The yeoman outside the earl's door did not know where he was,
only that he had left in unusual haste and without saying why. They
would have to wait. He could not say for how long. Tomasso sat
clutching the pistol while Christopher paced the antechamber,
stretching his fingers and listening for the sound of footsteps outside
the door.

When eventually Leicester arrived, they had been waiting for
an hour. He threw open the door and strode in, his look as angry as
Christopher had ever seen it.

'And what, pray, do you bring me, doctor?' he demanded, eyeing
the rolled-up cloth. 'The head of a traitor?'

Christopher took the bundle from Tomasso, laid it on the floor
and opened it out. 'It is the other pistol, my lord,' he replied. 'It was

concealed in a secret room in St Ann's. This is the reason James Kaye visited the churchyard. A look at this and Berwick will surely concede defeat.' He handed the gun to Leicester.

'He might, but first we have to find him. Her Majesty is much displeased that we have not already done so. She wishes him to be brought before her.'

Christopher's elation at finding the pistol drained away. Leicester opened the door to his study and went to his desk. From a drawer he took the other pistol and laid them side by side. They were identical.

'We found other things hidden with the pistol,' said Tomasso, 'the trappings of a Catholic priest. Rosaries, vestments, incense. James Kaye must be questioned about them.'

'Do you think him a priest?' asked Leicester, as if such a thing were beyond belief.

'Possibly, my lord. The church is bare, as if awaiting the call to service. One can imagine Kaye donning the priest's robes, lighting candles, filling the church with symbols of his faith, spreading incense and saying a Latin Mass, while all the time rejoicing at the death of our queen and an end to the Church of England.'

'As ugly a vision as one might imagine. Blood and Catholics — ever bedfellows. The queen despairs of their cruelty in France. Her tolerance has been tested beyond measure.' He picked up one of the pistols and waved it at them. 'And this will do nothing to restore it.'

'At least we have it and Berwick does not,' ventured Sessetti.

'That is so, but we do not have Berwick. Have you any scholarly advice, doctor?'

Christopher took his time in replying. This was hardly the time to point out that Berwick should have been arrested with Kaye. 'Here in Whitehall, Her Majesty is safe from attack, but in three days she will go to Aldgate where she will be protected more by her faith than by her guards. Is it not likely that that is when the traitor will strike? If so, between this day and that, he must go to St Ann's church to collect the pistol.'

'So we set guards to wait for him and take him when he appears.'

'We do. And as the two who have suffered most at Berwick's hands are Roland Wetherby and myself, I request that we are the ones to keep watch and to have the satisfaction of catching him.'

'May I not accompany you?' asked Sessetti.

'Of course, Tomasso, if the earl agrees.'

Leicester shook his head. 'I do not agree, Signor Sessetti. You are a citizen of Florence, not England. I cannot endanger you unnecessarily.'

'My lord—'

'No, Signor Sessetti.' Leicester's tone precluded further discussion. 'Have you any other suggestions, doctor?'

'Just one. That rather than placing this pistol with its mate in your care, we replace it in the church, having ensured that it cannot fire.'

'Why? What is to be gained from that?'

'Consider, my lord. The fox is most alert when he approaches the hen coop. His ears are pricked and he is ready to flee at a hint of danger. He is at his least alert, however, when he has raided the coop. Then he believes there is no danger and is intent only upon getting away with his prize.'

'But if there is no prize,' interrupted Sessetti with a grin, 'he will know there is danger.'

'Exactly. We let him take his prize, albeit, thanks to Signor Sessetti, a worthless one, and surprise him when he is returning to the church door. The guards will be ordered to station themselves outside it when they have seen him enter. The fox will be trapped.'

Leicester looked doubtful. 'He will be armed.'

'So shall we,' replied Christopher.

Still Leicester was uncertain. 'What is your opinion, Signor Sessetti?'

'If the pistol is unable to fire, my lord, what is to be lost? Berwick can do no harm with it.' The plan clearly appealed to Sessetti.

'Dr Radcliff or Mr Wetherby might be lost. You, Signor Sessetti, will not be present. Can you be sure of disabling the pistol without Berwick knowing?'

Tomasso looked aggrieved, as if his professional competence was being called into question. He picked up the pistol from where the earl had put it on the table and peered at the dogs and the trigger. 'I can certainly disable it in such a way that Berwick will not notice, even in bright daylight. He will have dry powder and shot designed for the narrow barrels, so I cannot tamper with those, but I will make a small adjustment to the trigger.'

'What manner of adjustment?' asked Leicester, a hint of doubt in his voice.

'The top of the trigger is inside the stock,' replied Tomasso, pointing to a spot above the trigger guards. 'Here. If I remove the lock, remove the trigger, file the top of it so that it will not make contact with the sear, the spring will not be released and the pistol will not fire. When it is reassembled, the adjustment will be invisible. It will only be discovered if someone tries to fire it.'

'Can you be certain that neither barrel will fire?'

'Quite certain, my lord. And even in bright daylight no one would notice that it has been tampered with.'

There was a long pause while Leicester stood at the window and watched the rain now falling. 'Very well,' he said eventually, 'I am not entirely comfortable with this but you and Wetherby, doctor, if he agrees, are the ones who will be facing Berwick, not I. If this is the plan you favour, I will reluctantly agree to it. Be aware, however, that if anything goes wrong, if Berwick should somehow escape or if either of you is killed or wounded, it will be on your own heads.'

'That is understood,' replied Christopher. There was no more likelihood of Berwick escaping with the pistol than without and, as far as Christopher could see, no more danger to Wetherby or himself.

The earl had not quite finished. 'I will try the pistol myself before it is replaced and I shall station guards nearby. Berwick must not escape. And I daresay he will end up in Griffyn's hands anyway.'

Christopher held up his hands. 'Please order the guards to remain hidden until he is inside the church, my lord. If they are seen by Berwick, he will flee.'

Leicester rubbed his temples. 'This is irregular, doctor. The queen would not thank me for your death, or Wetherby's, and even less should Berwick escape.'

'Shall we agree then that there will be but two men on guard and that they will be well hidden?'

'You wear me down, doctor,' sighed Leicester. 'Berwick will surely come, if he comes at all, at night. The watch must be set before dusk. I shall speak to Wetherby. Take this and render it useless.' He handed the pistol to Tomasso.

Outside the apartment, Tomasso swore. 'Why does my being a Florentine preclude me from the task? Does the earl think Italians of no account?'

'The opposite, my friend,' replied Christopher. 'He does not wish to have to explain your death to your ambassador or to Sir

Francis. We must have the pistol back in place without delay. Set to, if you please.'

'I will.' He looked up at Christopher. 'You are determined to be the one who captures the traitor, are you not?'

'I am. Or the one who kills him.'

The light was beginning to fade when the four men – Christopher, Tomasso, Wetherby and Oxnard – entered the churchyard. Oxnard unlocked the door, Christopher opened the hidden panel, and the pistol, now rendered useless and wrapped in the altar cloth, was replaced just as it had been found. According to Tomasso, even pressed to a man's forehead, it would do no damage. 'It is a deal less dangerous than the dagger you carry,' he assured Christopher. 'I have tried it myself and so has the earl. It cannot fire.'

'Goodman Oxnard,' said Christopher, 'Signor Sessetti will escort you back to Whitehall. Mr Wetherby and I will remain here.'

'May God watch over you,' replied Tomasso. 'You have a long night ahead of you.' He clasped hands with each of them and was gone. Inside the church they heard Oxnard's key turn in the lock.

They did not light a candle but had brought blankets and food to sustain them. Wetherby had also brought a bucket, saying only that it would not do to defile a church. They carried loaded pistols and Christopher's poniard was in his belt. They spread a blanket behind the screen and settled down. Somewhere in the shadows outside were two of Leicester's guards, who would be replaced every four hours. They would keep vigil throughout the night.

Gradually their eyes grew accustomed to the darkness and their ears to the silence. Wetherby was first to break it, his breath misting in the freezing air. 'Relieved as I am to be out of the Gate House, I had not expected to spend the night in an icy church,' he said. 'The earl told me that it was you who suggested I keep you company, doctor. Why was that?'

'You too have suffered at the hands of Berwick. I imagined you would wish to witness his capture.' Christopher sat stretching his fingers inside the woollen gloves he wore.

'That I do. But I am not a man of violence and my courage is untested. A better man could surely have been found. Signor Sessetti, for example.'

'You are here, Mr Wetherby. That is enough to convince me of your courage and your desire to see Berwick safely in the Tower. Now, we have long hours before morning. Let us find matters to discuss which do not pertain to politics or religion or war. Have you ever visited Paris?'

For some time they talked of Paris and London, of painting and sculpture and of the food they most enjoyed. Wetherby proved himself well travelled and well read and skilled in conversation and argument. Occasionally they stood to stretch their legs and stamp their feet against the cold, making as little sound as they could and listening for footsteps outside. After they had eaten, Wetherby lay down while Christopher sat with his back to the wall, a blanket around his shoulders and pistol beside him. They had agreed that they would take turns to rest and keep watch.

The hours came and went, neither slept and Berwick did not come. At dawn an anxious Tomasso arrived with Oxnard's key. 'I am glad to find you unharmed,' he said, 'although I assume that our quarry did not appear.'

'He did not,' replied Christopher, his teeth chattering. 'Mr Wetherby and I will now retire and leave the day's watch to the earl's guards. We will return before dusk. He might come today or tonight. If I were he, it would be at night.'

Outside the churchyard they parted company. Christopher walked up to his house, let himself in and threw himself on his bed. That night he would take more to keep them warm. The next day was the third day of October, the day before the queen's visit to St Andrew's church. Surely Berwick would come soon.

He was woken around midday by Rose. Wetherby was at the door. Christopher struggled awake, straightened his clothes and splashed his face with water from his ewer. 'Mr Wetherby, I am barely awake. What news?'

'The earl sent me, doctor. Spanish ships have been sighted off Dover and yesterday they were joined by a small French fleet.'

'Have they been fired upon?'

'No. They are just out of range of our cannon.'

'Waiting for a signal before approaching closer, no doubt. How is the weather at sea?'

'Frighteningly calm, doctor. Cold of course but only a light wind from the north. Our ships, such as they are, could leave their harbours but would not last long against Spanish cannon. The militia are lining the coast but they are, by all accounts, a pitiful lot. The earl impresses upon us the urgency of the matter. He is disappointed that John Berwick did not walk into our trap.'

'No more disappointed than I that he did not arrest the man earlier.'

They were interrupted by Rose carrying a large pie. Without being bid, she laid it on the table. 'You must eat, sirs,' she said. 'Good work needs good food. And this pie is as good as any in London. Pigeon with onions.'

'Alas, goodwife, I have not the time—' began Wetherby.

Christopher interrupted. 'Thank you, Rose. Come, Mr

Wetherby, let us eat quickly. Rose's pies are not to be missed and I do not wish to return to the sharp end of her tongue.'

Rose grinned. 'No, doctor, you do not. I will bring a jug of ale to help you wash it down.'

They helped themselves to slices of pie. Wetherby brushed a crumb from his mouth. 'The Privy Council is meeting now. I understand that the queen will join them soon. The earl expects the council to advise that an emissary be taken out to the Spanish flagship to ascertain their purpose.'

Rose returned with the ale. Christopher waited until she had left before replying. 'Their purpose, Mr Wetherby, is surely clear. It is *Incendium*. We must pray that the traitor walks into our trap before it is too late. My guess is that Whitehall was due to be blown to rubble on the same day as the assassination of the queen. We believe that day is tomorrow. From the gathering of their force we must assume that they do not know that Whitehall is safe and that Kaye is in the Tower. They are waiting for a signal that the time has come.'

'I dare not imagine it, doctor.'

'Nor I, in truth. There is something I must do now, Mr Wetherby. We will meet again at dusk in the churchyard.'

'I shall pray for better fortune.'

When Wetherby had gone, Christopher sat, lost in thought. If the queen were dead and her palace a heap of smoking debris, how easily the Spanish and French would cut a swathe to London, sweep into the city and swallow it in a single mouthful. No queen, no heir, a convenient successor in Mary Stuart. Around whom would the people rally? Would they fight for their beliefs or would they shrug their shoulders, accept changes as they had accepted them before, find ways to feed their families and themselves, and carry on as best they could? That is exactly what they would do. And it would happen if Berwick were not found at once and every traitor with him. 'I shall return later, Rose,' he called out. He left the study and opened the door on to Ludgate Hill. Just in time he remembered. 'Excellent pie. Thank you.'

The rain still fell, Cheapside was quiet and most stalls were half empty. Groups of goodwives and traders stood and spoke among themselves in hushed voices. Children playing their games and scrounging for scraps were slapped into silence. Barking dogs were kicked. Kites fighting over morsels were ignored. The news had spread and London was holding its breath.

Christopher made his way between the stalls and up to Wood Street. Katherine opened the door and glared at him. 'Why are you here, Christopher? I have no wish to speak to you,' she said. 'Kindly go away. Doubtless your whore has greater need of you than I.' She made to close the door.

Christopher stuck out an arm to hold it open. 'You must listen to me, Katherine. Ell Cole is a whore, but she is not my whore. She is my intelligencer. Why can you not accept that?'

'Do you take all your intelligencers to your bed chamber?'

'Katherine, she was never in my bed chamber.'

'Go away, Christopher. You are not welcome here.' Katherine put all her weight on the door and forced Christopher to withdraw his arm. The door slammed shut and he was left outside. He thought of trying again, decided it would be useless and turned back towards Cheapside. She was a stubborn, obstinate woman, refusing to believe him, or at least pretending not to, and not even willing to speak to him.

In the alley off Cheapside, unusually, Ell herself opened the door. 'Dr Rad, I was wondering whether to call on you again or to wait for you to find me. I heard another whisper. Might interest you.

Come in and warm your toes by the fire.' She ushered him into Grace's parlour. It was a welcoming room where her customers sat with their wine waiting their turn to climb the stair. Stew or not, Christopher had always rather liked it. 'Grace is in her bed with the ague so I'm doing her work. Not that there is much. Very quiet these last few days.'

'Have you heard that Spanish ships are off Dover, Ell? French, too.'

'Everyone has heard, Dr Rad. Are we going to fight them?'

'We are going to stop them landing if we can. If not, they will soon be in London. I came to warn you. What is the whisper?'

'Don't ask me where it came from but there is a rumour that a man from the palace, an important man, was mixed up in that murder at Cripplegate. Him and Smith, they say it was, murdered your man and his wife. Nasty business, they say.'

'Where did this come from, Ell?'

'God knows, doctor. Where do whispers ever come from? Most are fit only for the jakes. But I sense there is a mite of truth in this one.'

'Any word on who he is?'

Ell shook her beautiful head. 'Not really. An important man, I heard.'

'He would not have been dressed for court. If he was thought to be an important man, the rumour must have come from Whitehall. No neighbour would have known him.'

'I thought that, doctor, and that you might know who it was.'

'I might, Ell. Thank you.'

Ell smiled. 'Always a pleasure, Dr Rad. Keep the Spanish away, please. And the French. Dirty buggers, the French. Don't hold with washing. We're all frightened of what they might do. Can't we sink their ships?'

'I wish it was that easy. They're too far away yet and we haven't got much to sink them with if they come closer. We'll just have to pray for a storm.'

'Pray? Hah, bugger all use that would be. The last time I prayed was with a priest who liked me on my knees for praying and swiving. Beat me about afterwards, he did. Evil swine.' She paused. 'Is this what that word is all about?'

'*Incendium*, Ell, yes, it is. And more.' He rose to leave. For a moment he was tempted to take her in his arms and try to reassure her. What hope would there be for a woman such as Ell if the enemy marched into London? One dead whore more or less would not signify. When he took her hand the slightest of blushes coloured her cheeks. 'Take care, Ell. Thank you for the word.'

By the time he was back in his study, the milky sun was very low. Darkness would come soon. He put on an extra woollen shirt and found a second pair of gloves in his chest. Bread and cheese from the kitchen and he was ready for another long vigil.

Roland Wetherby was already in the churchyard. He too was better equipped for the night and had brought Oxnard's key. A guard locked the door after them and they settled behind the screen with their pistols cocked and ready. In the darkness, Wetherby coughed lightly and leaned close to Christopher to whisper, 'The queen has refused to send an emissary to the Spanish flagship and is insisting on worshipping at St Andrew's church tomorrow at ten in the morning. She will not acknowledge the danger.'

'Yet she knows everything?'

'Her Majesty knows as much as we do. She is content to leave her own fate to God and the fate of England to its brave and loyal people. She will not hide away like a skulking papist. Those, Mr Heneage said, were her words.'

If the queen had reigned at the time of Harold, the Normans would never have attempted a landing. She had the courage of a lioness. 'Has the earl posted guards again?'

'He has. The yard has been watched all day. No one was seen entering it.'

'Nevertheless, I will make sure that our bait is where it should be.' He opened the hidden panel and ran his hand along the bench. There was the pistol, wrapped in the altar cloth. He closed the door and rejoined Wetherby. 'It is safe and sound and awaiting a caller.'

Some time later Wetherby asked, 'Do you ever think, Dr Radcliff, of the perversity of life? A Spanish fleet, now reinforced by the French, threatening our coast, militia called out to defend us as best they can, our people in fear of their lives and the lives of their families, our world in danger, and here are we sitting in a dark church waiting for a man who might never arrive. Absurd, is it not?'

'Put like that, Mr Wetherby, it does indeed sound absurd. Yet, if by spending the night here we can prevent the assassination of our queen, our night will not be wasted. Catch Berwick, show him to the Spanish, tell them the queen and her palace and her counsellors are safe, and they will trim their sails and turn for home. Do you not agree?'

'I do. We will not be rid of them by standing on the shore and brandishing our weapons at them like so many savages. Rather it is here in this dark church that they must be defeated. Do you care to sleep first or shall I?'

'You sleep first. I will rouse you.'

CHAPTER 36

Paris

The Bishop of Beauvais crossed himself. 'It was God's will. He is testing our faith.' He had arrived that evening, having ridden hard despite being drained of energy by the terrible news from England. A single candle flickered on the table between the two men.

The duc de Guise thumped a furious fist on the table, rattling their glasses and spilling a few drops of wine. The scar on his face was livid. 'My faith needs no testing. Have I not proved it by killing Coligny with my own hands and ridding Paris of his ungodly Huguenots? It is the incompetent English who test my patience. The powder found and Kaye in the Tower. How did this happen?'

The bishop's voice was calm. 'Leicester's man, Radcliff, has somehow survived. He found the common thief whom Berwick employed to help silence the troublesome stationer and interrogated him. The thief must have led him to the stationers and they to the powder. That is all I know.'

'If Kaye has not yet spoken, the rack will soon loosen his tongue.

He will reveal the names of our friends among the stationers and perhaps of others. It is a catastrophe.'

The bishop nodded and opened his palms in a gesture of resignation. '*Incendium* has failed.'

'Does the king know?'

'I shall go from here to the palace.'

'And what of Berwick?'

'If he has not been taken he will be in hiding. We know not which. I have sent word to Alba, advising him to return to port. When last I heard, there had been no sign of the English fleet.'

Guise held his head in his hands. 'It is an awful day. Our careful plans come to nought and the witch-queen alive. There is but one hope and that is that Berwick has escaped and will yet find a way to kill her. Then our efforts will not have been in vain and we may yet see the Queen of Scots in London.'

'A forlorn hope, Henri, I fear. Berwick would not only have to get close enough to the witch without being discovered but also be prepared to die himself. Is he capable of that?'

'Few would be.'

'Then we must put the thought from our minds. This *Incendium* has failed but there will be another. Let us pray for that.'

Chapter 37

London

It had been another long, cold night. There had been no footsteps, no glimmer of light from a lantern, no hooded figure turning the key and creeping into the church. As dawn broke, they gathered themselves and their few possessions together and waited for Tomasso.

'I will retrieve the pistol,' said Christopher, trying to stretch the stiffness from his legs. He limped over to the hidden panel, pulled it open, stepped inside and felt for the bench. His fingers touched the rosaries, the vestments, the incense. He felt about for the pistol wrapped up in the altar cloth. He could not find it. Disbelieving, he felt again, removing each item from the bench as he went. The disabled pistol had gone. How was it possible? He backed out of the narrow room and called out to Wetherby, 'It is not there.'

'What? It must be. How could it have been taken? The church has been watched all day and all night. No one has been here.'

'Someone has been here.' They heard the key turn in the lock and Tomasso stepped inside. He was carrying a torch. 'Come here, Tomasso. Bring the light. The pistol has gone.'

Tomasso shone his torch into the hidden room. On the floor lay the things Christopher had put there. There was no rolled altar cloth and the bench was empty. 'How?' asked Tomasso, taking half a step into the room and holding up the torch. 'How is this possible?'

'God alone knows how.'

'And who by? Oxnard, a guard, one of us?'

'Pass me the light, Tomasso.' Christopher took it and lowered his head to go as far into the room as he could. He held the flame up to a wall and peered at it. Then he did the same along the wall opposite the hidden door. He ran his hand down a corner and found a hole just big enough for him to insert two fingers. When he pulled, the panel opened without a sound. He stooped lower and stepped through the opening. Tomasso, wide-eyed, followed him. By the light of the torch, Christopher almost bent double, they followed a narrow passage which ran to their left before turning right to end in another wooden wall. Christopher felt for a latch, found it and pulled a panel open. Beyond it was another, stouter wall. Again he felt for a hole, found it a few inches from the floor and opened it. He crawled through, stood up and peered around. The others followed. They were in a bed chamber. It was a chamber he and Tomasso had seen before. It belonged to James Kaye.

Christopher sat on the bed. 'I am a fool,' he muttered. 'We tested the walls but we should have tried harder. This house is built almost against the old friary wall. It would not have been difficult to fashion a way through to the church. Berwick has entered through here and taken the pistol. I doubt anyone but he and Kaye knew of the passage. It would be a useful hiding place.'

'He went unnoticed because the guards were watching the churchyard,' added Wetherby. 'And he moved silently or one of us would surely have heard him.'

Christopher was on his feet. Rising panic had turned to icy calm. 'Tomasso, return at once to Whitehall and tell the earl what we have found. Mr Wetherby, with me.' They left the house by its front door. Christopher and Wetherby hurried off towards Leadenhall where the church of St Andrew Undershaft stood. The maypole from which it derived its name was long gone but the odd name survived.

The queen's visit to the church had been widely proclaimed by the criers and reported in the news sheets. It would be a public demonstration of her wish to be at peace with her cousin Mary and of her courage. She would be making herself vulnerable to show that she was unafraid and had faith in the loyalty of her people.

When they arrived, panting from the exertion, outside the church, townsfolk eager to set eyes on their queen were already arriving and yeomen guards stood in line to keep them in order. The queen had determined to be there and she would do it as befitted a queen.

It would be a perfect opportunity for a man armed with a pistol, a pistol capable of firing two rapid shots, to carry out his task and disappear into the lanes before he could be caught. If Berwick had checked the pistol, found it faulty and replaced it with another and if they did not find him in time, the queen would die. Silently, Christopher cursed himself for not having examined the secret room more carefully.

'There is little point in searching St Andrew's,' he gasped, hands on knees and trying to catch his breath. 'He is not going to hide in a place from which there is no easy escape. He will bide his time and mingle with the crowds.'

'And his face will be hidden,' added Wetherby.

'Indeed, and I hope Tomasso joins us before the queen arrives. The more eyes the better. The earl once told me that he had a hundred eyes. They would be welcome now.'

'What should we best do, doctor?'

Christopher looked up. 'There are windows at the top of the tower of the church, from which we will be able to look down on the street. We will watch from there.'

They entered the church and climbed a flight of spiral steps to the tower. At the top was a small rectangular room in which lengths of bell-rope were stored. From the windows they could see in both directions along the street below. 'Before the queen arrives I will go down and join the crowd,' said Christopher. 'You remain here. Signal to me if you see anything suspicious. I will be watching.'

'Do you think that the earl might be able to persuade the queen not to come? With an assassin at large . . .'

'I fear not, Mr Wetherby. If the queen is determined, ten assassins will not deter her.'

A troop of the queen's guard arrived first. They wore the red and gold uniforms of her yeomen and carried swords and short pikes. They lined both sides of the cobbled street along which the royal procession would make its way to the church.

Behind them, it was as if the Spanish fleet lay at the bottom of the narrow sea, the massacre in France had never happened and England was prosperous and at peace. The people were determined to salute their queen and had defied the cold and come out in their hundreds to do so. Excited children sat on their fathers' shoulders, women's handkerchiefs and voices were raised in song to the rhythmic beat of a drum and the shrill whistle of flutes and fifes. The thought occurred briefly to Christopher that the Master of the Queen's Horse, the man responsible for her progresses and royal ceremonies, had had a hand in this loud, colourful display of loyalty.

Christopher scanned the faces he could see, noticed nothing untoward and returned to the street. His height allowed him to see over the heads of the people in front and to watch for a face hidden by a hood or a cap pulled low. Berwick was there somewhere, he was sure of it, but it would not be easy to spot him. He glanced up to the church window. Wetherby saw him and shook his head.

The crowd grew until shoulder jostled shoulder and voices were raised in anger. The yeomen used the handles of their weapons to prod the front line back. Someone stumbled and was kicked out of the way. An over-excited child slipped between the yeomen and stood wailing in the street until she was rescued by her mother and dragged back into the crowd. Christopher looked up again to see Wetherby once more shake his head.

A quiet voice spoke behind him. 'The queen will arrive in a few minutes. Is there any sign?'

He half-turned. 'None, Tomasso. Wetherby is watching from the tower. Does my lord Leicester know?'

'He does. He is riding in the queen's carriage and will accompany her into the church.' Christopher felt Tomasso's hand on his shoulder. 'Do not worry, my friend. The pistol will not fire.'

At that moment, a single trumpet sounded, the crowd went quiet and heads turned. The royal procession, led by six mounted bodyguards, each with sword and short lance, came into sight. They were followed by the royal coach — black with a discreet gold trim and waisted in shape. The coachman and his assistant and the two footmen at the rear were also dressed in black. It was followed by a second and a third carriage, smaller and equally restrained. They would carry senior members of her household — Hatton, Heneage and Oxford among them. Finally, another troop of the queen's bodyguards protected the rear of the line.

By royal standards, it was a modest affair, in keeping with the solemnity of the occasion. The procession moved slowly down the street, unhurried and seemingly without concern. The men in the crowd doffed their caps and bowed low and the women bobbed curtsies as it passed.

Christopher and Tomasso scoured the crowd this way and that, glancing up to the tower for a signal from Wetherby. There was none. Outside the church the coachman reined in his blinkered horses and the royal carriage came to a halt. It was the moment when the queen, accompanied by Leicester, would step out of the carriage and disappear into the church. At that moment a finger of fear ran down Christopher's spine. He was wrong. Berwick was not in the crowd. He was hiding in the church and was willing to sacrifice himself to kill the queen. He knew Kaye had been taken, he knew the plot to destroy Whitehall had failed. And he knew that *Incendium* could still succeed if he killed the woman around whom the people of England would rally. If not, the invasion would fail or not be attempted at all. Berwick knew all this and was hiding in the church.

Christopher shouted above the noise for Tomasso to stay where he was and elbowed his way through the mass of bodies towards the church door. He must get inside. He was rudely shoved back by angry onlookers. He bellowed that the queen was in danger. No one paid attention. He tried to push through the line of yeomen and was forced back by pike handles. He shouted again but his words were swallowed by the cheers of the crowd. A footman opened the carriage door. Tomasso had disappeared. He looked up. Still there was no sign from Wetherby.

And then, from the corner of his eye, he saw it. A movement, a glint of light, a hooded face. He waved his arms above his head and shouted once more. Still he was ignored, his voice drowned out by the crowd's excitement. The hooded man stood at the back of the throng, half hidden by the corner of a lane running towards Aldgate. He was standing on something — a crate or a half-cask perhaps — and could see over the heads in front of him. He was no more than five yards from the church door.

The queen stepped down from the carriage. When Christopher had seen her in the Whitehall gardens she had been dressed in black and had worn but a single string of pearls. Today, her cloak was white, fur-trimmed and embroidered with gold thread. The crowd screamed their devotion. Christopher shouted again and tried to force his way past the guards. He was elbowed in the face and blood dripped from his nose. He wiped it away with a sleeve and shouted again. He was in a hellish dream in which he was watching a disaster unfold but could not move or make himself heard. His eyes were locked on the hooded man.

He held a pistol in his hand. It had two barrels. He raised it and took aim, using his left arm as support. Could no one but Christopher see him? The guards and the crowd were watching the queen. He was too far away for Christopher to reach him. He pulled the trigger. There was no sound and no smoke. Christopher did not take his eyes from him. The figure looked at the pistol, raised it again and pulled the trigger. Again nothing. Relief flooded through Christopher. He stared at the hooded head. As if sensing him, the face turned and John Berwick's eyes, burning with hatred, met his. Christopher struggled to hold his gaze. The queen had entered the church and her entourage were following her inside. Berwick stepped down from his vantage point and was gone.

That part of the city, like Cheapside and Smithfield, was a maze of filthy alleys and narrow lanes, many of them unnamed. By the time Christopher had struggled through the thinning crowd Berwick had escaped. There was nothing to be gained by searching for him or by alerting the guards. The assassin had escaped with his life, and so had the queen.

'I too saw him,' said Tomasso, who had made his way from the other side of the street. 'How many times did he fire?'

'Twice, I think. He was well positioned and well hidden. Happily for us, he had not checked the trigger. I saw no spark.'

'He has not abandoned hope. He has the pistol. There is still danger.'

'We can do no more here. I shall await the earl at Whitehall. Bring Wetherby when the service is over.'

Leicester swept into the antechamber where Christopher was waiting for him. He pulled off his cloak, threw it on to the table and glared at Christopher. 'Dr Radcliff, I know not which is greater, my relief or fury. I thank God that the queen is safe, yet you endangered her by allowing the pistol to be taken from under your nose.'

Christopher held his gaze. 'I too thank God for her safety, my lord. And there is more you should know. Berwick was outside St Andrew's church. He had the pistol. It did not fire.' It was a relief to say the words.

'God's blood. I should have found a way to keep Her Majesty safe in the palace. My blood runs cold at the thought of what might have happened. I should never have allowed myself to be persuaded to your plan. It was foolish beyond measure. Did you pursue Berwick?' The earl's anger was rising.

Keeping his eyes on Leicester's, Christopher shook his head. 'We would not have found him in that part of the city.'

'I should have you back in the Gate House. He must be found. He has the weapon. He has shown courage and skill and will be determined to finish what he set out to do. Find him, doctor.'

Christopher exhaled. He was being given another chance. 'Have I your authority to question James Kaye again?'

'You have. I will request the council to authorize the rack. Every constable in the city will be put to the search. Employ every source you have. Find Berwick.'

'Should a message be sent to the Spanish fleet to tell them that *Incendium* has failed? The use of the word might itself be enough to convince them of its truth.'

'Such a message might equally be taken as evidence of our weakness and provoke them into attack. I will seek the council's view. Go, doctor. Find the traitor.'

A spell in the Tower and a little of James Kaye's outward arrogance had gone. His eyes were red and his shoulders slumped. When he entered the room where Christopher waited, he stumbled over the chains that bound wrists and ankles. This time, Christopher did not invite him to sit.

'Stationers' Hall has been searched and several members of the company arrested,' he began. 'The second pistol has been recovered and John Berwick has fled.' The untruth was small. 'The Spanish fleet will wait no longer. Winter storms will soon be here. Your plot has failed.' Kaye did not respond but hung his head and stared at the floor. 'What have you to say to that, Kaye?'

Christopher had thought Kaye's spirit was broken. It was not. He raised his head and spoke in a firm voice. 'There will be another time. The godly will destroy the ungodly as they have in France. My life is of no account.'

'The use of the rack has been authorized.'

'I do not fear the rack.' Despite the chains, Kaye's hands were shaking.

'You are prepared to be racked before suffering a traitor's death?'

Kaye shrugged. 'Pain is but fleeting. God's love is permanent.' They were the words of a priest.

The urge to take the man by the neck and shake the truth from him was almost irresistible. Christopher took a deep breath and barely controlled himself. 'Where were you ordained, Kaye? Rheims, Paris, among the Jesuits at Douai?' Kaye looked up sharply. 'We found the vestments and the rosaries. Were you planning to celebrate your Mass today?'

'It is God's will. There will be another day.'

'Are you a priest?'

'I am a humble servant of God.' His voice was just audible.

'You are a priest. How did you become a warden of the stationers?'

'That is of no account.'

'No matter. We will find out. Meanwhile we want Berwick. Your courage may not be enough when you lie on the rack. Very few can resist its embrace. Better for you that you tell me now where he will have fled. Where is he hiding? Who is sheltering him?'

Kaye smiled. 'There are many in London who would gladly shelter John Berwick.'

'You will give us their names.'

This time Kaye shook his head. 'I shall not. I may die but they will live to light the fires.'

It was as if there were two James Kayes. One the self-important stationers' warden, the other an unshakeable Catholic priest. And that, of course, was exactly how he had wanted it. When the time came the priest would emerge from the warden's shell. Until then he remained hidden. Christopher stood. 'I can wait no longer. Take him away and acquaint him with Mr Griffyn's rack. I shall return later.'

It would take too long to walk. Christopher borrowed a horse from the Tower stables and rode. At Cheapside he dismounted to lead the beast through the market and found a boy to hold it, for the promise of a shilling.

Grace opened the door. Before she could speak, Christopher was past her and up the stair. 'Gently, doctor,' she called after him, 'Ell is occupied.' He ignored the warning and burst into Ell's room to find her naked and astride a big-bellied, grunting man with his breeches around his ankles.

When she saw Christopher, Ell jumped off the man and burst out laughing. 'Dr Rad, you're in a rush. Hold tight until I've finished and I'll be all yours.'

'No, Ell. This is serious. I need you now. Get dressed and come downstairs.'

Ell caught his tone. She patted the fat man on the cheek. 'Won't be a minute or two, my lovely. You stay here.' The fat man was too astonished to speak. He simply stared at Christopher wide-eyed and disbelieving. Ell wrapped herself in a gown and followed Christopher to Grace's parlour. Grace was sitting by the fire.

'Urgent business with Ell, Grace. Could you wait in the kitchen?'

Grace gurgled. 'My, doctor, you are in a state today.' She heaved herself up and waddled off to the kitchen, muttering about extra payment.

Christopher was breathless after his ride, but he wasted no time. 'Ell, we are in danger. There is a traitor hiding in the city. He would have murdered the queen this morning and will try again. His name is John Berwick, although he might go by any name. He is five and a half feet tall, well spoken, brown hair, about twenty years old. He might have an unusual gun — a pistol with two long barrels. I need him.'

Ell threw up her hands. 'God's teeth, Dr Rad, how am I to find this man in the city? He could be hiding anywhere.'

'I do not know, Ell, but if anyone can, it is you. Spread the word. He won't be in a tavern or a stew. He'll be in hiding or sheltered by friends. Do your best. Go now.'

'What about my gentleman?'

He tossed her a coin. 'Let him wait.'

Christopher dashed down the alley, retrieved the horse and led it back through the market. It was asking much of Ell, might put her in danger, and had only a slim chance of success. The same would be true of Tomasso and Wetherby.

Within a half-hour, he was back at the Tower. Kaye had been brought to the room and was waiting for him. Christopher spoke to his guard. 'Has the prisoner been shown the rack?'

'He has, sir,' replied the guard. 'We used a goat.'

'Did you learn anything from the spectacle, Kaye?'

Kaye's face remained impassive. 'I do not care for goats.'

Christopher stepped forward and put his face a few inches from Kaye's. The warden's breath reeked and a sheen of sweat covered his skin. 'Levity — hardly appropriate, Kaye, at such a time. And it does not conceal your fear. Where will we find John Berwick?'

Kaye was unmoved. 'I cannot tell you and would not if I could. The rack will avail you nothing.'

Christopher's admiration for the man was grudging but real. He did not want to use the rack, or any means of torture, but Kaye's refusal to wilt was making it look necessary. Berwick must be found. He tried once more. 'Every constable in London is looking for him.

My own people are looking under stones and in dung heaps. He will be found and brought to justice. If you save us time, you will save yourself from an agonizing death.'

'I do not know where John Berwick is but I shall pray for his safety and the success of his mission. Do with me what you will.' Christopher stared into his eyes. Kaye was telling the truth. Like Patrick Wolf, he would not speak.

'Take him away. I will discuss with the Earl of Leicester what agony he should suffer.'

To Christopher's surprise, Thomas Heneage was with the earl. Leicester's face was drawn as if he had not slept for a week. 'Have you found him, doctor?' he asked immediately.

'No, my lord. Despite our efforts, we have learned nothing new and Kaye will not speak. I doubt that even the rack will make him do so and it is of course possible that he really does not know where Berwick is hiding.'

Heneage peered out from under his thick eyebrows and spoke slowly. 'My agent in the north has made inquiries about Berwick's family. He sent his report by sea. It seems that Berwick's mother was French by birth and her mother a member of the Bourbon family. Charles de Bourbon is the Bishop of Beauvais. He is close to the duc de Guise and is thought to be involved in the plot, despite having married the king's sister to Henry of Navarre.'

There was little point in asking why this had not been known until now. It should have been known when Berwick was first presented at court. The queen herself had been deceived. Heneage went on. 'What is more, Mr Wetherby, who serves me loyally, has suffered unjust accusation and imprisonment. His arrest was an affront to me and intolerable. Yet John Berwick, a traitor, remains free. Had Wetherby not been falsely accused and had proper inquiries been made, we would not now find ourselves as we do.'

'Mind your words, sir. You approached Dr Radcliff without my knowledge and were aggrieved at his rebuff. That is why you complain now about Wetherby.' Leicester spoke in a tone Christopher recognized – one of cold anger.

Heneage turned on Christopher. 'For offering you the chance of advancement in my service, you repaid me by imprisoning Wetherby and betraying my confidence.'

'I serve the Earl of Leicester,' replied Christopher, holding Heneage's gaze.

Leicester pushed back his chair, its legs scraping across the floor, and stood. 'Enough. Berwick must be found. This bickering is unhelpful. What else is to be done, doctor?'

'There are others to whom I would speak,' said Christopher.

'What others?'

'My lord, it is better that you should not know.'

Leicester glared. 'Dr Radcliff, a firearm has been levelled at the queen and the assassin has slipped through our fingers twice in a single night and a day. I tell you to find the man yet you have not. Why should I accept that it is better I do not know something? It is I who will decide what I should know and not know.'

Christopher was conscious of Heneage's eyes on him. 'Of course, my lord. I was seeking only to protect your good name. I have an agent with friends among the Marrano community. They will help find Berwick if I ask.'

'Jews. In London illegally, yet I have always admired them for their skills. Speak to him. Meanwhile, I have ordered all roads from London watched and every constable put to work in the search. Our southern ports are also watched. Go. Report to me tomorrow in the morning.'

*

Isaac was in his shop, busy with a customer. For all Christopher's impatience, there was a certain courtesy to be observed here. He needed Isaac's help but the goldsmith would not respond well to interruption. Christopher waited until the customer had left before speaking. 'Good day, Isaac. Can you spare time to talk? It is urgent.'

'And joy to you, Christopher. Of course I have time for you.' He locked the door and led Christopher through to his back room, where he offered Christopher the chair. A puff of dust rose from it when he sat down. Isaac sat facing him on a plain oak stool. 'I have few visitors,' he said, 'and my hospitality is not all that it might be. Yet I do have a bottle of Spanish sack. Do you care for a glass?'

Christopher shook his head. 'Thank you, no, Isaac. I have come to ask your help.'

Isaac's shrewd eyes narrowed. 'Something grave or you would not have come. Fires and Spaniards and stationers locked in the Tower, would it be?' Very little escaped the Marranos.

'It would. The Spanish fleet is still at sea, the certain destruction of Whitehall Palace has been narrowly prevented, an attempt has been made on the queen's life and one traitor is in the Tower. Another, the would-be assassin, escaped and we believe is somewhere in London. We must find him.'

'I see. And this, I take it, is the same man for whom the constables are now searching.' Christopher nodded. 'Of course they will not find him. A fugitive does not hide in a tavern or a whorehouse any more than a fox in a henhouse. A more subtle approach will be needed. I know you would not ask without good reason and of course my people will help you. For their own sake as well as yours. What is known of this man?' In Isaac's soft voice there was reassurance. Christopher's spirit rose a little.

He told Isaac everything they knew of Berwick, including the pistol. 'A man who has come this far, has deceived not only Leicester but the queen herself, and must enjoy the confidence of powerful men in France, is formidable and ruthless. I would not want you to underestimate him.'

'That we will not do. John Berwick, a courtier with a burning desire for revenge and a pistol that will fire two accurate shots. We will tread as carefully as Moses leading our people out of Egypt. Is there no thought as to where he might be?'

'Beyond that he is unlikely to have left London, none. Isaac, there is one final thing. This is *Incendium*. Listen for the word. If we catch Berwick, the plotters will lose heart and their plot will fail.'

'We will listen. The Catholics around Eastcheap might be helpful. They are peaceful, godly people. I will speak quietly to them.' Isaac rose and let Christopher out of the shop. 'I will send word when I have news. Until then, go carefully, my friend.'

'I shall be waiting. *Shalom*, Isaac.'

CHAPTER 38

November

Autumn rain had given way to winter cold. Christopher lay under the bed covers and wished for Katherine's warmth beside him. When he most needed her to share not just his bed but his thoughts, she would not speak to him. He turned on to his side and and tried to empty his mind.

It was impossible. Katherine one minute, John Berwick the next. What would happen if they did not find him? The traitor would try again, and this time with a working pistol. What would Christopher do if Katherine refused ever to speak to him again? He would write her a letter of explanation, which she would return unread. Damn her. He would catch Berwick and then demand to be heard. He would ask Ell to speak for him. He would approach Ursula Walsingham. He would employ Tomasso as an envoy.

He would do none of these things. He would wait patiently for Katherine to come to her senses and then he would explain why Ell Cole, a Cheapside whore, had been in his house.

Enough of this. He pushed himself up, lit a candle, and fumbled his way down the stair. Katherine must wait. He had a traitor to find.

The constables were searching, Ell was searching, Isaac Cardoza and his friends were searching. They had been doing so for weeks. Each had been going about their task in their own way. Surely one of them would find him. Berwick would be caught and interrogated and hanged. As a traitor — unless the queen forbade it — he would be drawn and quartered and Kaye would die with him. Unless he escaped. Then the spark of treacherous flames would still flicker and the queen would still be in danger.

He went to the study and lit the kindling Rose had made ready in the grate. He watched black smoke rise up the chimney and stretched out his hands to the flames. They offered some comfort.

He should have thought of Isaac's Eastcheap Catholics himself. They were a small group, who like the Marranos kept to themselves and caused no trouble. They trod a narrow path between loyalty to England and adherence to the old ways. But they were Catholics and the pope had called upon them to denounce their heretic queen. The papal bull, Ridolfi's plot to replace Elizabeth with the Queen of Scots, and now the slaughter in France — it would not be long before the narrow path could be trod no longer.

He dozed before the fire until Rose arrived rubbing her hands together and complaining of the cold. She gave him a cup of onion soup and a slice of bread, and soon after dawn he was on his way to Whitehall.

Leicester was unusually dishevelled, as if he too had found sleep difficult, and as ill- tempered as ever Christopher had seen him. His first words were a surprise. 'News has come from Dover. The Spanish fleet is nowhere to be seen. The first winter storm made them trim their sails and turn tail for home.'

'That is excellent news, my lord.'

Leicester seemed not to think so. 'The queen chides me for allowing a traitor to walk the streets of London,' he said, drumming his fingers on the desk. 'She calls me incompetent and suggests that I confine myself to arranging her progresses. She plans to recall Walsingham for what she terms "the serious work of government". How do you imagine this makes me feel, doctor?'

Christopher did not reply. In this mood, Leicester would rant until he could rant no more and nothing he could say would change it. The earl continued, 'Has Berwick been discovered in a foul stew? Have the Jews found him lurking in a synagogue? Has the stationer opened his mouth and spoken? No, no and no. You are here to tell me that you have learned nothing more. Am I not right?'

'It is only a few days since you authorized me to approach the Jews, my lord.'

'How long must I wait before I can tell the queen that it is safe for her to leave the palace? Or will it never be so? The stationer must be made to speak.'

'I have been unable to make him do so and have no experience of extracting information by force. Perhaps Mr Griffyn would have more success.'

Leicester's shrewd eyes narrowed. 'For that I do not blame you, doctor. I also could not inflict the rack or the wheel on a man, yet I find that I can, when necessary, order another to do so. Griffyn will be given his orders.'

'I have one other suggestion, my lord. If you call off the constables, Berwick might think we believe him to have fled London. If so, he will be more likely to make a mistake.'

'A perverse suggestion, doctor, if there ever was one. Call off the hounds to lure the fox into the open? Most perverse.'

'This is not a hue and cry. The constables will find nothing. We are much more likely to discover the truth by quiet questioning.'

Leicester scratched his beard. 'It may be so. Put Sessetti to work. Put yourself to work. Return later to report on your progress. I will decide on the constables then.'

Christopher bowed. 'As you wish, my lord.'

'And pray that the queen has not lost patience and sent me back to Kenilworth, for your own departure would swiftly follow.'

Christopher hurried along Fleet Street, Leicester's words ringing in his ears.

Tomasso had arrived at Ludgate Hill. 'What awaited you at Whitehall?' he asked.

'News that the Spanish have gone home and an angry and frightened earl. He is to put the interrogator Griffyn to work on Kaye while we scour the streets and lanes. My agent Isaac Cardoza, a member of the Marrano community in Leadenhall, has agreed to help and Ell Cole is asking questions in places you and I would not care to visit. I have tried to sound confident to the earl but, in truth, our chances of finding Berwick are poor. There are too many places to hide and too many ways of slipping unnoticed out of London. We shall need a signpost to point the way — a word, a hint, a clue.'

'I thank God the Spanish have gone, but what of us, Christopher, what are we to do?'

'We will go to Stationers' Hall.'

The Hall was not the serene place of commerce and conversation that it had appeared before. Yeomen stood guard outside and inside the entrance. The building had already been searched and the members questioned but Christopher doubted the thoroughness of either. There would be something there, something to incriminate or suggest. Griffyn, meanwhile, would force from Kaye whatever he might be hiding. A brave man, but unlikely to resist the rack or the wheel.

Ignoring the whispering stationers huddled in the grand reception room and the liveried servants scurrying from group to group with trays of bottles and glasses, Christopher and Tomasso climbed a staircase to the upper floor. The rooms there were unoccupied and devoid of books or documents. They had been cleaned out by the earl's searchers and the papers taken to Whitehall for examination. So far they had revealed nothing. They looked in chests and coffers and drawers. All were empty. The business of the stationers must have ground to a halt while the search went on.

They returned down the stairs. There was little to search in the reception rooms, each of them guarded by a yeoman. Christopher felt eyes on his back. For stationers guilty or innocent it must be a frightening time. Their business disrupted and who knew what might be found in the Hall or what one might say about another? A second flight of stairs led down to the kitchen and cellar. In the kitchen two cooks were busy preparing food while a maid scrubbed dishes. They paid the two men no attention. No doubt they were accustomed to their kitchen being invaded.

A single door led off the kitchen. 'What is this?' asked Christopher.

'The members' wine store,' replied one of the cooks, a young woman with a thin mouth that turned down at the corners. 'No one may enter without permission of a warden.'

'The wardens are engaged in other business. Where is the key?'

The cook delved deep into her smock and produced a large key on a short length of twine. 'I tell you that the store has been searched, sir,' she said. 'Nothing was found but bottles. The men took what they could carry.'

'I have no doubt that they did. Unlock the door, goodwife. We will see what remains.'

Inside it was dark and cold. The walls were lined with racks of bottles and draped in cobwebs. Christopher stepped inside. As his eyes grew accustomed to the gloom, he could make out a wooden crate in a corner at the back. He lifted the lid. The crate was full of what seemed to be old sacks. When he pulled away the top one, a small cloud of sack dust rose into the air, making his eyes water. He dried them with a corner of his cloak and peered inside the crate again. The next layer revealed was not another sack but a pair of leather gloves and a leather coat. A plague doctor's coat. There were others beneath. He called to Tomasso to come and look.

Tomasso came and stood beside him. 'And here are masks,' he said, reaching in and pulling one out. He held it up by the beak.

Christopher brought out a coat and gloves, Tomasso the mask. There was no doubt now where the fire-setters came from. The searchers had been too busy filling their own cellars to be bothered with a pile of old sacks. It was a wonder they had left any bottles at all.

In the grand reception room the stationers were still standing about in groups, engrossed in their conversations. Christopher stood at the door, held up the mask and called out, 'Which of you claims ownership of this?' The murmur of conversation ceased and every head turned to him. 'It is a plague doctor's mask. Why would I find it in your wine store?' There was an astonished silence. 'Nor was it alone. There are others.'

In their faces Christopher saw alarm and surprise, but no guilt. He went on. 'The recent fires in the city were lit by men in plague masks. No doubt your Senior Warden will be able to explain why this was hidden in your Hall.'

An elegant young man in a crimson doublet detached himself from his companions and stepped forward to speak. 'Sir, I am Hugh Curteys, Middle Warden of the Stationers' Company. We have recently become accustomed to the presence of strangers in our Hall and to the disruption of our business. We are aware that our Senior Warden James Kaye is held in the Tower, our members have been questioned and now you, sir, admit yourself to our wine store. Who are you and who granted you this right?'

'I am Dr Christopher Radcliff. This is my colleague, Signor Tomasso Sessetti. We serve my noble lord, the Earl of Leicester. We believe that there are traitors among you.' At this, voices were instantly raised and fists waved in anger. It was exactly what Christopher had expected. 'Are all your members present, Mr Curteys?'

'No, doctor. Most have gathered while this monstrous affair progresses but three or four are not in London.'

'Be so good as to write their names for me, sir.'

Curteys bridled. 'I hardly think that giving you their names would be proper or pertinent to your inquiry, sir.'

'On the contrary, Mr Curteys. The names are entirely pertinent and any attempt to withhold them would be improper. Kindly remember whom I represent in this matter.'

Curteys stared at him, then shrugged and went to a writing table in the corner of the room. He took a sheet of paper and a pen, wrote the names, dried the paper with sand and handed it to Christopher.

'Thank you, sir. This should prove illuminating. Come, Tomasso, our business here is finished for now.'

Outside, Tomasso asked, 'Why the names, Christopher?'

'If Griffyn extracts any names from Kaye, I'll wager they are the same as these. Four traitors who fled when Kaye was arrested.' He folded the paper and tucked it under his shirt. 'Come now, Tomasso, we have something for the earl. Let us return to Whitehall at once.'

The meeting with Leicester was brief. 'Four members of the Stationers' Company, whose whereabouts we know not and who might or might not be complicit in the plot.' The earl tossed the paper on which Curteys had written the names on to his desk.

'If Griffyn were to be given these names, my lord,' replied Christopher, 'it might aid his interrogation of Kaye.'

'Yes, yes, Griffyn shall have the names. But what of Berwick? Are you any closer to finding the man?'

'It would help if the constables were called off. Their searches serve only to drive the fugitive further into his lair.'

'I will call them off only when you bring me certain intelligence of Berwick's hiding place.' He peered at Christopher. 'Do I take it then that you have found no trace of him?'

'I have put the Marranos to work and am confident that they will find him.'

Leicester thumped a fist into his palm. 'Your confidence carries little weight in the circumstances, Dr Radcliff. When will they find him? When he appears from behind a tree with a pistol pointed at Her Majesty? Or when he is seen in the Louvre Palace hatching another plot with the French king?'

'My lord, I assure you that we are doing everything possible to find him.'

'Then go. And do not return until you have Berwick.'

They left the palace by the Holbein Gate. 'We can hardly blame him, my friend,' said Tomasso. 'I dread to think what indignities he is suffering in the royal presence. Come now, let us find a passable inn where we might settle our nerves.'

They found an inn near the house of Thomas Heneage, ordered food and drink and sat at a quiet table in a corner. Tomasso waited until Christopher had taken a glass of strong Rhenish wine before speaking again. 'What of Mistress Allington, Christopher? Is she well?' he asked.

Christopher could not disguise his concern. 'As far as I know, she is well.' Tomasso looked quizzically at him. 'There was a mis-understanding. It will take time to resolve.'

'By all accounts, a charming lady, Christopher. Do not allow her to slip through your fingers.'

'You are the second person to advise me so. There are complications. As it is, I must wait and see.'

'Wait and see what?'

'The earl is not an easy task master. One day he is encouraging, the next he accuses me of incompetence. There are times when I am thankful for the opportunity he has given me, and times when I would rather be elsewhere.'

A serving girl put a large platter of meat on their table and trenchers for them to eat off. Tomasso cut a thick slice of goose and placed it in front of Christopher. 'Eat that, Christopher, and it will help restore your spirits.' For a minute or two they sat and ate, not attempting to talk while they did so.

Christopher licked goose fat from his fingers. 'I should have fore-seen that there would be another way in and out of the secret room,' he said quietly, 'and I should not have put the pistol back where we found it.'

'If you had not, what would Berwick have done? Found another weapon — one that worked — and used that? Or taken fright and ridden to Dover before we could stop him?'

'But it was a risk. We were fortunate that he did not check it.'

'The queen approved the plan. She must have had trust in your judgement.'

'Perhaps. Yet it is I who most lack trust in my judgement, Tomasso.'

'Would you wish to turn your mind elsewhere?' asked Tomasso. 'To return to teaching perhaps?'

Christopher shook his head. 'No. Educating young minds in the niceties of the law is a comfortable profession to which I believed I was suited. Now, however, I find that danger and discomfort make peace and plenty all the more worth striving for, and the more to be valued when they come.'

'Your experiences in France have not put you off?'

'Quite the opposite. They have opened my eyes to the threats that England faces.'

'They must have affected you.'

Christopher sipped his wine. 'They have, of course. The dreams are terrifying and I fear for our future.'

'Find Berwick and the path to glory will stretch out before you.'

The bottle was empty and most of the meat eaten before Tomasso returned to Whitehall and Christopher to Ludgate Hill. He felt an unexpected affinity with the dark-eyed Florentine whom at first sight he had been inclined to distrust. It gave him hope.

Isaac Cardoza arrived at Ludgate Hill that evening. He wore a long woollen coat, gloves and a hat trimmed with fur. 'I do not care for the cold,' he grumbled, when Christopher let him in. 'My family lived in the sunshine of Portugal, not this dismal English chill.'

'Come in, Isaac, and sit by the fire. I will fetch you a glass of hippocras. You will have heard about the Spanish fleet.'

'I have and thank God for it.' Isaac took off his hat and wriggled out of his coat. 'Thank you, my friend, that would be welcome.'

With glasses of the spiced wine beside them, they sat by the fire. Isaac stretched his hands out to its warmth. 'I wonder sometimes at our city,' he said. 'On the surface, a busy place of merchants and artisans working to keep their families housed and fed, loyal to their queen and worshipping as they are expected to, yet underneath a hotchpotch of men and women living lives quite different to those we see. I do not mean the thieves and beggars and vagabonds, although they too are there, but rather those with opinions and faiths at variance with the majority.'

Christopher did not interrupt or try to hurry Isaac along. It was not Isaac's way to rush, even at a time of danger. He had never heard the soft voice raised in anger or excitement and he knew that Isaac would say what he had come to say in his own time. He sat quietly and drank from his glass.

When he was ready, Isaac went on. 'I am referring to us Jews, naturally; also the Puritans favoured by your earl, even the few of no faith, the *nulla fidiantes*, and now those ardent Catholics who not long since were tolerated but now are more and more shunned. I speak, too, not only of religious groups but also of those who embrace radical ideas of governance and philosophy. They too must guard their tongues and hide in dark corners. And new groups with new ideas are forming – often artists, players, writers, philosophers, even physicians. Having a common interest in survival, we help each other.' He smiled and shrugged theatrically. 'We Jews are accustomed to this. Others are not.'

Still Christopher stayed silent. When Isaac spoke again his voice had taken on a more solemn note. 'This morning I visited a friend among the Catholics in Eastcheap. Better you do not know his name as he is no longer welcome in this country. Like us Jews he is forced to practise his faith away from the gaze of others. He is a good man and a good friend.'

'Has your friend heard anything, Isaac?'

'He said little, as is his way, but I sensed that he does know something. He said that the thought of the Spanish landing an army on English soil terrified him. He fears another massacre like that seen in Paris.' Isaac sipped from his glass and nodded appreciatively. 'Excellent.'

'As do we all.'

'He knows, of course, about the attempt to destroy Whitehall and has heard a whisper concerning those who were responsible.'

'One of them we have, Isaac. James Kaye, Senior Warden of the stationers. It is the other, John Berwick, whom we seek.'

'Yes. It is he about whom my friend will make discreet inquiries.' Isaac sat back and took another sip of hippocras. 'Even you, Christopher, might be surprised if you knew how readily ideas and intelligence pass unseen from one group to another, thereby forging bonds between them. For example, a Jew thinks he has been robbed by a Catholic. He cannot go to a magistrate nor does he speak openly about his suspicion. He speaks quietly to a Catholic friend, who agrees to find out the truth of the matter. The thief is caught and warned never again to transgress. The victim's property is returned to him and neither the courts nor the gaols are ever involved. We police ourselves. It is just and effective.'

'And if the thief does not learn his lesson?'

'He will be thrown to the wolves. Happily, few are.' Isaac put down his glass. 'You must forgive my ramblings, Christopher. My children do not tolerate them and I have little opportunity in my shop to speak about such things to anyone other than myself.'

'You are forgiven, Isaac, and I am grateful for your help. But time presses. I ask that you act as quickly as you can.'

'I shall.' Isaac rose from his seat. 'And now to brave a wind cold enough to freeze my beard. I will send word or come again the moment I have news.'

'Go well, Isaac, and I pray you find Berwick.'

CHAPTER 39

December

Christopher left the house, huddled into his cloak and with his cap pulled down over his ears. The first flurry of snow had come and with it a bitter wind from the east. Since Isaac's visit there had been no news. Nothing from Isaac, nothing from Ell, nothing from the Tower. Constables and militiamen were knocking on doors and searching stews and hovels. Nothing. He dreaded a messenger from Whitehall and news of another attempt on the queen's life. And no word from Katherine. For all he knew she had returned to Cambridge.

From a chestnut-seller on the corner of Fleet Street he bought a handful of nuts and warmed his hands at the man's brazier. The news sheets were reporting that the queen had held a service of thanksgiving for the deliverance of the country from the ungodly Spanish and, now that her health was restored, she intended to ride daily in the fields at Holborn or in the park at Richmond. The threat of attack had gone with the Spanish fleet, at least until the spring, and London could breathe again. What few knew was that somewhere in the city, in some dark, secret place, John Berwick still lurked, and for as long as he did, the queen was in danger.

Head down, he walked along Fleet Street. Fallen leaves and discarded news sheets danced in the wind; as fast as the snow fell it turned to mush, and the few people about slipped and sloshed their way around the filth that waited for street cleaners and dogs to clear it away. It was a day for staying at home, not walking aimlessly. But Christopher could not have stayed at home. He had to get out and stretch his long legs. He had to suck cold air into his lungs. He had to clear his mind. It was ever thus: in Cambridge, the river path and the meadows of Grantchester, in London the streets and markets of the city.

He hesitated outside Isaac Cardoza's door, decided against entering, and went on. The streets were safer in this weather — too cold even for beggars and cutpurses — and he walked unmolested. Where Fleet Street became the Strand there was someone hurrying towards him. As the figure approached, he saw that it was Tomasso. He called out. Tomasso raised a hand in greeting and came up to him. 'Christopher, you have spared me a most unpleasant journey. The earl has sent me to give you the news. Kaye is dead.' Tomasso pointed to an inn where candles had been set in a window. 'That place appears open. Let us seek warmth there.'

The taproom was quiet. They ordered ale and sat as near the fire as they could. 'Why anyone would wish to invade a country with weather like this is beyond my understanding,' said Tomasso. 'It is intolerable.'

Christopher had no time for pleasantries. 'Did Kaye speak, Tomasso?'

'At the last he did. He gave up four names.' Tomasso took a scrap of paper from his pocket. 'These are they.'

Christopher read the names. He knew them. The missing stationers given to him by Warden Curteys. 'So we know who were Kaye's accomplices. That is something. Thank God it was not I who had the task of extracting them from him.'

'The earl will order them found and arrested. And it is possible, of course, that one of them shelters Berwick, although more likely, I fear, that they have fled London and are in hiding elsewhere. It will take time to find them.'

'Have you other news for me?'

'Only that this weather is confining the queen to her rooms. Even she does not wish to ride. Leicester professes himself relieved. Meanwhile he speaks of Jews and whores and is threatening to put more militiamen to work. Have you learned anything, Christopher?'

'No. At least, no more than the tiniest glimmer of light, not enough to report to the earl. My two best agents, both loyal and clever, are aware of the urgency of the search and I am at a loss as to what more might be done. How does one find a single man among near two hundred thousand?'

'Does one set a trap?'

Christopher laughed shortly. 'Our last trap proved less than successful, if you recall. I hardly think another will work better. Berwick is no fool.'

'Indeed he is not. Yet the cleverest fox might be tempted if the bait is juicy enough.'

'What bait have you in mind, Tomasso? Surely not the queen herself again?'

'No, not the queen, Christopher. You.'

'Oh come now, you jest at my expense, Tomasso. Why would I tempt Berwick out of his lair? I am neither a courtier nor a counsellor. I have no influence at court or in the government of the country.'

'I assure you I do not jest,' replied Tomasso. 'You were the one who exposed Berwick as a traitor and you rendered his attempt on the queen a failure. He saw you at St Andrew's church. He will want revenge.'

Christopher sipped his ale. 'He would need to know of the bait and be assured that it is not poisoned.'

'That is so. I will put my mind to it. Remember that I am a Florentine. We have a long history of trap-setting.' Tomasso stood up. 'I shall report to the earl that you are making progress.'

'Scant progress, I fear.' He spoke more sharply than he intended, and immediately put a hand on the Italian's sleeve. 'You must excuse my humour, Tomasso, and my lack of courtesy.'

Sessetti smiled. 'It is nothing, Christopher. When we find the traitor, your spirits will be restored.'

It was near dusk when Ell arrived at Ludgate Hill. She had learned nothing and wanted to know if she was to continue asking questions about a man who was hiding from the law somewhere in London. Christopher asked her to keep trying and told her that there were others looking. Berwick would certainly be found.

'What's he done, this Berwick?' she asked.

'He is a traitor and a dangerous one. While the queen remains at Whitehall, she is safe. When she ventures out, as she will, she will be in danger.'

'Did you say he has a gun with two barrels, Dr Rad?'

'He has.'

Ell laughed. 'God's wounds, I'd like a man with two barrels. Keep a lady happy that would.'

Despite himself, Christopher could not but laugh. 'Try, Ell, please. We must find him.'

Soon after Ell had gone, there was another knock on the door. Rose too had gone home. Christopher expected it to be Isaac. It was not. It was Roland Wetherby, whom he showed into the study. 'Dr Radcliff,' said Wetherby, twisting his cap in his hands. 'Forgive my coming uninvited. I wished very much to speak with you.' His eyes were red and his face sunken. Christopher wondered if he was ill or merely fatigued.

'Mr Wetherby, this is not the first time you have called at this house uninvited,' replied Christopher with a smile. 'Have no care of it. What do you wish to speak about?'

'It is this. Mr Heneage has told me of your meeting with the earl and I was unhappy at his outburst. He had reason to be angry at my unjust imprisonment, although no more reason than I, but if we are to find Berwick and bring him to the executioner's block, we must all cooperate. Mr Heneage spoke intemperately.'

'Certainly the earl thought so. His face showed as much. You speak of cooperation, Mr Wetherby. Do you wish to cooperate in the search for Berwick, despite Mr Heneage's opinion?'

'I do, doctor. If it were not for you I might yet be in the Gate House living on crumbs and scratching at lice.'

'And Mr Heneage?'

'Mr Heneage need not know. Please allow me to assist, doctor.'

Christopher straightened his fingers while he considered. 'How would you do so?'

Wetherby cleared his throat and took a deep breath. 'There are certain houses I frequent that are able to satisfy my tastes. I am sure you take my meaning, doctor.' Christopher inclined his head to signal understanding. 'One meets men of all stations and beliefs in such houses. Sometimes one becomes privy to matters that would otherwise remain secret. I could make inquiries.'

Ell was already making inquiries in her world. Should Christopher allow Wetherby to do likewise in his? It would be difficult and perhaps dangerous. A whore might get away with the pretence; a young courtier surely would not. 'Mr Wetherby, I cannot allow it. Not only would it be contrary to Mr Heneage's instructions, it would put you at grave risk.'

Wetherby's face fell. 'Dr Radcliff, I—'

Christopher held up a hand. 'However, it is possible that your service might be useful in some other way. I sense that steady hands will be needed.'

'Will you call on me, doctor, when the time comes?'

'Be assured, sir, that I shall.'

Christopher took Wetherby to the door and ushered him out into the cold. He felt a pang of sympathy for the man. Anxious to please, yet always disappointed. Twice Christopher had turned him away empty-handed and once Berwick had had him thrown into the Gate House. A young man with passions of which Christopher could not approve, but honest and discreet and loyal. He should not have spoken quite so sharply to him.

The summons to Whitehall was not long in coming. In his study Leicester was occupied with the queen's plans for the Christmas festivities and wanted to hear that Berwick had been killed or captured. A log fire warmed the room. 'It has been a year as terrible as any since Queen Mary burned a hundred and more in the name of Catholicism,' he told Christopher. 'Norfolk's execution, the massacre in France, the miserable little duc d'Alençon pressing his absurd suit, a Spanish fleet in our waters, an attempt to destroy Whitehall Palace and all within it, yet another plot to replace our queen with her Scotch cousin, and now an assassin in our midst. An assassin, furthermore, whom the queen herself trusted. That she finds hardest of all to bear and still, I think, hopes that his innocence will be proved. I know not how she has the strength.'

'Her gracious Majesty is a remarkable woman,' replied Christopher, 'and a brave sovereign.'

'That she is, doctor. She does not fear Berwick, and since the departure of the Spanish fleet she has recovered much of her spirit and is planning to celebrate Christmas at Hampton Court Palace. It is I, of course, who must arrange the progress of the household and the planning of the festivities. We shall have twelve days of feasting, dancing and games, and three entertainments from my players. The foresters are taking every scrap of mistletoe and ivy from the woods, and the keepers every duck and swan on the river. It will be a celebration worthy of a great monarch.'

'I have no doubt of it, my lord.'

Leicester stood with his back to the fire. 'There remains only the matter of the traitor Berwick. Would that I could serve his head up in place of a boar's at the Christmas feast. Sessetti claimed that you were making progress. I did not believe him.' His voice had taken on a harsher note.

Christopher swallowed a protest. 'The stationer James Kaye delivered the names of four plotters before he died. If any one of them can be caught, we may discover more — even the whereabouts of Berwick.'

'I am aware of that, doctor, and be sure that you do discover his whereabouts. I want his head on a plate and I want it before the court moves to Hampton. That would ensure the success of the celebrations. Without it, a cloud will hang over them. Not over the queen, who has no fear of him, but over those of us who do. Have you any real prospect of finding him, doctor, or shall I abandon that hope?'

'If he is in London, my lord, we shall find him.'

'Dr Radcliff, I tire of your use of the future tense. The next time we meet I shall expect it to have been replaced by the past perfect. Have found, not will find. Do I make myself clear?'

'Perfectly, my lord.' Leicester could hardly have been clearer. Time, and Leicester's patience, were running out. Danger or not, the traitor must be found before the festivities began.

Chapter 40

The following day, snow fell again — this time not in fleeting flurries that turned quickly to mush but in blankets that covered the streets and the rooftops and painted London white. Christopher sat in his study, rubbing Isabel's salve into his hand, and wishing Katherine was with him. He had not tried to speak to her again and she had made no approach to him. No Berwick and no Katherine would not make for a joyful Christmas at Ludgate Hill. The worst of it was being inactive, just waiting and waiting for a morsel of good news that might never come.

Rose had served his dinner and gone home. Christopher hoped that her roof, repaired by her nephew after the summer storm, would withstand the snow. He had lit candles and tried to read. It was no good. The words could not hold his attention. He closed the book and shut his eyes. A heavy knock on the door jolted him back to the present. Half-hoping it was Katherine, he went to open it. Without having to be told, he knew at once who had fathered the two boys standing outside in the snow. Strands of russet-red hair hung from under their fur caps and their black eyes shone with sharp intelligence. Isaac Cardoza had sent his sons to Ludgate Hill.

'Come in at once and warm yourselves,' said Christopher. 'I can guess who has sent you.' The boys stepped inside and removed their gloves and caps. Snow fell from their coats and boots. 'Have no care of it. Snow melts. Come and tell me why you are here.' He led them in and threw a log on to the fire. 'Now, you are the sons of my friend Isaac Cardoza, are you not?'

The taller boy, perhaps fourteen years old, replied. 'We are David and Daniel Cardoza, Dr Radcliff. Our father has sent us to guide you to our house in Leadenhall.'

'At this time and in this weather? Why so sudden?'

'There is a man at our house whom our father wishes you to meet. We are to tell you that the man will help. That is all we know.'

If Isaac had sent his two sons out after dark in the snow to fetch Christopher, he had good reason. He collected his cloak and cap, slipped the poniard into his belt, and followed them out into the cold.

The snow was falling harder and it took them a good half-hour to trudge through it to Leadenhall. The boys led him through the market and down a lane running in the direction of the river. This was the ward in which many Marrano Jews lived, worshipping in their own way in their own places and bothering no one. Unlike some, this community had long since given up the pretence of conversion and no longer attended Christian services. They openly observed the sabbath and the Feast of the Passover and some even walked without shoes at Yom Kippur. All this Christopher had learned from Isaac, but he had never before been invited to his house.

They turned off the lane into another which ended in a small yard surrounded by three houses. Daniel Cardoza knocked on the door of one of them and waved them in when it was opened. Isaac embraced his sons and sent them up a flight of stairs. He grasped

Christopher's hand in both of his. 'Christopher, you are welcome in my house,' he said. 'Give me your coat and cap and come into the warm. There is someone I want you to meet.'

Christopher followed Isaac into a room lit by a dozen candles and warmed by a good log fire. It was comfortable and friendly, not large but the walls were hung with fine tapestries and the furniture decorated with delicate carvings of roses and lilies. A large book lay open on one table, a bottle and three glasses on another. Three chairs had been set before the fire. In one sat a man of about fifty with hair the colour of the falling snow. He rose to greet Christopher, transferring the rosary he held into his left hand. 'Dr Radcliff, I wish you happiness.' The voice was deep and throaty and the eyes clear. 'You do not need to know my name. For you, I am Paul.'

'Christopher, you will take wine with us, I hope,' said Isaac, filling the glasses with a rich, red liquid. 'Let us sit and talk.' Christopher took a sip of wine — it was strong and sweet and immediately he felt warmth returning to his face and hands.

'I have known Paul for many years, Christopher. In this house you may speak openly to him. He knows all that I know about you and will not betray a secret.' Christopher smiled at Paul. His was an open face, one a man would instinctively trust. 'I will let him explain why he has agreed to be here.' Isaac raised his glass. '*L'Chayim*. To life.'

'Dr Radcliff,' began Paul, 'I am a Catholic. I worship in the old way and believe in the supremacy of His Holiness the Pope. I do not, however, believe in violence. I deplored the uprising led by the earls of Westmoreland and Northumberland and the Duke of Norfolk's futile and misguided plot to replace the Queen of England with the Queen of Scots. Before those events I and my family and friends worshipped quietly and without interference.' Paul paused and took a sip of wine. 'Now our lives have changed. We are feared and despised by many who were once tolerant of us and must be ever watchful for those who would serve us ill. It is not surprising. Recent events in France, although certainly exaggerated, have done us immeasurable harm.'

'I saw the bloodshed for myself, sir,' replied Christopher. 'There is nothing, not even the threat of an attack on Paris, that could justify it. I saw women and children slaughtered in the name of I know not what. Such barbarity must never be seen again.'

'Much of the barbarity was the work of criminals and opportunists. Nevertheless, the murder of Coligny was what gave rise to the opportunity and should not have happened. I too do not want to see it repeated in France or in England or in any godly country. That is why I am here.'

Christopher stared into the Catholic's blue eyes, searching for any sign of dissembling. He saw none.

'We Jews have much in common with Paul's Catholics,' added Isaac, 'mistrusted, reviled, ready scapegoats for any misfortune. Jews are Jews, Catholics are Catholics. A shoal of herring is made up of many thousands of fish yet who concerns themselves with but a single one? One herring is the same as another. It is the shoal that matters.'

When Paul smiled, his eyes lit up. 'Isaac has an unusual way with words. A shoal of Catholics makes for a strange picture.' He paused. 'Since the *Regnans in Excelsis*, doctor, we have been preparing as best we can for what is to come. We are realistic. The queen's tolerance is much strained and life can only become more difficult for us. There are few of our priests remaining in London. Soon they will all be gone. Our places of worship will perforce be hidden from hostile eyes and there will be those, as there are now, who wish only to see us suffer.'

'And you are preparing places of hiding,' said Christopher. 'This is known, or suspected, although not where such places are. If the Jesuits do send priests from the college at Douai, you will need them.'

'Quite so, doctor. If they do.' For some moments none of them spoke, the silence broken only by the crackle of the fire. Then Paul went on. 'Now let us consider your purpose in being here. There is a man you seek, a man of resource and unshakeable determination. While he is in London, he is a threat to you. He has powerful friends in France. He is also a threat to peace in England and thus to all of us. We wish him to be gone.'

'If you know where he is, sir, hand him over to me and you will be rid of him. The threat will disappear.'

'I do know where he is hiding and we have considered handing him over to you. We are not going to do so.' Paul sat quite still and showed no emotion.

'Why, if you really wish to eliminate the threat?'

'Because we cannot send a man, any man, to the traitor's death that would await him. The queen would not be as lenient as she was with Norfolk. The man would suffer beyond imagining.'

'He is a murderer as well as a traitor. Others have suffered at his hands.'

'An eye for an eye, doctor? That is not our way.'

'If I report this meeting to the Earl of Leicester, he will hunt you down and drag from you what we wish to know.' It was a struggle to remain calm. This man claimed to know where Berwick was hiding but would not tell him.

'You will not do that, doctor, because it would be a betrayal of Isaac's trust and would put him in danger. I know from him that that is not your way. Allow me, rather, to make a suggestion. Your quarry can do nothing because it is too dangerous for him to leave his hiding place. We do not wish to harbour him but will not see his head on a spike at London Bridge. You do not know where he is. If a way can be found to put him on a boat to France, I believe he will go.'

Christopher narrowed his eyes and toyed with his bent fingers. It was a proposal but a dangerous one. 'I would be acting without authority. My position would be in jeopardy, perhaps even my life.'

'You would be acting in the best interests of your country and it would be done in secret. We would arrange in due course for the earl to be told that the man is no longer in England.'

'What would prevent him from returning?'

'He will be discouraged from doing so. His face is known to us and he would be taking a grave risk by returning here. We would not be as sympathetic a second time.'

'You ask much of me, sir,' said Christopher, 'and I cannot at once see how such a thing could be done. However, I will give it thought.'

'We must not delay, doctor. Let us be rid of him before Christmas.'

'And if I cannot accept this proposal?'

'An opportunity will have been missed and he will remain where he is. Think hard, doctor.'

'My sons will escort you home, Christopher. I shall be in Fleet Street tomorrow. Visit me there,' said Isaac.

Paul rose and held out his hand. 'And remember, Dr Radcliff, I trust you because Isaac Cardoza, an old friend, has told me that I can.'

Christopher glanced at Isaac before taking Paul's hand. 'The Earl of Leicester also trusts me, sir. I must tread carefully.'

CHAPTER 41

Christopher had visited Isaac's shop in Fleet Street and told him that he was ready to meet Paul again, and a little after dusk, Daniel and David Cardoza arrived at his door on Ludgate Hill. They escorted him to Leadenhall where he was greeted by Isaac and blindfolded by Paul. From there he was guided by Paul's hand on his arm for about fifteen minutes through the snow, turning him this way and that so that he could not have said in which ward they eventually arrived.

They entered a building and descended a flight of stairs. He heard water dripping and guessed that they were in a cellar. He found that he was shivering with the cold. His eyes still covered, he was led along a passage narrow enough for him to touch both walls at once and up another stair. A door was opened, he was guided inside and the blindfold removed from his eyes.

He was standing in a room made bright by a score of candles and laid out in the manner of a tiny church. The nave was filled by three rows of low chairs, and separated from the sanctuary by a wooden chancel railing. A cross, flanked by two tall silver candlesticks, stood on the altar table. When they entered, a figure kneeling at the railing crossed himself and stood to face them. Christopher suppressed an oath. It was John Berwick. Paul spoke quickly. 'In God's house let there be no voices raised in anger.'

They sat, Christopher and Paul on one side of the nave, Berwick on the other, their chairs turned to face each other. Berwick's eyes held no trace of fear. Paul continued, 'John Berwick is here because I wished to show you that I have been telling the truth. He has been sheltered by us but it is now our wish, and his, that he be granted safe passage out of England. In return he will confess to his part in a plan to destroy Whitehall Palace and will take an oath never to return.'

Christopher stared at Berwick. 'You attempted to assassinate the queen. You are a murderer and a traitor. Your oath is worthless. I would see you hang.' With an effort he controlled his voice and his temper.

'Why then have you come, doctor?' asked Paul quietly.

Christopher's eyes were still on Berwick. 'You have been receiving orders from France. I want names.'

For the first time, Berwick spoke. 'That is conjecture, Dr Radcliff.'

'Do you deny it?' snapped Christopher. Berwick did not reply. 'I want the names of the principals in France and their agents in England.'

'What will you do with them?'

'Perhaps nothing. Simply knowing who they are may suffice.'

'And what do you offer in return?' asked Paul.

'I offer him passage to France. In return for the names a trading vessel will take him from Fresh Wharf to France.' In the expectation of reaching agreement, albeit with Paul as intermediary rather than with Berwick himself, Christopher had already arranged the vessel.

'How are we to know that we can trust you?' asked Berwick.

'Both of us will be taking a risk. If you attempt to escape or if you give me names that prove false or if you refuse my offer you will spend the rest of your life being hunted down. We both have more to gain by honouring the agreement than by dishonouring it.'

'You will set a trap,' said Berwick.

'I have given my word to Isaac Cardoza that I will not. Accept my offer or decline it. There can be no further discussion.'

Paul and Berwick exchanged a glance. 'Very well,' said Paul. 'Your proposal is accepted. When will the ship leave?'

'It will sail on the noon tide the day after tomorrow. I shall be waiting there. The captain and crew are accustomed to carrying passengers across the narrow sea and believe you to be an agent of the Earl of Leicester. They will be well paid to deliver you safely to France. Bring your list of names.'

The meeting was over. Christopher's eyes were covered again and he was led by Paul back to Leadenhall. He told Isaac what had been agreed and hurried home. This time neither Daniel nor David accompanied him.

Snow was no longer falling but it was bitterly cold. He left Ludgate Hill early and found a wherry at Blackfriars stairs. He wore two thick undershirts and was glad of them. The river upstream of London Bridge was quiet. Beyond the bridge, it would be busier. Whatever the weather, traders had to trade and fishermen to fish.

Fresh Wharf was close by the bridge on the north bank of the river. It had newly been granted a licence for trade and was used also by fishing boats and eel-catchers. The wherryman steered them through the arches of the bridge and pulled up at the wharf. Christopher jumped out and ran up to a row of timber store houses built a safe distance above the high-water mark. There was no one about. He watched the wherryman turn his boat and head back upriver.

Not long after dawn on a freezing December morning, the wharf was a miserable place — bleak and uninviting. The shore nearby was littered with fishbones fought over by screeching gulls, scraps of iron and lengths of rotten timber tossed from the boats that moored there, and heaps of filthy sail cloth. Scavenging crabs scuttled about in search of a morsel of food. The stench of fish and human waste filled the air. Trying to ignore it, Christopher stamped his feet and rubbed his hands together.

A single ship was tied up at the wharf — a stout, two-masted vessel designed to ply its trade in coastal waters and across the sea to the ports of northern France and the Low Countries. Christopher clambered on board. He assured himself that all was as he had arranged and stepped back on to the wharf. Taking care not to slip on the slime-covered timbers, he made his way around the side of a store house, checked that his poniard was in place and settled down to wait in the lee of the wall.

An hour later, Tomasso arrived. He too had taken a wherry. He joined Christopher behind the store house, put down the leather bag he was carrying and stamped his feet against the cold. 'Is all ready?' he asked, his breath clouding in the freezing air.

'It is. Remember, Tomasso, you will not show yourself without my signal. If he hands over the list as agreed, which I doubt, he will be allowed to leave. If not we will act.'

'We could take the names and then kill him.'

'I have given my word that we will not, although he will expect an attempt.'

Tomasso spat into the dirt. 'A liar believes nothing.'

It was a long, cold wait. In his bag, Tomasso had cheese and bread but Christopher found that he could not eat. He also had the pistol Christopher had brought back from France. In Holborn Fields, he had hit three targets out of four at a range of thirty yards. Afterwards, he had cleaned, primed and loaded it with painstaking care. He took it out of the bag and laid it down ready to fire.

As the morning passed, the river grew busier. Fishing boats tied up to the wharves to unload their catch, pushed off and were away again in search of more. The price of fresh fish in the markets could double in winter. Traders came and went; sailors and rivermen shouted friendly insults at each other; carters and labourers heaved crates on and off the boats and, above them, gulls circled and squawked. Fresh Wharf remained quiet. Christopher had invented a story about a valuable delivery from the Earl of Leicester to Sir Francis Walsingham in Paris and requested of the river authorities that, other than by his ship, the wharf should not be used that day.

The two men stood huddled behind the store house, stamping their feet and rubbing their gloved hands together. Tomasso was first to hear the rattle of wheels. He touched Christopher's arm and pointed to where a coach was drawing up in the lane that ran down to the river. The horses' breath rose thick into the air and the coachman's face was hidden by a cap and a kerchief tied over his mouth and nose against the cold. From where they hid they could see the coach but would not themselves be seen. Christopher waited until a hooded man climbed down before he walked around the river side of the store house to emerge on to the wharf as if he had been waiting there. Christopher stood there with his hands on his head.

John Berwick pushed back his hood. As he walked down to the wharf, the coachman behind him dismounted and opened the coach door. He reached inside and dragged out a figure with a sack tied

over its head and its hands bound with rope. The figure stumbled
and was roughly hoisted back to its feet by the coachman. Berwick
did not look round but kept his eyes fixed on Christopher. The coachman untied the sack and pulled it from the figure's head. Christopher
gasped. It was Katherine.

Berwick took a pistol from inside his cloak and held it pointing
steadily at Christopher's face. It was not the twin of the one in
Tomasso's hands. He spoke slowly and without a trace of nerves. 'If
Sessetti is nearby, doctor, I suggest that you tell him to put down his
weapons and show himself.'

Christopher could not look away from Katherine. Tears ran
down the grime on her face, blood caked her forehead and one eye
was swollen. The coachman held her by the hair with one hand and
removed the kerchief hiding his face with the other. He grinned at
Christopher and sent a stream of spittle to the ground. 'Lovely lady,'
he croaked. 'Wish I was going with her.' The coachman was the
interrogator Griffyn's assistant, Pygot.

Christopher reached for his dagger and took a step forward.
Berwick raised the pistol in warning. 'That would be unwise, doctor.
On a word from me, Pygot will slice open her throat and throw her to
the fish. Then I will shoot you.' Christopher stood still. 'Sessetti, if
you please. I have no doubt that he is here.'

Christopher longed to drive the dagger into Berwick's heart and
throttle Pygot. He breathed deeply before shouting to Tomasso to
show himself. When the Italian emerged from behind the store
house, he was unarmed and walked slowly. Berwick ordered him to
stand beside Christopher, both facing him.

'Now,' said Berwick, 'Pygot will help Mistress Allington on
board. I will join her and you will order the crew to make sail for
France.'

'The crew will return presently.'

Berwick eyed Christopher suspiciously and for a moment Christopher feared that he would fire. 'Why are they not here?' he demanded.

'It is not yet midday and they have a long voyage ahead. They are filling their bellies.'

Berwick took a step forward and pointed his pistol at Christopher's eyes. 'If there is any trickery here, Radcliff, you will all die.'

'The trickery is yours, Berwick, and I shall require the list of names,' replied Christopher, hoping that his voice did not betray his fear.

Berwick laughed. 'Require as you will, doctor. Surely you did not think I would oblige you with such a list? Mistress Allington will accompany me to France. Once there, I will decide what is to be done with her.' He took another step towards Christopher. 'Stand aside. We will await the crew on board. If they do not come by midday, she will travel no further.'

Christopher moved a little to one side, unable to keep his eyes from Katherine. Still holding her by her hair, Pygot shoved her forward and bundled her over the gunwale. She landed on the deck with a grunt of pain. Pygot stepped back to make way for Berwick. As he did so, there was a shot and blood spurted from Berwick's arm. He screamed and dropped the pistol. Roland Wetherby rose from below the gunwale, a pistol in each hand. He fired again and Pygot fell, his head exploding in a mist of blood and gore.

Christopher and Tomasso moved at the same moment. They grabbed Berwick by the arms and forced him to the ground. Christopher held him down while Tomasso retrieved his pistol and pressed it against Berwick's eye. 'You are a fool, Berwick,' hissed Christopher. 'Had you kept to our agreement, you would have escaped to France. But I knew you would not, so I took precautions. Surely you did not think I would not?'

Berwick did not reply. His eyes closed and his head lolled to one side. He was pale and losing blood from his wound.

'Tomasso, get him back to the coach. Bind his arm. He must live.'

Tomasso hoisted the barely conscious man over his shoulder and carried him up to the coach. Christopher climbed over the gunwale.

Wetherby was kneeling beside Katherine, his arm under her head, and whispering gently to her. Her eyes were closed and she did not speak. 'She is cut and bruised, doctor,' he said. 'Nothing more, I think.'

'Thank God. Can you drive a coach, Mr Wetherby?' asked Christopher.

'I can.'

'Good. We will carry her up to it. Leave Pygot to the gulls.'

Wetherby drove as fast as he dared over cobbles made treacherous by the snow. Inside the coach, Christopher sat silently beside Katherine. Tomasso had staunched the flow of blood from Berwick's arm with the strap from his leather bag. 'Is Wetherby skilled enough to have deliberately wounded him thus or did he miss his aim?' he asked.

'That you must ask him, Tomasso,' replied Christopher. 'Whatever the truth of it, Berwick is alive. I thank God for it for he has much to tell us.'

They delivered Katherine without explanation into the care of an astonished Ursula Walsingham in Seething Lane. Berwick they took to the Tower, where, at Christopher's request, the Warden found a small cell for him and agreed to send for a physician. From there, they drove to Fleet Street, where Christopher spoke at length to

Isaac Cardoza. Finally, as the feeble sun was beginning to set, the coach drew up outside the Holbein Gate. 'You would make a fine coachman, Mr Wetherby,' said Christopher. 'I shall leave you to report to Mr Heneage. I will call on the earl.'

'And I shall retire to my apartment,' said Tomasso. 'I have dispatches to write.'

CHAPTER 42

An hour later, Leicester knew all that had happened. He had sat unsmiling through Christopher's account, never interrupting and showing no glimmer of emotion. Eventually, when Christopher had finished, he spoke. 'It seems to me, Dr Radcliff, that the fates have smiled upon you. It might most easily have been otherwise, in which case your career on my staff would have been over. You would either be on your way out of London or floating in the river.'

Christopher was in no mood to be cowed. 'Kindly note, however, my lord, that I have not used the future tense. Berwick has been taken and is in the Tower. And Her Majesty's Christmas feast may now proceed as you have planned.'

Leicester grunted. 'Be that as it may, you put yourself and others in danger and, most heinous crime of all, you would have let Berwick escape to France.'

Christopher allowed his voice to rise a little. 'My lord, Berwick would never have escaped to France. As I expected, he had no intention of handing over a list of names, or of leaving me alive. He anticipated the presence of Signor Sessetti but not of Roland Wetherby. If he had killed us, Wetherby would have killed him.'

'And Mistress Allington, would she too have been killed?'

'I had not foreseen the presence of Katherine. But, yes, she too might have died.'

'Again you surprise me, doctor. I had not thought you capable of this.' Was there a hint of praise in Leicester's voice?

'Half a year since, my lord, I would not have been. But the sights and sounds of pleading women and screaming children being hacked to pieces while their houses burned . . .'

'A tragedy. I thank God that I did not witness it myself. The reports alone were beyond Christian understanding.'

'And what now of Berwick?'

'We will see what Griffyn can squeeze from him before he meets his executioner.'

'May I be permitted to speak to him first, my lord? There are questions I would put to him myself.'

'If you wish, doctor, but Griffyn shall have him when you have done. Go now. I must inform Her Majesty of Berwick's capture.'

John Berwick was brought into the room in which Christopher had questioned James Kaye. His wrists and ankles were shackled and a fiery bruise spread across one cheek. One arm was covered with a bloody bandage. Defiance burned in his eyes. Christopher wasted no words. 'Did you kill Nicholas Houseman and his wife?' he demanded.

'What matters it if I did?' Berwick's voice was a painful croak. The Tower guards had not been gentle with him.

'It matters to me. They were my friends.'

'They were your spies. I am pleased to have held the knife that slit their throats.'

'Did you order me killed?'

'I did, and regret only that my order was not carried out.' Berwick was clearly in pain but he stood upright and showed no fear.

'Did you have Elias Smith and Patrick Wolf killed?' Christopher would give him no respite.

'It was necessary.'

'Why, Berwick? What has led you to this and will lead you to a traitor's death?'

'Christ died on the cross. I shall suffer no more than did he.'

'Do not be so sure of it. You have yet to make the acquaintance of Mr Griffyn. I ask again — why?'

'Allow me to sit and I will make it plain.' Christopher signalled to the guard, who brought a chair. Berwick went on, 'My father opposed the rising led by Westmoreland and Northumberland. He was a Protestant, loyal to the Crown. My mother was French and a beautiful, devout woman. As a child, she brought me up quietly to worship as she did. That is all you have to know.'

'It is all I wish to know. Mr Griffyn, however, will wish to know more. He will want the names of all who aided you both in France and in England. It will go easier for you if you tell him without delay.'

'I shall never tell him.'

Christopher rose. 'As you wish.' At the door he looked back. Berwick was staring at him. 'May God forgive you, Berwick.' He closed the door quietly, leaving the prisoner in the charge of his guard. John Berwick would not see the light of day again until the morning of his execution.

Cheapside market was busy despite the cold. No threat from the Spanish or French would stop any family that had the money from enjoying their Christmas feasting. Ducks and geese hung in rows on vendors' stalls, pies and chestnuts and sweet biscuits and every sort of winter vegetable waited to be taken home to a warm kitchen. They did not have to wait long. Goodwives swept them off the stalls and into their wicker baskets while their husbands drank spiced wine and laughed at each other's jokes. A small child grabbed Christopher's gown and demanded a penny. He got a farthing and was glad of it. Another wailed that his mother had died that day and got nothing; not far away a young woman sat on an upturned half-barrel watching him. Christopher paid sixpence for a bag of minced pies, hoping Ell would be pleased with them. For the first time in months he could enjoy the bustle of the market without a heavy weight around his neck.

The door was opened by Grace, unsteady on her feet and much the worse for ale. 'Gone away again,' she said, when Christopher asked for Ell. 'Might have gone to her old father, might be lying in the Fleet Ditch. Won't be back, mark my words.'

How disappointing. He so wanted to tell Ell that all was well. 'I think she'll be back, Grace, and when you see her, tell her Dr Rad brought minced pies for her. You have them. They smell good.'

Grace took the bag. 'Won't be back. They never come back.'

'If she does, Grace, tell her that word I spoke of — it's over now. She can forget it.'

'I'd tell her, doctor, but she'll never come back.'

'I think she will. Goodbye, Grace. Tell her I was here.'

Katherine did not speak when Christopher was shown into Isabel's parlour but sat silently, her hands clasped in front of her. Her eye was still a little swollen. 'Will you permit me to explain?' he asked quietly.

'Explain your whore or why Berwick was allowed to attack me and take me as a hostage?'

'Ell Cole has never been my whore.'

'So you have said. I do not believe you. She was in your house.'

Christopher swallowed a flash of anger. 'Katherine, if you will not believe what I say, there is little point in my being here.' He made to leave. 'I wish you joy of the season.'

'Sit down, Christopher. I have more to say.' Christopher pulled a chair to sit opposite her. Katherine took a deep breath. 'If we are to be as we were, I have two conditions. First, you must never see the whore again. Never.'

'Katherine, she is a good intelligencer. I cannot afford to lose her.'

'Never.'

'And the second condition?'

'In future, you will hide nothing from me. Your secrets must be my secrets. I wish to assist you in your work.'

Christopher stared into the fire and rubbed his hand. Eventually he said, 'I will agree to seeing Ell Cole only in your presence. Then you will be privy to the intelligence she gathers and will soon come to realize that she is not my whore.'

'Very well. Reluctantly. And my second condition?'

'The Earl of Leicester would not condone your involvement in my work. If we are to work together, it must be kept from him.'

'But he already knows of my involvement.'

'In future it must be our secret unless I see fit to tell him.'

'Two conditions from me, two from you. Let us agree that is how it will be.'

'We are agreed.' Christopher rose to embrace her. Katherine held up her hands.

'You must give me time. I am not yet ready. Call again when Christmas is over. We will talk more.'

'As you wish, Katherine. Send word when you are ready. You will find me at Ludgate Hill.' As he had in the Tower, he stood at the door and looked back. Katherine was wiping her eyes with a handkerchief. 'When Christmas is over. I shall be waiting.'

CHAPTER 43

Paris

The two men sat in the warmth of the duc de Guise's Paris house. Word had arrived that day from England. Berwick was in the Tower, Kaye was dead. If there had been any doubt, there was none now. *Incendium* had failed.

Guise drained his glass and hurled it into the fire. 'It was the fault of the English. We should not have trusted them.'

The bishop shook his head. 'Berwick's mother was French. Wolf was Irish, Mackay Scotch. Only the priest-stationer Kaye was English. A self-important oaf, who I always thought was out to better himself at our expense. It is no surprise that they failed. The plan to destroy Whitehall was misconceived and had no real purpose. It was the death of the heretic queen that we most desired.'

'Alba is unhappy and speaks of recompense. He claims that arming and victualling his Spanish fleet was costly and expects a contribution from us.'

'I doubt that he will get one. The king is also unhappy. What started so well has ended badly. The price of failure is great.'

'Let us not speak of failure, Charles,' said Guise, suddenly more cheerful. 'Rather, let us plan more carefully and trust no one but ourselves to achieve our aims. A Catholic queen in England, a return to the old ways and a true ally against our enemies. Perhaps even a marriage between the Queen of Scots and a French prince. Our chance will come again.'

'With God's help, it will.'

ACKNOWLEDGEMENTS

I owe huge thanks to all those who advised, assisted and supported me in the writing of *Incendium*.

First to my wife Susan who uncomplainingly put up with mood swings which varied according to the day's work, and my son Tom, who read early drafts with a sharp film-maker's eye.

Jonathan Ferguson, Curator of Firearms at the National Firearms Centre in Leeds, provided generous expert advice on firearms of the period, as did Giles Fagan at Stationers' Hall on the history of the Stationers' Company. Jennifer Bench and Laura King kindly advised on possible symptoms of the stress suffered by Christopher after his experience in Paris.

My agent, David Headley of DHH Literary Agency, was unfailingly supportive and somehow found the time to read my drafts. And, finally, my long-suffering editor, Simon Taylor of Transworld Publishers, devoted a good deal more of his time and expertise to the book than I deserved. Without him, it would be a much poorer affair.

After reading Law at Cambridge, **A. D. Swanston** held various positions in the book trade, including being a director of Waterstones and chairman of Methvens PLC, before turning to writing full-time.

Inspired by a lifelong interest in early modern history, his Thomas Hill novels — *The King's Spy*, *The King's Exile* and *The King's Return* — are set against a backdrop of the English Civil War, Cromwell's Commonwealth and the early Restoration. He is also the author of *Waterloo: The Bravest Man*. The first in a new series set during the reign of Elizabeth I, *Incendium* introduces academic, lawyer and intelligencer Dr Christopher Radcliff.

A. D. Swanston lives in Surrey.